TURN OF THE LYKOI

Andrea Norwich

Pacey —
Never give up on your dreams! You never know which ones will come true!
Happy Reading,
♡ Andi Norwich

Copyright © 2011 by Andrea Norwich
The moral right of this author has been asserted.

*All characters in this publication are
fictitious and any resemblance to real persons,
living or dead, is purely coincidental.*

All rights reserved.
No part of this publication may be reproduced,
stored in a retrieval system, or transmitted, in any
form or by any means, without prior permission
in writing of the publisher, nor be otherwise
circulated
in any form of binding or cover other than that in
which it is published and without a similar
condition
including this condition being imposed on
the subsequent purchaser.

ACKNOWLEDGMENTS

Words cannot express the gratitude to countless encounters of inspiration in my life:

Mom, we have come to understand so much and grow because of that understanding. I'm glad that we have become close friends and have established such a strong bond as mother/daughter. I appreciate the continued support and encouragement that you give to me.

Sis, you are one of my best friends. You and I laugh, we fight, and we stick our noses where they don't belong. What it comes down to in the end is that we have and always will be there for one another. That makes me happy

Dad, No matter what is going on in our lives; I will always love you and will always look to you as one of my heroes.

Marley Gibson, thank you for being such an inspiration as a paranormal resource as well as a great friend. We have been through transitions in our lives and leaned upon one another, as we know we would be there always. You are the reason I kept reaching for my dream.

Laura, Keith, The Team (You know who you all are <3), all of my family members, all of my paranormal peeps and all of my friends who continue to be points of light in my life. I'm truly blessed to know and love each of you. I hope that I'm able to repay you for the endless gifts I receive from you every day, just by interacting with you.

To my missing link and final editor: I didn't know what I was missing until I found you. What you have given to me and what you have been to me, has meant more than I could ever have imagined. I can't help but be a better person with you and for you. Every day is a good day when I start by waking up next to you. There is nothing this world can throw to us, which we can't beat into submission. It's just how we roll.

Go Team Norwich

To my son: My angel and one of the only reasons for living. How I love viewing the world through your eyes. You inspire such imagination within me and you have awakened the inner child that had been asleep for so long. I hope you always find wonder in the world and in those that inhabit it. And no matter what you do, do not stop believing in yourself or others.

*Love Always,
Your Mommy*

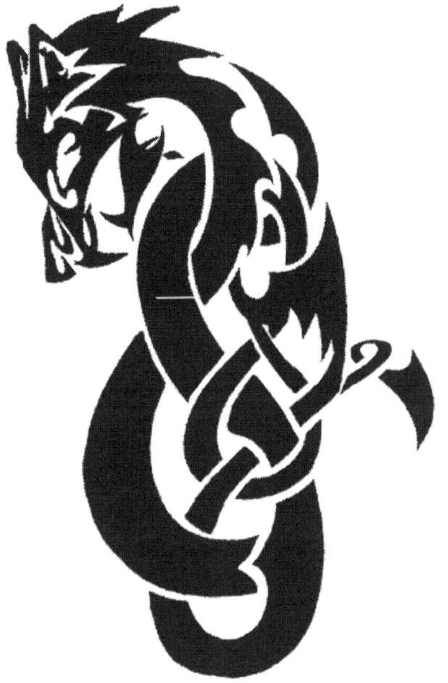

CHAPTER ONE

Fog surrounded her as she ran through the night. Trees whispered as she made her way through the darkness. Every turn, every hidden area of the forest called to her as it opened itself beneath her feet. Energy coursed through her veins and each step she took fell silent on the cold earth. Her breath-labored, as she struggled through the thickets.

A deer awaked in its lay, by movement in the distance, and took to flight. The fear the animal permeated filled the air with a pungent scent. The scent served as a beacon, pushing her in a frenzied pace. As a primal need arose in her, she sensed a change in the atmosphere. The need to pursue the animal was so powerful she could not stop until the prey lay in her hands.

Dodging through the overhanging tree limbs and vines, she moved through the grounds as she had a thousand times before. Each path etched in her memory from childhood. The only map she needed to trap her prey lay in the recesses of her mind... an inbred hunter's instinct.

Ominous clouds covered the landscape in its dark embrace and slowly parted to illuminate the prey in flight. The scent of fear excited her and made her hunger grow. The need to experience the kill for the moment was lost to the thrill of the hunt. There was no escape for the deer as fear leaves a scent. It marks the path leaving a target for the hunter and writes a death warrant for the prey.

They had reached a small clearing in the foliage. Closed in by the rocky bluffs the deer found itself trapped with no escape. Poised in a stance of confusion the deer looked at the pursuer, a deer trapped in the headlights with no way to turn without facing death. With a sense of defeat evident in its eyes; the prey, trapped could only watch as the hunter lunged to finish the task. The end came quickly as small sounds escaped the deer; the struggle to free itself ensued with desperation.

Intoxicated from the chase and from the conquest, the hunter raised her head as the moon shimmered and filled her with power. Eyes met eyes, the hunter and the hunted locked in the final moment of battle. She plunged at the deer's neck, ripping the throat open. She savored the moment the blood drained from one and filled the other. A primal scream ripped through the night air. It was not that of the deer's final gasp of breath, it was the scream of the hunter's soul released.

Samantha Harris awoke with a desperate jerk. Her scream vibrated through the night. The room, which was so familiar in the daylight, was lost in the throes of night. The looming darkness engulfed her. Consciousness made a feeble attempt to force its way to the surface as she shook her head. The smell of sweat filled her nostrils. It soaked her bedclothes, making her long dark hair lay heavily against her face. She struggled to release the haze of the dream and bring herself to reality. A strange yet familiar smell captured her. It wafted through the room, the smell of blood.

The sensation of the deer's torn flesh lingered in her mouth. The memory in perception was as real as the dream and had created a sense of morbid understanding. Still caught between that fine line between sleep and awake, Sam scrambled to the head of her bed as she struggled to wipe the blood from her nightshirt. The scream that escaped was that of a primal wild animal celebrating its kill and that of a soul trapped.

Claire ran into the room, startled by the scene that met her, she quickly put aside all of her fears and rushed to aid her niece. Reaching for Sam she struggled as the girl fought to loosen her aunt's comforting embrace. The screams that continued to tear through the night air raised the hair at the nape of her neck with an electrifying impact. Nothing more could be done than to hold onto Sam and let the unseen trauma that had attacked her sleep slowly clear her mind.

"Sam! Can you hear me?"

The familiar voice cut through the haze. Sam heard her aunt's voice call out to her though it sounded strained and far away in her mind. The depth of blackness waned as reality surfaced and the dream diminished.

"Sam, wake up!" Claire shouted, shaking her.

Watching the girl for signs of recognition, Claire continued to shake Sam's shoulders until she pulled herself from her dream state.

Freezing in place, Sam's amber colored eyes were wide with fear as she struggled to catch her breath. Claire was visible in a fragment of moonlight that filtered through her bedroom window. Slowly she brought her shaking hands to her face to see if the blood was there. Nothing but her sweat-dampened hands met her gaze.

"Look at me, my child. Look." Claire said sternly.

Sam moved into her aunt's comforting embrace, letting the soft voice calm her and protect her from the unknown demons haunting her nights. She moved to bring herself closely to the warmth her aunt's embrace offered, she felt her body burn with an inner fire, every muscle withering in pain.

Claire watched her niece and she could not deny that this time Sam's eyes were indeed glowing. The signs were emerging. The knowledge that the passage had now opened, Claire pulled her attention back to comforting Sam and away from the ramifications that knowledge unlocked.

"Listen to my voice." Claire's voice continued to sooth the young woman as she stroked her fingers across Sam's forehead, creating a melodic tone that floated through to her, as calm as water on a still day. It sounded as if she were calling Sam from another room. A part of all things, the words vibrated as they moved through the night penetrating the darkest corners of her mind. Claire's voice streamed through Sam's veins, calming the fire of her fear, quenching the hidden beast within her.

"You're here with me, you're safe." Claire's voice sent a tingling sensation along Sam's spine as it continued to soothe her fears. The seemingly hypnotic words took her to a trance like state.

Voices came and went, laughing and talking but never clear enough to make out a single word. Senses dipped and flowed with every movement of her aunt's hands across her face. Finally, reality won the battle over darkness and Sam's shaking body slumped in defeat.

Claire grabbed her wrap throwing it around her shoulders as she lifted her hand to her neck to assure the silver charm hung securely. This scene had played before and had brought only horrific memories to mind for Claire. The perceived dreams were growing in intensity and although she loved her niece, she knew inwardly the power held by the young woman, and protected herself against that moment when the child's dreams might become reality. A memory came flooding back to Claire, one of her own childhood.

"Claire, are you afraid of the night?" The simple question seemed odd to ask, but the answer needed spoken to protect her best friend.

"Not so much Paulie." The nickname flowed off Claire's lips as it had for so many years. Reaching into the pocket of her nightshirt Paulette pulled out a necklace and presented it to her dear friend.

Moving her hair back, Claire turned to allow Paulie a clear view allowing her to clasp the necklace around her neck. The silver charm hung midway between the cleavage of her forming breasts and was framed by her dark flowing locks of hair. Roses surrounded a silver cross with a silhouette of a wolf's head peaking from behind the rose vines. The wolf had a distinctive look, but though Claire had studied the gift many times over the years she could never distinguish what made the charm magical to her.

As if prompted by Claire's voice, a light breeze brushed Sam's cheek. The late October night dried the sweat from her body.

The sounds of the night eased her mind drawing the deepest fears away. Steam rose from the surface of the lake, covering the ground in fog as they walked along the bank. The sound of the water lightly touching the shore echoed when it retreated. They found a stone bench that was situated between the forest and the lake and that is where they chose to sit.

"Take a deep breath of this wonderful night air."

The soft command of her aunt broke the serenity of the soothing trance Sam had given into. Eyes, amber in color, fought to find focus. She was no longer in her room, but on that stone bench. She brought her head around to the direction of the guiding voice. This was not the first time their journey had brought them to this bench.

Like a child searching for safety in her mother's arms, Sam laid her head on Claire's shoulder. Claire took a moment to look at Sam before she welcomed her warmly. Sam's long hair appeared black in the light filtering into the forested nook, shining from the moonlight as if it were a living creature.

"My, my, child. What are we going to do with you?" she asked as she twirled Sam's long, dark hair through her fingers.

"I'm sorry…" Sam started to say but Claire hushed her and patted her head.

"There's nothing to be sorry about. We will find the underlying cause of this. For now, though, I think we need to get you back to bed. I will make you some of my special tea before you go. It will help you sleep."

Using the chill of the night as an excuse to leave their surroundings, she maneuvered her niece in the direction of the house.

"I didn't hurt you, did I?" The anguished question escaped, as they began their walk to the house.

"No, it wasn't like the last time."

Claire's mind flashed to Sam's last dream. Sam had clasped Claire by the throat like a savage animal tearing at its prey the last time. Only the spell of protection, chanted in desperation against her own niece, had kept Sam from killing her.

Sam's words during that last episode still haunted her.

"It's all your fault this is happening, sheer ignorance has brought me to this point, I should have been told."

The look of hatred, the words spit with disdain. This was not her Sam speaking so savagely. She didn't know who it was, but she knew in her heart that it wasn't her niece.

"This dream must have been calmer."

Sam looked at her aunt in sheer disbelief. "Calmer? I feel like my heart is going to jump out of my chest and this one was calmer?"

Claire didn't respond. She didn't know what else to say. Sam shook her head and they didn't say another word as they walked back to the house.

Sam's dream didn't go unnoticed to another person as well. There was someone watching them from just beyond their range of vision as they walked back to the house, someone who had always been watching. The guardian shook his head as he watched the door close behind the women.

Claire's property laced large mountains which the guardian had established a base camp, a shelter from his compound some miles away. From this vantage point, he could monitor Sam from a distance and not be obvious in his actions. He walked back to his campsite and thought to himself. "Crazy old woman, thinking the silver cross around her neck would protect her." Generations ago, this might have helped, but the genetic pool had changed and little could be done once the mutated cells emerged.

The campsite was located in a large split in the mountain's side where a dormant spring had once made its way through. The sides were lush with vegetation, completely covering the entrance of a cave. The stranger walked through the heavy growth to sit at his small campfire within the cave. He pulled out a pad and a pen.

"Saturday, October 10th. The nightmares are intensifying. Two months ago, they became more frequent and since the beginning of October, she has had one every night. Claire has done what she can to soothe the young woman after each episode. Mutation has begun, not much to do but watch at this time. (I still have to decide if I will send word to the council and take the necessary actions requested of me some time ago.)"

Placing his pad and pen back into his bag he moved to bed down for the night. His plan of action for the future ran like a movie in his dreams, the Council, the young lady, the old woman, the beginning, all merging into a complex puzzle.

The house was silent, only the sound of the unseen insects and frogs filling the still air. Claire guided Sam to a seat by the kitchen table while she steeped the tea.

The kitchen was one of the largest rooms in the house. The cream covered wallpaper with the slightest wisp of flowers ran from the floor to the ten-foot ceiling. Sam had found herself welcomed by her aunts' loving embrace as she entered through the walkway from the back door into the kitchen, for more memories than she could remember.

Clarence Davis, Claire's great-grandfather, had built the large, 6-bedroomed house in the early 1800's. Migrating with his family from Ireland, his travels had brought him to the northeast corner of Kentucky. Instantly recognizing a place where his family could flourish, he bought as much land as he could acquire, and thus established the family homestead.

Starting with two hundred acres, it didn't take long for Clarence to procure an additional two hundred and plan his family's future. His land was set in the Appalachian mountain range, the land offered valleys excellent for farming. With the additional land in the mountains, the wood for expansion was readily available, and cut for personal use as well as for sale. It added income to the family fortune already well established. Through the line of succession, the farm had passed to Claire as an inheritance.

The family home was built to endure the changing seasons, civil war unrest, and the hands of time. Standing three stories tall, Claire's grandfather had renovated the house during the Victorian era, where the house's ambiance felt perfectly arranged. The wallpaper in the kitchen had been replaced many years ago, matching the pattern that had adorned the walls of past days. It had taken a trip to Chicago to find a company willing to produce the needed pattern. The result as pleasing as it must have been to Claire's ancestors.

Sam glanced at the clock. Feeling exhaustion overtake her, she lowered her head and wept quietly into her hands. Claire tried her best to distract her with a plate of butter cookies. Sam wiped her face hurriedly with her hands forcing a grateful smile.

Claire was about to say something soothing when the teapot started to steam. The woman jumped, startled by the sudden screech, and slightly chuckled with the foolishness of her reaction.

"Well, I guess its tea time."

Claire got up to retrieve two cups and the teapot. She returned to the table and placed a metal tea strainer in each of the cups. Hot water dropped over the strainers, instantly filling the room with a sweet, heavy aroma. Sam stirred the mixture as she watched the steam rise from the cup.

"I have added something special to the tea. Let us see if you can pick it out."

Claire's voice flowed rich with the refined drawl of an educated southern woman. Her father had been adamant that his children be raised with refined tastes and not in the style of the hillbilly genre, which had swept that part of Kentucky. Eight children had been supplied a disciplined education with private tutors brought from the East. The children's tutors lived with the family and led their young charges in studies, shielding them from the education offered with native teachers speaking the rogue dialect of the territory.

Sam placed the rim of her cup to her lips and took a sip.

"There's chamomile, vanilla, vervain, lavender and…" The taste escaped her as she struggled to identify the last ingredient. Slowly she brought the glass to her lips taking another sip, letting it linger in her mouth. Still vague on the ingredient, the need to know was lost to the teas calming effect on her throbbing headache.

Her blood warmed in her veins, streaming its way through her body. Her eyes suddenly became heavy. She looked up at Claire and saw her smiling and she noticed that she never once took a sip of her own tea. Sam looked back down to her cup and savored the inviting aroma. She picked the tea cup up to take one last drink.

"Is it jasmine?" she asked, as the sudden weariness encased her body and mind.

"You forgot the most important ingredient." Claire said with a smile.

Sam knew this answer. She smiled and slumped a bit in her chair. Her eyes felt as if her lids had been tied to weights and she fought hard to keep them open. The cup in her hand began to waver and Sam quickly sat it on the table for fear of spilling the magical potion in her lap.
    "The most important ingredient is love."
    The words hung heavily on her lips as she succumbed to the sweet lure of exhaustion that had overtaken her. Leaning forward she put her head on her hands and drifted into a deep slumber.
    "Indeed it is, my child. Indeed it is."

CHAPTER TWO

Light filtered through the muslin drapes of Sam's bedroom windows. Most mornings she enjoyed the shafts of golden light and rainbow colors dancing on her walls. Her eyes, still heavy from the deep slumber of night, refused to open completely. The sun signaled the start of a new day and invited her to join. Her heart was unwilling to face the day. She stretched the aching muscles that ravaged her body, yawned and rubbed the residual sleep from her eyes.

Her room, which was a warm cream color, came alive with the streams of sunlight reflecting on them. With the sun glistening through the drapes, the setting created the semblance of a sun-laden cloud. Hardwood floors with handmade, knotted area rugs strewn throughout gave a comforting ambiance to the space. The rugs were made of old, worn quilts that Claire and Sam couldn't find the heart to throw away.

Windows adorned the room facing east to southeast. Her room situated on the third floor. Two small adjoining rooms; which had, through time, been used for boarders. Upon turning twenty-one Sam had insisted on renting the space from her aunt.

Sam grew up in the house, living under the doting tender love of her aunt. She had ventured outside of the nest only once to live with her first love. Claire's distrust of the young man should have been a strong indicator for Sam, but love blinds the heart to reality. Home again after a broken relationship with the young man, she had found comfort in all those things familiar to her since childhood.

To the right of the bedroom a small sitting room held the collection of Sam's rare books, a place where she could close herself to the world and escape into the stories shrouded in mystery and adventure. Pictures littered the tables and covered the walls, all silent symbols of her past. Separated enough from the main floors of the home the space afforded Sam the independence she needed yet kept her close enough to her aunt to alleviate the loneliness that consumed her at times.

Those moments of loneliness, were more often than not, those involving the memories of her parents.

Sam's mother, Paulette Cory, was one of the areas reigning beauties. She had done well in school, but her beauty had been the key to a successful marriage. Steve Harris, Sam's father, was lost the first time he had looked into her childish eyes. Paulette's voice haunted him; her rich laugh seized him as a siren luring wayward sailors to run aground.

The tragic accident had claimed Sam's parents immediately. It was only right that they go into death as they had lived in life. Together as one, separated they were nothing. At five years old, Sam found it hard to understand the absolution of death. Living in a world rich with love, being sheltered, pampered and adored by two becomes a chasm of emptiness with death. Running from room to room searching for her parents had been Sam's undoing. Screaming their names while frantically throwing open doors, eventually collapsing in anger, awash with inner turmoil.

The funeral had been full of people attentive in their salutations. Nevertheless, Sam had not missed them shaking their heads when discussing the poor child left without parents to guide her through life. All the while Claire had stood at her side, comforted her, picked her up and carried her when her little heart could bear no more. Her parents had chosen well placing Sam with the devoted godmother and the bond between them had grown through the years.

There was a small living room/library combination off to one side of the bedroom and a master bath to the other. Her parents had left every piece of furniture to her and it adorned the space Sam now called home. She enjoyed the independence of her own space, but also enjoyed staying with her aunt Claire. Here in this house Sam belonged when she had found no place to exist outside of its walls. The uneasy feeling that there was more to her destiny continued to plague her and it was only in the confines of the ancestral home that she found true solace.

Sam arranged her personal effects in the living quarters on the third floor of Claire's home. It had been difficult in the beginning to adjust to the strange environment but with time, as with all things this changed. This space, this home, this woman had all become Sam's lifeline to life.

The terry cloth robe hugged Sam and became a welcome barrier against the slight chill of the morning air. As she opened the door and walked down the staircase, she paused midway. Claire was on the phone, her voice frantic and tense against the backdrop of the quiet house.

Sam felt foolish in her endeavor to eavesdrop, her concern growing as the anguished words of her aunt penetrated her mind.

"Yes, the nightmares are getting worse, more frequent." Sam stiffened as she heard Claire pause and speak to the unknown voice on the other end of the phone.

"Of course it has begun, do you think me a fool?" Sam stood quiet, shocked by the tone of her aunt's voice. She had never known her aunt to speak a cross word to anyone.

"I understand they normally go through this when they mature." Silence hung in the air as the person on the other end responded.

"She should have been guided, this should have been finished before now, and maybe we made a mistake in not exposing her to the influence of her heritage."

The silence loomed as Sam sat on the step, her balance threatened to give way under her trembling legs.

"I've done what I can. This is beyond me now, she must be with you, and I will make the arrangements for next weekend. Yes I understand. I will bring it. It's for the best."

Sam waited until she heard the click of the phone returning to its base on the foyer table. Only then did she yawn loudly and make her way down the rest of the stairs. The smell of coffee met her as she stretched her lanky frame and kissed her aunt good morning.

She walked over to her friend, the coffeepot, and poured a freshly brewed cup of coffee. Retrieving the creamer from the fridge, she looked at Claire, sitting at the kitchen table staring at the sugar bowl. "Hello? Aunt Claire? Earth to Claire." Sam said jokingly. Claire snapped out of the daze that she was in.

"Hmm? Oh! Good morning, sweetie. Did the tea work for you?"

Sam not being one to beat around the bush, asked. "So, who was on the phone?"

Claire sighed. She looked at Sam with love and sorrow and replied. "Sammy, I think that we need to have a talk. I need to get something first. I will be right back."

She rose and left the room returning quickly with a wooden box in her hands. She placed the box on the table between them and sat back down. She opened the box and, reaching in, drew out a golden locket, placing it in Sam's hand. The locket's face wound in an intricate, Celtic knot. The knot held a large emerald. Sam opened the locket that housed a picture of her mother and father on one side, and a picture of Sam when she was a baby on the other. Sam's eyes burned as she turned the locket over and read the engraving. *"I accept myself for who and what I am. There is no beast greater than my own."*

Sam didn't understand what the inscription meant, but judging by the look on Claire's face, she was about to find out. Claire's eyes turned serious, her face set in stern determination as she began to speak.

"You need to listen first to what I have to say. I have to get it all out before you say anything. So just sit there and hear me."

Sam had never seen Claire so stern before, especially not with her. She knew that it was something to be taken serious just by watching her Aunt twist her embroidered handkerchief between her fingers. Claire continued to speak as Sam sat in quiet fear of the unknown.

"That was your mother's. You should keep it now, since it pertains to your circumstance."

"My circumstance?"

Sam was confused by that simple statement and started to say more when her Aunt's hand rose in front of her to silence the barrage of questions she felt sure her niece was about to unload.

"Yes. Oh, I'm finding this difficult to explain. I want to start with a story of your mom, one I have not shared one with you before.

You know that your mother and I had been friends since we

were very young. We had always considered each other sisters. No matter how close we got though, I knew that she kept something from me.

Once we became teenagers, I began to delve deeper into my studies at school. One special occasion, my tutor had drawn me aside and informed me that I was to join a new group that following winter, to further my studies. The study program would place me in a new area away from home and for the first time in my life, away from my family. After I had shared my news with your mother, we decided to treat ourselves to the Dog 'n' Suds for a celebration of my accomplishments."

Claire's gaze moved beyond Sam, attempting to visualize the memories from that night, making it easier to explain them to the captivated audience. She continued her story.

"It was a beautiful yet humid evening. I wanted to change clothes before heading out, so your mother went ahead of me. We planned to meet an hour later. After changing, I started on my usual way to the Suds. I walked alone, like I had so many times before. It was around nine that night."

Claire's narrative became abrupt one liners so unlike the yarns she had spun in the past that were full of magic and wonder at each new spin spoken.

"The moon had shown so brightly through the clouds that crowded the night sky, so much so that I could almost pick out distinct colors around me. I felt someone following me as I walked through the park so I started to walk faster. I felt as if I was being stalked. The danger surrounded me. I screamed for help."

It was evident even to Sam that the memories were coming to Claire through a hard fought battle to retrieve them from where they had laid, hidden for years. She poured herself a glass of water, taking a sip then clearing her throat Claire continued.

"I was so afraid, but I was running out of energy. I knew that I would have to face whatever was stalking me. Fear is our own worst enemy and running from it useless. I had come to a clearing in the trees. I stopped to draw a breath into my straining lungs.

Eyes met mine, golden orbs turning red. We stood there, one afraid, the other curious. The moonlight revealed a wolf raised on its haunches. The animal sidestepped and began to circle around me, not to advance, but to establish its perimeter. I moved backwards, not daring to turn my back on the wolf.

The wolf gave a low growl and started towards me. My fate was unfolding before me. My mind was void, only intense fear of the beast occupied my thoughts. The animal lunged and I screamed and slumped to the ground. I covered my head in some vain attempt to shield my face."

As if on cue, or triggered by the memory her arms raised and folded to cover her face. This simple demonstration caught Sam's heart in mid beat, remembering the dream and the lunge to the throat of the deer; she cringed with self-loathing.

"It was all so eerily surreal and before he could close the distance, something intercepted him. I could hear more than see as the unknown savior slam into the animal. There was a heavy thud as the two bodies met in mid air.

The savage fight ensued, one animal bent on destroying the other. A dog protecting its master without thought of its own danger.

All I could see were those eyes of the wolf. He was now in front of me once again and ready to attack. I could see that it was another wolf that came to my rescue. It positioned itself behind him. It was as if it knew what it was doing. The wolf's intelligence was more than a mere animal could have had. Each movement was calculated in preparation of the others reaction to the attack.

Something connected and my need to run overrode the fear which had consumed me.

Just as I thought the end was eminent, the beast struck once more from behind. Starting low to the ground she leapt into the air and landed on my enemy. Catching the flank of the male wolf, he whipped his head around in shock at the unsuspected attack. Grabbing the attacker in her jaws the female wolf shook her victim flinging him back and away from me. The smell of blood filled the air, and for some reason I knew that this would be a fight to the death for one or the other.

I knew the battle had ended, with a sigh of death the male lay motionless on the ground. The female looked to me and moved to limp away. She was wounded in her attempt and success in saving me. I called softly to her; timidly she turned to look at me, then slowly, almost as if unsure of what to do, she moved toward me. The fear that had held me with the other wolf was now replaced with an unknown courage.

How odd that her eyes were so familiar to me, as if I had looked into them a million times before. Such sorrow also lay in those eyes. She looked from me to the dead wolf just beyond us; the sorrow evident in her eyes that touched me as nothing had in life prior to that moment. It was almost as if the deed done, you could see in her eyes that she had no other choice.

The wolf moved near me and nudged at my elbow where I had unnoticeably been bleeding. I must have sustained a scrape when I had fallen to the ground. The beast laid herself in my arms I lowered my head to bury myself in her fur and began to cry in reprieve. The clouds had parted and the full moon occupied the night sky, wide and brighter than I have ever known it to be.

I raised my head from my companion and ventured a glance to where the mortally wounded wolf lay."

"Claire I...." Her aunt stopped her in mid sentence, admonishing her to listen until she finished.

"Where the wounded wolf had landed a naked man now lay. The moon illuminated the wounds on his body where the wolf had suffered each blow. The hunter dead, a life sacrificed to save the hunted. I felt her soft pelt and buried my fingers under her neck embedding and moving them in soft strokes on her chest. As I moved my hand to her back, I could feel the gaping wounds she had suffered on my behalf. She let me reach out and feel her soft muzzle. She winced, a sharp yelp escaping when contact was made with one injury. Laying my hands on the wound, I called out a prayer of healing, learned from my mother when just a small child. It was the least I could do for such a valiant warrior who defended my life.

Where moments before any incantations had failed me, I now felt the ebb and flow of healing rise within me and pass to the wolf. I had not lost my powers. I let the warmth of the ancient ways wash through me and allow me to be an instrument in healing. Alerted to some unseen danger, or feeling the call to return to her lair, the wolf moved away from me. There was nothing more I could do but sit and watch as she left. She remained in sight until she reached the edge of the park and disappeared into the tree line. She glanced back as the canvass of night covered her in her retreat.
    I left the park shaken by not only the encounter, but by the knowledge that I had just discovered a dark secret of life. Looking again at the naked man lying on the ground I somehow found the courage to stand. I moved in an arc around the body and ran as quickly as I could toward home.
    Your mother and I did not meet that night. The joy of the occasion lost for me in the shadow of that night.
    It was best, I was too shaken to ask the questions and learn the answers that I knew would come the next time I met with my dear friend. That night was not the time to grow in understanding."
    Claire took a short break from her memories and rose to refill her teacup. The telling of the story was taking a huge toll on her already stressed emotional resources.
    After a brief interlude of concentration, she again sat at the table and continued to fill in the missing links of the story.
    "The next morning I called Paulette and we agreed to meet at Newberry's restaurant for brunch. Before I left the house I snuck into mother's room and pulled her chest from under her bed. Pulling bottles from the inside, I quickly mixed a salve mother had used many times before on my wounds. When I arrived, Paulie was standing in the corner waiting for me. I could see the apprehension in her eyes. I walked to her. Moving to face her, I reached up and moved the long locks of hair hiding her neck. We did not speak, but I saw the mark I sought. I took her hand and led her to the alley out along the side of the building. I opened the bottle with the salve and applied it to her wound.

The red incision burned as I touched it, but the salve quickly extinguished the fire of infection.

She didn't avoid my questions, answering them honestly and without reservation. She explained the mutant gene which dictated her existence, and the rights of her clan. The wolf and she one, the moon their guide, the battle to rule supreme, all laid before me in that one discussion. Werewolf. The word had held only humor for her in the past. Stories my grandfather would tell us children on a slow summer's night, now alive with her explanation, her secret escaping her lips as quickly as she could form the words. Paulie explained all to me.

The beast within was referred to so many times during the conversation that I could not ask its meaning. She had trusted me with her secret and while conveying the legacy she assumed I understood the meaning of the legacy and the beast. It was not until much later that the understanding dawned and filled me with fear beyond any I had known in life."

Claire shared how Paulie broke down the certain sense of responsibility one had when faced with such gifts. She explained how she was termed a Trueblood and that Paulie was from the Myric clan. The Myric clan noted for their clerics and healers and the same group who accepted Claire to study with them. The true nature of the Myric teachers always kept hidden from her until that moment, how she had been chosen to study with her clan and how she had been the only human to be given that privilege. After a long pause to sip her tea and to read Sam's reaction, Claire found Sam had no signs of any emotions.

Sam stood and grabbed the coffeepot to refill her cup; agitated at the sheer irony of her aunt's words she moved to place the pot in its bay. The motion stopped when she felt her aunt's arms move around her neck, slowly moving Sam's hair from the nape she clasped the locket into place. As the emerald dropped to just above her heart it began to glow with an eerie hue.

"It is your destiny child, it is your heritage." The words spoken in a low fervour.

A sarcastic laugh came; there was no stopping once it had escaped. Sam moved her hands to circle her sides as she doubled over in hysterics. Trying to speak she looked to her dumbfounded aunt and again the laughter grew in intensity. Something stopped her, maybe the look that met her, or the tears, which slid so freely down her aunt's cheeks. Something dawned on Sam that this was not a laughing matter.

"So, let me get this straight. You are trying to tell me that my mom was… a werewolf?" Sam struggled to wrap herself around such nonsense and shook her head at the incredible feeling of ironic humor she found in the story.

"Yes, dear, that's what I'm trying to tell you," Claire stated with such force that it left Sam shaken by the conviction in her dear aunt's voice.

Sam dug the locket into her palm as she balled her hand into a fist. "A werewolf."

Claire saw the disbelief in Sam's eyes and tried to reassure her. "I know it's hard to grasp that yes indeed, your mother and your father were both… special. There's more if you would like me to go on. I can tell you how your mother and father met, how their love was inevitable and how they were so excited about having you and how much they loved you."

Claire fought to find one shred of hope to give the young girl in front of her.

"Wow, my mom brought new meaning to the word bitch."

Claire shot back in her chair as if Sam had slapped her. "How dare you. How dare you talk about your mother that way!" She got up and walked away as Sam sat there wishing that she could stick her foot in her mouth.

Claire walked out onto her front porch that wrapped around half of the house, and sat on the porch swing. She visibly shook, cursing all who had worked to hide this truth from her young niece. She said a few words to herself under her breath and the anger began to slowly melt away. She said a small prayer of thanks and continued to figure out a way to convince Sam to cooperate.

Sam was a very stubborn woman, but if she wouldn't cooperate with Claire this time, she might perish despite Claire's efforts to bring her full circle in understanding of the dangers she now faced. Claire went to prayer, but this time the prayer was one of clarity for Sam.

Sam came out onto the porch and sat in one of the white rocking chairs that situated near the swing. Claire looked out onto her property averting her eyes from the young woman until she was sure she had total control of her own mixed emotions.

"I'm sorry," said Sam. She waited for the comforting words of forgiveness and was surprised when the familiar phrase did not come.

She continued. "From what I remember of my mother, she was a wonderful person. I haven't thought about her or dad in years and doing so now has unleashed a five year old that is still waiting for her parents to come home. I have tried to be strong and push them back into my mind with what whit I do possess. I guess looking back at it; no-it wasn't something I should have said. But to find out that your mom was a werewolf? I know that living with you; I have been exposed to some weird stuff. Nevertheless, this is bizarre. My mother... the Werewolf. It sounds like a movie title rather than true life."

"Werewolf or not, she was still your mother and she loved you and deserves respect from you in death as she did in life." Claire spat the words out as she worked to maintain the anger that threatened to consume her at that moment in time.

"I know," Sam answered Claire still never looking at her.

"You never really mourned their death, Sam." Her aunt looked to her with the same tenderness she had shown so often when talking of the young girl's parents and their death. As the anger subsided, Claire tried to imagine the position her niece was in and how the news of her legacy would affect the duration of her life and how it would be lived. A small sigh escaped as she struggled to withhold the tears that threatened to escape as she continued to seal the young woman's destiny.

"I mourned in my own way. Just because I didn't cry in public for days on end or because I didn't break down at every mention of their names doesn't mean that I didn't mourn." Sam's voice went from reason to anger.

Sam went on. "You weren't there at night when I cried silently into my pillow. You didn't see the little girl who had to put her parents out of her mind and grow up faster than what she should have had to. Every day I promised myself to be strong in the hope that my parents would see that I was a good girl and come back to get me, to take me home."

Claire turned and looked at the woman now curled up in the rocker, sobbing into her hands. She wanted to confess that she had been there, but not in the way that Sam would have understood at the time. She wanted to go to her, to comfort her, but Sam had denied comfort so many times that Claire had become self-conscious about it.

Finally, Claire's emotions and love for Sam overtook her own emotions and she went to her. She leaned over Sam and wrapped her arms around her. Sam, overwhelmed with sorrow, clung to Claire and cried, as she should have done so many years ago. This episode was the true mourning that should have come long before now.

Sam pleaded through her hysteria. "Please Aunt Claire, don't leave me, too. I take it back, I promise. Please don't leave me!"

Claire pulled Sam closer and began to weep with her. "My dear child. I have always loved you like my own and I always will. I promise to never leave you. Not even death could part us."

Claire let Sam weep for the tears brought much-needed and long-awaited healing.

It was a while before Sam regained herself. She wiped the unshed tears from her eyes and took a deep breath.

"Ok." Sam took in a deep breath and exhaled slowly. "I think that I'm ready to hear the rest of the stories. Just as long as my dad wasn't the monster from the blue lagoon, or along those lines."

"Sam, sometimes your sense of humor is unbecoming of you. Your father was also a Trueblood." A grin found its way to Claire and worked to soften the intensity of the moment.

"So both of my parents were Werewolves?" The question came as a shock to Claire, she had not thought to explain Sam's father's role in all of this knowing the importance that the alpha female played out in the whole dynamic of her existence.

"Yes, born and raised as such by parents as devoted to them as yours were to you."

"And me?" Twisting and turning like a roller coaster going its course, one question led to another. Thinking to herself Sam wondered how many more turns she could withstand before growing weary of the ride. "Are you a Trueblood? Are there others?"

"No, no child, I am not a Trueblood. Carol Sinclaire, you know her well, and she is a Trueblood and of the same clan as your mother. Over the years I have kept her informed of all signs you have displayed. She and I were chosen to care for you in the event of a tragedy with your parents. She agrees with me that there is a chance with the signs I have seen that you also are gifted as well."

This question was the one that Claire had dreaded facing. The inability to answer it honestly created an unavoidable stir within her. Determined to see this through to the end she ventured forward figuring those questions with no answers would create an uncertain dilemma, but at least they would be problems with a face.

"We are not sure yet." Claire played with the strap on her purse nervously. "Who is we?" The reality of the situation dawned fully on Sam. There would logically be more members to the clan than her and with that one question, she hoped there would be those she could trust to fill in the blanks her aunt seemed unwilling to complete.

Carol, like Sam's mother, had always been a part of Claire's life. A holiday or a birthday would not be complete without Carol popping her head in the door to drop off a special treat and as quickly as she had appeared, she would make her exit. Sam had always chalked that up to her nervous energy, now she pondered if there were in fact a deeper reason.

"Wow," she stated, mesmerized. "So what do the dreams symbolize?" Claire ran her hand through Sam's hair.

"I will answer as many of your questions as I can at this time, but I think that I have informed you of the biggest news thus far and maybe it would be best if we moved to your room to continue to rummage through the memories."

Sam however felt the need to sit alone and go through the memories, and encouraged her aunt to do her gardening and give her some time to collect her thoughts and calm down.

The rest of the morning was lost to Sam. Seated in the sanctuary of the third floor she rummaged through the chest that her Aunt Claire had pulled from the back of the storage room. Pictures unseen for years now lay on the table in front of the small love seat. The locket around her neck had changed color again, moving from the flaming red to soft amber. As she drew a new item from the chest the stone would change again in color, sometimes green, other moment's blue, only once did it again burn red.

Trueblood was the term her aunt mentioned. One which comes from the unspoiled lineage of royalty, one whose responsibility lies with the clan it leads, rich in the gifts of the ancient ones. Sam moved to the windows facing her aunt's rose garden. The sun slowly waned giving way to early evening as she watched the older woman kneeling, removing dead foliage from the late summer blooms. Sam shuddered to think of the anguish this woman had carried to protect her. Moving back to the chest she found one last item tucked into the folds of the silk lining, hidden from the casual eye.

The book bound in rich leather, the language on the pages alien to Sam, but the meaning of the words easily understood. The genealogy leapt out of the pages, names appeared then disappeared as new ones fell into line. Hundreds of generations graced the pages, each with a story unread beside the name. At the end of the book, her name appeared just below those of her mother and father. As with the lineage coming down the names appeared in gold, it was not until she got to her father's name that the ink burned through her senses. Written in blood it stood out among the many names printed in gold guild.

This was the story of the Myric clan, once noted for their clerics and healers, the same clan she agreed to study during this summer internship. It was evident now to her that this was not an act of random selection, rather one carefully chosen to bring her home. Eighty years, that is what the head mistress had said when she had told Sam of her acceptance into the program, eighty years since one name had been chosen from their school.

As if not trusting her ears to hear what was being spoken, Sam returned to her aunt who was kneeling on her worn gardening pad and weeding away at her herb garden. Sam dove right into conversation. "I still can't wrap my brain around it all. You are trying to tell me that my mom was a werewolf." The statement was more of a rhetorical question. Just to feel the words roll off her tongue brought her a sense of peace. It now made sense to her, the dreams, and the strange need for the night. The whole discussion with her aunt ran rampant through her mind.

Sam unlatched the locket from around her neck and ground it into her palm. As she balled her hand into a fist a primal scream escaped from her lips, the cry of an animal in pain running from the truth.

The hairs on the back of Claire's arms rose at the sound. She had heard this before. Claire dusted herself quickly and rose to her feet. The sun was slowly setting, creating a warmed hue around the young lady standing in front of her. She braced Sam with her hands on either side of her and gave her a look of confidence, of support. The look that said. "Overall, I believe in you". They made their way back to the house to make room for the night as the moon hastened her need to seek refuge in her own room. The time to protect her niece was lost to the survival instinct that warned that it was time be in a secure location. Claire and Sam turned in for the night, adjourning to their own rooms. Once securely behind her own door, Claire slipped the deadbolt into place as the primal howl continued throughout the night.

Sam remained in her room for two days and continued to study the contents of the chest. When she finally ventured out she found her aunt patiently waiting for her. Claire spoke first.

"I know this is hard for you to grasp but it is a certainty, as real as the air you breathe, your inheritance as leader of the Myric clan lies in your future. Your mother and father were both, shall we say, 'special'." She waited for Sam's response and when none came she continued with the discussion as if the need for approval was of little consequence.

Wanting to allow time for Sam to digest everything, Claire suggested they have breakfast and continue the conversation after they had met their physical needs. "I have informed you of the heart of the story; the rest can wait until we have eaten." Claire ran her hand through Sam's hair as she moved to the front door. "Besides, I need to run to the open market later and if you would like to go, lunch is on me." Sam smiled at Claire's attempts to keep her happy.

After a light breakfast and a hot shower Sam was ready to face the world. Relaxed for the first time in days, she quickly grabbed her sandals and jacket for their trip to the farmer's market.
Sam forced a smile as she ran through the door. Claire was waiting by the car, watching her run down the steps of the porch, she had to hand it to Sam. Her ability to bounce back from adversity was uncanny. She lost herself in some random memory when Sam's approach startled her. Sam threw her hands in the air in mocked surrender. "Whoa, it's just me. Aunt Claire, what's wrong?"
"Nothing." Claire took a deep breath. "You should not go sneaking up on old ladies like that!"
"I thought that you would have heard me on the porch. Are you sure that you're ok?" The look on Sam's face masked the deep concern she harboured for her aunt during this ordeal.
"Yes, I'm fine-I'm fine." Claire took another deep breath. "Well, are you ready?"
Sam, watching Claire closely and answered. "I am if you are."
"Let's go then." Claire gave a fleeting glance in the general direction of the trees bordering the yard. She could sense someone watching from beyond, but didn't loiter on the idea for long. "Let's go have some fun." Claire ignored the look that Sam was casting upon her. She smiled awkwardly as she passed.
They climbed into Sam's 1978, bright red Scout. The Scout was a gift she had bought for herself using inheritance money from her parents' estate.

The stranger began to journal the morning's events as they had played out:

"October 11th, mid-morning. Claire tried to explain to Sam where she came from and the truth regarding her parents. Claire did not get that far before Sam weakened in a hysterical fit. She is feeble in her human state, soft at heart and easily manipulated (i.e., see volume 113, page 48, reference Danny McDaniel.).

I will continue my recording until I can find the precise time to carry out my mission. Another messenger came to relieve me of my station. I politely declined his offer. I sent the message back to the Council, along with his body. I'm sure I will be receiving an expeditious response in return. I await their acknowledgement."

He then placed the journal in a satchel and made his way from the property.

CHAPTER THREE

Kenny Staiten and Aimee McDonald sat across from one another at Boone's Burger Joint. Aimee's daughter, Katie, restlessly kicked her feet beneath the table. The girls normally ate breakfast at home, but Kenny had invited them to join him in meeting the two newcomers that had arrived in town. Katie continued the persistent kicking as she dipped her French toast sticks into the plastic container of syrup.

"Katie, please. Mommy can't think straight with you swinging your legs like that." Katie stopped abruptly and replied. "Sorry mommy. Kenny, when are they going to be here?" Kenny looked down at Katie. "Anytime sweetie."

"Why do you think they were called to the area?" Aimee's voice held a hint of apprehension evident in the softly whispered question.

With his answer, he tried to convey a nonchalant attitude that was not from the heart. "I'm not sure. It might be a midpoint until they can assign them to permanent duty."

"Why would the Council want information on the Daniel Boone National Forest?" A trivial question she was sure, but the need to pass the time waiting was better spent with silly questions rather than tortured silence mingling with her daughter's anxious banter.

"Who knows? All I was told was that they were given my number to call when they got into town. I was instructed to keep an eye on them and make them feel at home." A mission he was sure would not be to his liking. Entertaining strangers had never been his strong point; he tended to be wary of them, watching for signs of danger. The council would better spend his time assisting the old codger in the hills than babysitting more agents sent.

"What are their names?" Aimee asked as if at this point, names held any special meaning.

"John and Marc. Rumor has it that they were working on a project funded by the Valdens when they were attacked accidentally. Somewhere out in Utah. Bum rap, taking both of them like that."

"And they both survived?" Aimee's voice, incredulous with disbelief.

"Yes, now they are like some dynamic duo the council depends on for special assignments." Kenny's brow drew into a deep furrow as a thought crossed his mind. "It's odd, they are still new, only a couple years or so. I don't think they even know what is going on, yet the council trusts them with so much information."

"Poor kids," Aimee said. More empathic than sympathetic.

"Kids? They're your age Aimee." She lowered her eyes and drew a sip of the hot coffee into her mouth to stop herself from saying more. Shaking his head, Kenny also drew a taste of the coffee in his cup. He spit the brew back into the cup thinking it a crime that fast food establishments had the audacity to call the nasty concoction, that he was forced to choke down, coffee.

"I realize they might be *my* age, but I've lived with this a lot longer…" The sentence lost to ending as she spat the words, anger beginning to flare, her eyes taking an ominous turn in color. Kenny raised his hand in front of her and interrupted the thought process that threatened to overtake her at that moment.

"I know what you meant. I just hope they don't end up like the last guy."

"You mean, Paul? Whatever happened to him? One moment he is in everyone's face, the next not a word or sight of him." She continued to drink her coffee as she glanced to see the progress Katie was making with her breakfast.

"He vanished." Kenny snapped his fingers to make his point. "Just like that. Piss someone off bad enough and that's that." Aimee looked down at Katie.

"I'm glad that we are not a part of it. Has your husband found a clan yet?" A moot question he knew, but the hope was always there that some reasonable compromise could be found.

"No, but his business has kept him occupied lately. He said something about a rumor of one in Colorado. We might check there in the spring." She moved quickly to mop up the spill of Katie's drink as the girl on hearing Colorado turned in excited anticipation.

"Are we going on vacation, mommy?" Katie's voice, filled with excitement, spat out the question as well as small fragments of food still in her mouth.

Caught by the exhilaration in her daughter's question she answered with guarded enthusiasm. "We might. We will have to see."

"Almost nine thirty, they should be arriving at any moment now." Searching the room Kenny strained to see if he had missed any unfamiliar faces.

Something stirred in Katie, where she had fidgeted the morning away now she sat motionless, so much so that both Kenny and her mother turned to her. Katie was looking past the breakfast crowd at the counter, past the restaurant door, into the gift of her visions.

"By accident these gentlemen have come to be. But an accident that was meant to happen cannot be an accident. They didn't even foresee such events; they still do not see the potential. They are both good at heart and though turned, one holds Trueblood." Aimee brushed Katie's hair from her face. "Katie, is that all?" Katie seemed to snap back into her seven-year-old personality. "Uh-huh. They are really nice, and they are here." Aimee and Kenny both sensed them as Katie pointed toward the door.

They turned and looked at the two men walking through the entrance. They noticed Aimee and Kenny right away as well. The two men walked straight up to the table. Kenny and Aimee were both on their feet, waiting to greet the men. The taller of the two was standing closer to Kenny and seemed to be the representative. He held out his hand to greet Kenny. The other offered his hand in friendship to Aimee.

"Hello. I'm John DesRosiers and this is Marc O'Mara. You must be Kenny Staiten." Kenny sensed nothing but goodness from the men. He smiled as he motioned for them join them at their table.

"This is Aimee Parks. The lovely child over there is Katie, her daughter. Thank you for meeting us here. You will understand my concern for the child and mother's safety." This simple statement warning the two strangers to be wary of their actions while in this town and on his watch.

They all sat down. John speaking first. "I don't really know what to say. I have never been assigned to any one particular place." Aimee looked at John suspiciously while ruffling her hand through Katie's pigtails. "Weren't you working on a research project near Lake Tahoe, for the Valden Corp?"

Aimee smiled. "Then you had been assigned before, you might not have known it but you were. Have you found a place to stay?"

Marc replied. "Yes. It's the Cottonwood Apartments just outside of town. Our orders state that we might be here for a while. The accommodations were arranged for us, by our project supervisors, we are supposed to do some research on the Daniel Boone National Forest."

Kenny turned to John. In his late forties, he was tall but not over six feet. His salt and pepper hair was straight and thick from the Indian bloodline inherited from his mother's side of the family. He had it braided to keep it away from his face. He looked like a tough biker with the thick mustache and leather vest, rough exterior, but upon meeting him, realized it was nothing more than that, exterior.

"Do you know what you'll be researching?"

"No, we haven't received those orders yet. We were pulled from the Tahoe project and sent here. The amount of money they were going to pay us, we couldn't refuse." How strange Kenny thought, somewhere in the depth of his confusion he searched the faces of the men looking for a trace of untruth in the newcomer's eyes.

The sound of Aimee's voice interrupted his train of thought. "Do you two go everywhere together?" Marc and John both laughed nervously. Aimee chuckled and added. "Sorry, I mean it just strikes us as awkward that they would assign both of you, at the same time."

John looked at Aimee. "Marc and I have been working together for what, eight years now? I guess they think we make a good team."

"I see. Well, there isn't much to do here in town, small town, small activities." Kenny smiled. "My brother owns a bar at the other end of town. You can meet Chaz there tonight. He's on assignment right here in town. He works for the town during the day and watcher by night."

Marc asked. "Aimee, you said your husband was away?" "He's a contractor of sorts. He's on a job right now, but is due back any day. He will want to meet the two of you. Word of warning, he's not as big of a bear as you think, just as mean as one." Aimee winked at them.

Katie, getting tired of all of the formalities, got up and walked over to John. He greeted the blue-eyed angel with a hearty salutation. "Well, hello Miss Katie McDonald." Aimee watched carefully as her daughter climbed onto the man's lap and stroked his face. Alerted, Aimee kept her focus on the man's eyes watching for any change that would signal danger, relieved she saw only the intense blue eyes deepen in color displaying pure affection for the child. "I want you to play with me."

"Now Katie, I'm sure they want breakfast." Aimee tried to corral Katie from John.

"That's ok, I need to work up an appetite," John offered.

"Let's go to the playground." Katie grabbed John's hand and pulled him toward the restaurant's play area before her mother could protest.

"You've got 10 minutes!" Aimee shouted towards Katie.

Marc caught Aimee's attention. "You would just let your daughter run off with a stranger like that? I mean no offense, but are you sure?"

"Marc, I'm not in the same class as you. If he were to threaten or harm my daughter, I would know before he would have time to act on his impulse. He wouldn't have time to run before I would intercede." To emphasize her point she looked to Marc as her eyes turned an ominous shade of crimson red.

Marc whistled. "Got it. I'm going to order our breakfast. Would you like anything?"

"No thanks, I'm full. They have descent sandwiches here," Kenny said. Aimee pushed her tray away from her thanking the stranger as she declined his offer. "I will be right back." Marc rose from his seat to walk toward the counter to place his order.

"Well, they seem nice." Aimee tried to rationalize, although as she spoke she ventured a glance at the playground where she watched, her daughter and the strange man involved in a heated round of hide and seek. She trusted her own instincts when it came to Katie, knowing that even if hers were weak at any given moment, her daughters unique gift would have alerted her at the first hint of danger.

"I don't think that Katie would have given them such a review if they weren't." Still agitated, she struggled with her own doubts about the two men.

"You will forgive my hesitation then, there are pieces of this puzzle which do not fit. Until they do, I still have reservations. Blame it on the human side of me." He shrugged his shoulders as Aimee silently appreciated his apprehension.

Aimee watched Katie taking John by the hand, showing him each slide. As if pulled by the force of a powerful magnet Aimee left the table to join her daughter in the play area with John.

"And this one is the curvy slide. It's scary but a lot of fun at the same time."

"I bet. That's one thing that you miss as you get older, slides." Aimee was enthralled by the ease in which John conversed with her daughter.

"Then why don't you just slide?" The statement simplistic in the eyes of the child.

"It's not that simple, Katie. I wish it were. But life sometimes makes it feel like you are on a slide."

John smiled down at Katie watching as the seven year old girl changed as she spoke to him. "You shouldn't be afraid of what others will think of you. You should do what your heart desires and not listen to that voice inside of you that says you are being foolish." John didn't move from her, but she felt him tense. He sensed that somehow she knew how he felt. This was a little unnerving coming from a seven-year-old.

"Katie, you are wiser than you let on," he spoke trying to alleviate the tension he felt. Katie's eyes lit up with her smile.

"It's a gift."

"A gift, you say?"

"Yes, from the ancient ones. They said that they like the way that I giggle and so they gifted me." She seemed surprised by the skeptical look on his face. All of the adults in her life had known of the gift and accepted it without question.

Suddenly uneasy with the child he suggested they return.

"Why don't we go back to the table with your mommy and Kenny? I still need to eat breakfast." As they moved toward the door John noticed Aimee watching them, her eyes were burning a luminous red color. He heard the soft growl as she bent to hug her daughter as she ran into her waiting arms.

Katie led the way through the door, skipping and humming to a song that no one else heard. "I hope she wasn't too much trouble." Aimee took Katie in her arms.

"On the contrary, you have a very beautiful and bright young lady." John tried to establish the groundwork of trust with the woman, but wasn't sure her response gave him much hope.

"You hear that mommy, I'm beautiful and bright!" Katie's eyes danced at the sound of the compliment rolling off her tongue.

"You know you are, you silly girl!" Aimee tickled Katie.

Marc approached the table with a tray full of food. "John, I ordered for you too." Marc handed John a large cup of coffee. Kenny and Aimee sat across from each other and talked as the two men ate their breakfast. A wry smile between the two, wondering if their guests would show their disgust for the 'coffee' too.

Katie bored with the adults asked if she could go back into the playground area. Aimee agreed and watched Katie's pigtails bounce as she skipped towards the door.

Kenny carried most of the initial conversation while the men listened intently. "Beyond Chaz and Brad, there are no others in the town or county. There is a Myric about three hours from here. There has been some suspicion that agents have been sent to watch the woman, but we've not been able to sense them."

"As far as humans go, are there any people we should stay clear of?" Kenny and Aimee went on high alert at the question, their thoughts the same, were they asking as men or beasts.

"Most people here are really nice. There are a few thugs

around, some white supremacists and then there's Danny McDaniel. He's the hothead cop in this area. We believe that he's compensated to give safe passage through town, for some drug traffickers. He's nothing but an ass, and a dumb one at that. So, watch yourself. He likes to poke his nose in everyone's business." Kenny's last statement, spat with venom, made them wonder what issues this guy had with the local authority.

Aimee smiled at the men and added. "Other than that, it's a really nice town. You don't have to lock your doors at night. There's also more than enough hunting to be had. We have a lot of friends in town that own hundreds of acres and have given us permission to hunt their grounds."

"We haven't been hunting since we got here." Marc said with a hint of need in his voice.

"Then you really need to meet Chaz. He goes out almost every night. But you have to understand, because of his size, he needs it." The group talked over numerous refills of coffee and sandwich wrappers until Marc and John were finished.

"Well it's been nice meeting you, but Katie and I have to get going. We need to get to the market before it gets much later." As Aimee stood to leave both men in unison stood to shake hands with her.

She looked at John and Marc. "It has been nice meeting the two of you. If you need anything, give me a call." After saying her good-byes, she turned and walked to gather Katie from the playground.

Kenny turned to the guys. "I'm afraid I have to leave also, I have to get the bar ready for tonight. You should come and check it out. Like I said before, Chaz will be up there for sure." He shook both their hands as he stood to make his exit. John and Marc cleared the mess from their table and headed toward the door.

"So, you want to check out this market they were talking about?" Marc asked as they stood on the sidewalk outside of the restaurant. "Why not, what else do we have to do this morning?" The two men parked their black suburban on Main Street and meandered through the market.

CHAPTER FOUR

Sam and Claire arrived in town around ten that morning. It was usual to see the hive of activity bustling through the streets on a Saturday in Pinbrook, KY. The town closed down Main Street once a week to hold their "Open Air Farmer's Market". Most of the businesses in Pinbrook would participate as well as many of the farmers from surrounding areas. The market attracted tourists and many residents from this and adjacent counties, boosting the small town's economy.

The market spanned four town blocks. Main Street had always resembled a postcard from the late 1800's. The cobblestone streets still echoed with the passing traffic. The decorative light post's lining the streets were new, but fashioned to maintain the antique ambiance of the town. Buildings were all original structures from that era with the exception of updated electrical wiring and indoor plumbing. Scattered among the parking spaces there were once hitching posts placed for the Amish families that would come to town for supplies.

Businesses catered to tourists, set ideally on the route most had to travel to arrive at the Appalachian Mountains. With a plethora of state parks engulfing the surroundings, the town merchants thrived on the tourist trade. Familiar faces and those of strangers mingled during market day. Pinbrook always welcomed visitors, strangers, any walks of life, just as long as they spent their money as they passed through.

Sam turned to Claire. "I hope the Jenkinsons are here, as I've run out of her homemade strawberry jam."

Claire rummaging through her purse glanced up casually, searching for the booth. "I need to see if Carol is here too, you run along and shop. I will meet you at the Sacred Grounds Café at eleven thirty. We'll have lunch then." Although she was disappointed she could not spend all her time meandering through the market with her favorite person, it was essential she speak with Carol alone.

Sam agreed and started on her way, the wicker basket in a nearby booth catching her eye. She loved Sacred Grounds, the food selection offered was some of the best in the area, and the dessert pastries were to die for, exactly the type of medicine she needed to brighten her mood. Sam had brought her large cloth satchel to carry her purchases, learning the hard way years ago that it was a pain to carry a bunch of separate bags. Turning the basket over to admire the intricate artisanship, she laughed to herself.

Claire's father may not have liked the backward ways of the Kentucky Mountain people, but there was no denying their work was some of the best in the country. She knew most all of the vendors and what they sold, The Wrights sold breads, cakes and other desserts and this was Sam's next stop after purchasing the basket for her aunt Claire.

With her mouth full from a sample of cinnamon roll she got at Wright's booth, purchasing two for herself of course, she continued down the line. Before she arrived at the next booth, she felt a tug on her satchel. She looked down at the young girl in pigtails who demanded her immediate attention.

"Hi Sam! What are you doing?" asked Katie.

"I have to get some jam, I've run out and my toast hasn't been the same since. What about you?" Bending to take the child into her arms she commented. "I swear, Katie, you get cuter every time I see you." Sam watched as the beautiful little girl blushed through her dimples. She had long hair that was a sun-kissed brown, it would have appeared longer but the pigtails disguised the length.

It was amazing to watch Katie at seven years old studying with Aunt Claire. Since she had grasped the English language at a young age, she had come to their home to be taught the ways of the ancient ones. It was evident even then that she had unique powers. Carol had contacted Claire and with Aimee and Brad's approval, Katie had begun her studies at age three. Claire agreed to the arrangement only after another student, Nicki, left her to begin her studies with the Myrics.

"Mom and I are shopping for a gift. I got two A's on my last report card."

"Good for you, Katie. Keep up the good work." Sam patted Katie on the head. Katie took Sam's hand and started to walk with her.

"Where is Aunt Claire?" She glanced behind her, turning so that Sam's arm became entangled and looked like a giant pretzel the child was connected to. Twisting to follow the pull of the child's hand, she was turned in a full circle.

"She's looking for Carol Sinclaire. She is going to meet me at the Sacred Grounds later, if you would like to join us?"

"I would but mom and I have to get back to the house. We are waiting for a call from daddy. He's working." She said quite matter-of-fact.

Sam knew what line of work her father, Brad, was in. He was a valued bounty hunter. He brought in criminals and missing people all of the time. She never really had the chance to sit down with him and talk about his profession. She had known Brad and Aimee all of her life, but always felt uncomfortable bringing it up. Aimee and Brad had been in all of her school classes growing up. It was hard to go through life in a small town and not have your life intertwined with those around you.

"Is he far away?" She knelt to brush some of the crumbs from Katie's blouse, dropped from the cinnamon pastry Sam had shared with her.

"No, not far." Sam knew that Katie had a way of knowing things, without ever being told and did not press the matter. A casual conversation with the child could be trying at times. One was never sure if they were talking to Katie the carefree child, or Katie the seasoned cleric.

As they continued to walk towards the next booth, Aimee came up behind the girls. "Katie, have you deserted your mommy?" She joked as she nudged her daughter,

"No mommy," Katie said as if her mom should know better.

"Sam's my friend. You are my mommy. There's a difference."

Aimee and Sam had a hearty laugh as they hugged. "I hear that Brad is working right now." Sam stated.

"If he isn't hunting people, he's hunting everything else. Oh, I guess that didn't sound right."

"I know what you meant." Sam smiled.

"He's supposed to be back sometime tomorrow. He's been

gone for almost two weeks. Katie and I miss him, don't we honey?"

"Yes, he'll be home before you know it." She looked up at Sam. Sam saw something in Katie's eyes that caused her do a double take, just as in the restaurant that morning Katie had gone still, reaching up to stroke the side of Sam's face she said.

"It is as it is."

Returning to her usual self Katie looked up and smiled. Aimee glanced from her daughter to her friend and a cold shiver crossed her body

"Well, I have to get back to my shopping." She released the hold she had on the child's hand and spoke to her. "Are you coming over Monday?"

"Yes, after school." As she skipped away, she yelled over her shoulder. "I will see you then." Odd thought Sam, Aimee did not say goodbye.

Sam stopped at the next booth that belonged to the Jenkinsons. She browsed the many offerings the booth held and, finally deciding, she bought her favorite jar of strawberry jam. She placed the jam in her satchel and continued on to the next booth, hoping that Claire had not already purchased the needed supply.

Henderson's booth caught Sam's eye, loaded with new and used books, she could spend hours just browsing the titles offered. The traveling bookstore as Sam put it, reminded her of a gypsy gathering. The Hendersons always watched the customers to assure them they would not lose merchandise to unsavory characters. Specializing in rare books, the covers in the old leather style aroused her senses each time she entered their booth. Sam said hello to Mr. Henderson as she skimmed through the 'New Release' section. Rarely finding the new books appealing, she would skim the titles to see if anything caught her fancy. Her heart, her passion lay in the antique literature.

She browsed through the titles of the antique books, some gilded in gold, others in red lettering, all stacked in a meticulous row of inviting adventure. 'The Tale of Two Cities', '1904 Farmer's Almanac', 'Fannie Farmer's Cookbook', 'Folklore, Legends and Myths of the Werewolf'. Sam stopped, her heart caught in her throat. Picking the book up, she leafed through it and then quickly closed the pages. Cautiously she looked around to see if anyone had noticed her reaction to the title.

She took the book as well as two others to the front of the booth, handing them to Mr. Henderson as she reached into her satchel, pulling out her wallet to pay for her purchases. Mr. Henderson, who'd normally read the titles of each of Sam's choices, read the spine of one book and looked up at Sam. Sam startled by how quickly Mr. Henderson's facial expression changed. He went from jovial, to lifeless then back to happiness in a breath of time. Sam had seen and noted the change. After silently placing the books into her bag, Mr. Henderson tried to force a smile.

"Werewolf legends eh? That's not your normal choice of reading material Sam." His voice unsteady as he struggled to maintain their normal banter over her purchases.

"Oh, you know, getting close to Halloween. I thought that I would broaden my literary horizons," replied Sam.

Mr. Henderson lifted an eyebrow over his sunglasses and when he lowered them, his tension eased a bit.

"If you like this one let me know. I can find more books on legends for you." All he had to do was choose from his own private collection, stored carefully on the shelves adorning every wall in his house.

"Thank you. I'll let you know next week, if I have time for this one it will be a miracle." Thinking in the back of her mind that with the new revelations concerning her life she just wasn't sure how the next moment would go let alone the next week. Would there still be time for her reading passion?

"I'll be here." He moved toward his wife, thus dismissing Sam to her thoughts.

Sam ambled slowly down the right side of the market when she noticed the town's vagrant sitting on the curbside. He was looking at her and talking to himself. She walked over to him and handed him the extra cinnamon roll from her bag.

"Good morning, Gabe."

Not looking up he took a bite of the roll and mumbled with a full mouth. "Good morning Samantha."

"Good business today, huh? Really busy." Idle chatter was better than watching him devour the roll with the passion of a pig at the trough. Gabe didn't acknowledge her, he just grunted and continued to chew.

Knowing the conversation had ended, she turned away.

"Well, have a good day, Gabe." She said over her shoulder.

Gabe mumbled almost sarcastically. "Sweet dreams."

"What did you say?" Startled by his words Sam turned around.

"Sweet things," he repeated as if that was what he had said. He held up the pastry and smiled with a large piece of roll in his mouth.

Sam smiled suspiciously and nervously added. "Yeah... bye."

She turned around and vanished into the crowd once more. Gabe watched Sam disappear into the throes of people while he chewed on the roll. He waited only a moment more before he leaned to the side and spit the roll out of his mouth. He threw the rest on the ground and retrieved a notepad and pen from his pocket.

"October 10th, continued. Sam greeted me in the market today and gave me a sweet roll. Her heart for those less fortunate will get her killed one day if she is not careful. She has bought jam, two rolls and a book... on werewolves."

He turned his attention back to the crowd when he was taken aback. No sign of Sam, seeing only Katie standing in the middle of the crowd, staring at him. She didn't move, nor did she blink, she just stared at him with her intense blue eyes. She could have been made of stone from the lack of expression on her face. Gabe let out a low guttural growl, which made the few birds that had swooped in for the discarded cinnamon roll, fly away.

Gabe's focus wavered for a moment by the fleeing birds and quickly returned to where Katie was standing. She was gone from sight. The encounter unnerving, he quickly pushed the scenario out of his mind. Not alerting 'young' Katie to the council, a deliberate oversight on Gabe's part.

An unusual sensation overtook Sam as she made her way to the other side of the street. As if it happened all at once, she lost all hearing excluding the thudding of her own heartbeat. Losing track of time, things seemed to move in slow motion. Pulling herself from the haze, she looked up just as she ran headlong into a man. Hitting his chest, so hard that her balance was thrown off, and his momentum forced him back three steps. Her heart sped up and her breathing became hard from the impact. When she tried to right herself, she dropped her bag, the thud resounded with the clink of breaking glass.

An arm reached out to catch her, but she was oblivious to the touch. Moving quickly to evaluate the damage in her bag, she blurted in a rushed voice. "I'm so sorry." Kneeling she struggled to pick up her bag.

"Geez. Sorry lady. I didn't see you, are you OK? Let me help you with that." The man's voice rang in her ears and coursed down her spine like a warm blanket, as he knelt and tried to assist her with the mess. She was suddenly aware that she could smell him. He smelled of cologne, the mixture of sweat and earth as it swirled in her mind like a welcoming breeze. She inhaled deeply and staggered from the enlivening scent.

"Hey, are you OK?" the man asked again.

"Huh? Oh yes, I'm OK, sorry, I'm such a klutz." Sam opened her bag to view the damage. Her jar of Strawberry jam was broken the contents seeping into the silk lining.

"Is this yours?" the man asked as he handed her the leather bound book she had thrown from the bag. His voice still saturated her senses as achy muscles reacted much like to a warm relaxing bath. As Sam started to take the book from him, her hand brushed his. Looking up she met his gaze, and the surge of power ran through her body like a thunderbolt.

"Thank you." The words suspended in the air, her voice heavy with anticipation. She couldn't move, she couldn't speak, her eyes wide from the surprising magnetism between the two strangers. As if drawn to the man's eyes she lifted her own, what met her were the most intense eyes she had ever seen. Locked in the moment as she was, he could only stare back, unable to speak himself.

As she reached to retrieve the book, their hands met again. An electric charge surged through the air, cracking, causing both of them to jump back. The world blurred into nothing as time stopped, Sam lost in the young man's blue-grey eyes. His eyes glazed over, he began to close the space between them outnumbered by the sheer desire just to be close to her.

Someone tapped the man on the shoulder, breaking the trance the two were caught in.

"John, are you alright man?" asked Marc.

John? Yes, that fits. He looks like a John. Sam's odd thought crossed quickly in the recesses of the haze.

"Huh?" John blinked and brought himself back to reality.

"Oh, Uh-yeah, you see, this girl..."

Damn man, pull yourself out of this, he thought to himself, it's just some silly country girl.

"Sam," she offered innocently. John looked back at Sam as if her name called to him.

"Sam?" He rolled her name off his tongue, savoring the homespun feeling of mom and apple pie, of belonging it had invoked in the pit of his stomach. He cleared his throat and forced himself to look at his friend.

"Sam and I seem to be directionally challenged, weren't watching where we were going and well...," John shrugged looking down at the mess in front of them. His friend looked at Sam, and though he was not as enthralled at John was, he could feel an immediate connection.

"I'm Marc O'Mara and this is John DesRosiers." Both men reached to assist her in rising, one grabbing the bag, the other taking Sam into his arms. Standing, Sam brushed at the knee of her slacks knocking the loose gravel from its folds, smiling at the two of them.

"Nice to meet you both. Samantha Harris." She moved closer to John without knowing she was doing it. While her shoulder brushed his, she looked straight at Marc, trying to break the spell they were both under.

"So, are you two just passing through?" Following Marc's gaze, she realized she and John were standing in the middle of the road holding hands. His hand was warm and inviting, with a sense of strength under the tender grasp. Uneasy with the contact, Sam politely yet quickly removed her hand from his. John looked startled, and just as embarrassed as she appeared to be. They both chuckled. John answered her since Marc just stared at his friend in bewilderment.

"We're here on business, on assignment studying the ecosystem of the Daniel Boone National Park."

Sam didn't pay attention to the words as much as the man who spoke them.

"Are you scientists." Still stunned by his friend's fascination with the girl, Marc just stood there.

Again, John picked up the lull in the conversation his friend seemed to be struggling to maintain.

"No, more like research specialists. Isn't that right, Marc?"

Shaking his head Marc smiled as he found his tongue.

"Yeah, research specialists. We study the environmental impact of the dwindling ozone on foliage and wildlife."

John chimed in. "Are you a tourist?"

"Oh God, no. I've lived in this town almost all of my life." Sam couldn't get over the sensation that was still coursing through her body as she once again met the man's intense gaze.

The rest of the shoppers passed the three talking in the street. As in any crowd, Sam was bumped and jostled a couple of times. By instinct bred in most men, they separated to be on either side of her, protecting her from harm's way. A low growl threatened to escape John's throat when one rather scraggly looking character moved into Sam with a purposeful bump.

"Excuse me Sam, you ought to move to the side of the street if you want to gab, make room for the rest of us." Sam looked to Gabe taking the suggestion as if the man's words were a command.

"Well Marc."

She turned to see those intense eyes waiting to join her own. "John."

She smiled at Marc as she reached to retrieve the bag he still held in his hand never taking her eyes from John.

"It has been wonderful meeting you, but I have to go and wash out my bag before I ruin all my other purchases."

"Can I at least buy you a new jar of jam?" John spoke hastily, desperate to keep the girl near him for a few more minutes.

"Thanks, but that won't be necessary, I'm sure my aunt has bought the same as I have so we'd have double anyway."

Holding her gaze on John as long as she could she turned to walk away, the gaze breaking only when she ran into a man standing in her path.

The stone around Sam's neck began to glow with a deep blue color, vibrating, enhancing the already tingling sensations ripping through her. Amazed at the connection she had felt with John, she moved behind a booth just a couple of spaces from where the confusing encounter had occurred. Sneaking a peak from around a rather large man, she held her glance on John. He was tall, well over six feet, not thin but not overweight either, well built you might say. His shoulders were broad and muscular, as if they could hold the weight of the world on them, her world.

The muted green long sleeved shirt with matching unbuttoned flannel vest over it suited John well. The sleeves were rolled up showing his contoured forearms, the veins pushing against the brawny skin. Weight lifting, this she was sure was the only answer to such muscles, each rolling perfectly into the other, joining, flexing, she shivered as she thought of them wrapped around her in the throes of passion. Now where had that thought come from, it was not as if she had never had sex, but sex without passion is wasted energy, as she had learned during her short-lived engagement.

This feeling, this sensation was new to Sam and she struggled to overcome the urge to run back into the arms of the man standing in the street. As she continued to watch the man, the sunshine caught just right on his light brown hair. Cut short but stylish, it glimmered from dark to light as he moved his head, looking at the miscellaneous items on the booth table. Turning just the right direction, he afforded Sam a good view of his contoured jaw line, strong, as was the rest of his bone structure. His face hadn't seen a razor in days, which only added to his masculinity. She couldn't see his eyes anymore, they hid behind the dark glasses that had fallen from his nose during their brief encounter, but she remembered them for sure.

Those intense eyes, definitely his best feature, sliding her gaze down his nose she came to his full lips, shivering with the need for those lips to claim her own. And, like a child caught with her hand in the cookie jar, he turned casually to meet her glance. He smiled and with a slight nod of his head, he chuckled low under his breath. He moved only to disappear into the crowd.

Since she could not melt into the pavement in sheer embarrassment, she turned and lost herself in the familiar faces milling about the booths.

Walking to the door of the little mom and pop grocery store she hurried to the back restroom where she worked at cleaning the lining of the bag. Harry's was the only 'convenience' store for twenty miles. Lined with shelves on each wall and two double-sided shelves in the middle of the room, people in the community still did business with the brothers on an honors basis. "Put it on my tab, Jay." Words spoken and accepted as the only contract needed to ensure payment.

Sam moved to the front of the store from the restroom. Jay, seeing her dilemma, gave her two plastic bags, one for the saturated cloth bag and another to hold the purchases made with the street vendors. Thanking him, she walked through the door into the market chaos once again. Glancing at the Town Square's large chiming clock, she decided she had enough time to purchase another jar of jam before meeting her aunt for lunch.

The Jenkinsons had sold the last jar of jam by the time Sam had made her way back to the front booth. Mrs. Jenkinson put her name on the list of pickups for next week's market. Disappointed, Sam thanked her and walked to the Sacred Grounds Café.

The aroma of coffee beans and sweet pastries met Sam as she walked through the café's door. As luck would have it, there was a free table in the middle of the front window, she made a beeline straight for it. The server stood to the side of the table and waited for Sam to stow her bags and take her seat. Without hesitation, she looked to the young girl and ordered a Caramel latte, knowing the smooth mixture would calm her rattled nerves.

Sam loved to people-watch, as she savored her java-laden beverage. She took a few sips of her coffee and then continued mindlessly stirring it while she enjoyed the crowd. She brought her cup up to her lips, to take another sip, when she received the same sensation as before. She put her cup down and searched the crowd until she found who she was looking for.

As John and Marc walked along the booths Marc looked to his friend in amazement. "I can't believe you," he shook his head as they continued along their path.

"What?" John tried to play off his friend's shock.

"Why in the hell did you just buy six jars of strawberry jam from that lady?"

"It looked good," John said nonchalantly.

"It's because of that chick you just ran into, isn't it. You don't even know if you will ever see her again." The statement burned through John's gut, cutting a course to his heart, a feeling he had thought he would never feel again.

"Then I guess I will be eating a lot of toast, now won't I?" John started to get peeved at his friend's persistence, but Marc continued.

"I'm just saying that that's a hell of a lot of jam."

"Just drop it," John replied. He was just as uncomfortable about the purchase as Marc seemed to be. Although he liked strawberry jam, his tastes did not warrant buying six jars of the homemade concoction. He knew that he had bought them for Sam, and found it odd but was unable to stop himself. Try as he might, the touch of the girl's hand was now permanently set in his skin's memory, the scent of her embedded for life within his soul. He had continued his slow pace through the numerous booths, trying to loosen the strain in his gut.

"Don't get me wrong, she's cute and all-" Marc's statement was cut short by the angry glare which met him.

"Look Marc. I bought the damn jam. I will eat it right out of the jar if it will stop your constant prattle, anything to get you off the subject ok. Just drop it."

"What is your problem, you eat some bad meat or something?" Marc asked as if John's tone had wounded him.

"No." John slumped. "Look, I haven't been getting a lot of

sleep since we moved here." He looked to his friend, the anguish of uncertainty evident in his eyes. Bending to sit on the curb, he slumped forward putting his hands to his forehead, looking as if the weight of the world, was indeed lying across his shoulders.

"No kidding. I've seen your sheets at night and you rip them to shreds. Eating right before bedtime is not a healthy habit."

Marc sensed John's need to talk, to deal with whatever was haunting his nights and causing the night terrors.

"That's just it. I can never remember my dreams, only enough to know that they are stressful. When I do remember them, they have nothing to do with me. It's like watching a suspenseful movie, one where you sit and shout at the victim for running upstairs. I have no control over them and yet I feel every emotion, every sensation."

"Have you tried drinking until you passed out?" Marc slapped his friend on the back and the both of them laughed drawing looks from the people in Henderson's booth.

"Your home remedy for everything." Shaking his head to clear the mood he had been in, John glanced at the old gypsy behind the table. With the dark glasses hiding his eyes, it was hard for John to evaluate the old man, but something had his hair on the back of his neck on end. The old man caught John's gaze and with a nod of his head, he made it clear that nothing escaped his watchful eye.

"Well, if you haven't tried it yet." The sentence hung in the air as Marc reached for a flyer lying on the table as they made their exit from the booth,

"Randy's, live music, good food, good spirits and good times."

Marc thought, this is just what the doctor ordered, a night on the town to alleviate the road weary strangers. It would be an ideal opportunity to size up the community and the native population.

"We can come back tonight, talk more with Kenny and meet this Chaz character. You might even run into your girl and be able to give her the jars, at least get that weight off your shoulders. If she isn't there you can get smashed and use the jam to dip your pretzels in." The program sounded good to Marc if not to John.

"Why the hell not? I need a break." John slumped as if his spirit were completely drained. The thought of seeing Sam again made his tension ease, although the thought caused a shiver of anticipation to rip through him.

Sam sipped on her coffee as she watched as the two men made their way from one booth to another. She saw Marc pick up the flyer on the edge of Henderson's table then watched them as they moved past the front of the café. She continued her vigil, savoring each moment she could feast on the sight of pure masculinity. Another set of eyes also watched the two men move through the crowd.

The men, too busy with their own conversation, did not notice Gabe watching them as he followed. Gabe would stop to dig in various trashcans for bottles to maintain his cover as the town vagrant. No one paid attention to the old man, least of all the strangers mixing with the locals.

Sam drank in the sight of John, the sturdy jaw, the broad shoulders, and the package a feast for hungry eyes. His hips were slim in his worn jeans, and his backside nicely complimented the tailored fit. Licking her lips, she watched John's mouth move as he talked to Marc. She reached to touch them, running her fingers slowly in a circle; she encompassed the perimeter of her mouth. She ached to have more of him than her own fingers caressing her lips. It broke her focus on the men's progress.

The hair on her neck suddenly stood on edge. Glancing out of the window, she struggled to find John and Marc in the throng of shoppers in the street. Finding them near a booth just outside of the café, her senses sharpened. An awareness of need awakened, unlike any she had known in her life, consuming the moment. All she wanted was to walk into the street and into his arms.

The feeling beyond physical attraction came over Sam. It was an animal's unquestioning commitment to its mate. Odd, she thought to herself, wherever had that thought come from? She tried to play the feeling off by thinking how silly she was being. Yet she was unable to stop the emotions rampaging through her already rattled nerves. She continued to watch him: The way he fondled the items on each table, his interaction with his friend, each gesture a symphony of superiority. The dance of the Alpha male, perfect in its deliverance, achieved with little exertion.

Her heart began to race again, the sensations consuming her, she watched as he slowly turned and sniffed at the air. Wanting to draw her attention from the man, Sam was startled when he turned and looked past his friend, past the people clogging the avenue of booths to meeting her eyes. He locked her in place with his gaze.

The moan escaped before she realized she had spoken aloud. A moan of pleasure and need, the emotion so strong it brought her to tears. Grabbing her napkin from her lap, she quickly buried her face in its folds, wiping away the tears she struggled to maintain control of her response to his gaze. Looking quickly around the table she sat at, she watched to see if anyone had heard the moan or seen the tears. When she braved another glance out of the window she once again met by the deepest blue eyes she had ever seen.

Tilting his head to one side, he took a questioning stance, a smug smile spread across his face as he lifted one hand in a wave of recognition. Sam flushed, trying to look away, almost subconsciously, she returned the wave. Biting her lip in a seductive response, she managed to maintain her composure long enough to hold his attention for another moment.

Sam felt like a schoolchild experiencing her first crush: knees weak, heart pounding, 'have- no- clue- what- to- do', pupil crush. John hadn't moved since they first locked eyes. Marc watched his friend become transfixed with the woman in the window, alarmed only when a small growl escaped his friend's lips.

John moved as if in a trance. He made his way without conscious effort, waving, smiling, all for the benefit of the young woman, all to hold her fascination with him long enough to heighten her need. She would be his, this he was sure. Without the taste of her, he would live an empty existence. Whatever it took, he would make sure this rendezvous happened. Lifting his head, he once again sniffed the air embedding the scent of her in his mind.

The weight of sexual desire turned her body into a volcano threatening to erupt from the pressure building within its depths. Matching his actions her face rose as she drew in a deep breath through her nose. Holding her breath, she let the scent mingle with hers.

John walked into the Café and headed straight for Sam. She tried to act surprised when he stopped at her table, but the truth was, she had sensed him long before she saw him enter.

"Sam?" John interrupted her concentration. Turning slowly to allow herself to gather her senses, Sam looked up at John. She immediately blushed. She had always been prone to shyness and this moment was one of the worst she had experienced in her life. As she struggled to find her tongue, she smiled at him, her amber eyes suddenly alive with the sight of him.

"Hello John." It came as a whisper, a seductive whisper, as she moved her head to send an invitation of promise to the man in front of her.

"Do you know much about this place?" He handed her the flyer, thinking about her statement concerning Pinbrook being a small town and added. "Stupid question. Let me rephrase that. Is this a nice enough place to go, in town?" John's mind was really asking if she went there but he hadn't the nerve to ask.

Her hand moved to take the paper without conscious thought on her part. Holding the paper in front of her, she tried to focus on the words and caught only 'Randy's' in bold print.

"Randy's? Oh sure, from what I've seen. I've been there a few times and it's a pleasant place to get to know the locals. The owner and his brother are real nice guys." As she handed the flyer back to him, her hand trembled as it slightly brushed his.

"Oh, so you don't hang out there?" John enquired.

Funny she thought. The looks just like a schoolboy pouting when he realizes his favorite toy is broken. Sam couldn't help but smile bigger.

"I haven't had a reason to go. I have a girlfriend who constantly bugs me to go with her, but it's normally the usual crowd." Sam put her tongue to her cheek and answered. "I've been invited tonight, I might consider going." She lowered her eyes, holding her breath hoping he would give some sign of his plans.

"Marc and I are thinking of going too. If you're planning on going, let's make a night of it. With someone familiar with the local residents it might offer us a way to be introduced. We'd have someone familiar to... you know," John smiled. "Talk to."

"That sounds wonderful. I haven't talked with my aunt to confer on our plans. If it doesn't interfere with hers we'll be happy to join you." There, the words were spoken, the deed done. Sam had never felt so brazen in her open flirtation, nor had she ever felt the alpha-male, alpha-female attraction that loomed before her.

"Great... Ok... Yes." John started to back away, not being able to turn from her. Moving backwards, he bumped into a server carrying a tray of food and only when it splattered across the floor, did he stop and turn around. Swinging in a full circle, managing to keep his balance he reached into his pocket and pulled out a fifty-dollar bill. Handing the waitress the note, he told her to buy the customers, whose breakfast had been ruined by his clumsiness, anything they wanted, then to keep the change. When the wrong had been righted, he turned his attention back to Sam who sat at the table in hysterics. A sheepish grin crossed his face as he moved once again to the table where she sat. She could do nothing more than bury her face in her cloth napkin, trying to gain control of the laughter that racked her body.

Contagious, that is what her laugh was, the sound of a siren calling the sailors of a thousand lonely nights at sea. The elixir of the Gods... it was the music to sooth a man's heart.

"I forgot to give you this." He handed her the bag that he had been holding. Taking the bag, she opened it slowly and gasped in amazement. While she was examining the contents of the bag, John took the moment to move silently toward the door.

As she counted the jars of jam, she once again broke into hysterical laughter, turning to thank her benefactor she saw only the waitress bent cleaning up the mess on the floor. Her glance went to the slightly ajar door where she saw John standing. Lifting his sunglasses, he gave her a nod of the head and moved out of the door. Given no time to protest his generosity she sat back in the chair and let the laughter once again overtake her.

"Oh my God... John." She held the bag to her chest. Turning quickly toward the window she watched to see if she would catch one last glimpse of him in the street. Once he was outside of the door, he turned and through the large picture window, he waved to her. She mouthed thank you. He said. "You're welcome," and backed into the rush of people. He joined Marc with a smile and a renewed vigor in his step.

"Where did you go?" The question was more to fill the quiet between the two men than it was for the need of an answer. Once John had come back without the bag Marc knew where he had been. The thought of his friend falling over himself because of some woman was a bit disconcerting, but knowing his friend for as long as he had, he knew that John did not fall into anything without careful consideration.

"I went into the coffee shop. I thought that someone in there might know a little about Randy's." The fact that John tried to shrug off his question with a vague answer somewhat threw Marc off guard.

Suspiciously, he asked his friend. "Well? Did you find out?"

John's eyes began to flash. "Yes."

Marc stopped his friend and looked at him incredulously. "What's going on?"

Happiness was one thing, but concern grew that John might cross the line jeopardizing their assigned mission.

"Nothing. Can't I just be in a good mood?"

Good mood, how ironic that was, until they had been assigned to come to this little hamlet in the middle of Kentucky John had spent months in a brooding stupor.

"You? Lately? Hell for months you have been a bear to be around. So, my answer would of course be... you can be in a good mood, it sure beats the alternative."

John laughed at his friend and slapped him on his back.

"Things are looking up my friend, certainly looking up. Come on, let's get some lunch." John's step intensified as he worked his way to a booth selling hot sausage sandwiches.

Not letting things lie, and just for the fun of being able to egg his friend on, he continued to ply John with questions.

"Hey, where's your bag?" He almost lost it with that question, laughter threatened to escape but raising his sandwich he took a large bite to alleviate the need to burst into hysterics.

"I dropped it off." John didn't look his friend in the eye, seeing him stuff his food into his mouth to cover the laughter he did not want to run the risk of making the poor man choke to death.

"Oh, I see," said Marc. The statement had drawn out through the last swallow of food. Like a man intent on finding the last piece of the puzzle, he continued searching for the missing parts. Marc put the puzzle pieces together.

"So, was *she* in there?"

Weaving through the crowd, the last of the sandwich in one hand, his purchases in the other John with a full mouth grunt and a nod of the head answered Marc's question.

"Dude, she'd better have a friend!" Marc exclaimed.

Trying to act nonchalant with his friend's inquiries he simply stated. "We might find out tonight."

There was enough strawberry jam in that bag to last Sam until next spring. She sat stunned while the server refilled her coffee cup. A surge of pent up emotions began to course through her. Needs which had lain dormant since her childhood fantasies about love and marriage, suddenly and with a vengeance, surfaced, causing her a moment of panic. It had been so long since a man had caught her attention and to have one so obviously sensing the same attraction created a frenzy of conflicting turmoil in her body.

She had been on a few dates here and there, either the men were boring or they did nothing to hold her attention for more than one evening on the town. Not that they weren't nice, she had been careful to choose men she felt would fit into her plans for her future. But none had aroused her to the point where she would consider spending more time to develop a lasting relationship. Aunt Claire had met a couple and liked them, but Sam had known in her gut that none of them could be someone she could commit the rest of her life to.

When closing the door to a relationship she couldn't explain to them what it was that held her back. She couldn't explain to Aunt Claire that she just wasn't going to settle down before she was ready. The time to make a commitment was something to consider once she finished school and found her way in the world.

Her reaction to John startled her. Honestly, she had never felt a connection so intense with another living being. The urge to run after him, to touch him, just to be near him was alien to her. Mulling over the events of the afternoon in her mind she tried desperately to make some rational sense of it all.

An explanation escaped her for the moment, and replaying the chance encounter with the stranger was going nowhere now. She decided to talk it over with her Aunt, not willing to let it go without some input from someone she trusted with her heart. Learning from experience her aunt was a wise old sage.

At that moment, Claire entered the café, summoned by Sam's thoughts. As she watched her aunt make her way to the table by the window, it dawned on Sam that she had done this since Sam had come to live with her as a small child. Sam watched her move through the crowd, walking the same path to enter as John had used to exit. Sam waved to her, but Claire could not see through a crowd that had finished their meal and were standing to leave the Café. Sam stopped waving when she figured out that Claire couldn't see her and she stood hoping to catch her aunts searching gaze.

"Sorry dear, I couldn't see clearly through the window, I couldn't remember if we were to meet inside or outdoors."

Glancing at her niece, Claire's voice took on a concerned tone. "Are you ok?"

Looking at her aunt, she weighed the question in her mind, struggling to find just the right way to approach the subject of the stranger.

"Yes, I'm fine, a bit confused, it's been quite an afternoon." Sam couldn't hide the smile on her face. As if Sam had not even spoken, Claire continued with her own conversation, not a second thought to the question she had asked the young girl. As she turned to place her bags on the chair beside her, she happened a glance at Sam's flushed face. "I should say so."

Gathering the girl's hands in her own she spread her arms as if she were a tailor. "Yes indeed, your aura is ablaze! Someone stirred something deep inside of you."

Sam could feel the color rise in her cheeks as her aunt watched her carefully.

"A young man perhaps? The question went unanswered, as the color grew deeper on the inexperienced woman's face.

"Aunt Claire!" Sam exclaimed.

"Oh I have to have fun too, you know."

The moment was a rare one that sparked between them; usually Sam would clam up when it came to talking about her gentlemen friends. She had met a couple of mousy little characters to say the least.

She had known that none of them could hold Sam's heart. The last one had been a threat, but with the gentle placement of a harmless spell, the man had fallen by the way side. As much as she had hated the defeated woman who had returned to her home, she had known at the time it was for the best.

"I want your opinion of him. I want you to look into my memory," Sam asked.

Claire pulled away from Sam, the invitation she knew had not come easily for her niece. Only once had Claire dared to enter the mind of the child. A feat she was not anxious to experience again, the moment had come after the first dream.

Sensing her aunt's turmoil Sam pleaded. "There is something about him. Something I can't put my finger on. I need your help figuring it all out."

Claire shook her head searching frantically for an excuse not to grant her niece this one request.

"Have Nicki do it, I don't want to feel your deepest desires. They are too private and uncomfortable for me."

"Please?" Sam asked. When she saw that Claire was not going to budge, she grudgingly gave up the quest.

"Fine, I will have her do it after dinner tonight."

She knew she had been abrupt and possibly hurt her niece, so she quickly changed the subject.

"So, are you hungry?"

"Starving!" Sam answered as they opened the menus.

Claire sniffed the air. "Why do I keep smelling Strawberry jam?"

CHAPTER FIVE

They placed their order while each woman showed the other her purchases for the day, Sam careful not to let Claire see the gift she had gotten for her. They lingered over lunch, watching as friends passed in front of the big window.

The day of shopping over, they made their way back to the car and the long ride home. The accidental introduction made the return home a silent one as Sam withdrew into the sweet memories of the day, and Claire's mind wandered where it chose. Sam drifted off into a lazy slumber, the rhythm of the moving car lulling her to rest her weary body. The dreams came, but those of love and seduction, an altogether different kind of hunt, a different kind of hunger.

Claire was preparing dinner, humming to some long ago song floating through her mind, as she danced around the island in the middle of the generously sized kitchen. Cooking had always been her passion, for her, food was love. You cooked for those you loved and you ate the meals of those who loved you enough to cook for you. Simplistic in its philosophy, it had served to bring generations of her family closer at the beginning or end of a long day of work. She was also happy to see Sam in a good mood.

The morning didn't start out as she had hoped, but she was glad that the market was such an event for her today. She let herself replay her conversation with Sam and the chance encounter with the young man. Claire didn't need to walk through Sam's memory to know that there was something particularly interesting about the young fellow. She had an idea as to what it was, but thought better than to say anything too rash. She would watch Sam and see if she was right. Even though she did pray that this chance encounter with the young man could break through Sam's solitary existence. She whistled a tune and returned to her recipes.

Sam and Nicki were in Sam's apartment, talking.

"We should really go to Randy's tonight," Sam suggested as

she watched Nicki pick through her closet.

"What?" Nicki turned to Sam.

"What do you mean what? I just think it's time to get out of the house, that's all." Sam struggled to hide the crimson color rising in her cheeks.

"Why the sudden change of heart? You have been content on not socializing for over a year now." Looking to her friend, the sentence caught in mid air as she noticed the way Sam averted her gaze. The color in Sam's cheeks peaked as her friend looked at her with sudden realization. "It's because of that guy, isn't it?" Sam just shrugged, turning to occupy her hands picking up the garments Nicki had disregarded from her closet.

"Oh, you can't just leave it at that. Don't tease me, girl!" Sam had always loved the way her friend could see through her emotional barriers. Words could be unspoken for days and if Sam was in a funk, her friend would appear from nowhere.

"He came into the Sacred Grounds with one of Randy's flyers and he asked me about the place." Sam had turned to her, the look on her face took Nicki by surprise. She could sense the longing in her friend's demeanor. The need so great it consumed the girl to the point where Nicki felt concern for her dearest companion.

Treading carefully, she asked. "Did he ask you out?"

"Not exactly," Sam appeared puzzled by the question as if she were trying to decide if he had or had not asked her out. Her brow furrowed in thought.

"So, he just asked you about the place?" Nicki turned away from Sam, going again to her friend's closet to search for something to match the red mini skirt she had chosen to wear that night. Trying to act nonchalant, she pushed first one top then another to the side as she listened for an answer.

"He said that he and his friend were thinking of going up there tonight." She couldn't hide her excitement, try as she could.

"Friend?" Nicki whipped around to face her friend.

"Single? Oh please tell me he's single." Nicki folded her hands as if in prayer and lifted her eyes to the ceiling.

"I couldn't say. I didn't see him with anyone." Grateful to have her focus on anything but the memory of the man who ravaged her mind, she now felt a hint of humor at her friend's desperation.

"Is he cute?" Thoughts of high school and the nights spent in the very house, talking of dreams and boys with her friend crossed her mind. Nothing much changes does it she thought to herself, time passing is the only constant.

"Which one?" The giggle came without hesitation, growing into a belly laugh, which sent both of the girls across Sam's bed. Sam enjoyed teasing the young woman at her side.

"The friend! Oh, you are just toying with me now." Nicki flung the blouse she held in her hand across Sam's face. In retaliation, she grabbed the nearest pillow and began to pummel her friend with its soft fullness, laughing harder with each blow.

"Ok, ok, I give, but seriously, is he cute?" Nicki was still searching for an answer. The girls stopped the childish fight.

Sam, looking to her friend, answered. "Yeah, he's cute. He's a little on the skinny side."

Sam had always preferred muscular men. Those that were the linebackers in school had been her favorite part of the sport. Watching the masculine bodies move as they attacked the enemy on the field.

"Sorry if not everyone likes the linebacker guys you normally go for." Nicki moved to Sam's dressing table where her makeup and jewelry adorned every inch. Picking through to find just the right match for the outfit she had chosen, she looked in the mirror to find her friend's reflection staring from behind her.

"There's nothing wrong with a little meat on the bones."

Sam threw the pillow at the back of Nicki's head.

"Come to think of it, you only dated one guy that was slim, but the least said about that the better." Nicki knew that it was a sore subject and if brought up it would ruin Sam's mood. Sam chose not to acknowledge the statement, choosing instead to act as if she had not heard it. She surprised herself by her own reaction. In the past, the simple statement would have sent her into a funk for days. Baby steps to recovery. That is what Aunt Claire had said. One moment, and one day at a time would become her mantra.

She looked up at Nicki and saw her rubbing her hands

together accompanied by an evil laugh. "He-he-he, fresh meat."

Sam smacked Nicki on the hand as she walked past her sitting at the dressing table. "You're so bad!"

"So bad I'm good!" Nicki had always had a carefree attitude; Sam had envied the girl for her lack of inhibitions.

Nicki was about five and a half feet tall with long loose curls of red hair and brilliant green eyes. She was very petite, almost too thin for her frame. She had lost a lot of weight since her ex-fiancé dumped her months ago, to marry his mistress. After a three-year relationship with that loser, Nicki was devastated. Once she had come to her senses, she realized it was for the best. Thoughts of revenge had consumed the girl. This subsided only when she had ventured a meeting with Kristi Fare, the new wife.

The newly married couple had moved the month before and Kristi felt better with more distance between her and Nicki. Although Nicki put on a strong front, Sam knew that deeply hidden in her friend's psyche was a broken woman still in love with her ex. The hurt was evident during those rare moments when Nicki let her guard down.

"I think you're too skinny to wear my clothes." Sam watched as Nicki donned the outfit she had chosen. She was stunned that it hung so loosely on her friend, where months ago they were clinging to Nicki's body. The skirt and blouse were billowing on her small frame.

"Don't be silly, it's because you have a better rack than me, you fill out your clothes, so what if I am thin, some men like thin." Sam saw the surprise in her friend's eyes as she summed up the outfit in the mirror.

Sam knew her friend saw herself for the first time in months. Reaching into her closet, she drew out a pristine green silk dress she had found in a boutique in Chicago. She had not worn it when she returned home. Although at the time she had bought the dress she had loved the way it laid across her body, it seemed out of place in the small lazy hamlet in Kentucky.

Flinging the dress at her friend she said. "Here try this, it'll set off those intense eyes of yours, what man could resist? But before you do, could you do something for me?" She turned to her friend knowing what she asked was breaking a golden rule between them.

Hesitantly she continued. "I want you to walk through a memory of today. I need you to see what I saw, it is all so confusing."

Nicki whined, trying to evade the subject. She turned to face her friend

"Can we do it after Randy's? You know how it wipes me out." Anything to buy time and allow her to work at the next evasive maneuver she could create. Nicki had walked through Sam's mind once before, the dark depths of which she was not eager to experience again.

"Ok, we can do it after." Sam watched as her friend donned the dress and matching heals, amazed at the way it brought out the color of her skin and eyes. It was as if the dress had been made just for her.

"Deal." Nicki stuck out her hand to shake on it. Sam giggled and shook her hand.

"Dinner's ready!" They heard Claire sing the melodic invitation for the girls to join her.

"Give us five minutes Aunt Claire, I am still dressing."

Hurrying to touch up the makeup around her eyes and lips she gave one last glance at the mirror before grabbing her sweater and heading downstairs.

"How do I look?" Nicki winked at Sam as they headed out the door.

"If you're out to kill with looks, you've succeeded."

John and Marc pulled up to Randy's bar. Though the sun had already set, the night was still early to have a crowd. They walked in to see the night staff gearing up for the crowd they eagerly awaited. The guys sat up at the bar and a female bartender came to take their order.

"Evening, what'll it be boys?"

"Two beers... and is Kenny here?"

The barmaid looked over their shoulders and shouted over the bustling staff.

"Hey Kenny, newbies want your ear." She turned to them and returned to a pleasant tone. "Two beers coming up." As she walked away, Kenny entered the back of the bar.

"Glad to see you guys came out."

"Nice place you got here." John answered. Eagerly looking around.

"This place? Just wait a couple hours when it's packed."

Kenny seemed to have a tone of pride to his statement. John and Marc grabbed their beers and they both mindlessly took their first drink.

"So, where are you two originally from?"

"I'm originally from Texas. Marc is from Connecticut. We met in the army when we were stationed in Kentucky."

"Ah." Kenny said as he pieced the puzzle together.

"Ah?" Marc asked inquisitively.

"We've just never seen two people assigned to the same project who were accidently gifted at the same time." Kenny tried to keep his conversation tactful.

John smiled. "Marc and I were rookies just like everyone else when we joined. That's where we became friends. We found that we worked well together. We moved up the ranks quickly for our short stint in the military."

"Why'd you guys quit?" Marc took this chance to answer. "It was our three year tour. We paid for our college with our time. We decided to get going before they sucked us into becoming lifers. We went to different colleges, but ended up working for the same company and on the same team. We thought it was an unlikely coincidence until after we were both in our 'accident', we kinda pieced some things together. They had been notified of our progress and our talents as…"

Kenny cleared his throat and John stopped talking while the female bartender walked by.

"As regular Joe's. And what a better way to make the Joe's better…" John's tone was not that pleasant.

"I did two tours in Nam, but I had already been gifted." Kenny laughed at the new term that John had stated.

"How long?" Marc asked.

"Let's see. I was 16."

"Fucking 16 years old!?" Marc was amazed.

"Ah, it was my fault. I was a rough neck. I got what I

deserved. Don't ever fuck with the underdogs. You never know what you are going to get."

It was Kenny's turn to sound unpleasant.

"But when I turned 18, they enlisted me in the Special Forces. Over there, we were myths. We became their nightmare."

John and Marc both had to shake off Kenny's look. Kenny noticed and cheered up the subject.

"Anyway, Pinbrook's a nice town. Peaceful, beautiful and rich in history."

"So, where's this Chaz character?" Marc retorted.

"Oh, you didn't meet him when you got here. That's right, he was playing pool. Hold on."

Kenny whistled and turned his attention back to John and Marc.

"He'll be over in a second. So, you guys want something to eat?"

"You serve food here too?" Marc asked.

"We do it all. I'll grab you some menus, but you'll have to take a table." John and Marc stood and went to turn when, without warning, their view was blocked by a very large man. John, at over 6 feet, had to look up. He met the eyes of the very tall and very pale man, who in the darkened bar, appeared to glow from the whiteness of his skin. The man's eyes twinkled.

"Hey there. What's the rush?" Chaz tried to sound tough.

Kenny chuckled at his friend. "Chaz, this is John and Marc. They're new to town."

"So I can sense. Come on boys, come have a seat." Chaz let John and Marc pass by and followed behind them. Once John and Marc sat down, Chaz took his chair and turned it around so that he was leaning the back of his chair against the table.

"How long have you been in town?"

"Only a week," said John.

Chaz nodded. "Yeah, I kinda thought it was around that time. Are you guys settling in ok?" Marc tried to hide his chuckle through a swig of beer.

John tried to cover his friend's reaction. "We went to the market today."

Chaz eyed them suspiciously. "You ain't starting trouble in

my town, are ya?"

"Your town?" Marc snickered.

Chaz stood up for a moment just to try to be intimidating. "Yeah that's right... my town."

John thought he saw a glimmer of humor in Chaz's dark hazel eyes and decided to take his bluff and stood up.

"I hope there's room for us all or there will be trouble." John looked at Chaz as seriously as he could before he blew a kiss to him.

Chaz couldn't hold his bluff any longer, not after seeing a guy only a few inches shorter than himself blow him a kiss. Chaz started to laugh and clapped John on the back.

"You're alright man." They all sat back down and continued to talk through two more rounds of drinks. Chaz was the one to end their visit.

"Well guys, it's been fun, but I have watch tonight. Duty calls." He shook John and Marc's hands. "If you guys want, you can come out and hunt with me."

John's eyes twinkled. "Maybe some other time. There's someone we might be meeting here tonight."

Chaz lifted an eyebrow. "Anyone I might know?"

"Sam Harris," he replied.

Chaz's facial expression turned serious.

"Be careful. She's like the little sister of this town. You mess with her and there will be many people out for your ass. She's already been fucked with before. It won't happen again."

"Chaz. I just met her today. I have no intentions of being mean or messing with her."

Chaz eased up. "Well, if you were able to talk her into coming in here after a year of hiatus, then maybe you ain't that bad. Tell her I said hi. Gotta run."

He threw a twenty on the table and walked away.

"Damn that was one huge dude," Marc stated.

"Yeah, nickname tree trunk," John scoffed.

"Are you sure this chick isn't too much trouble for YOU?"

"Ah, what the hell. Someone told me that I needed to go after things without worrying about what other's thought."

"You are too much." Marc pointed at the pool tables. "Why

don't we start a game?"

"I'll get the balls, you save the table," John said. With that, both men got up and went about their task.

Sam kissed Aunt Claire on the cheek. "Don't wait up. I'm going to be late and I may even stay with Nicki tonight."

Claire hugged her. "Be careful and have a good time. Call me if you need me."

Claire shut the door and the girls were off. Sam rode with Nicki in her convertible Camaro. Nicki was always one to be flashy where she could be. Clothes and cars were her favorites. Anyone in town could hear Nicki coming from a mile away, with how loud she played her radio. Sam winced each time the bass would strike.

Nicki smiled ruefully and only once she was parked and turned off the engine did she speak.

"Hey, I can't hear my radio when I have the top down."

"It's October. You should have the top up! It's freezing."

"I have to enjoy it while I can. Now let's get inside, I'm cold!"

Before they walked into Randy's they gave each other the once over. Nicki picked out Sam's complete attire. Sam wore a pair of tighter than usual, low-riding jeans, boots and a faux suede midriff halter with a tailored brown leather jacket. She always felt uncomfortable when she let Nicki pick out her outfit and this time was no exception. Nicki's outfit was no better. She was wearing a very short black skirt, a green tank top with a cardigan to match, and heels. Sam wouldn't give in to wearing heels. She only wore heels to funerals and weddings. Sam smiled to herself with the thought that Nicki probably wore heels jogging.

They walked into Randy's and were immediately immersed in smoke and drumming music. Randy's was the usual small town bar and pool hall. It had room enough for two bars, six pool tables a dance floor and small tables littered about. The place was surprisingly packed. It had changed since Sam had been there last. A couple more pool tables and a bit more space for dancing, nothing to exciting. There was a band playing cover songs and many patrons dancing away. Sam drank in the energy of the place. If she wanted to, she could go by each person and run her fingers through their auras. She had had a gift since she could remember. She could take snippets of their auras and eat them like fine chocolates. The place was buzzing with alcohol and lust, just like any bar. Sam kept an open mind and hoped that no one was there that would spoil her evening.

She and Nicki went up to the bar and ordered their drinks. Nicki demanded a margarita on the rocks with salt and Sam ordered a bottle of beer. They sat there for a while and talked.

"So, is the guy that you ran into here?" Nicki asked before taking a sip of her drink.

"I don't know yet. We just sat down, Nicki." Sam chuckled at the same time straining her neck to see if he was here.

"Don't mess with me, girl. I can tell you're looking for him."

"Just so you can meet his friend, that's all," Sam said, only half jokingly. "Look, I'm not going to get my hopes up."

"What? The man bought you six jars of strawberry jam. I think that it's safe to get your hopes up," offered Nicki.

"But what if he's some weird psycho or something?" Sam was already trying to talk herself out of another relationship.

"Trust me, you would know it firsthand."

"Danny wasn't at first." The sadness of the statement matched the remorse still buried in Sam's eyes.

"Sorry to break it to you honey, but yes… he was. You were just too in love to see it."

"Was I really that blind?" The thought that she had left herself so vulnerable to another person's influence and control had haunted Sam since the day she had walked away from the relationship. Always confident it was a real awakening to find herself prone to vulnerabilities in love, this was unacceptable to her as a liberated woman.

"You were so happy to be out of that awkward tomboy stage that the first person that took notice of you got your heart, your everything." Nicki motioned her eyes to Sam's crotch. Sam covered herself with her hands.

"Alright, I was stupidly blind. You don't have to make me feel dirty about it."

"Sam, the guy who is lucky enough to end up with you will be just that, lucky." Sam lowered her head and smiled as she blushed. Nicki decided to change the subject. "I'm just thankful that Randy started advertising and brought in a band on Saturday nights. It's really helped his business and brought in some new meat. He's even thinking of opening up something outside, with a grill."

"Why doesn't it surprise me that you know the scoop about the town's bar?" Sam said, rolling her eyes.

"Well, a girl has to have some fun." Nicki smiled and looked around the bar. "I'm going to scope out the place, order me another margarita and order us our shots. We are going to celebrate tonight!"

Before Sam could protest, Nicki had walked away. Sam sighed with a smile and turned back to the bar, flagging the bartender. "Kenny! Could I get another round and two tequila shots with lime?"

Kenny stopped in his tracks and turned slowly. He came down to the end of the bar where Sam was sitting and acted as if someone shot him in the heart.

"Be still my beating heart. Who may this beauty be, seated before me? Oh, Tis, the long lost Sammy. How the hell are ya girl?"

There had been many nights where Sam spent more time talking with Kenny than anyone she came with.

"Sorry it's been a while. I'm good. Working hard. I haven't been out much…"

"It's understood. You look great," he proclaimed.

Kenny knew her ex, Danny, and he didn't blame her for not wanting to come in.

He reassured her. "He's on patrol tonight so he won't be bothering you in here… just watch it when you leave."

"Thanks for the heads up." Sam continued. "Well, I heard that you and your brother are in the marketing business now."

Kenny answered as he poured the shots. "It was my idea. We started with just flyers on the cars at the market, and then went to a whole booth about our fine establishment." Sam smiled and nodded. Kenny didn't waver. "I would have thought that you might be scared of coming in here."

Sam took a drink of her beer. "I have backup tonight, somewhere. Nicki brought me."

"Some backup? You'll end up saving her before the night's over."

"I bet you're right." Sam went to pay and Kenny refused her money.

"This round's on me. It's good to see you. We've missed you."

"I've missed you too. I promise not to stay away so long next time." Waiting customers pulled Kenny away. As he walked away, Nicki plopped back down on her chair.

"Oh there's a lot of eye candy here tonight!" She picked up the shots and handed one to Sam. "To Saturday night," the girls proclaimed a toast together. They took their shots like they had some years ago, straight down and then threw the lime over their shoulders without eating it. Sam's mouth puckered at the bitter taste of the tequila. Nicki was already hanging over the bar, ordering another round of shots. Sam looked at her in protest.

Nicki interjected the look. "You haven't been out in so long. We're going to be here a while. We will celebrate and be sober before we leave." Nicki grabbed the next round and handed her the second shot of tequila. "To Saturday night." Nicki sang.

"You already said that," shouted Sam.

Nicki's devilish side came peering through. "I know and I'll keep saying it until something happens to make it a good toast."

Sam started to feel the alcohol warm her blood. She could feel the effects start to wear on her inhibitions. She also felt it give way to something she had never felt before. She suddenly felt more confident, sexy even. Wow, what a few shots could do for a girl, Sam thought to herself. Her cheeks began to fill with a rosy glow.

Nicki saw this and a gleam sparkled in her eyes. "We haven't been here twenty minutes and I already have you drunk?"

"Just buzzed…" Sam blinked slowly. "And in about ten more minutes the rest of the alcohol will kick in and you'll be certifiably tanked.

Sam shrugged in an overly exaggerated way. "Oh well. So

it's been a while since I've been out. I'm going to make up for it tonight."

Nicki took Sam by the shoulders. "Just warn me if you are going to dance on the bar."

"Why, so you can join me?"

"Hells yeah!" Nicki exclaimed as she smiled. The girls both laughed as Nicki got up to look in the mirror.

"Now sit here, I have to see how this looks."

Before Sam could focus on Nicki, she was out of sight once more. The effect of the alcohol began to slowly seep in as she lost her rational train of thought. Her face felt a bit numb and her mind became enveloped in a warm fuzzy blanket. Sam finished her beer and ordered another one. Before she took the first sip, she saluted to herself. "To Saturday Night." And took a drink.

No sooner had she tipped the bottle back to take a draw did Nicki come racing over to her.

"Oh my God, Sam! I just met the cutest guy on the way to the bathroom. Tall, well for me anyway, blonde hair, blue eyes, thin," she exclaimed. She looked Sam square in the eyes. "He said that he had a friend and they were over playing pool if we wanted to join them."

Sam just stared at her, trying to decode the fast-talking that Nicki was doing. That fast paced cadence that her friend fell into whenever she was amazed by a turn of events or became excited about the possibilities of life unfolding at that moment. Through it all, Sam continued to drink her beer and down shots of Tequila in a frugal attempt to bury the past, and the memories held in this local dive. Here she had experienced how it felt to hang on the arm of a man and here is where she experienced the betrayal in that love. The beer was not helping, and neither were the shots. The memories hung in the air surrounding her like a dark cloud.

As she snapped out of the past she looked to her friend as she continued in her frenzied excitement.

"Oh please, oh please!" Nicki began to shake Sam by her jacket lapels that served to pull her from the past and back to the future.

Sam giggled. "Ok. I will take one for the team, but if I see my friends, I'm going to join them. You so owe me big time just remember that for the next time I need a favor!"

Nicki squealed again and kissed Sam on the cheek, leaving a perfect kiss mark in lipstick. Taking Sam by the arm, they worked their way through the crowded dance floor to the pool tables. As they walked up, Sam saw the two men her friend had so excitingly drug her over to meet. Her focus was unbalanced by now and combined with the low lighting of the area it was difficult for Sam to determine which of the men had caused such a stir in her friend.

As she stood there allowing her eyes to adjust to the lighting, one of the men walked over to talk with Nicki. The other had his back turned to the girls and was bent over the table about to take his next shot. Sam was busy staring at the stranger's nicely shaped butt as she thought to herself. "I have certainly seen that butt before..."

Her scent filled his nostrils as he concentrated on controlling the animal that threatened to present as he struggled to make his last shot on the table. As she continued to stare at his back, a sense of belonging consumed her. Knowledge yet to be understood, imbedded somewhere deep within her, came alive. As she was in the midst of enjoying the moment, he slowly stood and turned to face those piercing eyes. She gasped in sheer delight as the stranger broke into a brilliant smile that engulfed her.

Nicki and her gentleman friend walked up to Sam who was still staring at the man standing within inches of her, where he had moved upon the moment of recognition. Unlike his friend, he knew the urgency in staking his territory. To break her resistance he had positioned himself between her and anyone who thought they might have a chance to sway the local beauty's attentions.

"Sam?" Nicki tried to get her attention. "I'd like you to meet Marc O'Mara." Sam turned and cupped her hand over her mouth to stifle a laugh as she watched Marc break into a grin of recognition.

"Well, well, we meet again," he said as he turned to

reintroduce his lifelong friend. "I'm sure you remember John." Nicki realizing that the three of them had met before that moment hit Sam in the arm and whispered close to her ear.

"Again? You've been holding out on me!"

Sam answered back. "These are the guys I bumped into today, at the market. Remember the strawberry jam incident?" Sam tried to whisper.

Nicki's eyebrow rose. "Oh! Yeah."

"Would you like to join us for a game of pool?" Marc asked as casually as his heart would allow him to.

Sam looked at him. "Doubles?"

Marc turned to grab Nicki's arm as he stated. "Nicki can be my partner, and you can have John."

Sam and Nicki looked at each other. "I think we should start girls against guys."

Sam smiled and the words came pouring out of her mouth before she had time to think of them.

"Trounce away, if you can." Sam's expression must have been worth a thousand words. She took Nicki by the arm and walked off to grab some cues.

"Wow, Sam! I can see why your senses went haywire for John." Nicki said as she examined the pool cues.

Sam had already picked one for herself. "Yes, but there is something more there that I just can't put my finger on, something more than physical attraction, though he is a hottie, isn't he?"

Nicki looked over at the guys and saw Marc racking the balls.

"Hey, Marc's no dog. I find him highly attractive."

Sam looked at Nicki's gaze and scorned her. "You'd better behave yourself."

"And you'd better not." Nicki scorned back almost instantaneously.

Sam shook her head. "Middle of the road?" It had been a term they had used since grade school, for deeming compromise.

"Deal," said Nicki.

"I need a harder drink," Sam said jokingly.

"Oh, you bad girl." Nicki cooed. "Should we go easy on the first game?"

"Sure, and then we will throw in a little girl power." Sam nudged Nicki. They turned, and hand in hand, walked back to the guys. Marc and John were watching the girls from across the room.

Marc shook his head. "Hot damn, those girls look nice."

"Incredible." John said mesmerized. "What a great little town."

"Marc, try to be a gentleman."

"Who me? What's that?" Marc joked.

"I mean it, be nice."

"I plan on being nice…" Marc said as he rubbed his hands together. He stopped his actions when he saw John's expression of disapproval. "Ok… I'll be nice."

The girls walked up to Marc and John. Nicki went over, stood next to Marc, and looked at Sam as to say. "Well, go on…" Sam walked over to stand next to John. She held her cue tight; to keep from letting her hands wander. She could feel the buzz of energy radiating from him. She closed her eyes slowly and sighed. Between the alcohol and John's energy, she was feeling warm.

She turned to John. "Would you hold this?" She handed him the cue so that she could take off her jacket. John watched her as she arched her back slightly to let the jacket slide off her shoulders. He watched her flip her long dark hair out of the way. Her perfume was suddenly prominent in the stale, smoke filled room. And he could do nothing more than stand there and watch every motion she made while he struggled to control the beast threatening to take her where she stood.

"John, what do you want to drink? Yo, John!" He heard Marc yell.

"Huh?" he turned to see Marc and Nicki staring.

"What do you want to drink?" Marc asked.

"A beer would be fine."

"Me too." He heard Sam holler from behind him.

"Thanks, I'll take that back now." She went to take the pool cue and deliberately brushed her hand over his. Once again, there was an instant charge of energy.

"Who's going to break?" Sam tried to play it off and focus.

She turned to Nicki who was draped all over Marc. Nicki seemed to be happy with whatever Marc was telling her.

Sam tried again. "Nic, middle, middle!" Nicki looked at Sam and mockingly smacked her own hand. John looked at Marc who was shrugging at him.

Marc answered. "You can have break," and turned his attention back to Nicki.

John turned to Sam. "Can you play?" Sam grinned.

"A little." Nicki chimed in.

"Sam, you break. You know I'm no good at it." Sam positioned the cue ball on the table. She looked around at her group. Nicki was now sitting in her own chair; she might as well have been sitting on Marc, the way her arms were draped over him. She looked over at John, who was watching her intently. She could feel the weight of his stare and her senses rolled in it. Sam winked at John, which took him back a moment.

"Watch out. I don't know my own strength sometimes." Sam turned back to the cue ball and let her mind go blank. Many people had tried to teach her how to play pool, but she could never really follow them. One day, she picked up a cue and decided that she wasn't going to concentrate on any one thing. She let her mind react as if she were looking at one of those novelty 3-D pictures. The ones that if you don't focus, you don't see it, but focus too much and you won't see it either.

She wasn't going to look at each shot like a geometry question. She wasn't going to make sure that she set herself up for the next shot. From that day on, she won more games than she lost. She took a deep breath and as she exhaled, she shot at the cue ball.

The shot was a good one, sending in two solids and a striped ball. She heard Marc whistle.

"John, I think we have a hustler on our hands."

"Very impressive," agreed John.

Sam's cheeks flushed as she thought of the statement.

"I'm very impressive at a lot of things," she quipped. She looked over at Nicki and saw her staring back in amazement. Looking back to John she saw the same expression. She came to realize that she had indeed thought that statement aloud. She heard Nicki start to laugh uncontrollably. John only raised one eyebrow and let a grin slide over his beautiful lips. Sam just smiled and swallowed her embarrassment.

"I guess since I shot in two solids, we'll take those. But by all means, take the striped one that I shot in for you, as a consolation prize." Sam started to make her way around the pool table to take her next shot when John blocked her path.

"Oh, a hustler and a big talker," he said, as he reached to move a stray strand of hair from her face.

"I'm only cocky when I'm winning." Sam met his gaze and felt the pull of his eyes. She walked up to him as he stood his ground. She motioned for him to bend down closer to her. He bent his head down to her level where she whispered in his ear.

"You're blocking my shot." Sam was sending herself with the way she was acting. She could hear a small voice in her head telling her to behave. She also heard another tell her to take John right there on the pool table. She decided to tune out both voices. Middle of the road, she thought to herself.

"Would you like me to move?" John stepped closer to her, which made Sam weak at the knees.

"For now." Sam breathed into his ear.

She pulled away slowly, matching his advances. She was never this brazen with a stranger. She decided that she wouldn't drink for the rest of the night. Then again, maybe she would just let herself go and see where it would take her. She had tried all of her old ways before and things never ended up the way she wanted. She talked herself into giving in to the unknown. Such a revelation came as a shock and a comfort. Who knew that she would be open to next?

John moved out of her way but only enough to allow her to squeeze by him forcing her back to rub against his chest. Such a simple move caused Sam's eyes to close. She heard John's breath shudder for a mere moment and knew then that he was as bad off as she was. Sam smiled and opened her eyes. She worked her way to the end of the pool table and bent down to take her next shot. She looked up from the cue ball and saw John leaning up against the wall, watching her.

Sam smiled and looked back at the cue, and took her shot. She had made the shot and began to follow the cue ball, to shoot again.

John watched her as she made her way to the next shot. She was positioned on one of the sides of the table so he got a great side profile of her. She was long and sleek and toned in the right places. She didn't come off as one that went to a gym. He made a mental note to ask her what she did to keep in shape. He watched as her breasts rested on the bumper as she leaned onto the table to take her shot. The halter left a lot of her back bare. Her hair covered her when she was standing. While she was bent over, however, John was able to see her muscles work under her skin.

Sam was staring at Nicki before she took her shot. Nicki was staring back at Sam when her eyes averted to Sam's chest, where she let out an astonished laugh.

Sam stood straight up. "What?"

"You can see straight down your shirt."

Sam looked down at her own breasts in her shirt and then back to Nicki. "Is it bad?"

"Not really, but I'm sure you're flashing more than you want."

Sam's thought went to John and how just moments before, was watching her as she shot. The next feeling she felt wasn't that of embarrassment, but of empowerment and sexual confidence. She shrugged and leaned back down to take her shot.

"You can't see nip, can you?" The question made Marc spit beer onto the floor.

Nicki burst into laughter. "No, you're fine. Just don't wiggle while you are down there."

Sam started to laugh and bury her face into the felt of the table. She didn't know where she was getting the boost of confidence, but she didn't mind it. She took her shot and missed, she was sure from too much laughter. She bowed and went back to sit next to John.

"I missed," she said, in innocent humour.

"I couldn't tell." John raised an eyebrow as he thought of Sam and Nicki's conversation.

"Your turn. Remember, you're the striped ones."

John stood up and made his way to the table. His position had him looking straight at Sam. She was staring at him while she made slight suggestive gestures to her cue. John shook his head and took his shot and missed.

As he walked back over to his chair, he shouted to Nicki. "Your shot." and took a drink of his beer.

"You missed," Sam teased.

John smiled and leaned closer to her chair.

"If you hadn't been trying to distract me, I wouldn't have."

Sam looked at him innocently. "What?"

"You were," he mimicked her motions. "Fidgeting."

Sam's face went a deep red. "I was not."

"Oh yeah you were."

"I'm so embarrassed."

"Yeah, just trying to win by any measures, I see." John tried to ease her mind.

"I don't need diversion to win... I'm an antsy person. I never sit still."

"And you pick that way to fidget?" Sam feigned innocence as she picked up her beer and took a drink. As she placed the bottle back in its place on the table, John added. "And now you are drinking my beer." He couldn't help himself the look on her face as she choked on the swig of beer she had just taken caused him to lose his composure and the laughter slipped from his lips easily.

Sam put her head in her hand. "What's wrong with me?" She said quietly.

She heard Marc yell for her. "Sam, your turn."

She was relieved that it was her turn to shoot. As she found the cue, it put her bending over the table right in front of John. Before she bent over, she turned around. "Could I have another drink of your beer? I'll buy our next round if you order for us."

John handed her the bottle. "I order and it's on me. Here."

Sam took the bottle and drank the rest of his beer. She handed him the empty bottle and before he could object, she bent over to take her shot.

John was going to say something about her drinking the last of his beer when he lost his words. He saw her bend over the table in front of him, pulling her jeans tight against her backside. He could see her hair spill onto the table while part of it lay rested in the middle of her back like a pool of soft black water.

She couldn't believe what she was doing and whom she was doing it in front of. She felt the room warm where John was sitting. She looked back at him while she stayed bent over the table and saw him try to hide the fact that he had just been staring at her ass.

She grinned at him. "I'm not blocking your view, am I?"

"Not in the least," John said. Smiling like a Cheshire Cat.

Sam's grin turned into a smile and she turned to take her shot. She looked over at Nicki and saw her and Marc whispering to each other. Marc was caressing Nicki's hand, which rested on his knee. She looked around at the bar and took a moment to soak in the crowd. She drew threads of each person's auras. She mixed them together and drank them like sweet wine.

She drew a ragged breath and regained her focus as she shouted to Nicki. "Think it's time?"

"Yeah, do it girl." Sam smiled and shot. She made her shot, and the next and then the next. Clearing her team's contingent of pawns down to the final eight ball. She looked up at John, who just sat there, still smiling at her.

"Eight ball, side pocket." She bent down and as she took the shot, her sight never wavered from John. The ball went in, as she knew it would. She heard Nicki in the background shout.

"That's right, sister. Show them what it's like."

Sam laid her pool stick on the table and walked over to her seat next to John. She picked up her beer and took a large drink as she watched Nicki and Marc start to walk away.

Nicki rang out. "Marc and I are going to dance. You can play with John." Nicki's words held double meaning and Sam knew it. She wasn't able to think long on Nicki's words before John broke her concentration.

"My my. You are good."

"Well, I practice some."

"Some?" John said with raised eyebrows.

Sam couldn't hold it in any longer. She began to giggle.

"I have a pool table at home."

"Ah-ha! I knew you couldn't be good looking and a hustler at the same time. What other games do you have at your house?"

"Darts, foosball, air hockey, ping pong…"

"Do you run an arcade or what?" John stood and made his way to the pool table and started to rack the pool balls.

Sam laughed. "No, I live in my aunt's house. Her attic had long ago been set up as a studio apartment. She use to take in lodgers, but once I became a permanent resident of the house, she stopped taking in people. In our basement, we have a family/game room. I haven't been out much."

She wanted to take back the last part. She didn't want him knowing that about her.

"Sounds like a fun household."

"I like it." Sam stood up and chalked her cue. She lined up her shot and broke the balls. She didn't make anything in. John followed the cue ball, never taking his eyes off Sam

"So, Sam, what do you do for a living?"

Sam sat down, took a drink of her beer, and answered. "I'm a stable-girl," she said with great pride.

"A what?" He made his shot and walked to the cue to take his next turn.

"A stable-girl… a farm hand? I work with horses, on a farm. I have since I was 16. It's hard work, but it's worth it."

"So that's why you look so toned." He was pleased with himself for finding a way to broach the question in a gentlemanly manner.

"Are you saying that you were checking me out?" Sam purred.

John made his shot and missed. He made his way back to the table and before he let Sam pass, he stood face to face with her.

"You put your ass in my face, I can't help but look. I'm a nice guy, but I'm still a guy." He moved to the side to let Sam pass by.

Sam nodded. "Point taken. I normally don't act this out of character. I guess something (or someone she thought to herself) is bringing it out in me"

"I'm not complaining." John reassured her as he leaned against the wall. "Did I mention that you look great tonight? I mean different than from this afternoon… not that you looked bad this afternoon…"

Sam looked up before she shot. "I know what you meant." She smiled and went back to lining up her shot. "Nicki dressed me. I haven't been 'out' in a little over a year. She's my out. I normally just live through her stories." Sam made her shot and continued to the next.

"That's not living," he mused.

"Have you taken a look around this town?" Sam asked. "Not much to choose from, and I'm a sad person to be so damn picky."

"Well, I for one am glad you're here now."

"So am I." Sam moved to take yet another shot as she cocked her head and asked. "Can I ask you something?"

"Sure." John's tone lifted to a quizzical one.

Without missing her shot, she kept talking and moving to her next turn. "Have you, I mean do you? Oh, how do I put this…?"

Sam was having a hard time concentrating with her hand in his. "When we bumped into each other, I felt a sense of belonging or longing I am not quite sure which I felt, but it was almost as if destiny had reunited us in some way from a past existence…"

She looked to him for some type of acknowledgement, which he gave. "Energy! Lots and lots of energy."

"Exactly!" Sam bolted straight up, excited. "I have honestly never felt such a powerful attraction before. That sounds like such a line."

Easing back, she took her next shot. "I know it sounds corny, but it's the only way to describe it. Half of me find's it comforting. The other half finds it unnerving."

"Yes! Ordinary people just don't find that kind of connection every day. Eight ball, corner pocket," Sam stated. She shot and made it in.

John walked up to her. "You are far from ordinary."

"Oh, now that was a line," Sam chuckled.

John put his hands over his heart. "I'm hurt."

Sam tried to act ashamed. "Sorry. My sense of humor is dry enough. It's magnified with alcohol."

They both sat down and ordered one more beer to share between them. Sam moved her chair closer to John. She rested her head in her hand. "So, John DesRosiers, what else is there to know about the handsome, mysterious man who came walking into MY town today?"

"Handsome? And why does everyone keep referring to it as their town?" John raised one eyebrow.

"I told you, we are set to do research at the National Park."

"On what?" she asked.

"Creatures."

"Big ones?" Sam leaned closer.

"All kinds." John matched her movements. Sam leaned into John to whisper in his ear. She motioned him to move closer. He leaned in slowly. She brushed her cheek up against his as her lips glided over his ear. She knew she was flirting with him. She wanted him to know that. She wanted to feel that exhilaration of being attractive to someone.

"I don't believe you," Sam said slowly.

As she spoke, she could feel John's body lean further into her. He whispered back to her. "You don't?"

"Na-uh. I think that you were sent here to put a smile on my face."

John laughed quietly. "You got me. Normally I would have to take you out for knowing my secrets, but I think I can let you slide just this once. Just don't tell the others."

Sam brushed her cheek up against his. "Our secret, and I'll take you up on taking me out." John was puzzled for only a moment, then realized what he had said could have been taken either way. Regardless, he didn't mind the response she gave.

Nicki and Marc danced away on the dance floor. Nicki spotted John and Sam whispering to each other.

"You know, you can almost feel something between them," Marc stated. "Like from a past life or something. If she breaks his heart, it'll kill him, and anger me." Marc looked into Nicki's eyes. Nicki became very sober at that moment.

She looked deeper into Marc's eyes and said one simple word. "Ditto."

Marc tried to recover. "I'm just saying that I've been friends with John for years now and he's more like a brother to me… twenty years," he said as the memories once again surfaced from their past. "You and Sam have been friends for…?"

Nicki interrupted Marc. "Twenty years." She softened her eyes and replied. "Sam has always been the heart broken, not the heartbreaker. I don't think that she has it in her to be that way."

"God, they are a good match." Marc chuckled to himself as he whisked Nicki around where they could no longer see their two friends. "Enough of them. Let's focus on something more interesting."

He pulled Nicki tight to his chest and smiled.

She let out a startled "Oh."

He heard. "Us."

With the way that Sam was acting, she was not only driving John mad, she was doing it to herself as well. She knew that she was playing with a fire that could rage out of control at any minute. But she needed this. She pulled away from him and looked into his eyes. She could see the reaction she was looking for. She did have a major affect on him. She smiled with an ironic sense of contentment.

John and Sam talked at breath about family and friends, Pinbrook and his hometown. She found out that he had a brother and sister. He was the oldest of the three, his sister and then his brother. He hadn't seen his family in a year or so, his work kept him from it. He remarked that he wrote to them all of the time. Sam had talked quickly about her parents being killed in an accident. John could sense that it wasn't a subject to be explored at this juncture. It showed that it was hurting her enough to tell him as much as she did.

He stood up just as the band began to play a slow song. He held out his hand to Sam.

"What?" Sam asked.

"Would you dance with me?" John smiled at her.

Sam hesitated for a second. "I haven't danced in years." She gave him her hand anyway.

John took it and helped her out of her seat. "I promise that I will not make fun of you."

"Gee, thanks," Sam said.

John pulled her through the dance floor to the corner of the room. Sam looked around at their final destination. They were literally in the corner of the dance floor and of the room.

John answered her puzzled look. "This spot keeps us out of the spotlight."

"Thank you," Sam said softly.

John moved into her space and held out his hand. She placed her hand in his and he immediately wrapped it around so that the back of her hand was against his chest. He slowly slid his hand across her lower back, to ready himself to lead. John took advantage of the exposed skin showing through the halter-top Sam was wearing, and glided his hand over her bare flesh. Sam wanted to writhe under his touch, to follow it with her body, but she contained herself with what control she still had. She felt her body temperature rise and how parts of her body tightened just by his touch.

She knew then that she had denied herself the simple pleasure of human contact for too long. She also knew that the man, with whom she was dancing, was no ordinary person himself. John's body lightly pressed against hers. He began to sway, leading her in his moves. She couldn't bring herself to look in his eyes, but she was not going to look down. She settled on watching his pulse dance on his neck and fought valiantly to keep from leaning in and kissing it.

"I want to thank you again for the jam."

"I felt bad about breaking your jar. To be perfectly honest, I couldn't stop myself from buying it."

"Concerned about a perfect stranger?"

"I wouldn't deem you a perfect stranger. You said yourself that there's a definite spark between us that was felt the moment we ran into each other."

"That's true, but you bought me six jars." Sam couldn't help but smile. She wanted to go that extra length to kiss his neck, but forced herself to pull away just a bit, mere inches, but it was enough to keep control.

"I couldn't help that either," he said.

She felt him tense. "It wasn't a bad thing. On the contrary, I have just never had that kind of affect on a guy before."

"Oh, you do need to get out more. You are kidding me, right?"

"There was Tommy in the second grade. He gave me an unopened piece of gum."

John listened to her intently.

"Hey, this was coming from the boy that used to eat his boogers. I took that stick of gum as true love. Of course, I couldn't get past the fact that he... ate his boogers... so that was the end of my first true love." Sam felt John chuckle and ease a bit. There was a moment of complete silence and Sam couldn't help but tense a little. John felt her stiffen.

"Am I making you nervous?" he asked.

"Why do you ask?"

"It's just that you relayed your charming tale of true love with Tommy what's-his-name in under a minute, then suddenly silent."

Sam rested her head on John's chest, which was easy since he was taller than her by approximately five inches or more.

"I'm sorry. I talk a lot when I'm nervous."

She lifted her head and rested it against his jaw line once again. She could feel his breath on her temple. She concentrated on keeping her breaths even and normal. She couldn't help but lean her head against his lips. He caressed the bare flesh exposed by her shirt, running his thumb under the bottom of the shirt as he teased the acceptable boundaries.

Sam felt him lean to the side of her head and smell her hair. Her body ached for more. She pressed against him, to lose any space left between them. He took her hand out of his only for a moment to brush her hair back to expose her neck. Sam's heart was in her throat. She burned inside with hopeful anticipation.

He took her hand once more and leaned down to run his nose and mouth close to her neck and shoulder, never making contact with her skin. He started at her shoulder, slowly and to the beat of the music, moved up to her neck and then to her ear. She could hear his breathing, which had become long, drawn-out breaths. John maneuvered away from her ear in a path for her face. His face was in line with hers. She had in the meantime, tilted her head up to meet his.

They were so close, face-to-face that they were unable to focus on one another. Sam's hand rested on his shoulder as she caressed his neck and ran her fingers through his hair. She could feel his breath against her lips. They moved in slowly, bridging the gap between them. She could feel his lips so close to hers.

Their lips barely brushed each other before they pulled away in utter shock from a lone voice shouting at them.

"Middle, Sam, middle!"

Sam began to see stars from the overwhelming emotions running through her at that precise moment. Her ears started to ring.

John noticed Sam sway and grabbed hold of her. "Whoa. What's wrong?"

Sam moistened her lips with her tongue. "I need a seat."

Nicki obviously didn't understand what was going on. She continued to poke fun. "The music stopped about ten minutes ago. You two were the only ones left on the dance floor. They've already called closing time." Nicki began to giggle.

"So much for being out of the spotlight," Sam said. Contemplating the need to cry, or vomit, or maybe both. She had gone so long feeling that she would never find someone who wanted her. Now that she found someone interested in her, she couldn't take the interruption. She was able to contain her emotions, but barely. John came up from behind her and placed his hands on her shoulders. He bent down and whispered in her ear.

"To be continued." Sam smiled and leaned against him.

Nicki could see the sorrow in Sam's eyes and tried to think through the intoxication. "Sam what's wrong?"

"Nothing, I'm fine."

Nicki knew better, she had known her friend long enough to know when things were not right in her world. She could hear it in her tone. Sensing her friend's need to escape, she excused them from John and Marc's presence for a moment to talk with Sam alone. "What's up?" Nicki asked with concern.

"Why?" Sam asked as she struggled to overcome the heavy sensation of danger hanging around her.

"Honey, you're going to have to be more specific than why." Nicki said as casually as she could at that moment.

"Why would you do that to me?" She asked with confusion.

"Hey, I thought that we had a deal. We talked about it earlier. We said that we would be naughty, but on the nice side. I was just following your orders."

Sam buried her head in her hands. "I'm so embarrassed and this isn't helping me any, I'd like to leave - now."

The panic that threatened to overcome her senses was now at a dangerous level and the need to escape that bar and the throng of people became an urgent quest for freedom.

"Are you sure?" Nicki's tone was now serious.

"I just need some fresh air."

"Then fresh air is what you'll get. So, middle is out the door?" Sam knew that she was not only asking for Sam's sake. Sam didn't care at the moment if Nicki had ulterior motives.

"Yes." Nicki grinned. "Great! Hey Boys," she shouted the latter.

John and Marc came back to the table.

"We need to get out of here," she stated.

John turned to look at her. "There is no way I'm letting you drive," he looked at Nicki. "Either of you."

Sam's eyes were glazed over by controlled emotions. "I need to get out of here."

John looked over to Marc. "Are you ok?" he asked, as the hair on the back of his neck rose in alert to the impending danger they all faced at that moment.

"Yes." She answered. As the fog, threatening to consume her, slowly began its mission of consumption.

John turned to Sam. "I'll drive Nicki's car for you girls and Marc will follow."

Sam quickly responded. "Just because I need to get out of here doesn't mean that I need to get away from you."

John's expression softened. "We'll talk in the car."

Marc looked up at everyone. "Is the party over?"

Nicki wrapped her arms around him. "We're just relocating."

"Where to?" said Marc.

Nicki got excited. "To the lake!"

John looked at Sam as she said just above a whisper. "The Lake?"

Nicki answered the questioning look on the men's faces. "Sam's place has a beautiful lake."

Sam's expression was neutral. "We could go there if you wanted to." She didn't want to show any signs of anxiousness. Everyone just looked at each other.

Nicki took the initiative and answered for everyone. "Then it's settled, to the lake!"

She stood up and pointed to the door.

Marc joined her and they both repeated. "To the lake!" Marc grabbed Nicki and in a mock dance step, headed for the door.

CHAPTER SIX

Sam and John smiled as their friends weaved through the crowd. John took Nicki's keys from Sam, and took her hand.

"Are you sure that you're alright?"

"I'm sure. I'll be fine. Thanks."

As they walked to the car, John asked. "Thanks for what?"

"I suppose, for being at the right place at the right time today."

They reached the car and John opened the door for Sam. She thanked him and got in. After she was in, she maneuvered herself to push Nicki's seat back before John got in. John noticed the gesture.

"Thank you."

"It's a habit. Besides, if you would have gotten in with her settings, you would have knocked your teeth out with your own knees."

Sam gave him directions once they were on their way. Marc and Nicki followed at a safe distance. The rest of the car ride was silent, but the air was filled with hidden messages, whispers. As they drove, John reached over and put his hand on her knee.

He glanced at her and asked. "Is this ok?"

"Yes, yes it is." Sam smiled.

He could have done many more things to her, asked that same question, and still received the same answer.

Once they got to Sam's house, she told John where to park. Marc followed. The group got out of the cars and stood in front of them. Nicki looked cold, so Sam gave her her jacket. Nicki protested something to the fact that she wouldn't be wearing it long, but Sam's mind wasn't listening. Nicki and Marc started down the open path to the lake, while John and Sam went over to his truck.

John opened the passenger door and flipped his truck seat back. He was blocking Sam's view to peek at what it was. John handed her a flannel jacket. "I don't want you to catch a cold."

John watched as Sam put the jacket on. Though the jacket

was lined with a sweatshirt material, it was still large a
It made Sam look like she was a kid wearing her father
Her hands weren't visible through the sleeves and it hu
mid thigh. She gave John a sarcastic look.

"Two people could fit into this."

"Really, you think?" John moved closer to her. "Let's see." He slid his arms inside the jacket and wrapped them around her waist, pulling her close.

She leaned in and hugged him. He hugged her back as their hug turned into a full body press. She draped her arms around his body, holding him and then tried to close the jacket. She laid her head on his chest and heard his heart racing. She became warm with desire. He caressed her body as he held her. They pulled away at the same time, slowly. Sam swallowed hard. She knew that it wasn't yet the time to go further. She smiled and bit her lip.

"Almost," John smiled.

Sam couldn't speak. She was still tingling from head to toe.

She asked him if he would like to walk the path with her. He put his arm around her "to keep you warm" as he put it and they started to walk. Sam kept leaning to the side to sniff his jacket. John saw this and laughed.

"What?" Sam scoffed.

"Nothing," John grinned.

"It smells good," Sam protested.

"It's dirty."

"Yeah." Sam snuggled into it more.

"So you got a thing for dirty clothes?" John teased.

"It smells like you. It's warm. What's wrong with that combination?"

"Nothing I guess."

"And it can't be that dirty if you let me wear it." They walked the edge of the lake and continued to follow the path. "Don't let what Nicki did tonight, bother you. She's a really nice person, but when she gets to drinking she loses her common sense."

"Marc's the same way. I guess they're a good match."

"I wonder if I'll ever find a good match." Sam realized she'd thrown John a loaded question.

She felt John grin. "Let's see. Maybe? If you're talking about for you, you'd need someone who was a kind-hearted person, someone to match your good looks…"

Sam interrupted with a scoff. But John continued.

"Someone to help you overcome your modesty, someone to bear your stubbornness. Last but not least, someone to help you carry some of the world that's on your shoulders."

"All of that from just getting to know me? Pretty perceptive."

"Did I mention that you wear your emotions on your sleeve?"

"Well this IS a big enough jacket!" Sam snorted at her own joke. John brushed off her attempt at trying to change the subject.

"How long has it been since you received a compliment?"

"Aunt Claire," she said, without hesitation.

"Aunt Claire doesn't count." John interrupted.

"I can't remember."

"You're kidding me."

"Didn't you hear me when I said that I haven't been out in years? There was no reason to."

"Was?" John answered with an enquiring grin.

"NOW who's toying with whom?" Sam tried to change the subject teasingly.

John replied in the most. "I know if you were around me, you would hear compliments all of the time."

"Are you trying to give me a reason to come around you more?"

"Hoping," John said under his breath. Sam heard him and looked up. He looked at her and smiled.

They walked a little further and came upon a stone bench, the same stone bench that had met Sam each night, with Aunt Claire. Sam paused and inhaled/exhaled for just a second. She conquered her inside demon and asked John if he would like to sit down.

John sat.

"I would love to hear the story of what just put the world back on your shoulders, sometime."

"Maybe some other time. Now's not a good time."

He saw sadness fill her eyes once more and thought of a remedy. He wrapped his arms around her and pulled her close to him. Still bundled in his jacket, she laid her head on his chest and they gazed at the still waters in pure silence. He could feel her tension ease. He caressed her arm and leaned over to kiss the top of her head. Sam smiled. She pulled away to face him.

"I'm seriously not bipolar. I just have a lot on my plate right now and sometimes I falter."

John moved into her space. "Do you have time for this?"

"Time? I need this so much right now," as she leaned into him. "I really do."

John didn't wait. His hand came up and cradled her face. He leaned into the position where they were so rudely interrupted earlier. His lips scarcely brushed her, as he whispered to her softly.

"I think this is where we left off…" he said.

He met her soft, warm lips with his. He kissed her gently as she melted where she sat. He pulled away and ran his thumb over her cheek. He looked longingly into her eyes as he moved back in for another kiss. Once they made contact, their connection, their power, grew to fever pitch within them. He kissed her harder, longer. She tried to press against him the best she could while sitting beside him. He grabbed her, pulled her up off the bench, and laid her down on the ground in one swift move. He was stronger than she thought. He balanced himself on his hands to gaze at her for only a moment before he moved into her space. He overwhelmed her with passion. His kisses became hot with desire, so much that Sam whimpered at his touch. She wrapped one of her legs around his waist and the feeling set John reeling. The battle of control was being lost between them.

John broke away from her kiss to move to her neck. She tilted her neck back, inviting him to feast. He moved against her body as he kissed her. He slid his hand under her shirt and caressed her soft skin. She gasped at his touch in what John wrongly interpreted as a motion to cease. Sam realized his retreat and ushered his hand with hers to continue.

She pleaded. "Don't stop. Please."

John let out an inhuman growl, which sent Sam's heart pounding. He pulled away to look at her in the moonlight. Her eyes glowed a bright amber color, as if they were radiating their own light. He slowly moved in and they began to kiss once again. Something unknown awakened in Sam. She could feel it as it paced back and forth inside of her, like a caged tiger waiting to be freed. She felt its power. She felt it connect with John. What surprised her most was that she was not afraid of it. She welcomed this secret beast deep inside of her.

She ran her hands down his back as he moved against her. She moved with his body. With every thrust against her body, her body reacted to him. She moved with him, writhing in anticipation. She motioned to take the jacket off when John stopped her. Holding her breath, she searched his face for an explanation. She looked at him and tried to figure out what was different about him. His features were the same but somehow different. His eyes had changed to a lighter blue. She stayed as still as a rabbit.

John looked around and sniffed the air. He looked directly to the woods and growled. Sam heard something rustle in the woods and in that instant, John was up and running for it. She could barely focus on him as he ran for the tree line. She heard him call for Marc, at least she thought it was him. It was John's voice but it wasn't. She found it hard to concentrate. She saw Marc out of the corner of her eye running towards the forest. Sam's adrenaline began to flow. Her pupils dilated and the hair on the back of her neck stood on end. She noticed that her hearing became crisp. She could hear the water lightly lapping against the shore, small things scurrying in the woods, and Nicki off the way cursing at herself. Sam got up and ran to the gazebo.

John looked back to make sure that he was well hidden in the trees before he started his change. He stripped from his clothes and readied himself. The change came fast, barely ten seconds needed. His breath grew ragged as the sounds of popping and stretching rang through his body. His body jerked wildly, but he was able to keep his balance. His skin turned to a grey and hair began to flow over his body where none had been. His face contorted into a muzzle with animalistic eyes. He looked to be stuck somewhere between human... and wolf. He took off running towards the other being. He noticed that Marc caught up to him and ran beside him. Marc was in form as well, his skin and hair shining in the moonlight, a dark chocolate color.

Both John and Marc were able to close the distance between them and the unknown entity. John motioned to Marc and they parted to come up on the being from both sides, John made great time. The shadow of the figure was right in front of him. John could smell the beast, another 'Were'. John lunged for the other werewolf and brought it to the ground. John wrestled with the beast until it kicked him off his chest.

The werewolf stood up and geared up for an assault when Marc attacked it from behind. John took advantage of the distraction that Marc was providing and jumped on the front of the were, but it only lasted a moment. Marc was grabbed by the shoulder and thrown against a tree. The attacker then turned his attention. He backhanded John, which sent him to the ground. John's face immediately began to bleed from the slashes the werewolf inflicted. The beast jumped on top of Marc and began to slash into his flesh. John got up, kicked it off Marc, and jumped on him, landing hard onto its solar plexus. The werewolf was winded for only a moment, but long enough for John to slash at its body. Deep pools of blood formed on the beast's face with a cheek hanging slack from muscle damage. Marc was on his feet, but holding his stomach, blood seeping through his fingers. He was breathing fast and shallow, but stood his ground and readied himself to strike again. John only sustained minor wounds that would heal before the night was over. He and Marc stood face to face with the werewolf. It snarled at the two assailants. John accepted the challenge and took a step forward when he saw Marc fall out of the edge of his eye.

Sam made it to the gazebo where she found Nicki putting the last bit of her top back on. Sam and Nicki looked at each other in search for an explanation as they listened to the sounds of terror ringing from the woods. Their eyes widened with each snarl. Sam grabbed Nicki's arm and started to run. They were closer to the other side of the lake, which meant that they had a long run ahead of them. Nicki didn't try to fight Sam. They ran as quickly and as quietly as they could.

John looked over at Marc and then back to the beast. The werewolf was already gone. John snorted and turned back to his injured friend. He picked Marc up and started running towards Sam's house. Marc had begun to return to human form, which was not a good sign. A Were either had to will the change or be dying. Since Marc was unconscious when he started to change back, John knew he had to get Marc to the house quickly.

John ran up on the porch and laid Marc down on the front step. He was about to leave when the door opened suddenly. Aunt Claire stood there in her robe, looking at John. She looked down at Marc's injuries and then back to John.

"I need you to bring him inside." John looked behind him from where he had been with Sam.

Claire sensed his concern. "They are still at the gazebo, but I don't know for how long. I can help him, but I cannot carry him... Please."

John sighed and hurried inside with Marc in his arms. Claire led him to the library where she motioned for John to set Marc on an antique chaise longue. He laid him to the chair and turned to Claire. She looked at John in his transformed state, quite unperturbed. "Once you go out the door, go down the hall to the kitchen. Use the door to your right. You will be able to get back to the woods. Thank you for helping him, now go."

The girls, alarmingly, heard the sounds suddenly stop. They were halfway to the house when dead silence came over the area. No more thundering growls, no more tiny crickets chirping in the night. It was quiet, too quiet. Sam felt something take over. She felt something primal and instinctual spew forward in her. She crouched down and walked swiftly while still holding onto Nicki's arm. Nicki mimicked her friend's actions and continued down the path. Sam was in a state of survival. She scanned the area before making any moves, following an invisible path to the house. Sam became annoyed by Nicki's slight whimpers and turned to her. Nicki gasped at the sight of Sam. Her eyes were glowing. Sam's expression was intent. She held her finger up to her lips and smiled. Nicki didn't make another sound. Sam turned back around and continued on the path to the house. Once they reached the house, Sam headed towards the closet to get her shotgun. Nicki ran to find Claire.

John vanished from the house just as Nicki rounded the corner to the kitchen. She didn't see John outside the door thanks to the unlit porch light. Nicki ran into the room and saw Claire tending to Marc. Nicki couldn't focus. She couldn't let her mind process what was going on. She saw Marc laying there, his intestines swelling out from his body. There was blood everywhere. Claire started chanting above his body, words which no language before uttered aloud. The room began to glow. Each word she spoke melted into the next that formed on her lips. Wind from nowhere blew in the room and around Claire. Her hands began to glow a brilliant gold color. She placed her hands on Marc's wounds and repeated her words in a more forceful tone. A light flashed in the room and then everything dimmed. Sam was on the other side of the door about to enter when they saw the flash and then the darkness. Sam ran through the door and found Claire on the floor. Sam went to Claire while Nicki ran to exam Marc.

"Aunt Claire?!" Sam picked her up to lay Claire in her lap. Claire started to come to. She was pale and sweating. She could barely open her eyes. "What happened?" Sam asked her.

"She has helped Marc, though he still needs help," Nicki answered.

Claire looked up at Sam as if those were her own words. She nodded slowly.

"I'm going to call 911," Sam said steadfastly. Claire used what energy she had to grab her arm. She frowned and shook her head.

Nicki called out. "Sam, I can help them but I'm going to need your assistance." Sam looked down at Claire, saw her nod, and close her eyes. Sam gently laid her on the floor and grabbed a pillow from the nearby chair to place under Claire's head.

Sam went to Nicki for instruction. Nicki never took her eyes off Marc.

"I will need some bandages, medical tape, a pitcher of water and a glass. Oh, and some blankets if you can manage it."

Sam ran to retrieve the requested items.

In the meantime, Nicki began to heal Marc the rest of the way. She looked at Marc and saw that though his bleeding had stopped, there were deep wounds in his chest and stomach. She caressed his face, said a prayer for strength and began her concentration. She made her mind focus on Marc only. She moved back from the chair and closed her eyes.

She began to chant the words that Claire had been chanting earlier. The room began to glow a brilliant white. The source of the light, coming from Nicki. Wind blew fiercely throughout the room, knocking books off their shelves and pictures from the walls. Nicki felt the power flow through her. She walked back over to Marc and laid her hands on him. The power crackled in the air, through her body to his.

Her power ran wild, connecting with Claire and anything that she could touch with it. Sam stood in the doorway, with the blankets and bandages when Nicki's power reached out and touched her as well. Sam's back bowed and she dropped the items as she went to her knees. Nicki could feel what was happening and pulled her concentration back to Marc. Sam could feel Nicki sever her connection with her, but left her with renewed energy. Sam blinked as if she had just awakened from a deep sleep. She felt more focused and assured that this would work. She ran to Claire and helped her to the nearby chair.

Nicki pulled all of her power from the outpouring vessels and collected it above Marc's body. Her power hung like a disco ball above Marc. Nicki began to chant faster and louder. Sam and Claire saw the energy ball slam into Marc's body. His body bounced off the chair and hovered two feet above it. Nicki motioned her hands over his wounds and watched the broken bones begin to mend, she watched the severed muscles begin to reattach like some invisible force sewing his insides back together. Nicki was able to mend Marc's wounds as best she could, before her power started to wane. She took the last of her power and lowered Marc onto the chair. Nicki slumped to the floor, only bracing herself against the chair where Marc was still sleeping. She hung her head and sighed.

Sam went over to Nicki and put her arms around her.

"Are you gonna be ok?"

"I think so. I need to rest." Nicki rested her head on Sam.

"The blankets are for Marc. We'll need to bandage the rest of his wounds, but I think that he's going to be ok."

Sam suddenly got a chill down her spine and she stiffened. She supported Nicki against the chair and stood up. "…Where's John?"

Claire looked at her. "Who's John?"

Sam said it again, this time to Nicki.

"Have you seen John?" Nicki started to answer but Sam was already out the door.

Sam ran back to the linen closet, pulled out their 12-guage shotgun, and checked to make sure that it was loaded. She stuffed extra shots in her pocket, just in case. She ran out onto the porch and gave herself a moment to get adjusted to the darkness. Once again, her senses were heightened. She thought that the extra energy running through her, compliments of Nicki, were heightening her senses. She was hearing and seeing better than she ever had at night. She walked out into the yard and started for the path. Sam had used the shotgun many times in more instances than just target practice. She had a run in with a bear once. She didn't kill the bear, but by shooting it, the bear has not been back since. It had snuck up on her campsite on the back of Claire's property.

Sam walked the path, looking from side to side. She was listening for any sign of movement. She was trying not to let her thoughts escape to the worst. After seeing how bad Marc was, she could only hope that the same hadn't happened to John.

About halfway to the lake, she started hearing movement. She stopped in her tracks and stopped breathing. Her pupils dilated as she felt a presence moving in the shadows. She started to ready herself as she heard a sudden noise behind her. She took a deep breath and turned toward the sound in the darkness. In the midst of her turn, John knocked the barrel away from the line of fire, which pushed the gun back on Sam as she fired.

The shot missed John by a mile, but the sound rang in their ears. John closed the gap between them and looked fiercely into her eyes. She returned the look. He went to take the gun from Sam but she jerked it away in anger. He grabbed the barrel, ignoring the heat of the gun and yanked the gun from her grasp. She tried to keep the gun, but his strength was too great and she gave up the tug of war she was locked in with the man and the gun. She scowled, threw the extra ammo at him as stormed off in the direction of the house.

John kept an eye on his surroundings while he picked up the ammo and jogged in hot pursuit of the young woman. Sam brushed away an angry tear as she kept her brisk pace, she never looked back for fear he would see the tear, and she would give into her need to be comforted. He followed her closely, still watching the shadows for any danger that might emerge. Sam reached the porch and motioned to open the door, John intercepted her movement.

"What in the hell was that for?" John said in a loud voice. He was still having problems hearing anything beyond the ringing in his ears. He could barely hear himself talk let alone what anyone was saying to him.

"What in the hell was that for?" Sam retorted. "What in the hell were you doing, sneaking up on me like that?"

"Whoever taught you to shoot without seeing what, or whom you were shooting at, should be shot," he spat in an angry tone.

"Normal people would have notified the person with the gun that they were coming up on them," she replied with the same vengeance she had heard in his voice.

"I didn't want to scare off whatever you were tracking you fool." He ran his fingers through his hair as he realized that she was shaken by the whole experience of the night. He saw the tracks the latent tears had left on her cheeks and he struggled to stop his finger from reaching out to wipe them away.

"Oh, I think that we managed that quite nicely, thank you." Sam looked down at his hand, which was red and blistered.

"And why would you grab the barrel like that."

"I sure as hell wasn't going to give you a second shot."

"I wasn't tracking YOU, I was looking for you. I was worried." Sam's tone changed.

Through the light drowning onto the porch, John could see the tears well up in her eyes. John suddenly felt like an idiot for arguing.

"I'm fine."

"But you could have been... like Marc. He's pretty bad."

"Is he dying?" John said, obviously concerned.

"No, Nicki healed him enough, but he's still out."

Tears began to stream down her cheeks. John reached up with his unscathed hand and wiped the tears from her face. Sam hung her head as if she were embarrassed.

"Don't cry. I'm sorry I got so upset," John said softly.

"I have never seen anyone that bad off before. He was laid wide open." Deep yet silent sobs poured out of Sam.

John sat the gun on the floor and pointed it away from them. He pulled Sam into his chest and held her tight. She cried so hard that she began to hiccup. John simply let her have it out. He stroked her head and kissed her cheek.

When John felt Sam was calm, he pulled her away to arms length and stared into her liquefied eyes.

"We're ok. We're going to find out what's out there, but for now, we need to go inside. Are you going to be ok?"

Sam sniffed and nodded. She felt ashamed for breaking down like that in front of John. She had been on such an emotional roller coaster tonight that she didn't think that she could take much more. She ran into John once again, to gain a bit more strength from his embrace. He smiled and held her close.

She pulled away and smiled. "Ok. Let's go in"

They walked into the house to find Claire sitting on a chair in the living room. Sam could see that she was trying her best not to smile. Sam's ears were still ringing, but the deadening, throbbing initial sound had subsided.

Claire grinned and nodded at the two. "So, who shot who?" Sam just gave her a disgusted look.

John answered. "She almost shot me."

"Don't start," Sam said.

Claire tried to ease the tension in the room by diverting the conversation. "Don't put that gun back in the closet while it's still hot, I don't want you burning the house down."

Again, Sam could hear the humor in Claire's voice. Sam just laid the gun behind the couch, on the floor and walked to the kitchen. John followed. Claire stayed in the living room, smiling at a hidden joke deep inside.

Sam poured her a glass of water. She saw John walk in and offered the glass to him. He took it and drank the rest of her water. She didn't know how she was ever going to think straight being around him. As she watched him drink from the glass, all she wanted to do was press her bare flesh against his. She wanted that physical contact with him. She felt her body begin to react to him and she decided that if she stayed angry, maybe it would help her think clearer. She turned to the sink and splashed cold water on her face. As she wrung her hands across her face, John walked up behind her to put the glass on the counter. His chest brushed against her back and it sent her body into overload.

She felt her body press back against him as her mind protested. He held his ground, to let her make the contact. His hand moved up on her shoulder and she was unsuccessful in willing herself to move.

She looked into the sink as she spoke. "I can't," she flatly stated.

"Cant' what?" John asked.

"I can't do this right now."

"Again, what?"

Sam turned. She could feel her anger push her desires down and she felt better for it.

"I am in a weakened state right now and I feel that you can sense that. And you are just eating it up that I can't seem to keep my hands..." she paused "... or any other part of me off of you right now. I bet you're getting a real kick out of the chick that has needy issues. I'm probably doing a damn fine job feeding your ego aren't I?"

"You aren't making any sense." John started to sound angry.

"I can't be close to you right now. I have to save some part of my dignity. You have to keep your distance. Stand over there." She pointed to the other side of the island.

John stormed over to the other side of the island, but was not about to back down from the discussion.

"Have you even listened to anything I said tonight? After the stories that I told you of myself, do I look like a guy who would prey on lonely women?"

"Oh, so I'm lonely?" Sam started to raise her voice.

John met her tone. "You aren't with anyone are you?"

Sam was looking for a reason to be mad at that point. "But that's not what you just said. You said lonely, not alone. There's a biiiiiiig difference."

John saw through her rouse and replied accordingly. "That's not what I meant and you know it, but you are a woman who can twist what a man says and make it sound horrible."

"Hold your hand out," Sam said unexpectedly.

"What?" John practically shouted out of confusion more than anger.

"Hold your hand out. I want to check it," she said in the same dead tone.

"My hand's fine," he answered.

Sam turned back to the counter and focused on making an ice pack for his hand. John continued. "Don't change the subject. I'm not calling you lonely. Hell, I'm the lonely one." John wanted to put his foot in his mouth the moment he said it, and then changed his mind when he saw the reaction that Sam had to his statement. Her back was turned to him, but he could see how her posture changed. Sam stalled for a moment, taking in what he had just said. She shook it off and walked to the freezer to put ice in the dishtowel. She couldn't get out of her head what he had just revealed. Her anger began to melt away. She tied the dishtowel in a knot to hold the ice and walked over to John who stood in silence, gently taking his hand and raising it to see the damage. His palm was lined with quarter-sized blisters. She lightly placed the ice pack in his hand. He couldn't help but wince. She looked up at him and saw the burning sorrow in his eyes.

"I'm sorry," she said.

John looked at his hand. "You weren't the one that grabbed the barrel-"

"Not that." Sam interrupted. "I'm sorry."

John took a breath and softened his guard. "I'm sorry too."

Sam lowered her gaze and realized that John's hand wasn't the only wound he sustained. She shot her gaze back to his face. "You're wounded."

"I am?" John said. Looking down at the blood soaked shirt. He watched as Sam began to unbutton his shirt. He fought not to think further than his wounded hand. He couldn't focus on Sam's hands earnestly undressing him, even if it were to check the severity of his wounds.

"Oh my God! John, these are bad! Aunt Claire!" Sam shouted. She was fixed on the deep gash on his abdomen, under his right peck. Sam reluctantly paid no mind to how smooth his chest was or how his abdomen rippled with muscle. She could only see blood and beyond that, bone. Some of John's ribs exposed from the deepness of the gashes. Sam put it down to shock that he didn't notice the extent of his wounds.

"Sit down John," she said, ushering him to the kitchen table. John was dizzy from Sam's presence, not from his wounds.

Claire made her way into the kitchen and saw John's shirt open, exposing his wounds.

She looked at Sam and said. "Go to the sewing kit and fetch me a needle and some thread, then get the alcohol from the bathroom closet." Sam nodded and made off. Claire walked up to John who was frowning. "Ah, come now big guy. If you can handle a wound like this, you can handle a measly little needle stitching it up."

John looked at the old woman with a stale gaze. "You know as well as I do that I will heal by morning."

Claire met his eyes with a smile. "Yes, but do you want her to know?"

John just stood quietly. He hadn't thought about that point.

She continued. "I have some healing herbal salve that is good for burns. I will also put it on your wounds. It will throw Sam off from your healing so quickly."

"Did you know that it was me?" John asked.

Claire shrugged. "Not at first. But now I see your eyes, your mannerisms. They carry over to your other forms. It could have also helped that I studied with the Myrics for about thirty years... but who's to say."

"Are you-?" John started to ask.

Claire interrupted. "I'm one of the few privileged humans to ever study with the Myrics. Nicki will be the next in line."

"You didn't tell Sam, did you?" John seemed anxious with his question.

She replied. "What, that you were the one that saved your friend? No. We hadn't talked about it. I'm just going to tell her that I found him passed out on the porch. I am also going to tell her that I threw away his clothes since they were beyond saving so you will have to do something with his clothes."

John scratched his head. "You didn't know who I was when I had Marc in my arms. Why would you trust a werewolf?"

Claire, humored by the young man's shielded vision. "I opened the door to a werewolf who was holding a human. He was obviously helping a friend. Why should I fear someone who was helping another being?"

Sam came through the door stating. "Here you go. I hope the thread isn't too thick. I thought I would try for a white color... might blend in better than colored thread."

John smiled. "But I always looked good in green."

Sam and Claire both shot John a look of surprise. John would have jumped back, but Claire was in the process of salving his wounds. "Sorry, nobody ever gets my humor."

Sam just smiled at John. She became fixed on his eyes, like the color of slate warming in the sun. She became dizzy. Claire had the needle in her mouth when she muffled. "Sam, you are no help just standing there and staring. Go check up on Marc and Nicki."

Sam and John both blushed. John broke their gaze and Sam left the room.

Claire chuckled to herself. "I never thought she'd find a suitor that shared her sense of humor."

"Look, I know that I've only known Sam since this morning, but-" John was cut short by Claire's response.

"When you know, you know," she said softly.

She hushed him. She knew that Sam was on the other side of

the door. Just as Claire went silent, Sam turned and stood in the doorway. John caught her gaze once again. He never flinched while Claire stitched his wounds. He and Sam shared a connection of unspoken words and of unknown feelings. He brought to mind, their interaction by the lake. His mind swam around the memory of her embrace. Sam watched as his aura began to rise from him like steam. The dark green colors wisped around his body.

She thought to herself. "Well what d'ya know? He does look good in green."

Claire looked up and saw John looking towards the doorway. She tied a knot in the thread and patted his shoulder. John shook his head to come back to the present.

Claire sighed. "All done." She turned and saw Sam was beet red. She shook her head and smiled. "You two act like love-sick puppies."

"Hey," John said as if he were shocked.

She continued. "You remind me of a couple I once knew. Same chemistry. Good makeup. How long have you known each other?"

John blushed. "Since this morning."

Sam added. "He was the one I bumped into this morning."

"I broke her jam."

"Yes," Claire said as her focus went from Sam to John. "I would have thought she would have been more disappointed about that little incident. I can see now why she wasn't."

"I bought her the rest and gave it to her today," John said, looking to validate his action.

"Good boy." Claire winked at him.

She started to walk out the door passing Sam on her way out. She whispered. "He's all yours."

Sam felt her cheeks burn once again, they were alone. Sam walked up to him to inspect Claire's work. John stood there and let her look. Sam let her eyes wander down the 6-inch line of stitches that stretched under his right peck to his side. There were three other lines evenly spaced under the first. She brought her hand up to touch it, but thought better of it and grabbed her own hand to keep from disobeying her own mind.

John broke her concentration. "Do you know what it was, that attacked us?"

Pulling the needle thru his tanned skin, she answered. "No. I had a feeling, but I don't know."

John, not paying attention to the nagging pain of the needle, continued his interrogation. "Did you feel how we were being stalked?"

"I would call it more watched than stalked," Sam said, matter-of-fact.

"Watched?" John was intrigued.

"There has always been something that watched me, ever since I was a little girl. I never knew what it was and I had never seen it. I just thought it was something or someone that Claire assigned to watch me, to protect me."

"A watcher?" John's voice became strained.

Sam's tone turned into more of a question. "I guess?"

"Have you told your aunt?" John didn't give her time to answer, he continued. "Did you know it was watching us the whole time tonight?" John crossed his arms over his chest to keep from touching her. He squeezed his arms and clinched his jaw to banish her from his mind.

"It has always been there. Always. And why are you getting mad at me all of the sudden?"

John's concern for Sam's safety was creating an unknown rage within him.

"Because if we would have known that you had a watcher, we would have never attacked it. Marc would be ok and still in the gazebo with Nicki... You and I..."

"You and I what?" Sam stared at John.

John felt ashamed to feel so selfish. She mimicked his pose.

"I just met you today. Whether something interrupted us or not, it wouldn't have gotten that much further."

With that, Sam turned away.

John took a few steps towards her and replied. "That's not what I meant."

"Look, I don't know what's out there. Knowing Claire and her abilities, I never thought to ask her or to tell people about it. I guess it's a logical question that I will now pose to her, but you can't blame me for not saying anything before."

Sam was about at her wit's end. She was about to continue the conversation when Nicki poked her head in the Kitchen.

"What in the world are you two fighting about?"

They both looked at her and in unison spouted. "We're not fighting."

They both felt the humor in their jinxing, but were not going to give into their own stubbornness to chuckle about it.

Nicki walked into the kitchen slowly.

"Well, I wish you would hold it down. I have a splitting headache." She reached into the cabinet and grabbed the aspirin.

"With all the powers that I have, all the spells that I know, nothing works better than good ole' aspirin."

Sam and John just stood there; doing their best not to look at each other, but neither could bring it upon themselves to leave each other's presence.

Nicki popped the pills in her mouth, chewed quickly with a sour face, and chased it down with a glass of water. She made a face and then looked up at the two.

She slumped a bit and reprimanded. "Marc's fine. We're fine. You two don't have the issues that you think you do. There's enough sexual tension in this room to spread it on a piece of toast and eat for a snack. Why don't you two just kiss and make up. There's no harm here. Now kiss and play nice."

Sam and John stood their ground and stared at Nicki. She looked back and shushed them. Finally, Nicki rolled her eyes and walked over to them. She took John's hand and Sam's hand and pushed them together. They looked at their hands interlocked and back up to each other. Nicki put her hand on each of their backs and began to push them together. John wrapped his other hand around Sam's body. Sam returned the embrace.

"Now that's better. John, I'm going to need your help moving Marc to the spare room on this floor. I will give you two a minute to recoup."

Nicki scooted out of the room, towards the library. John and Sam just stood there, holding each other.

John went to say something.

Sam stopped him. "No. Don't say a word. She's right. There's too much tension right now and too much has happened tonight. Let's not talk anymore tonight. After you take Marc to the room, I'm going to head up to my apartment. I need to rest. I would like to fall asleep knowing that we're good."

John squeezed her slightly. "We're good."

Sam knew better than to steal a kiss. Again, there was too much tension to go and start playing with fire. They both started to head to the library, hand in hand.

Once they were standing in front of Marc, John bent down and picked him up into his arms. Nicki and Claire both winced as they heard John's stitches popping under the pressure.

"Be Careful!" Claire exclaimed. "You'll pop them all before you get him to the bedroom. And don't bleed on my quilt in there."

John walked Marc to the room and laid him down. Nicki was there at his side, already tending to him. John turned around and streams of blood ran down his chest. Naked from the waste up and bleeding, for some reason Sam found this highly attractive. Claire stood in front of Sam to block the view. Sam fought to bring her mind back to Claire.

"I want you to go to your apartment now," Claire said.

Sam's shoulders slumped in defeat. "Yes, it's probably best I do."

She peeked over Claire's shoulder and caught John's eyes. "Good night."

John looked like a four year old being left at the sitter by his parents. "Good night."

John added, but to Claire. "Do you mind if I stay here tonight. I would like to be here for Marc, and…"

Claire gave John a sincere smile. "Of course, that's fine."

She looked back at Sam. "Go."

Sam turned around and walked the long hike to her apartment on the third floor of the house. Once she got there, she closed the door and leaned against it. "What's wrong with me?" she thought. "I've known the guy for what, 24 hours and I'm acting like a crazed looney… like a schoolgirl with a crush."

Sam paced her living room, trying to make sense of why she felt this way and couldn't come up with one logical answer. She went to her desk and picked up her newly purchased book to escape from reality for a bit.

Sam thumbed through the stories, stopping to read a few of the shorter ones. The book was very dated, but the stories intrigued her. She felt as if she could see past the words to those stories that were true and those that where definite fables. She finally put the book down and looked at the clock... 1:00am. She walked to her bathroom and changed into her nightshirt and underwear. She slipped into her bed and drifted away as soon as she hit her pillow.

John walked out into the kitchen once more and proceeded to remove the stitches. His wound had already begun to close. He would have no reason to be re-stitched. He was picking at his side when Claire walked into the room. "Could you help me with the ones on my side, I can't see them."

Claire walked over and began to pick at his side, pulling the tiny threads through his flesh.

John broke the silence. "Do you have an appointed watcher for Sam?"

Claire stopped picking at John and looked into his eyes. "No, why?"

John continued. "We attacked, or were attacked by another one of our kind."

"WHAT!" Claire stood up.

John continued. "He was very powerful. You could feel his power surge off his body. He could have taken us."

Claire tried to deal with the question.

"Why did you ask if I had appointed a watcher to Sam?"

"I asked her about it and she had said that she has always felt a presence and thought that you had just appointed something or someone to watch her while on the property."

Claire rang her hands on the dishcloth. "No... I have never! I would never interfere with her personal life, no."

John noticed that the topic was being taken out of context. He tried to reassure her as best he could.

"Not to spy, but to protect her."

Claire stood her ground. "No, I didn't appoint anyone."

John gazed into his own mind and spoke aloud. "I think you might have a problem."

"Yes, yes indeed I might. I'm going to have to call some friends. I might call upon you if I may?" Claire asked.

"Anything to keep her safe."

John turned his face towards the doorway. "Anything."

"We will talk more about that tomorrow. Right now, we are as safe as we can be." Claire sniffed. She tried to change the subject. "Let's talk about something else."

"You have a beautiful home," John tried to oblige.

Claire looked into the young man's eyes. "When you bought the jam for Sam this morning, did you know that you would see her again?"

John was taken aback by the question. He began to blush. He answered. "After we parted this morning, I didn't know if we would ever see each other again. I headed for the booth. I couldn't help myself. I was overcome with a feeling that I had to make her happy at all costs. She was nothing but a mere stranger to me. It was uncomfortable, not having control over what I was doing. Since this morning, I haven't been able to get her off my mind. Since being around her, I can't seem to keep my distance. I have to have some sort of contact with her."

Claire smiled. "You're a wolf. When you find someone who is a good match for you, you know it instantly. You will do anything for that person, die... kill."

John scoffed in disbelief himself. "A good match sure, but this is nuts. It's on the verge of obsession."

"Let me break it down for you. Wolves mate for life right? Well, have you ever known how they keep such a tight bond with each other? They encounter the one person or being that is supposed to be their mate for life."

"Are you trying to tell me that I bumped into the person that will be my life mate?" John asked with a skeptic tone.

"I'm just saying that you both have a really strong connection. You never know... you might have."

"But she's so strong-willed, so pigheaded," John practically growled.

Claire nodded as if to agree. "It's both her strength and her weakness."

"How have you lived so long with her, with that?" Claire had a slight chuckle to herself at the young man's expense.

She added. "She has a way of tugging at the ole' heart strings when you aren't looking."

John huffed. "Thanks for the warning."

Claire laughed. "She means well."

"For whose sake," John added as to cut off her sentence.

Claire sat back for a moment and sized him up. "She's really gotten under your skin, hasn't she?"

"What?" John brushed off her look of observance. "No..."

A twinkle sparkled in Claire's eyes. "Say what you will. However, old women like me have a knack for these things. All knowing, all seeing."

John shook the old woman off. "What's her deal anyway?"

"That is not my place to say," Claire answered honestly. "But there is a something, isn't there."

Her demeanor changed to somber. "Has she spoken with you about it?"

Now it was John's turn to look upon Claire with observing eyes. "No, I can sense it. There's something strange. Something that's not quite right."

Claire found this intriguing. "Why so strange?"

"I've never felt this before. I could swear that I can almost sense her... emotions."

Claire was pleased with his answer. "That's why I believe that you are life mates."

"Stop saying that. It's wigging me out." John almost shivered at the thought.

Claire stood steadfast in her belief. "OK, but you'll see."

"Have you known others that were life mates?" John asked.

Claire smiled, as she answered. "I knew a couple once. Their clans forbade their love, but they couldn't deny it. They tried... God knows they tried. Don't misunderstand me, being life mates doesn't mean total bliss. They would have their fair share of fights, but their bond kept them... well... bonded. Sometimes it helped matters, sometimes it worsened them. They finally got the knack of it."

"Truebloods?"

"Yes."

"From two different clans?" John asked, eyebrows raised.

"Unfortunately, yes."

"How did that go over?"

"They were assassinated."

"It's frowned upon that much, the mixing of the clans?" John said, startled.

"About as much as a Trueblood falling in love with a Turned."

John whistled.

She picked out the last of his stitching and told him to wait there while she bandaged him up.

"I'll let you sleep in one of the rooms on the second floor. I'm sure you'll not be able to pull Nicki from Marc's side tonight."

"Are they life mates?" John asked.

"No, but Nicki really likes him."

"Yeah, Marc likes her too."

"Good." She padded his chest. "Done. Let's get you upstairs. It's late."

She showed him to the room and bid him good night. John felt very comfortable in Claire's home. He felt nothing but good vibes. He could almost hear a memory hidden in the walls, of the laughter from a little girl from so long ago. The house loved Sam as well. He took off his shoes and pants and carefully placed them on the dresser by the bed. He turned down the covers and lay down.

Sam was once again running through the darkness of the night. She could smell the damp air in her mind; she felt the heads of wheat whipping past her as she ran. She heard the crickets pause in their singing, holding their breath in hopes she didn't hear them. They were not her targets. She ran at a good pace, zigzagging through the field. She followed her prey by senses instead of sight. The earth whispered to her; rites of passage. She readied herself in her stride and lunged for her prey.

It screamed, he screamed.

The clouds of the night parted and let the moon shine its luminescence down upon them. She preyed upon his fear, drinking it up like an elixir. He struggled to get away, which brought her back to her capture. Sam lunged for the man's throat. Sounds of ripping and snapping echoed through the field as did his last scream, a scream of death. Sam whipped her head and buried her face into his warm flesh, savoring the metallic taste of his blood as she gnawed. She looked up and screamed for her victory, screamed to wake up... screamed to save her sanity. She broke from the dream, screaming for real. She could still taste the blood in her mouth.

John was about to drift off when he heard Sam scream. He bolted upright and fled out the door. He didn't know where she was; he only followed her pleas, her screams. He made it to her door and burst in. He ran to her. She was still screaming, trapped between dream and reality.

He shook her. "Sam, Sam! Wake up!"

She looked at him without seeing him and began to growl low. John's beast came rising to the top and he fought to keep it at bay. She broke free of his grip and scampered to the top of her bed. John's beast came forward, in his eyes, in his mind. He moved closer to her and grabbed her violently. He held her to his chest, letting her know it was him, keeping her from seeing his eyes, his other side.

She fought him the whole time, trying to free herself. She felt someone pulling her from her state, into reality, into John's arms. She stopped fighting him and began to hold onto him as if her life depended on it, sobbing uncontrollably.

John kissed her head. "It's ok. It's ok. It was just a dream. I'm here, you're safe now."

He kissed her again and rocked her as he held her tight. It seemed a lifetime before he felt her body go limp, and then he knew that she was asleep once more.

Claire, who had run up the stairs when she heard the commotion, stopped at Sam's door when she heard John and Sam squaring off. She peeked around the corner and saw John holding her. She watched how Sam fought his embrace then finally give in to him. Her heart welled up. She snuck back around the corner, holding her heart in her throat. She hated to see Sam go through this.

When the dreams first started, they would happen maybe once a year or so. Now, they were almost every night. Claire knew that it was getting dangerously close and that they needed to act soon. She swallowed her heart and turned the corner to come through her door. She walked up to John who was sitting there with his eyes closed. He was still holding Sam tight. Claire put her hand on his shoulder. He inhaled and opened his eyes. He didn't flinch but she could see the statement in his eyes. She whispered into John's ear.

"I know this is asking a lot, but would you stay with her tonight?"

John just looked at her in confusion.

"I haven't seen her pull through a dream like that since she first started having them..."

Claire paused as Sam stirred, waiting for her to be still once again.

"You were her anchor. I believe that the connection you share has helped her. Maybe if you stay with her, she will sleep through the night."

John nodded in agreement. A look of anguish on his face as he wished he could do more for her.

Claire walked over to the other side of the bed and pulled Sam's blankets down. John positioned Sam where Claire was able to cover her up. She watched Sam snuggle into her bed. John lay on top of the blankets and pulled just the top layer of extra blankets over himself. He smiled at Claire. She kissed Sam and started to leave the room. Before she left, she whispered once more.

"I will let you both sleep in the morning. Just come down when you're ready." She waved to John, shutting the door quietly in the process.

John turned on his side and pulled Sam against him. Even unconscious, Sam sidled herself against him as much as she could. He wrapped his arm around her, kissed her ear, and slowly drifted off.

CHAPTER SEVEN

Sam felt the sun on her face. She started to come to, but kept her eyes closed. She could see the bright red color on her eyelids from the sun beating down on her. She felt John behind her, holding her close. She took a deep breath and stretched. He didn't move, which told her that he was already awake. He pulled her closer to him. She smiled to herself. He positioned his face near her ear.

"Good morning, sunshine," John said seductively.

The feeling of his breath on her neck sent chills down her spine.

"Mmmm-hmmmm..." Sam said, and started to stretch again. John loosened his grip on her and watched her arch in a cat-like stretch. She settled and turned to face him. He looked at her face. She had pillow creases on her cheek from sleeping so soundly, he caressed them.

"You're beautiful in the morning."

"Equipped with dragon breath no doubt. I knew there was a reason I didn't like to drink." Sam tried to look over John to see her clock, but his broad shoulders were blocking the clock.

"What time is it?"

"After twelve."

"WHAT?" Sam was shocked. She hadn't slept past twelve since she was sick a while back.

"Don't worry. Your aunt came up here about two hours ago to check on us. She told me to let you sleep. Therefore, being the nice person that I am, I let you dead-arm me for the past two hours. Do you know that you have a really heavy head?"

Sam smacked him in the arm and he mocked a flinch and said. "It's like a melon."

John sighed. "You know what? You have some really vivid dreams."

John wished he hadn't brought the subject up. He saw the happiness wash away from Sam's face. John tried to recover.

"I'm sorry for blowing up on you, last night in the kitchen."

Sam forced a smile. "Don't be sorry. I'm just as much to blame. I'm normally not like that. I was just overwhelmed by the attack."

Sam averted her gaze as John caressed her face.

"Like Nicki said, we're all ok. Scraped up, bruised and frustrated, but ok nonetheless."

Sam slowly looked back at John. "Speaking of frustrated."

John grinned at Sam. "Speaking of…"

"As much as I am attracted to you, I think we should get to know each other before we-"

John interrupted her. "I agree. I'm not all about that, though I do find it hard to control myself around you."

"Me too. And that's another reason I think that we should get up soon."

"Are you saying that I'm wearing down your control?" he teased.

"Oh, I think that being on a bed together, with not much clothing is definitely pushing the boundaries of control."

"Yes, I believe so too."

"I have to get up."

She went to get out of bed and he grabbed her arm. She stopped and turned to look at him. He stole an innocent morning kiss. She sank into his arms with that kiss. He didn't let it go any further. She let herself enjoy the moment. When he released his grip on her, she got out of bed. He lay there, purposefully showing off his bare chest.

Sam walked to the bathroom backwards. "No fair."

"No fair? This is coming from a woman in an oversized t-shirt and I bet that's about it?"

John stood up and walked towards her. Sam kept walking backwards slowly until a wall finally blocked her. She was trapped. She watched John walk up to her in nothing but a pair of boxer briefs. She noticed how strong his legs looked, how well defined his calves were, how slender his hips were. John closed the distance between them.

The look on John's face showed hidden intentions.

"Would you do me a favor before you get ready?"

"What?" Sam asked suspiciously.

"Would you check my wounds?" John held up his arm to stretch his side.

"Oh, sure," Sam almost sounded disappointed.

John gave her a second glance, but let the statement slide. He felt her hands make contact with his body. He felt her fingers work the bandages that Claire had placed there the night before. He felt the warmth in her fingertips; he saw how flushed Sam's face was. Sam was having a difficult time focusing on her task. She began to peel away the bandages that bound him. Sam knew she was flushed, but there was nothing she could do to stop it. She also knew that John was looking at her, which didn't help the matters. She swallowed hard and went back to her job. John's hands came to rest on Sam's shoulders to keep them out of her way. Sam was almost finished with the bandages. The last piece of course was stuck fast. She moved in closer and attacked it with her fingernails, with a vengeance.

"This piece is stuck." Sam was aggravated.

John smirked and flinched. Making her lose any progress she was making with that piece from the movement.

Sam became frustrated. "If you don't stay still, this piece will never come off."

John lifted her gaze by lifting her head with his finger under her chin. She saw the look in his eyes, ablaze with fire. His eyes were actually lighter in color.

"Leave it." He kissed her. He wrapped his arms around her waist, holding her to him. Sam became enraptured by the power that surged between them.

He moved his hands past her waist, to her backside and below. He grabbed and lifted Sam in one-step. Sam wrapped her legs around him as he carried her to her desk. He sat her on top of the desk and pressed against her. He kissed her fiercely, bruising her lips. She kissed him back with the same ravenous appetite. She glided her hands down his back, tracing each ridge and valley of his muscular structure. He slid his hands on the outside of her thighs to her waist. He was taking her nightshirt with his hands. She didn't care. He kneeled down and kissed her bare stomach.

Sam lost track of everything but her and John, pulling him to her face. She wanted to feel his lips on her. John obliged. When he stood up, he stood at arm's length from her. He had his hands on her knees and pressed his body against hers.

He cradled her face and kissed her passionately. Sam wrapped her legs around his waist that urged a low growl from John. She bit his lip playfully as she kissed him. He began to kiss her harder and began to thrust against her. Her body yearned for him. She was finding it hard to keep control. She pulled away from his lips and began to kiss his chest. She played with his nipple all the way to his collarbone, where she licked the line across his chest to his shoulder. She kissed his neck and bit down on his shoulder. He began to grab at her underwear as she bit down harder. Sam heard John's breath quicken and took on a lower tone. What she didn't see was John's beast rising to the top. He needed a release. His face began to contort and his eyes were completely changed to his other form.

Power exploded between the two in a flash and Sam bit down hard one last time. She heard John's voice.

"Oh shit." He said in a sex-filled voice.

Sam licked where she had bit him. The taste of sweat mingled with… blood. Startled, Sam pulled away and saw the blood all over John's shoulder. She looked at herself and it was down her nightshirt. She began to scream. John was instantly on the defensive. He pulled away from her and stepped back. She couldn't stop screaming. She stood staring at John's chest. She was in another place. She was in a field hovering over a man that she had been feeding on. John heard footsteps and bolted for the outside entrance to Sam's apartment. He busted open the door and jumped from her balcony to the ground, a 36 feet drop. Once he hit the ground, he ran.

Claire and Nicki rounded the corner and saw Sam. Sam stood there screaming at some unseen horror. Her nightshirt was drenched in blood, as was her face and hands. Her eyes were wide and locked on something in front of her. Nicki shouted a few words and Sam collapsed on the floor where she stood. Claire shot a stern look at Nicki.

Nicki shrugged. "Well, what other idea did you have?"

Claire and Nicki made it over to Sam. Claire propped Sam up in her lap. "This isn't her blood."

Nicki was taken back. "You mean. It's John's? How can you tell?"

Claire examined the spots more intently. "I know her blood and this is not it. You have to get her into her bed."

Nicki grabbed a hold of Sam from one side and Claire grabbed the other. They positioned her and literally dropped her on the bed. Nicki looked at Claire.

"You should do a walk-through."

"Oh, No! Definitely not. Sam and John were alone, together up here and now John is gone and Sam obviously has bloodied him. No, that's too personal." Claire paused. "But you could."

"While she's knocked out?" Nicki answered, shocked.

"Well, that was your doing now was it not?"

Claire carried on. "Don't go back too far. We just need the truth."

Nicki sighed and walked downstairs to grab the components to complete the process. Nicki's power was like no other, but her experience was lacking.

Once Nicki was back in the room, she laid the components on the nightstand near the bed. Claire pulled a chair up to the bedside. She would hand Nicki the components when she needed them during the ritual. Nicki sat at the edge of the bed, crossed her legs where Sam's feet rested on Nicki's knees.

Nicki took a few cleansing breaths and started the ritual. She lowered her head and closed her eyes. She began to recite the words.

"Dosal, Kipin, Halthah, Nict…"

Nicki grabbed for the first item, earth. She reached into the bowl that Claire held for her and dug her fingers deep into the black soil. She took it and threw it high over Sam's body. As the soil fell, it caught fire like tiny meteors racing to the earth over Sam. The particles burned in brown flashes of light.

Nicki's chanting continued.

"Lavan, Sypho, Ilta, Behn…"

She grabbed for the next item, water. She cupped her hand in the bowl and threw the water over Sam's body as she had the soil. The water drops burned in bursts of blue flame and disappearing over Sam's body.

"Eeto, Nortas, Faylos, glyn…"

Nicki inhaled and then exhaled slowly, blowing her breath over Sam. Nicki's breath came out like a thick fog that dissipated over her body.

"Cytan, Joskos, Omeer, Voc…"

Nicki took the brazier from Claire's hand, threw the burning ashes in the air, and watched them as the burst into bright red flashes and disappear over her. Colors of red, blue, green and white began to swirl around Nicki and Sam.

"Memory hear me, let me see, by the elements, so let it be."

The world outside of the sphere began to blur. Claire had vanished just as Sam and John appeared over by the desk. Sam was screaming….

"I need you to go back moments more, please." Nicki asked.

She saw the world fade and then come back into light. She saw John standing there while Sam checked his bandages. She saw them kissing, feeling what Sam felt. She felt the deep and hidden emotions that Sam was feeling. She felt Sam's aching need for John. She was about to delve deeper when she reached the end of the memory. She felt Sam bite into John. She could taste his blood in her mouth.

Nicki was hit with a power so hard that she was thrown from the bed. She hit the far wall before she hit the ground. The memory was still playing around her. The scenery had changed while she was being thrown. She was now running in a field of wheat. She saw the man that was her target. She could feel Sam tackle the man to the ground. She saw the monster that Sam was. She tried to scream for Sam to stop, but was frozen in fear. She saw Sam attack the man… killing him. She watched as Sam began to devour the man. The taste of the man's flesh was thick in Nicki's throat.

Nicki finally was able to scream. "STOP!"

As the dream began to fade, she saw Sam look up and scream, scream to escape the monstrosity, to free herself…

The sphere dissolved and Nicki braced herself on her hands and began to convulse.

"Nicki, what happened?" Claire said frightened.

"I think I know why Sam was screaming." Nicki was still dazed.

"Are you OK?" Claire asked.

"I need to rinse out my mouth."

Claire helped Nicki to the bathroom where she rinsed her mouth out with mouthwash. The memory was starting to fade from her senses and with it, the taste of blood and flesh. She splashed water on her face and before leaving the bathroom she took a few strengthening breaths.

"I think that I saw her nightmare from last night."

Claire's eyes widened. "I told you not to go back too far."

"But I didn't. In fact, that's what had made her scream. It was the flashback of her dream that made her react the way that she did."

Claire looked over to Sam in concern.

Nicki continued. "And yes, it was John's blood. They were kissing... and well, the power brewing between the two was just too much. She got caught up in the moment."

Claire frowned as disapproving parent would. "Oh, they only met yesterday..."

Nicki smiled. "Oh GOD no." She was astonished. "I know her too well, she would have never..." She looked at Claire.

"Seriously, they weren't. But, and this is a big but, there was much power or energy flowing between them. I have NEVER felt that before from any kiss I've received."

Claire became uncomfortable and tried to change the subject. "What about the dream?"

Nicki paled. "She killed a man and fed from him."

Claire stood up. "Oh dear."

"Your lil' darling over there turned into a super monster, killed AND fed off of a guy and all you say is 'Oh Dear?' Oh shit is more like it." Nicki swallowed hard. "She outright killed him. I felt no remorse in her. No conscious." Nicki shivered.

"It's time."

Claire walked out of the room.

"Time for what? If you are ordering a pizza, I'm not hungry... thanks."

Nicki walked over and sat next to Sam. She laid her hand on Sam's forehead.

"Wake and be at peace." She prayed over Sam.

Sam stirred and opened her eyes. Her actions went from sleepy to almost frantic.

"Where's John?" Sam got up out of bed. "I think I hurt him. I didn't mean to." She walked to the door. "I need to talk with him."

Nicki stayed sitting on her bed. "He's gone."

"What?" Sam was disoriented. "We… we were… well we weren't… but we wanted to. We kissed. Things got carried away." She hung her head. "I bit him. I bloodied him." Sam began to check herself for traces of his blood.

"We cleaned it off of you."

Sam shot her a look of fear. Nicki added. "You were unconscious, completely incoherent."

Sam smelled something acrid in the air. "Did I vomit?"

"No, that was me. So much for Sunday brunch." Nicki could tell that Sam needed more of an explanation. "I had to do a walk through."

"How could you?" Sam's question was mixed with disgust and amazement.

"Claire and I walked in on you screaming, blood everywhere and John was gone. We couldn't get you to stop screaming. Hey, at least it was me and not Aunt Claire." Sam flushed.

"Can I say something without you getting totally wigged out?"

"No, but I know you are going to ask me anyway. But thanks for the warning." Sam sat in the chair next to the bed.

"Ok, all I have to say is WOW girl. You two have some energy. And he's a damn fine kisser!"

Sam looked into Nicki's eyes. Nicki could see Sam's heart breaking as they sat there. Sam began to cry. Nicki sighed.

"Ah, why ya have to go and cry for? Don't cry. It was only a small bite." Nicki held Sam and let her sob.

John was in his truck in only his briefs, not wanting to go back inside for his clothes, but not having a way to leave since his keys were in his pockets of his jeans, still in the house. John hit his steering wheel with his hands and then rested his head on it. He spent a few minutes contemplating his next move when he heard Claire's voice.

"I know I should be asking what did you do to my girl, but what I'm asking is what did she do to you?"

John never lifted his head from the steering wheel.

"She's makes me have these uncontrollable feelings."

"I was talking about the bite mark, but ok, let's talk about that for a moment." Claire tried to smile.

John sighed and sat back in his seat.

"Why worry? I just scared the living daylights out of her not a half hour ago. I don't think that I will be invited around anymore."

"What I think you should do is give her a week of not seeing each other. Call her all you want, but give yourselves some time to get to know one another."

"Didn't you hear me? I scared her. I know my beast was beginning to surface. She saw me and screamed."

"And what I'm telling you is that if you don't call her tomorrow, werewolf or not, I'll tan your hide. She wasn't screaming about that. Trust me. Call her tomorrow evening say around six. And do not be late."

John looked defeated. "Six o'clock. Ok, if you say so."

Claire smiled from her victory. "Good, now here." She handed him his clothes. "You might need these."

"What are you going to tell Sam?" he asked.

"I'll think of something. If Marc wakes up, I'll have Nicki take him home. I'll make sure that Marc doesn't spill the beans."

"Sam's hiding something isn't she?"

"So well she doesn't even know what it is."

"But you do." John needed answers.

"I might."

"Should I be worried?"

"Hiding something or not and if it were just Sam we were talking about, yes," John smiled.

"Now get going, I have work to do."

Claire hit the hood of his truck and smiled. John slipped on his shirt and pants and started his truck.

He popped the clutch into gear and before he took off, he leaned out his window to Claire. "Thanks,"

"Don't thank me. You don't know what you're getting into yet."

Claire walked inside and picked up the phone. She dialed the number, waiting until someone picked up. The voice on the other end of the line was a woman's voice, but very heavy and very rough.

"Yeah?" the voice asked.

"This is Claire Williams," Claire stated

"What do you want?" the voice retorted.

"I would like to speak with Carol if she's available."

"She's busy. Leave me your number and I'll have her call you back."

"Let her know that it's imperative that she gets back to me today. It's a matter of life and death."

Claire gave the woman the number and hung up as she heard the girls coming down the stairs. She turned and saw Sam and how pale she was. She walked up to her and gave her a hug.

"I'm glad you're ok, sweetie."

"Embarrassed more than anything. I'm ok."

Claire tsk'd at her embarrassment and guided her to the kitchen.

"I have some coffee on, I'll make you a sandwich."

"I'll take the coffee, but hold off on the sandwich. I don't feel that great."

Claire poured Sam a cup of coffee and sat it down in front of her. She lifted the cup and let the aroma ease her mind, then took a few sips. Though it was probably placebo, she was already starting to feel better, not fully, but better.

Nicki sat beside Sam, and looked at her in wonderment. Sam felt her gaze and finally met her eyes.

"What?" Sam asked.

"You, I just don't get it. What is it?"

Claire sat down between the both of them.

She turned to Sam. "Is this something that you are going to share eventually with her?"

Sam sighed and answered. "If I didn't tell her, she would find out eventually."

Nicki sat there and listened. She started to get angry.

"Don't talk about me like I'm not here."

Sam and Claire looked at Nicki. Claire patted her hand.

"I'm sorry Nicki. I think that Sam has something she'd like to tell you."

Nicki turned her focus to Sam. Sam smiled at the awkwardness of it all. She rubbed the back of her neck with her hand and finally blurted it out.

"I'm not all human."

Nicki's mouth gaped open, staring in astonishment, mouth still open.

"Both of my parents were Werewolves."

"W-O-W," Nicki said astonished.

"It's not that big of a deal. I'm still Sam."

"But it explains a lot though."

"Explains what?" Sam was now curious.

"How you are always so in tune with nature. That thing that you can do with auras, I knew either you had hidden mystic abilities or something more was happening. Yes, I can definitely see it now."

Sam turned to Claire. "What's happening to me?"

Claire took Sam's hand. "Your body is ready for the change, for the beast to become one with your human side. I fear that keeping you away from werewolf influence through your life has had opposite effects on you."

Sam didn't know what to say. She didn't understand what Claire was saying.

"Truebloods normally have their first change during their stages of puberty. Some children go through it before or after, but that's about the time that it happens. In some rare cases, Trueblood parents have given birth to humans who never change. We watched you until you were eighteen. We decided then that you must have been one of those cases. We were wrong. Your beast is now trying to force its way out of you."

Sam looked even more perplexed. "Force?"

"The nightmares. It's your beast sending your brain signals that it's time, actually, that it's overdue. You need to go through your change."

"How do I do that? Does it hurt?"

Nicki was completely content listening to Claire explaining the process to Sam. She made no noise, she asked no questions.

"The very first time you change has to be performed as a ritual. It has to be done with a Myric. They have a clan not 50 miles from here. I was going to take you there this weekend. Friday is the next full moon and I don't think that you could survive it."

It was Sam's turn to stare with her mouth open.

"What?"

Claire's eyes began to glisten with tears.

"Yes, I think we've waited too long. I think that your beast will consume you if you don't."

"What would happen, exactly, if I don't get the help that you're talking about?"

"Your beast will split through your body. It will not have enough power or mass to keep its form and it will kill you in the process. Neither will survive."

"Talk about a turn of events," Nicki said whimsically.

"So, my beast isn't me?" Sam asked.

"It's you, but in a different form, almost in a different plane of existence if you will. From what I have been told, it's almost like having two minds fight for the same body."

Sam sat up in her chair. She mustered every inch of courage she had. "When do we do this?"

"As soon as carol calls me back, we'll know."

"Is Carol?"

"Yes, she is."

Nicki and Sam both looked at each other. Sam turned back to Claire. "Who else in this town is?"

"Well, there are two different kinds of Weres. There are the Turned and the Truebloods. Carol is the only Trueblood in this area, but there are a few turned in town."

"Who?"

"Kenny. From Randy's. Then there's Brad and Aimee Parks. Chaz Fitzpatrick from your graduating class, though Brad and Aimee are a different type of were…"

"Wait wait wait. So, you're telling me that Kenny and Chaz are werewolves. Should I ask what Brad and Aimee are?"

"Remember that hunting incident when they were in Alaska, where they got attacked by a bear?"

"Yes."

"They are a form of Werebear."

Sam took a moment to soak in the information. Her eyes widened. "Oh god, is Katie?"

"No, they were turned after Katie was born."

Nicki took this time to speak up. "I think that-"

She was interrupted by Claire's stern shot. Nicki changed the subject. "I think that there's a lot of them out there, huh?"

Nicki knew that it sounded like she was covering up something. Sam knew it too.

"What is it." Sam asked.

"Just there's so many of them in this town. I wonder if it's a meeting point for them." Nicki tried better to recover.

Sam wasn't biting. "What do you know?"

"It's just that I've always had a sneaky suspicion about that Chaz. He just struck me as odd. Different."

"He's just different, period."

Nicki replayed Claire's voice in her head from earlier. "She mustn't know that Marc and John are turned. John wants to tell her himself."

Claire, not keeping up with the conversation, laid her head on her hands.

"Aunt Claire, What's wrong?"

"I'm just worn out. I need to get some rest. Would you help me to my room?"

Nicki and Sam aided Claire on her walk to her room. Claire was not that old, yet she acted as if she were. She lay down on her bed and pulled a quilt over her legs.

"I'm going to take a nap. I don't mean to leave you with all of this, but I don't have the energy to go on. Please wake me in a while. I will make us dinner."

Sam hushed Claire and tucked her in tight. "I will take care of dinner. You get your rest."

Nicki and Sam left the room, left Claire with her thoughts.

She said a prayer for strength and then slowly drifted off to sleep.

Nicki and Sam were on their way back to the kitchen when they heard Marc stirring.

Nicki turned to Sam. "Would you go and get him something to drink. I want to personally greet him."

Sam grinned and walked away. Nicki knocked on the bedroom door. She heard Marc shuffle around. "Hold on…" She heard more shuffling. "Come in."

Nicki came in and saw Marc sitting on the edge of the bed with a sheet wrapped around his waist. He was rubbing his head.

"What in the hell?" he asked.

"You got fucked up pretty bad. John brought you to the house just in time for me and Claire to save your life."

"Who in the hell was that in the woods?"

"We don't know yet. Claire was going to call on some trustworthy Weres to help her in her search for the creature."

Marc looked up at Nicki. He smiled at her. "Damn girl, do you ever get ugly?"

"You haven't seen me in the morning. I'm a bear before I have my coffee."

"I have heard of Werebears but have never met one."

"No silly." She sat down next to him.

Marc peeked in the sheets. "I guess my clothes are still in the woods?"

Nicki smiled. "Nope, John put them in the truck for you. But since he sped off like a bat out of hell this morning, you're my captive. I'll decide if you get clothed."

Marc wanted to run with the conversation, but he was still stuck on John. "Why did he leave?"

"Sam and John were really getting into it upstairs, when she bit him. He thought that his beast was coming through, but what she was really screaming about was the blood and the flashback."

Marc rubbed his head. "Huh? Oh, this is too much."

"I will explain it to you later, but Sam doesn't know that you guys are Weres. John wants to tell her on his own, so we can't talk about it. Deal?"

"How did you know that…?"

"That you're a Were? You dive into someone's soul to hold

onto them for dear life, you get to know a person pretty well, and pretty quick."

"I can still feel something."

"It's the reverb of the healing. What's left of it is bouncing around in your body like a lil' nurse, trying to fix what ails you."

"You did this for me?"

"I am not going to lie, I would have done it for anyone, but I feel that my powers arched last night because it was you."

"Power surge?"

"Big time. I had energy spouting out of my toes. You put a lil' emotion in your healing and powers could be limitless. The only analogy I have is when a mom picks up a Buick that had just rolled on top of her kid. That kind of strength."

Marc smiled and winced at the same time. His hand went to his head.

"I feel like I've been on a 3 day bender."

Nicki went back to another subject. "So, you'll keep you and John a secret for now?"

"What do I get out of it if I keep the secret?"

Nicki put her hand on his thigh and gingerly played with the fabric of the sheet. "Oh, I'm sure there has to be a way that I could repay you for your secrecy."

"I like bribery."

He stole a quick kiss from Nicki. He pulled away and asked. "Now, are we going to take advantage of the naked prisoner or can I get something to wear? I'm starving!"

Nicki sighed. "I wish I could take advantage of you right now, but I don't think that it's good timing," she pouted. "So I will run and get you some clothes."

She got up to walk away and Marc smacked her on the butt to move her along. Nicki giggled and walked out of the room.

Once she got to Sam, she asked if she had any clothes that would fit Marc that he could wear. Sam ran up to her apartment and grabbed some sweatpants and a T-shirt. Nicki took them into Marc and he quickly got changed. Nicki stood there, watching Marc dress.

Marc couldn't help but make the comment. "See something

you like?"

"Oh yes I do. Yes, indeed." Nicki wasn't looking at his face.

Marc just smiled and finished dressing. After he had everything on, he looked at Nicki. "How do I look?"

Sam had given him the largest pair of pants that she had. She also gave him the largest T-shirt. Marc wasn't big, but he was tall. The sweat pants hit him above the ankles. The t-shirt had an old woman on the front, holding an empty coffee mug and a gun. The quote read. 'Talk to me before I've had my first cup of coffee and I'll shoot you.' Nicki started to giggle. Marc started to chase Nicki out of the room and towards the kitchen. She squealed as she ran.

Marc caught up to her and they walked the rest of the way to the kitchen.

Sam was pouring another cup of coffee. She turned and saw the two at the table. She could hear them talking under their breath and it was too much for her to bear. She turned back to the counter and held her breath. She felt the tears coming on and did her best to fight them back.

Nicki looked over at Sam. "Sam, are you going to join us?"

Sam didn't turn. She just lifted her head and answered. "Nah, I think that I'm going to go out on the porch and enjoy the afternoon. Marc, you can help yourself to something to eat."

She walked to the door without ever looking at the couple. She felt Nicki's gaze on her as she hurried outside. She held her coffee mug tightly as she walked to the porch. She could still smell John's scent outside and followed it to where his truck was parked. She stood there and thought about him, about how he held her as she slept, how he helped her through her nightmare and how the sheer presence of him calmed her. She barely knew him but felt that she had known him for ages. She breathed in his scent, letting it roll through her memory. She exhaled a sigh and turned to the porch. She saw Nicki sitting on the swing, watching her. Sam made her way to the swing and sat next to her.

"What's up?" Nicki asked.

"I'm just tired."

"Liar."

"I am. Tired of having a screwed up social life. Tired of everyone around me enjoying a love life, when I can't even seem to do right with the ones that ARE interested in me."

"You are doing right."

"I bit him. I bloodied him."

"He liked it."

"WHAT?" Sam was astounded

Nicki bit her lip. "From what I saw in your memory, he really liked it."

"But the human bite is the worst bite when it comes to infection. He's probably got a huge gaping, infected shoulder because of me."

"No worries, you're not human...remember."

"OH MY GOD....OH MY GOD!" Sam shot up, spilling her coffee on the porch.

Nicki grabbed her arm. "What's the matter?"

"I'm not human. I bit him. Infected him... Oh god, I could have possibly given him... this."

Nicki tried to keep the smile from her face. "You don't know if he was infected. Hell, we don't even know if you can infect someone that way."

"What am I going to do? I have to call him. I need to talk to Marc."

Sam got up and began to rush towards the door.

Nicki grabbed Sam's arm. "It's going to be ok. Don't freak out. Do you really want Marc knowing your secret?"

Sam stopped in her tracks. She had her hand on the doorknob, but didn't turn it to go in.

"How am I going to talk to Marc about it without letting him on?"

"You don't talk to Marc. You talk to John," Nicki said, soberly.

"Yeah, that's probably better." Sam was caught up in her own thoughts. Nicki squeezed her arm in reassurance.

"It's going to be ok."

"If you say so."

They both walked back into the house and headed for the

kitchen. They walked through the door and found Marc amidst a feast of food. He had pulled out every container that he could find of leftovers from the fridge and was stuffing his face. He was leaning against the counter, eating right out of the containers. He heard the girls walk in and looked up. He made an effort to smile even though his cheeks bulged with food. Nicki and Sam chuckled.

"I'm going to eat all of this, so don't worry about me putting back half empty containers."

Sam leaned on the island, trying hard not to think of John and what she might have done to him. "Save room for dinner."

"Oh this? This is only a snack."

Sam did a double take. Marc smiled again at the reaction.

"I've been out for a while. I need to get my energy back. Ma always said that I had a good appetite."

Sam shook her head. She walked over and got out her cookbook to decide what she was going to make for dinner. She set the book down next to a needle with blood soaked white thread hanging off it. The needle glistened in the afternoon light. Sam took the dishtowel and covered it from her sight. She didn't want to pick it up, but she couldn't let it distract her. She took a breath and thumbed through the recipes. She found an acceptable recipe and began to go to work.

Dinner was almost ready when Sam went to wake up Claire. Sam made it to her room and peeked through the door. She saw Claire staring out the window. She walked into the room and sat on the bed.

"Penny for your thoughts?" Sam asked.

"I wish you didn't have to go through all of this."

"It's ok. I can handle it."

"But you shouldn't have to." Claire sat up and took Sam's hand. "I wish you didn't have to go through this."

"Really, I'm ready for this. I feel that somehow, I have been ready for this for a while."

"But you will never be the same, never be normal again."

Sam gave her a sarcastic look. "When have I ever been normal?"

"But I'm going to lose my little girl, Claire said.

Sam put her arm around her.

"No matter how old or beastly I get, I'll always be your little girl." She reached over and hugged Claire reassuringly.

"Ok, now come on. I actually made dinner and I want you to come and enjoy. I'm starving!"

Claire patted Sam on the knee and nodded. They walked to the kitchen together to find that Marc and Nicki had set the table. Sam seated Claire then proceeded to serve everyone. Once everyone settled, Sam sat down to her own plate.

Claire took a bite. "Sam, this is good."

"Don't sound so surprised."

"I know I am." Nicki poked fun.

Sam went to take a bite when the phone rang. She got up and retrieved the cordless phone. As she walked back to the table, she answered.

"Hello?"

"Samantha Harris?"

"Yes, who's this?"

"This is Carol. I am returning Claire's call from earlier. Are you ok?"

"Um, yes and no."

"Nightmares?"

"Yes. I killed a man in my dreams last night. And today," she turned her back to the table. "I bit someone..."

"You bit someone?" Carol's voice was shocked.

"Long story. Chalk it up to young love, but yeah, I bit him on the shoulder."

Carol was quiet for a moment.

"Is that bad?" Sam asked.

"No, since you are not truly yourself yet, I think that he'll be ok. You will have to watch him for the next few days. If he complains about any awkward ailments, let me know."

"That's about all that has been happening here. I can feel my senses heighten in stressful situations, but I thought it was just adrenaline or something."

"How are you emotionally?"

"A wreck, but that's nothing new."

Carol was forward. "Ok. I'll come out to the house tomorrow. I'll be there around three. Tell Claire to have my room ready for me."

"I'll see you tomorrow."

Sam said goodbye and hung up the phone. She sat down and started to eat. She looked up as she was bringing the spoon to her mouth and saw everyone staring at her. She couldn't help but smile.

"It's alright. Carol will be here tomorrow at three. Aunt Claire, she said to have her room ready."

Everyone continued to eat. As they ate, Marc entertained the girls with outlandish stories of him and John. He had a captivated audience, but whether it was from his stories or from the four bowls of chili, he ate, it was not certain. He took the room when he finished his last bowl, and asked what was for dessert.

Dinner was finished and Claire was cleaning off the table. She brought the dishes over to Sam to load in the dishwasher. Sam went to open the dishwasher when the phone rang again.

She saw Claire look up at the clock and reply. "Oh, uh honey will you get that? I will finish up here."

Sam didn't think anything of it and headed towards the phone. Claire said a prayer of thanks and kept her smile locked inside her heart.

Sam answered the phone. "Hello?"

There was a brief silence, and then a voice. "Sam?"

"John?" Sam couldn't repress the excitement in her voice.

"I... I wanted to call and apologize to you."

Sam mindlessly walked out of the room and onto the porch.

"Apologize? I should be the one to apologize. I'm the one that hurt you."

"You didn't hurt me. It was nice, well, except for scaring you."

"I screamed from a flashback from my dream the night before. I saw your blood and I was automatically dropped back into my dream. I couldn't escape. When I came to, Nicki had me on the bed."

"So you weren't screaming because of me?"

"What? Why would I scream because of you?"

She heard John release a sigh of relief.

"I just thought... that maybe it was getting too much, too fast."

"Well, it was going a bit fast for my taste. I know your last name and a few stories about you, but I don't know you yet. But if I wouldn't have had the flashback." She stopped.

"If..." John stated as well.

"How is your bite mark? It's not infected, is it?"

"Oh no, it's fine. Almost healed. Is Marc awake yet?"

"Yes, do you want to talk to him?" Sam tried to keep her disappointment out of her voice.

"No, I called to talk to you." She could hear him smile on the phone.

"Good," Sam said, smiling back.

John and Sam talked for the rest of the night. They revealed all of their hopes and fears to one another. John told her what he had hoped to do with his life, while she told him about her plans for the future. She told him how she had been working as a stable girl for the same farm, for the past eight years. That she started in the 4H club in her sophomore year of high school and that once she graduated, they hired her permanently. She told him how she went to a community college, received her Associates in Science, and majored in business management. She went on to tell him how she had saved for the past six years because she was gearing up to go to Moorehead University the following year. He told her how he had already received his bachelors and masters in veterinary and animal behavior and that he was working on his doctorate for wildlife conservation research. For twenty-six, he had really made a life for himself.

She thought quietly to herself that there must be something wrong with him, to be single all this time.

As if he heard her thoughts, he asked. "Aren't you going to ask about my past love life?"

Sam could feel herself blushing. "Well, I was thinking about it."

"I have only had two major relationships in my life. Both ended quickly. I have been on a few dates, but never really found someone I connected with..." He deliberately paused as if to say something else but didn't.

"I have had one major relationship. It lasted a while, but I was stupid and young. He was not the nicest person in the world. I take that back, he isn't. Best part about it is... he's a damn police officer for this town. After I was hit enough, I decided to get out while I could."

"He, hit you?" John said slowly. Sam could hear the anger rise in his voice.

His question brought back a memory she wished would have stayed buried.

Sam ran frantically around the kitchen. She checked the clock for the time, 6:15pm. Danny would be home anytime. It had been one year since she and Danny started living together. Sam wanted to make the night special. She had made a wonderful anniversary meal, had a bottle of wine chilled, and a special dessert prepared. She set the dining room table and lit the candles. She ran to the bathroom one last time to check her makeup and dress before coming back out to the living room. She sat down on the sofa and waited for Danny to come through the door. She waited and waited. She went to the kitchen and checked the time, 7:30. She turned the stove onto warm and returned to the living room. She sat and waited. She slumped in her chair. The last time she checked the time it was 9:45. She turned off the stove and put the food in the fridge. She went to the room and got dressed for bed.

She was brushing the curls out of her hair when she heard the front door open and slam shut.

"Sam, where are you?" She heard Danny slur out a shout.

Sam exhaled. Her heart was broken. She couldn't shed any more tears even if she tried.

"Hey, where's my dinner?"

Sam walked around the corner with her arms crossed in front of her.

"Where've you been?" Sam asked without emotion.

"Where's my dinner?"

"Where've you been?" Sam's tone harshened.

"Look, bitch. I don't answer to no one. I'm someone in this town." He thumbed his own chest.

"Yeah, you're someone alright. You smell like shit."

"Who the fuck do you think you are? You high and mighty bitch." Danny was stumbling around the furniture to come close to her.

"Your dinner's in the fridge. It was warm and ready when you were supposed to be home four hours ago. Now, you can eat it cold."

She turned to walk down the hall.

"You'd better get back here and fix my dinner."

He walked down the hall after her. She was almost in the room when Danny grabbed her arm and yanked her back. She turned and he pushed her down the hall, on the floor.

"I said, get in that kitchen and fix me my fucking dinner!"

He kicked her in the rear further down the hall. Sam quickly jumped up and turned to face him.

"STOP IT! I'm tired of you treating me like this!"

Danny backhanded Sam across the face. Sam's face immediately began to throb with a dull pain. She didn't cry. She lifted her chin and stared him straight in the eyes.

"Don't you ever hit me again." Sam's voice shook with every word. Danny's eyes sparkled with humor.

"You threatening me?"

Sam slumped. "Look, it was supposed to be a special night. Tonight marks a year we've been together. I wanted to make it special for you."

"All you do is ride my ass, have to know where I am at all hours of the day. You never give up."

"You were four hours late. What was I suppose to think?" Sam's voice raised another octave. She tried to control her anger.

"Just sit down. I'll make you a plate."

Something in Danny's eyes turned. "Nah, I'm not hungry. A year huh? So, what were you going to do to make it special?"

Danny licked his lips as he glared at her. Sam took a step back.

"Well, I made dinner and dessert." Sam wasn't going to let on what else she had planned, which was a bath and a romantic night to follow. She didn't want that part of the night now. Danny knew that she was holding back on him.

"What else?"

"Nothing. I was just going to draw a bath for you. I would have thought that you would want to relax after dinner." Sam couldn't look into his eyes.

"I know what I want." He grabbed her arm.

"You're hurting me." Sam tried to pull away from him.

He pulled her to his chest and planted a sloppy kiss on her. Sam struggled to get away from him.

"Stop. Please don't do this." She tried to stay calm. Acting irrational would only fuel his fire.

"Don't you want to make it special for me?"

"Please, not tonight, not now."

"Come on. It's our special day." Danny mocked Sam. He dragged her down the hall to their room. Sam tried to struggle against him. She tried to hold onto the doorknob. Danny just yanked her from the door and threw her on the bed.

Sam tried to shield herself from him, but it only aroused him more. He ripped at her nightgown, exposing her chest. Danny fell on top of her and began to ravage her body. Sam kicked and punched at him. He laughed at her and punched her in the mouth. Sam was partially stunned by the hit.

Danny flipped her onto her stomach and ripped her underwear off. He grabbed her legs and pulled her to the edge of the bed, where he proceeded to rape her. Sam laid still. She didn't make a sound. When he finished, he got up and walked out of the room, leaving Sam halfway on the bed.

Sam inhaled quietly. She hadn't known that she was holding her breath. She knew that her face was swollen and bloodied. She let her body melt onto the floor. She tried to cover herself with her ripped gown. She knew that it was far beyond repairing. She sat huddled on the floor for what seemed to be hours, eventually getting up and walking to the bathroom. She turned on the light and examined her face in the mirror. Her whole left side was swollen and bruised, her lip split. She could barely see out of her left eye. Tears swelled up in her eyes, burning her left eye even more than it was. She searched the rest of her body and found bruises around her arms and around her neck. She turned off the light and headed back to the living room.

Danny was passed out on the couch. Sam quickly ran to the room and packed her clothes. This was the last time that she would let Danny do this to her. She took all of the pictures that had the two of them in them, and packed those as well. She had plans for those later. She finally got dressed and snuck out the back door.

She drove to Nicki's house. She didn't want to face her aunt just yet. Nicki answered the door and about fell down. She grabbed Sam by the arms and pulled her in the house.

"Sam! What in the hell!"

Sam lowered her head. "He..."

"He? HE? He's gonna pay!" Nicki shouted.

Sam put her hands in the air as to surrender.

"Please, Nicki. I have gone through enough."

"Oh, Sammy. I'm so sorry."

"Can I stay here with you, for a day or so. I can't go to Claire's yet. Not looking like this."

Sam began to cry the last part. She didn't cry from being hurt. She cried because she knew that she was no match for Danny. There was nothing that she could do to get back at him. She could go to the hospital and claim rape, but since she was in a relationship with one of the only cops in town, she was likely not to be believed. Danny had also made it a point to have his hand in every business in town, so having someone back her was almost impossible. She knew the only thing she could do was to leave.

Nicki held her gingerly. She could only imagine what Sam was going through. All she could do was hold her, be there for her.

"Would you like me to do something special to him, for you?"

"Ask me when I'm thinking rationally. You don't want to ask me that right now."

"Sure I do. Tell me what you would want to have done to him."

Sam pulled away and looked at Nicki. Nicki shrugged and smiled.

"Look at it as therapy. Don't let him control you even sitting here. Let's get you cleaned up and you tell me all about what you would like me to do to that creep."

Sam stood up and walked to the window to look outside.

"Nicki, could you hide my car?"

Nicki closed her eyes, chanted a few words and snapped her fingers. She opened her eyes and smiled.

"Presto!"

Sam looked towards her car and it was replaced with a pink truck. She turned from the window and gave Nicki a look.

"What? It was the first thing that I could think of."

"Only you would choose a pink truck."

"If I had a truck, it would be pink. So, there. Now, let's go get you cleaned up."

"Sam? Are you there?"

"Yes. Yes, sorry."

"What in the hell... What just put you in a whirlwind of rage?"

"I didn't think that it could be noticed over the phone."

John exclaimed. "I could feel the anger over the line. He was that bad, wasn't he?"

Sam tried to play it down. "Like I said, I was young and stupid. He was older, I thought he was cool... you know how it goes."

"It's no excuse. I hate people like that."

"So do I. Aunt Claire tried to warn me, but I wouldn't listen. It almost killed our relationship."

"Asshole."

"And then some. But once I opened my eyes, I saw what he was doing to me and I left."

"He let you leave?"

"Not exactly. He kept bothering me until Claire said something about having enough and made a call. He stopped harassing me. Now, he just pulls me over and gives me a ticket every chance he gets."

"How do you still have a license?" John mocked.

"Because the sheriff is sweet on Claire," Sam said playfully as to change the subject.

"I'm sorry Sam."

"Why are you sorry? You didn't hit me. I don't think that you're the hitting type."

"No. I'm not."

"Besides, I'm a strong person, I could take ya."

"Oh you think so, huh?" John played back.

They changed the subject once again and continued to talk. During their conversation she had said goodbye to Nicki and Marc as they left, and said good night to Claire, who had already got herself ready for bed.

He could hear her tiredness on the phone. He looked at the clock, midnight.

"What time do you have to be at work tomorrow?"

"5 AM, why?"

"Look at the time."

Sam looked and almost fell out of her chair.

"OH MY GOD! I'm so going to be dragging ass tomorrow." She giggled.

"I'd better let you go so you can sleep."

"I wish I could talk to you all night."

"We have talked all night."

"I'm scared," Sam said flatly.

"Do you need me there?"

"You don't have to," Sam answered.

"Do *you* want me there?" John asked in a different way.

Sam was silent. She so wanted to say yes. She so wanted to curl up in his arms and drift silently to sleep. She wanted to sleep with no dreams.

John could hear her silent pleas even over the phone. He knew that she was trying to be strong.

John smiled to himself and said. "How about I make a deal with you. I don't think that it would be a good thing for us to be awake at the same time, together, at least for right now. So if you could leave me a way to get in, I will sneak in and sleep with you, but I will leave before you wake up in the morning."

"That's a lot to go through." Sam tried to put him off.

John wasn't buying it. "I get to sleep with a beautiful woman in my arms? How is that not worth going to the ends of the earth for?"

Sam was silent.

John added. "OK, I'm going to leave now. I will be there in about 15 minutes or so. Don't fall asleep. Don't want you having bad dreams. What time do you get up in the morning?"

"4:30"

John's jaw dropped on the other side of the phone.

"Ok, I will leave at 4:15. Sound good?"

"I can't believe that you would do that for me." Sam was almost in tears.

"All you have to do is say the word and I'm there, but say it fast. It's getting late."

Sam paused. She gave into herself.

"Yes. Ok," her voice strained. She could feel John almost smile.

"I'm on my way." She told him where the extra key was hidden to get into the apartment and then said good night.

CHAPTER EIGHT

Sam hung up the phone and settled into bed. She couldn't believe that she had just agreed to make him drive all the way to her house just to sleep with her. What was he getting out of it? Sam tried to stay calm but her emotions were on overload once more. She began to cry silently into her pillow. She couldn't believe that someone would go through so much for her.

After a while, she wiped her eyes and turned off the light. No sooner than she settled herself into bed, she heard the door open. She never turned to face the intruder. He pulled down the covers and climbed into bed with her. He wrapped his arms around her and kissed her on the ear.

He whispered to her. "Good night. Sweet dreams."

The feeling of his body pressed against her gave her a sense of security. She fought sleep so that she could hold onto the feeling of his body against hers. She lost the battle and drifted off. She slept hard that night.

Sam woke up to the alarm going off, reached over and turned it off. She rolled back into place and noticed that a pillow was propped behind her, not John. She didn't know for sure, if he had come during the night or if she had just imagined it. Either way, she felt great. She had slept more than she had in months. Moreover, and best yet, she didn't dream. All she remembered was total darkness, sweet and silent darkness. She turned on her light and rolled out of bed. She saw an envelope on the pillow next to her. She couldn't help but smile. She opened the envelope that housed a card. There was a picture of a shooting star on the front. Inside the card was blank except for John's handwriting.

"Sam,
I hope that you slept as well as I did. I will call you tonight.
Yours always, John"

She read the card and then held it to her heart. She looked up and saw his eyes smiling back at her. She mouthed the words "Thank you." Before the eyes vanished in the darkness. She placed the card on her vanity and proceeded to get ready for her day.

John watched Sam wake up. He saw her turn the light on and find the card. He watched her expression as she read the card. He stood there and exchanged glances with her as she thanked him. He smiled and walked down the stairs. He knew that he had helped her. He also had slept great for such a short night. He got into his truck and headed back to his place, his mind never leaving the smell of honeysuckle and mint from Sam's hair.

Sam packed her lunch and made her coffee to go. She left a note for Claire and headed out the door. She could feel eyes on her, but this time it was not John. She fought past her fears and proceeded to her truck. She felt the presence get closer. She turned around to face nothing. She knew that someone was there, just out of sight. She put her stuff in the truck and turned back to the yard.

"I don't know who you think you are, but you can't keep doing this to me. This has gone on too long. I am not afraid of you."

She stood her ground, her heart in her throat. She waited a minute before climbing into her truck, started it and started to back up. She looked behind her to watch as she backed up. When she turned back around, she saw a beast for only a slight second, standing in front of her headlights. Sam gasped. Was that her imagination that was playing tricks on her?

She put her truck into drive and sped down the lane. She was about to the end of the drive when she peeked into her rearview mirror to see the beast once again. She shook her head and turned onto the highway. She shook the image out of her head. She let her thoughts drift back to the strong arms holding her as she drifted into her slumber. That memory calmed her.

Sam parked where she normally would, to start her day at Indian Creek Stables. She got out of the truck and was greeted by Jacqui Carpenter. Jacqui walked over to Sam before she could enter the barn.

"I have a pot of hot coffee in the house, if you would like to refill before you start you day." She knew the way to Sam's heart. Sam smiled and turned to look at her.

"Show me the way, Mrs. Carpenter."

The two walked into the house and sat down at the counter. Jacqui refreshed Sam's coffee mug and then filled her own.

"How was your weekend Sam?" Jacqui smiled as if she already knew the answer.

Sam exhaled. "I don't think that I've ever had a more interesting weekend."

Jacqui's smile widened. "You seem to have a spring in your step this morning."

"I met a guy."

"OH!" Jacqui tried to act surprised.

"Well, I did," Sam stated.

"Must be some guy." Jacqui stated over her coffee cup.

"I think so. He's got a really good heart."

"Want me to read him?" Jacqui offered.

Jacqui not only part-owned Indian Creek Stables with her husband, but she was also a medium. She taught weekly classes at the local community classes on how to communicate with your guides, hosted her own paranormal radio show, and was a published author on haunted locations in the area.

Jacqui was a classic American. She was average of height, with dark auburn hair. Her eyes were a deep brown that specked green throughout. She was of normal build, but her personality made her 10 feet tall and bullet proof. She had a way of knowing things, things you didn't want her to know.

She was good at heart and used her powers so often that it came to her like breathing and she used them when she didn't even know that she was. That made her dangerous in a good way, most of the time.

"No, that's ok. I pretty much know about him. I'm able to sense him." Sam shrugged it off.

"Oh, he really likes you," Jacqui purred.

"Jacqui!" Sam shouted.

"I'm sorry. It's a habit," Jacqui pleaded innocently.

"I have to get outside," Sam said in a half laugh.

"Go ahead. Greg's already out there." Jacqui handed Sam an extra mug. "And take this to Greg if you would. I have to go to town and buy some groceries."

Sam grabbed the cup and headed to the barn. She entered the front door of the barn, which led to the tack room, the feed room and the office. Sam walked into the office and saw Greg sitting there, going through paperwork. She cleared her throat. Greg looked up and smiled,

"Well, Good morning! Ah, you brought breakfast."

Sam handed him his mug.

Before he took a sip he asked. "Did you have a good weekend?"

"Everyone keeps asking me that." Sam smiled.

"It shows on your face," Greg laughed. He was not a psychic nor did he have any mystical powers. He was just a man who had known Sam since she was 16. He truly cared about her as if she were one of his own kids.

"Yes, I had a good weekend." Sam bowed her head in embarrassment.

"Good." That's all he said about it.

Greg wasn't one to get into the personal lives. If someone wanted his advice, they would ask him for it. He didn't give it freely unless it was something important. Sam looked at the man sitting in front of her. He was the closest to a father that she had ever really known. Greg was below 5'10", with his stoutness making him appear shorter. He kept his grey hair buzzed almost off. His glasses fogged as he sipped his coffee.

"She always puts too much damned sugar in my coffee."

"Too sweet?"

"As always." Greg sat the mug to the side and shook his head.

"We have the Cory Paint coming to stay for the week."

"How many stalls do you need ready, besides cleaning the others?"

"Three. I also need the tack room dusted and swept."

"I'm on it."

She went to walk out of the office. She stopped at the door

and turned to look at Greg once again. "Good morning to you, too." Greg returned her smile as she left the office.

She started with her usual daily tasks. She let the horses out into the pasture and began to work on the stalls. She cleaned them, laid new hay on the ground, filled their food, swept the walkway to the stalls, and refreshed the water troughs. Sam felt lucky to have such an enjoyable job. She never saw herself sitting behind a desk. She would always get antsy when Greg would have her figure the bills for the stables. Sam couldn't type more than twenty-five words a minute and more hunt and pecked for the letters on the keyboard than typed. She would rather be out, saddle-breaking a yearling. She loved the smell of the farm, the sweat of the horses from a good run and the hard work that left calluses on her hands. She felt that she accomplished more in one morning than most pencil pushers did in a week.

She laid hay in three more stalls at the end of the barn. She went into the tack room next and dusted everything down. She wiped down all of the saddles and bridles, and finally swept the floor. All in a day's work she thought to herself.

Before her workday was over, she called the horses back into their stalls. The horses knew her call. They knew it was lunchtime. The horses passed by her, one by one, each knowing which stall was their own. Sometimes a yearling would try to share their mother's and Sam would have to redirect them. Once all of the horses were in their stalls, she closed their gates and took time with each of them as they ate. Greg had seventeen horses of his own and fifteen that were permanent boarders. He favored Arabians but would let any horse board on his farm. Sam's favorite horse was Astra, one of Greg's Arabians. She was about three years old. She was tall for her breed, lean and leggy. She was also very stubborn. Astra had been named after her mother, who had died while giving birth to her. Sam spent a full week of nights with Astra after she was born. Sam slept with her, in hopes to keep her alive. It worked. Since then, Astra has had a fondness for Sam. Sam was the only one besides Greg that could ride her. Most people would just avoid her.

Astra was the last horse that Sam greeted. As Sam approached her stall, Astra put her head over the edge and eagerly waited for her. Sam made it to her and she nuzzled Sam's neck. Sam stroked her head and neck, whispering sweet nothings into her ear. Astra bucked her head a few times in play and Sam caught it and kissed her on the nose. Sam looked around at the other horses to make sure that they were not watching, and snuck Astra an apple.

Sam got close to Astra as she ate her present.

"I'm going to go home now. I'll be back tomorrow. You be nice to the others." Sam kissed her once again and ran her fingers through her mane before she walked out of the room.

Sam looked at the clock. 12:30pm. Sam was beat, hungry too. She said goodbye to Greg and drove to town. She was about there when she saw the inevitable flashing cherries in the rearview mirror. Sam sighed and pulled over to the side of the road. She put her hands on the wheel and waited for the officer to walk up to her window. The officer made her wait a while. Sam was about to take her hands off of the steering wheel when she heard him shout over his intercom.

"Ma'am, please keep your hands on the steering wheel."

Sam sighed out of frustration and put her hands back.

The officer finally got out of his squad car and walked to Sam's window.

"Driver's License and Registration."

Sam handed over the requested items and looked straight ahead as if she knew the drill.

"Do you know how fast you were going?" the officer asked as he wrote something down on his clipboard.

"No. I'm assuming the speed limit." Sam tried to keep the sarcasm out of her voice.

"Well now, if you don't know I guess I can write down anything on this ticket, now can't I?" the Officer smarted off to Sam.

Sam's eyes narrowed as she turned her head to him. "Why don't you give me the damn ticket, Danny, and let me go on with my day."

"That's Officer McDaniel to you, sugar."

"If there is nothing else," Sam talked through her teeth. "Officer McDaniel."

Danny looked at her driver's license and then stated. "I'm going to need you to step outside the vehicle, please."

"What's this about?" Sam was becoming angry.

"I need to search your vehicle."

"Please, step outside the vehicle ma'am," Danny repeated with a smirk on his face.

Sam stepped out of the vehicle and Danny ushered her to place her hands on her hood. He also kicked her legs apart. He proceeded to search her.

Sam was livid. "Officer McDaniel, may I state my piece?"

"Anything you say can and will be used against you in a court of law."

Danny continued to pat Sam down in a professional manner.

"If I even feel that you pat me down in anyway but a professional manner, I will make sure the employee relations hears of the harassment."

Danny paused for just a second. She could feel him burning with anger.

"Don't move. I'm going to check your vehicle now."

He opened her door and half-heartedly searched the cab of her truck. Finding nothing, he slammed her door and turned to Sam.

"I'm just going to give you the ticket for speeding. You're lucky I'm in a good mood."

Sam knew better than to spout back. All Danny was looking for was a reason to send her to the sheriff.

He allowed Sam to stand in a normal position and he handed her the ticket.

"Drive safely and have a good day," he said, as sarcastically as he could.

Sam folded the ticket and smiled at him. Her eyes were that of a savage beast, waiting to tear into his body. She hated Danny with all her soul. He had done things to her that made her skin crawl just to think of them.

She stood there and watched Danny pull away. He even waved goodbye to her. She wanted to rip his hand off and feed it to him. All she could do was stand there. Once he was out of sight, Sam unconsciously balled the ticket in her fist and gritted her teeth. Even now he still got to have his way with her. She felt pure and unadulterated hatred consume her. Something else rode the wave of that hatred... power. She felt a surge of power harness that hate and begin to manifest dark and hidden urges in her. She felt only primitive thoughts of war and death, victory and conquest. She felt her skin begin to burn with the power. She felt that anger turn into fear. She noticed that she was beginning to hyperventilate. She concentrated on nothing but her breathing, taking deep breaths in and out.

She waited a while before she moved from that spot. Once she had some control back, she climbed into her truck and checked her face in the rearview mirror. She wanted to see if she was as flushed as she thought. She turned the rearview mirror towards her and gasped.

Her face was ashen decorated with darker splotches on her skin. Beads of sweat trickled down the side of her face. Her eyes were on fire by their own light. They glowed. Sam once again concentrated on her breathing. She watched her face return to a normal color as she breathed. She put out the fire in her eyes with tears. She wasn't ready for this. She never wanted anything but a normal life. She wanted to be normal but always knew that something, would keep her from that. She never knew what that was. She knew now.

Sam hit her steering wheel and then hugged it as if she would fall out if she didn't. She let her mind go numb before she lifted her head. She knew what she had to do, lifted her head and dried her tears. She wasn't going to let it bother her. She would talk to Carol and Aunt Claire about it later.

She walked into Danny Boone's to grab lunch. She was wearing a pair of boots, worn jeans and a tucked in flannel shirt and covered from head to toe in dust. She wore her cowboy hat inside to hide the hat head underneath. She walked up to the counter and ordered her food. She was standing there waiting on her order, when she heard a voice from behind.

"Well, well. If it isn't lil' miss rodeo."

Sam couldn't help but smile. She turned around and looked

up.

"Hi Chaz. Getting lunch?"

"Yeah, the boys said it was time to feed the beast."

Beast was right. Chaz Fitzpatrick was over 6'5" and close to 300lbs. By all means, he wasn't fat, just built more like a brick shithouse. He was the tallest and biggest Irishman Sam had ever met. He looked more like a modern day Viking. He had shaved his head smooth or his hair would have been a deep dark red. His pale skin only made for a stark contrast to his 6 inch, red pharaoh's beard. When he wasn't pale, he was burnt. Sam quietly thanked the gods that she had more of an olive complexion. She could be in the sun for hours and never burn.

"What project are you guys working on now?" she asked.

"Water main, new pipes. Heh, I'm laying pipe."

Sam started to laugh as she jabbed him in the stomach.

"You want lunch company?"

"Sure. You buying?" Chaz hoped.

"Not likely," Sam stated.

"Was worth a shot."

Chaz laughed and pulled his attention back to the cashier but not before, he gave Sam a double take.

Sam noticed. "What?"

Chaz shook his head. "Ah, it's nothing."

"What?" Sam asked again. Chaz ignored her and ordered his food. Sam waited patiently while Chaz finished ordering. Once he got his food, they found a booth to sit in. Sam looked at Chaz again who was already starting on his burger.

"Why did you do a double take?" she asked.

"Don't know what you're talking about."

"Ok, I saw you double take, what's up?" Sam pressed.

"There's just…" Chaz swallowed a mouthful of food. "Something different about you than last I saw you. Can't put my finger on it."

Sam shot him a look.

"I'm not hitting on you. I'm being honest."

Sam shook her head and began to unwrap her sandwich. She brought it to her mouth to take a bite, but stopped short because she was so wrapped up in Chaz' lunch. He had ordered three double deluxe Boone Burgers, 2 large orders of onion rings, a pie turnover and a shake.

"Don't tell me that you are going to eat all of that?"

"Ah, this is nothing. I'm trying to watch my weight."

Sam scoffed in disbelief.

Chaz continued. "I could eat you as an appetizer, and still have room for dessert. I'm a big guy," he gruffed as he hit his chest with his fist. "Big guy need much food."

Sam's smile faded from her face, though her eyes never lost their humor.

"I know of others who have appetites such as yours."

Chaz looked up at her from his meal. He didn't bother chewing the food he had put into his mouth, he merely swallowed. His eyes shot signals of warnings.

"Guys like me?" he said half-jokingly, half-serious.

Sam took a bit of her burger, showing no sign of fear from his stare. She didn't know where her courage was coming from but she was going to take advantage while it was hanging around.

"Mmmm." Sam chewed her food to one side of her mouth. "You know guys and gals," she said as if it were nothing.

Chaz leaned into the table, never breaking eye contact with Sam. She mimicked his gesture. Chaz sniffed the air between them. His expression never changed, but his amazement in his eyes gave him away.

He leaned back. "Mother fucker," he said calmly.

Sam smiled at him.

"Why haven't I noticed that before?"

"Probably because it's a new development," Sam answered.

"Holy Shit. You're telling me..." He paused to lower his voice and to steal an onion ring at the same time. "You're telling me that you're a fucking Trueblood?"

"I think so. I haven't gone through my first change yet."

"Don't fuck with me Sam," Chaz said in disbelief.

"I'm serious. I am getting signs that it's close." She looked beyond Chaz. "Very close. But I haven't yet turned."

"I know a few Truebloods. They all went through their change when they hit puberty or closely thereafter. You are a WAY late bloomer."

Sam sighed. "I was hoping to talk to you about it."

"About what?" Chaz asked, finishing of a second burger.

"About *IT*. Does it hurt? What's it like once you're fully changed?"

"Never thought we would have this kind of talk over lunch." Chaz laughed.

Sam laughed slightly.

"I'm sorry. I guess I'm being a big scaredy cat."

"More like a scaredy wolf."

"Smart ass."

Chaz smiled at her statement as if she were giving him a compliment.

"Well?" Sam persisted.

"Damn girl, you are pushy."

"If you don't want to talk about it, we don't have to. I just know that you will give it to me straight."

Chaz shook his head. "Finally, a subject that I could teach you on."

"I was only better than you in school because I applied myself," Sam teased.

"Now who's being the smart ass."

Chaz went on to explain some things in detail for her. Sam excused his talking with his mouth full because she knew she was taking up his lunch hour just to talk to her about something that she would have to experience eventually anyway.

"It hurts the first time, bad. No lie; it's as if your body is splitting in two. And it takes a long time. Truebloods get the help of the Myrics. The Myrics give their healing and prayers. Those of us who are turned, we have to face it on our own." Chaz took a sip of his shake. "Sure, the Myrics are there to watch us if you will, go through our first change, but they offer no support."

Chaz's tone changed to disgust. "They're there to dispose of those who don't make it through the change. I've seen it, it's not pretty. Only the strong survive."

It was Chaz's turn to stare beyond Sam.

"I'm sorry." Sam couldn't think of anything else to say.

Chaz switched back to his normal self. "It's no biggie. I made it. I actually like it. It fits my personality, don't you think?"

"I just hope you're on my side," Sam said jokingly

Chaz became very sober, very unlike him. "Whenever you need me, I'm there."

Sam was taken aback by his response. "Thank you?"

"It's not easy, but it's sure as hell a lot of fun. When do you think you are going to go through with it?"

"I'm supposed to meet with a Myric tonight." Sam suddenly felt ashamed.

Chaz tried to make her feel better. "Ah, don't feel bad. So, you have some privileges. It's ok, take what you can get. They don't offer much, not even to their own kind."

"But since you're a werewolf, wouldn't that make you one of their kind?"

Chaz about choked on his last burger. He coughed a few times and smiled through his fit.

"Are you kidding me? You're kidding, right? Shit girl, you are not going to make it far with that attitude. We Turned. We're shit as far as the Truebloods are concerned. The only reason they would care if we lived or died would be for losing a literal servant. We do their dirty work. We support their lazy asses, no offense. We are forever slaves."

"But that's not fair," Sam said in anger.

"Yeah, but who's going to go against the council or even the clans for that matter?"

Sam just sulked.

"Well, my lunch is up. We should get together again tomorrow and eat. I will tell you more about it and you can buy me lunch." Chaz grinned.

"Whore," Sam said.

"The easiest way to a man's heart…" He put his hand over his heart.

They both got up, and after throwing away their trash, left at the same time. As Sam was walking away, she shouted to Chaz.

"It was good seeing you."

"It's because I'm just that pretty," Chaz shouted back.

As Sam got to her truck, she found a single rose on her

windshield. She smiled and bit her lip and smelled the bright red rose. She read the small card that was attached to it.

*"Thinking of you. I'll call you tonight.
Your secret admirer."*

She looked around to see if John was still around. She wondered if he saw her sitting with Chaz. She would bring it up tonight, to let him know that Chaz is an old school friend and nothing more. She thought about that mental note for a moment and questioned herself as to why she felt she owed John an explanation. Sam was always making excuses or explaining situations to people. "I guess I get into a lot of situations that need to be explained. I need to work on that." She laughed to herself. Sam got home around two. She placed her rose in a thin vase on the coffee table. Claire came around the corner and saw the rose.
"Oh, where'd you get that?" Claire smiled. She had a hint, but she wanted to see Sam talk about it.
"It's from John!" Sam's face was aglow. "I can tell by the handwriting on the card that was attached to the rose. Isn't he sweet?" Sam drifted off with a sigh.
"A very sweet boy indeed."
"And he's going to call me again, tonight!" Sam perked up.
"He must really like you." Claire added fuel to Sam's blazing heart.
"Yeah." She smiled to herself. "I think so."
Claire hated to, but she changed the subject. "Carol will be here in about 20 minutes. Do you have anything planned out to ask her?"
Sam's expression became one of determination. "Yes indeedy."
Claire looked at Sam with suspicion. "What do you have up your sleeve?"
"I ran into Chaz Fitzpatrick today. I remember you telling me that he was turned. We had lunch together where he answered some of MY questions. The answers only brought more questions that I will ask Carol tonight. But for now." She

walked towards Claire and kissed her on the cheek. "I need to take a shower and get ready."

Claire nodded, smiled and watched Sam walk up the stairs. She knew that Sam was a stubborn woman and would speak her mind even if she didn't have all of the facts, but she hoped that she didn't upset Carol, who was Sam's only help right now. She sighed and headed back to the kitchen where she finished preparing an early dinner.

Sam reached, closed the door to her apartment and at that moment, everything went black…

CHAPTER NINE

She slowly came to. Her head was hurting and her eyes were out of focus. She rubbed her head and brought her hand back to find it splashed with blood. She fought to stay conscious. The room spun out of control as she fought to stay conscious. She leaned over and threw up on the floor next to her. The pressure seemed to ease a bit, but her focus was still off. She rubbed her bloody hand on her pants and tried then to rub her eyes. She was able to see things closest to her. She was in the corner of a room, with nothing around her but a bowl and a pile of hay. The smell of her own vomit was making her nauseous so she struggled to sit up. The room began to spin again so she steadied herself against the wall. She noticed that her hands and feet were bound in chains. The room started to come into her focus. It was a large and narrow room. Everything was cleared from her reach. There was a drain in the floor close to where she sat. She saw a fireplace on the other side of the room, a table and a cot. There were only two windows on other side of the room. There was only one door, also on the other side of the room.

Sam surveyed the area where she was being held captive. The walls were made of stone, the floor seemed like concrete. Sam could see old blood stains on the walls and floor where she was chained. She looked at the chains. They were long enough for her to stand and walk out about four feet, but she was having a hard enough time sitting. She knew she would be pushing it if she tried to stand. She could feel the blood drip onto her shirt. Her hair was matted in blood. She must have taken a good blow to the head. Head wounds always bled more than any wound. She tried to use the sleeve of her shirt to soak it up.

She was working on her head when she saw the door open. She stopped and steadied herself. She tried to prepare herself for what walked through the door. It was the beast that she had seen that morning. He was tall and monstrous looking. He was a dark grey color with coarse hair growing throughout his body.

Even through his hair, she could see that he was a male.

He didn't look at her. He went to a shelf where he pulled off a large bound book. She could see him write something down in it and then put it back on the shelf. She saw the beast stand up and look out the window. He suddenly turned to face her. She was startled at first, but curiosity overcame her. His eyes were... familiar. If she was correct, then she knew who lay behind those eyes. She would have never thought that he would have hurt her before. Why was he now? He saw the recognition in her eyes and averted his stare.

"Could I have something for my head?" Sam asked.

He didn't move.

Sam persisted. "I'm still bleeding. I need to stop the bleeding."

He walked over to a counter where he pulled a jar and a rag. He placed it in a box and walked over to the boundary of the room. He kicked it to her.

"Wipe your head and put that on. Take the rag and hold it to your wound. It will stop bleeding shortly."

She had a hard time understanding him. He stood where she couldn't focus on his face. She took the jar and opened it. The smell of the salve inside about made her vomit again. It smelled like dead animals and feces. She wiped her wound as best she could through her hair and smeared the salve on the wound. She closed the jar and placed it back in the box. She pushed the box back towards the boundary and put the rag to her wound.

"What do you want from me?" she asked.

She received no answer.

"You've always been there, out there, haven't you?" Again, she received no answer.

"You showed yourself to me this morning. I saw you. Why are you watching me?"

He snarled. "No more questions. Be silent or I will silence you myself."

Sam looked at him.

He walked over to the door and left. Sam's head had stopped bleeding and the throbbing had started to subside. She closed her eyes and tried to think of her situation, only to fall asleep.

Claire went to answer the door. Carol was standing there in her tailored suit, holding a matching overnight bag. Her nails were manicured, her bottle blonde hair bobbed at her shoulders, and her makeup precise. She looked like a politician's wife in her mid-50's.

Claire wrung her hands on her apron and opened the door. "Carol. Thank you for coming."

Carol handed Claire her bag. "Thank you for calling me. I feel honored that you called upon me for this."

Claire knew that Carol was only going through the motions. Carol knew that she was the only Myric around in a three county radius, which made her invaluable.

Claire played along for Sam's sake. "No, we're honored to have you in our home, to receive your assistance."

Carol walked through the door and inspected the living room. "You've always have had such homegrown tastes."

The comment was almost an insult disguised as a compliment.

"Simple, country, down-to-earth feels better to me. I'm more comfortable with that style." Claire stated as if she took Carol's remark as good intentions.

"Mmm, yes," Carol said as she sat on the couch.

Claire offered her some tea. Carol did have one passion, Claire's homemade tea.

"That would be lovely. Your blend, correct?"

Claire smiled. "Of course."

"Thank you." Carol said as if a nice person peeked through her stuffy appearance.

Claire disappeared to the kitchen. Carol gazed at the rose and other items on the coffee table. She went to pick up one of the magazines on the table when she stopped. She sniffed the air and shot up off of the couch. She ran to the door and out onto the porch. She looked around, trying to see what she sensed. The hairs on her neck were standing on end.

A voice came from behind her. "Carol, what is it?"

"Something's wrong. I can taste it." She smelled the air in a way that put her completely out of character. She looked like Jackie Onassis acting like a coon dog.

Carol mindlessly walked out into the yard, Claire followed.

Carol followed her senses to the side of the house, where the steps led to Sam's apartment. Carol spun around and Claire about kissed her, she was that close.

"We need to check on Sam, NOW!" Carol demanded.

The two of them ran back inside and up the stairs. They opened Sam's door and found the place empty except for the drops of blood on the floor. Claire gasped. Carol turned to Claire.

She began to undress. "Claire, take these. I'm going to search around. Send for help."

As Carol spoke, she started to change. She stopped in her Curreno form. Carol had to duck to get out of the doorway.

"I'm going to be going south on the trail. "Carol spoke slowly so that Claire would understand her. "I will leave markings. Your help will be able to follow me. Please hurry."

Claire nodded as she stood there with Carol's clothes in her hands. She watched Carol's golden form jump off Sam's balcony. Claire hung her clothes in a hurry and grabbed Sam's phone. She wanted to call John, but didn't know his number. She called Kenny.

"Randy's."

"Kenny!" Claire said frantically.

"What's wrong?" Kenny answered.

"Sam's missing. Carol is here and already on her scent. She said that she's going south to follow the trail. She needs help."

Without answering, Kenny hung up the phone. Claire knew that he would be here in no time. She took a breath and then called Nicki. "Yes," Claire thought to herself. "Nicki would have Marc and John's number." She got Nicki's voicemail and hung up. She tried her cell phone.

"Hi Sam..." Nicki was cut off.

"Nicki, call Marc and John, now! Sam's missing and we need their help. Tell them to get here as soon as he can!"

Claire hung up before Nicki could ask any questions.

Claire ran down to the library and started pulling different books. She knew that she needed to get started with preparations on finder spells. She pulled books off the shelves that didn't pertain to her need, unceremoniously throwing them to the ground. Claire stopped only because she couldn't stop the outburst of tears. She held onto Sam's cordless phone and wept. She allowed herself only a moment's weakness because she needed to find Sam at all costs she thought to herself. She continued her search.

Nicki stood in the coffee shop, holding the phone out from her ear. She had just sat down to enjoy a cup of coffee when Claire had called. Claire hung up the phone faster than Nicki could process the conversation. It hit her like a ton of bricks... Sam was missing. Nicki hung up her phone and searched for Marc's number in her phone's contacts list. She dialed their number and it rang only twice before someone picked up.

"Yeah?" the voice answered.

"Marc?"

"No, John."

"JOHN, YOU NEED TO COME QUICK! SAM'S MISSING!"

"I'll bring Marc and meet you at the house! Thank you for calling me!"

John and Nicki hung up. Nicki got up and walked out of the coffee shop, leaving her purse and coffee on the table. One of the workers followed her out of the shop.

"Miss, Miss, you left your purse!"

Nicki turned around and grabbed her purse in a daze. She turned and walked to her car. She knew she had to concentrate on driving. She was 10 minutes away from Claire's house. She knew the route by heart. The last thing she remembered was getting into her car. She was now on Sam's porch. She didn't notice that her car did not come with her. She walked into the house. She walked to the library where she knew Claire would be. She walked in and found her pulling different components. Claire never looked up.

"Nicki, we need mandrake. Go to the kitchen."

Nicki never left the library. She knew where the mandrake was in the kitchen and somehow, it now lay in her hand. She handed it to Claire. Claire never paid attention.

"Earth... I need soil."

Nicki manifested a bowl of soil in her hands. She handed it to

Claire. Something inside of Claire made her turn and look at Nicki, to see what was going on.

Nicki was a blur of color. Her eyes had bled to green as if someone had replaced them with emeralds. There was no other color than green. Claire selfishly thought that Nicki's trance could help them in their time of need. Claire never bothered to pull Nicki out of it.

"Where's Sam, Nicki?"

Nicki was looking at the window. Her voice came from some distant place.

"She is further away than we think."

"Where?" Claire began to walk towards Nicki slowly as to not disrupt the connection.

"South and to the West… Hills and valleys… Trees… Thick vegetation… The room is small… My head hurts? I'm chained… I'm scared and confused… A known face…"

"What?"

"Carvings on the building… Ancient ruins… Hidden from those who try to find him… Carvings traced in fresh blood… The pit… Death… Vicious and no remorse…"

"Sam?"

Nicki's voice changed to Sam's. "Aunt Claire? I don't know where I am. Someone attacked me from behind in my room. I'm scared. Please hurry."

"Sam!" Claire screamed. She severed the link between Nicki and Sam. She saw Nicki's eyes go back to their normal state as she collapsed into her arms.

"Sam! Come back!" Claire screamed at Nicki.

"She's not here. I've lost her scent." Carol's voice came from the doorway. Claire held Nicki tight to her chest as she let the both of them drop to the floor. Nicki started to come around.

"What the fu..? Claire?" She looked at her, not knowing what had just transpired or even how she got to Claire's library.

Carol was still in her form. "Do you have help coming?" she stated.

Claire nodded silently. She couldn't talk. Carol snuffed and turned for the living room.

Nicki looked at Claire and asked. "How?"

Claire laughed lightly. "You teleported."

"Sam?"

"You connected with her. You saw where she was, but not enough. I am afraid that I broke the connection."

"I saw her in my mind. She was chained to a wall. She has a wound to the back of her head. She is worried but not as afraid as she should be. She doesn't know what lies beyond the building where she's being held. There's a type of pit..."

"We have to find her," Claire said looking into Nicki's eyes.

"I will do my best."

"You have done far more than expected already but I thank you for your help."

John hung up the phone and called out to Marc. He came out of the kitchen with a sandwich.

"We need to go now. Sam's missing."

Marc and John raced out of the house and sped away to Sam's.

Kenny called Chaz to ask for his help. He left the job for 'emergency' purposes and headed for the bar to pick up Kenny. Kenny also called Aimee. She told him that Brad was out on a mission but that if he got home anytime soon that she would send him out. She also offered to come over and watch the house while they went looking for Sam. Kenny told her that would be a good idea and closed his phone. Chaz pulled up to the Bar and Kenny jumped in. They sped off to the other side of town.

John and Marc were at the edge of town when they saw cherries in their rearview mirror. John was going to keep going when Marc stated. "We don't need the heat after us too. Pull over."

John gruffed and pulled his truck over. Danny got out of his vehicle; hand on his gun as he approached John and Marc. John sat there, looking ahead. Marc did the talking.

"What seems to be the problem officer?"

"License and registration."

John's jaw clenched. He reached into his back pocket

"Whoa there, cowboy. Slowly," Danny added. He could see

that he was getting to John.

John handed the license to Danny and Marc handed John the registration out of the glove box.

Danny wasn't even looking at the items. He was busy staring John down.

Marc tried to intervene. "Officer, I'm sorry if we were speeding but there has been an emergency in my family and we are just trying to get to the hospital."

Danny never let his gaze falter from John. "Well sir, you must not be from around here. The hospital is the other way."

"I'm sorry sir. Noted. Thank you sir. May we go now?"

Danny backed away from the window and drew his gun. "I believe that I will need you two to step out of the vehicle."

John looked at Marc. Marc could already see the change coming out of John. Marc tried to calm him as best he could.

"John, if we get into trouble, we'll be of no good to Sam. Be cooperative, for her sake."

John fought the beast and got out of the truck.

Danny spouted. "Hands on the truck where I can see 'em."

They did as they were told.

"I don't think you have an emergency at the hospital. Looked to me that you knew exactly where you were going." Danny felt proud of his observation.

"Hey!" He looked at John. "What's your problem buddy? You not feeling well?" Danny said in a condescending voice.

John was sweating from the effort that he was putting forth to keep his beast at bay. He knew his emotions were playing a big part in his lack of control.

Marc whispered to John. "Just a bit longer. Hold on."

Danny pointed the gun at John. "No whispering. Might make me nervous whispering."

John could suddenly smell Danny sweating. He could taste Danny's fear on his pallet. John was taken for a moment by another smell that swirled on the officer. He knew then that Danny had touched Sam earlier. He could smell her on him. There was no control left to be had. John went into a rage.

His beast came busting through before Danny could even take his shot. John turned from his truck and headed for Danny.

Danny began to back away and fired at the same time. Each time he shot John, John grew angrier. John kept walking towards the officer. John grabbed the gun and pulled it from Danny's hand. He threw it into the woods behind them.

He grabbed Danny by the shoulders and threw him in the same direction as his gun. John walked over to the squad car, ripped out the radio, and slashed two of his tires on the way back to the truck. John hopped into the bed of the truck and lay down.

John said one thing. "DRIVE!"

Marc didn't answer. He climbed into the driver's side and sped off.

John and Marc reached Sam's house in no time. They pulled in just as another truck was pulling in behind them. They all pulled up to the house and jumped out. John was still in form. What mattered is that he needed to find Sam. John walked up to the porch with Marc. Marc was already knocking on the door. Marc turned and saw Kenny and Chaz walking towards the house. They met up on the porch just as Carol answered the door in her robe. She looked at John and demanded. "Change before entering the house."

John snarled under his breath and changed back to his human form. Carol let the men inside. They all sat in the living room, except for John. He walked through the house to the bathroom where he retrieved a towel to wrap around his waist. She met up with Claire and Nicki as they were walking out of the library. At any other time, John's appearance would be humorous. Not this time.

The three walked into the living room and John sat down. Nicki walked over to Marc and put her hand on his shoulder. She saw carol give a disgusted look to the gesture, which fueled Nicki to lean over and kiss Marc.

She pulled away from Marc and whispered. "Thank you for coming out to help." She looked back at the woman who glared at her and then turned to look at Claire.

Claire spoke up. "Thank you all for coming to help. There are traces of Sam's blood in her room." She saw John stand up and quickly added. "Not a lot, but enough to know her true scent. Nicki was able to sense her and she's not in this area... I think. My property meets up with the Daniel Boone National park. I believe that she's in there somewhere. I have maps here. We can trace out where each of you will go. Nicki and I will come with you."

Carol butted in. "I think that the humans should stay here. They are of no use to us in our search."

Claire gave attitude. "If it weren't for us humans, you wouldn't have the clues that were given to help you find her." Her voice got low. "Now we will go with the group to find her. If you don't like it, you can sit your ass on my couch and sulk." Claire didn't care at that moment if she were stepping over the boundary of human and Were, but she knew that she had enough 'friends' there to protect her if she needed it.

Carol stood up and walked out of the room. Upon which she heard the remark. "Fucking stuffy Trueblood."

She turned and began to change in the presence of the men. The men in turn started to change as well. Claire and Nicki both felt the energy, pulled together, and set forth a blinding flash of light that stunned the group.

Nicki announced. "Us humans will not have you Weres tearing at each other when our focus is Sam. Carol - you need to leave the room. Guys, sit the fuck down."

They all did as they were told. Claire and Nicki knew that they were walking a fine line between surety and insanity. They settled the guys down and once carol was out of the room, they began to go over the logistics.

"Nicki, you go with Marc and Kenny. I will go with Chaz and John."

John spoke up. "Wait a minute, Marc and I are a team." He looked at Chaz. "No offense man."

Claire answered. "I need you two split up because you are both too close to each other. You won't be so distraught if your assigned partner gets whacked." Claire added. "No offense." The guys all smirked with what humor they could hold onto. John turned to Chaz. "Glad to see you here, man."

"Sam's like a little sister to me. I have to help. Nice to see I have back up though," Chaz smirked.

Kenny looked around the room and replied. "If everyone is calmed down now, let's get up to Sam's apartment and grab a scent." They all made their way up to Sam's room. John was the last one to leave the living room. He looked back and saw his rose in a vase on the coffee table. He swallowed hard and headed up the stairs.

Claire went to Carol's room where she found her dressing and packing her things.

Carol turned to her. "I have never…"

Claire held up her hands in surrender. "My baby girl has been abducted. We are all friends of hers and we are all very upset. We just want to find her, to save her. I apologize for all of us."

Carol stopped for a moment and turned to Claire. "You have humans and turned…" She paused in disgust. "Mingling together. That's not right."

"Thinking that it's not right is what's wrong," Claire added. "Just because one is…" Claire was careful. "…'special', doesn't mean that they can't have feelings for each other."

"It's wrong."

"Maybe in your society, but in the real world it's accepted. I'm sorry if you were offended. Please stay."

"I can't. Besides, there is nothing that I can do now. I will go home and if she starts to go through the change, bring her to me I guess." She sighed out of obligation.

All Claire could do was shake her head and leave the room. She had other things to worry about. She walked out of the room to meet up with Nicki who was already in one of Sam's hiking outfits. She had packed two backpacks for Claire and herself to carry. Nicki took extra canteens and walked to the kitchen. Claire followed.

"She's going to be ok," Nicki reassured Claire.

"We don't know that." Claire had a way of letting the worst-case scenario run through her head.

"I know Sam. She is one tough bitch. She's also smart. She'll be fine I'm sure. All we can do is find her and help her out."

Claire nodded.

Carol snuck out the back door while the group was devising a plan. Once carol was in her car, she pulled out her cell phone and began to dial. She turned onto the main road as the line began to ring. Carol tried to regain composure, readying herself for her conversation. The other line was answered. "Green Residence."

Carol cleared her throat as she spoke. "This is Carol Sinclaire. I need to speak with Mr. Green."

A pleasant yet lifeless voice answered. "I will see if he's available. Please hold."

The line went silent as the maid searched for Mr. Green. She found him in the library with a man. The young man was shirtless and sitting next to Mr. Green with an adoring gaze. The maid watched as Mr. Green caressed the man's cheek.

"Excuse me, Mr. Green." The maid spoke out meekly.

Mr. Green rolled his eyes and sighed an answer. "Yes, Elizabeth... what is it?" Never wavering his attentions from the young man.

"Ms. Sinclaire is on the line."

Mr. Green's piercing stare turned to the maid, which made her lower her gaze to the floor. "I will take the call in here." Mr. Green excused the young man and walked to his desk.

"This is Mr. Green."

"Mr. Green? It's Ms. Sinclaire. I have news."

He smiled to himself as he spoke. "Ms. Sinclaire, please, call me Riley."

Carol felt herself flush with happiness. "Ok, Riley, I have news on Samantha."

Riley sat back and twirled a pen mindlessly in his hand. "Do tell, Carol, do tell." He purred the words to her, sending unseen vibrations through the phone, which made Carol fall further under his spell.

"She's showing signs of the change." Riley put the pen down and leaned against the desk. "Hmmm... interesting."

Carol continued. "Claire called me Saturday morning and told me about her episodes. I went to their house to exam her."

"What did you find?"

Carol swallowed hard. "That's just it, she wasn't there. Someone has taken her."

Riley cursed under his breath and Carol tried to rebut. "Riley,

I had nothing to do with this. When we found out that she was gone, I did what I could to catch her scent. Once I came back to the house, Claire's dogs-"

Riley butted in. "Now, now, hush. Carol... I know you did what you could. I have an idea who it might be. Carol, word of your cooperation has been stated with the council and they are very pleased with your actions."

Carol smiled and waited for him to continue.

"This can only help further your standings within the Myrics. I will contact you later once we have been able to deliberate over further actions. Thank you very much Carol."

"It's my pleasure, Riley." Carol hung on his name as he hung up the phone.

Carol listened to the dead air for only a moment before putting the cell phone back into her purse.

Riley sat at his desk, swiveling back and forth slowly until stopping suddenly to pound his desk. The cracking sounds of wood echoed through the dark office. He walked to the window and stood there with one name on his lips. "Gabriel".

With resolution, he turned back to his desk and began to propose a letter of termination of Gabriel. He called for the maid once more. "Elizabeth, I need you to take this to Mistress Anya, right away."

Elizabeth took the envelope from Riley's grasp without looking into his eyes. Riley got up out of the chair and moved towards her. She didn't move but she did tense. He lifted her gaze to his and held her in place.

"Please don't be this way. It's for her own good. They need to know." A single tear rolled down Elizabeth's cheek, the only sign of battle between the mental persuasion of Riley and her own will. She smiled and nodded. He patted her cheek and ushered her out the door. "Remember, hurry." Elizabeth ran out of sight. It was more to get away from Riley than to hurry on her mission. Riley went back to his office and poured himself a glass of single malt scotch.

The rest of the group had finished picking up Sam's true scent from the dried blood. Marc walked over to John and put his hand on his shoulder.

"We're going to find her."

Chaz looked at John and realized that he was more than just a friend to Sam.

"Dude, he's right. We'll get her back..." A wry smile formed at one side of his mouth. "... then do what we will with whoever's responsible."

John looked into Chaz's eyes. Chaz knew by that look, that there was nothing that he could do that would be any worse than what John had planned. Chaz, for the first time in his life, shuddered. The other side of his mouth completed the smile.

"Oh yeah, I think that we're gonna get along just fine."

John's expression never changed.

CHAPTER TEN

Sam's was shaken to consciousness, which did nothing for her head. She was about to vomit again but was torn away when she heard a voice.

"Wake up. If you fall asleep, you might not wake up. And don't puke." She opened her eyes to see the beast in front of her. She could smell him. His scent she had smelt before. She knew him. She squinted at him and he turned quickly.

She spoke up. "I know you, don't I?"

He never answered. She watched his mannerisms. She finally recognized him.

"I know you! I know who you are! At least, in your human form. You're Gabriel, the homeless man. I don't know how I know but I know it's you."

He never moved.

She continued. "Why are you doing this, Gabe?"

"Shut up! I can't hear myself think with you talking. Talk, talk, talk... don't you ever SHUT UP!" He proceeded to pace the other end of the room.

Sam sat on the ground, huddled in a corner. She began silently weeping to herself.

"Oh and don't you even start to cry or I will kill you right now."

She sucked it in and held it tight, bottom lip still quivering.

"I have to think. THINK. What to do? So many things to consider."

"You can let me go."

"SILENCE!" he snarled.

Sam watched Gabe walk around, talking to himself. She stayed as quiet as she could. She knew not to test the waters again for the time being.

Gabe paced the room as he talked to himself. She could only hear a word here or there, mostly incoherent sayings. Gabe stopped and raced over to Sam. He grabbed her by the shirt and shook her.

"And stop staring at me!"

Sam covered her eyes and started to cry.

"Stop it. Stop crying. Why do women always CRY?" he screamed at her.

"BECAUSE WE FUCKING CAN! Why don't you make up your fucking mind?" Sam screamed in his face.

Gabe began to emit a low, evil laughter. She was too angry to back down now. She knew that the mental torment she was going through was too much for her to handle. Better to be dead quick then to be tortured for days, she thought to herself. Gabe started to stand, while still holding onto her. He lifted her into the air and held her in front of his face.

"Stare at me now, little girl," he said in a dark voice.

Sam stared into his eyes. "Like you've watched me all these years? You fucking psycho! What? You get off watching little girls turn into women? Oh, I bet you got a sight the other night," Sam hissed.

Gabe scowled at her and threw her against the wall. She hit with a thud and then dropped to the ground hard enough to knock the wind out of her.

He walked to the door and before he left, he said. "You don't have your precious DOG with you tonight so you better not fall asleep. I don't need you turning in my house. You start to turn and I'll kill you on sight."

"You keep making idle threats and I'm going to think that you don't have any balls under that form." She was deliberately trying to piss him off enough to finish her. He knew it. The last sight she saw of him was a sadistic smile ride across his wolf-like face. He walked out and slammed the door behind him.

"FUCK YOU!" she screamed as loud as she could. She winced in pain from what she felt like a broken rib. She felt along her rib cage and one on her left side was off-kilter.

John led Chaz and Claire down the side of a mountain. He was glad that he was in full form. He knew that he would better handle finding Sam this way. Besides, he knew that she wouldn't be able to tell that it was him, not immediately anyway. He was beginning to get antsy. He would scout ahead and then have to wait for Chaz and Claire to catch up. He knew that it wasn't Chaz that was holding them back. Once Chaz and Claire caught up, John motioned for Chaz. John communicated to Chaz more sensory than physically. John mentally sent a message that Claire was holding up the search.

Chaz answered. "Dude, I know she's a burden, but you saw her power. We might need her."

John shook his head. He gestured for Chaz to pick Claire up and carry her.

Chaz sighed. "Man, I have to carry the old broad on my back? Shit, fine." He looked back at Claire. "I'm glad that she's not a fat chick." John didn't stick around to hear Chaz complain. He took off through the brush, in his zigzagged scouting pattern.

Chaz walked over to where Claire had sat to rest. He was the one that got to break the transportation changes to her. She looked up to him in question. He put his hands behind his back.

"John thinks that we would make better time if... if..."

"If you carried me?" Claire added. She knew that she was holding up the party.

"Um, yeah," Chaz answered uncomfortably.

"Fine, bend down. I'll climb aboard." She ushered to him hastily. "You'll have to hold onto me though. I can't hold on quite as well as I could when I was younger."

Chaz' mind went to that dirty gutter place that only he could go, but he had enough control not to speak aloud.

He bent down and Claire climbed onto his back. Chaz hefted her weight higher on his back and braced her by wrapping his arms around her legs.

"Ok, I'm going to be quick. If I start to scare you, close your eyes."

"Got it. Let's roll."

Nicki was holding the GMRS radio when a call came in from Claire,

"Nicki, you need to ride on Kenny's back."

Kenny and Nicki both stopped and looked at the radio and then at each other. It was as if Claire could see them.

"Kenny and Marc will be able to make better time if we aren't so... slow"

Kenny shrugged and walked over to Nicki. Nicki couldn't help but start to giggle uncontrollably. She radioed back. "10-4, Big Mama."

"Don't call me that," Claire said.

"Roger."

"That either." Claire chuckled. The humor masked their worry.

Nicki climbed onto Kenny's back and once they were settled, Kenny took off. Marc made it back to Kenny and stopped to give them both one of those dog looks when they hear a high-pitched noise. Nicki chuckled and felt Kenny do the same. They saw Marc shake his head and turn to continue scouting.

Nicki leaned into Kenny. "Hey, at least I'm light."

"Thanks for that," Kenny stated at he took off in a full sprint.

Chaz was covering ground at an alarming rate. Claire leaned close to his ear. "Are you still following John's tracks."

"Yes, why?"

"We seem to be moving awfully fast."

"And believe it or not, he's about a mile ahead of us. He's on her scent; I can smell her as well."

"Besides John and Sam, do you smell any other?"

Chaz was quiet. Claire went silent. She hunkered down on his back. The wind that he was creating from moving so fast was making her eyes water. Her nose had also begun to run as well. Chaz felt her almost curl into his back like a cocoon. He patted her on the legs.

"Relax, we're making good time."

Claire nodded her head against his back but said nothing. She perked her ears when she heard Nicki's voice. "Claire, do you read me?"

Claire picked the radio out of her pocket. "Yeah. What is it?"

"You should be getting closer to us, John's found Marc and he's picked up a definite trail. I think you're a little over a mile from us."

"I'll see you then."

Claire could hear Nicki's tone and tried to shrug it off. She didn't want to let her mind go to the worst.

The light in the room had gone dark. There was no fire, so the only light was coming in from sparse beams of moonlight through the trees. She could hear the crickets singing beautiful lullabies for her. She heard nighttime rustling in the woods just outside the windows. She moved the chains back and forth on the walls, trying to free herself from the bands. Her wrists were worn and bloody from her attempts to free herself. She stood up at one point and tried to yank the chains in different directions, so see if there was any give. It was no use. Sam was losing hope.

She hadn't seen her captive for about 4 hours. She started to sing to herself song after song, to keep herself awake. She tried walking through different memories, but that didn't help. She started to talk to herself, making lists of things that she needed for the house. What she had for her one meal that day, she threw up. She was hungry, thirsty and tired. She fought to stay awake. She thought about John, letting her mind roll to the day that she met him, how they bumped into each other. She let herself fall into that comfort of his embrace during their dance that night at the bar. She felt the energy between them and she pulled from that energy that she kept stored deep within. She used her emotions to stay awake. She stood up and started to pace her area. She walked back and forth, back and forth, all the time swinging her chains slightly. She heard the door open and she stopped. She quickly sat back on the floor, against the wall. The light from outside came pouring in.

Gabe's presence blocked out all of that light as he passed through the door. He slammed the door and there was darkness once more. She could hear him rustle around his side of the room. She heard him strike a match and the room went ablaze by one matchstick. She watched him light a lantern on the table and proceed to make a fire in the fireplace. Once the fire was started, the room began to fill with waves of warmth and Sam had wondered to herself how she didn't notice that she was so cold. She could barely make out colors on her side of the room, but she could tell that his fingernails were blue.

"I know that you may have some padding, but I'm only human and I'm freezing over here," Sam said flatly.

Gabe never looked up. "You're not human."

"I am right now. And right now, I'm on the verge of hypothermia," Sam exclaimed through the chattering of her teeth. The days during this time of year were mild 60's but the nights were low 30's. She had only a pair of jeans and a flannel shirt on. It only provided so much warmth.

"You have a bed," Gabe stated.

She looked around and saw the pile of hay. She looked back at him in disbelief. He wasn't looking at her.

She added. "Could I at least get something to drink?" Gabe stood up, grabbed a bowl and filled it with a ladle that was in a bucket. He walked over to Sam and thrust it into her hands. Half of the water spilled out onto the floor. Sam tried to steady the bowl to keep the rest of it inside its container. He turned his back to her and started to walk away.

"Thanks, Gabe," she said sincerely.

"Don't use my name," he added.

"Then just thanks," She added again, trying to keep her impatience from her tone.

He went to sit back at the side of the table that faced the fire. He didn't need it for warmth, but more for the light. He rummaged around at something on the floor. Sam brought the bowl to her lips and smelled the water before she drank it. It smelled musty, but she had no other option. She held her breath and drank. The taste of iron instantly lay heavy upon her tongue. Well water. She finished the water and put the bowl to the side. She watched Gabe stand up, holding something in his hands. He walked over to her and threw a dead rabbit at her feet.

"Dinner."

"What?" Sam asked.

"Your dinner."

"I'm not eating that, you've got to be kidding me."

"That's what you get, take it or leave it," Gabe shrugged.

Sam pushed the rabbit away with her feet.

"We will see what you say tomorrow, if I let you live that long."

He turned to walk back to his side of the room. "If you aren't going to eat it now, push it against the wall. The cold will keep the meat fresh."

Sam could see his shocked reaction to his own statement. Why would he give her a helpful tidbit like that if he were threatening to kill her? He looked away from her to keep from showing any other reactions.

"Or do what you will. I don't care."

Sam stood. "I have a feeling that you do."

"Think again, little one."

"Then why are you keeping me alive? What's the importance of keeping me here? Why don't you just off me and be done with it?"

"I saw you pacing the room to keep yourself awake. One would think that you have had training," he changed the subject.

"Training?"

"They want to kill you. They want you dead. You are a threat to their every belief," he stated.

"Who?" Sam humored Gabe. She knew that he was crazy. She also thought that playing along might get more answers out of him.

"All of them." There was no tone or inflection as if she knew who he was rambling on about.

Sam stared at Gabe's back when she asked. "You?"

She watched as Gabe's posture shot straight and rigid before answering. He took a deep breath in, and answered. "I do as I am told. I don't care if you live or die."

"You keep saying that. You're trying really hard to convince yourself of that." Sam tested the waters once again as she huddled in her makeshift bed. She had even scraped the hay around her in hopes for warmth.

"Not because I want you alive. I just don't trust them."

"You keep saying them. Who's them?"

Gabe walked over, lay on the cot, and closed his eyes. Sam sighed and sat against the wall, away from the rabbit.

CHAPTER ELEVEN

Chaz ran swiftly through the woods. Claire had long since buried her face into his back. The wind bit at her hands and head. She leaned up a moment and asked,

"Are you still following John's tracks?"

"Yes. We'll catch him in about 10 minutes or so."

Claire couldn't help but ask. "Can you sense Sam?"

"Her scent is mingled with John's tracks."

Claire hunkered down once more and wiped her tears on his back. Chaz felt what she had done and didn't make a comment or motion. He picked up the pace and hoped to get to John soon.

John was pacing. He was at a point where he needed to stop and wait for the group, but he didn't want to. He wanted to leave them behind, but he knew that he would be risking too much if he did. If the beast was the same one they encountered in the woods before, was the one that had Sam, he was going to need help. John stopped and looked to his right. He saw Marc coming up to him. He waited until Marc was a meter away before he started his change to his Curreno form to talk to him.

"Any sign?" John asked as Marc changed also.

"None of Sam I'm afraid. Lots from some other fella."

"You think it's the same guy."

"Yeah, stinks like him," Marc snuffed.

Marc saw John's restlessness. "Can you sense her yet?"

John's head bowed. "No. Not yet. I need to get closer to her."

"We will... We will. I'm going to find Kenny and Nicki, and we should stop for a bit."

John shot a look at Marc.

Marc continued. "Our group is labored by the girls, yes, but you never know if we are going to need them to save Sam... the way that they saved me."

John turned and looked beyond the trees. "Fine, but we can't stay for long. The longer we wait-"

"I know," Marc interrupted. "We'll get moving as soon as we can. Besides, we all need to eat. We need the energy."

Marc took off in the direction that he came. John back tracked a bit and found Chaz racing towards them.

John spoke to Chaz and Claire. "We need to rest, but only for a moment. We need to replenish our energy to press on later tonight."

Chaz lowered Claire to her feet and then plopped onto the ground.

"Claire, you're not heavy by any means, but carry someone over 25 miles on your back…" he paused to take a breath. "… It takes its toll ya know. PHEW!"

"Thank you." Claire put her hand on Chaz's shoulder.

"No prob." Chaz patted her hand.

Claire walked over to John, to catch him before he turned to leave again. "John, a moment of your time… Please." Claire called out. John stopped and sighed. He turned back to her.

"I know you're worried, we all are. But if you think that getting there now and not resting to gain our strength back is a good idea, think again. You know what you faced in the woods the other day. That's who has our Sam. We need our strength."

John turned back around and disappeared into the darkness. Claire went back to Chaz and found Nicki, Kenny and Marc joining him. Nicki had started to gather wood, to make a fire. Marc walked over to Claire before she got to the group.

"Where's John?"

"Back that way." She motioned her head. "Try to talk some sense into him. I know that his emotions are running on overload right now, but we need him. Sam needs him."

Marc answered. "I'll do what I can. I'll make sure we bring back dinner." He turned and followed John's trail.

Claire helped Nicki build a fire before she dug two sandwiches out of her sack for their dinner. She handed one to Nicki just as she put up her hand to refuse. Claire had no patience. "Take it."

Nicki was shocked into taking the sandwich and immediately began to take tiny bites from it. Claire sighed and drew her coat closer to her body. Nicki swallowed her sandwich and spoke up.

"There's got to be something we could do, to help out the

guys. I don't like feeling like a backpack."

"There are a few things that we could do, but they might be too risky."

Nicki's eyes lit up as she replied. "I can try that flight thing that you have had me study on."

"Soaring, it's called Soaring, and no. You have just started studying the art and besides, you don't know the area. You might get lost. I can't think of losing you and Sam all in the same day."

"You know that I can do it and I won't get lost if you keep a flashlight pointed high. Just tell me what I should look for."

"Are you sure you want to chance it?" Claire tried to keep the pleading tone to a minimum.

Nicki saw the hopefulness in Claire's eyes and she smiled.

"Yeah. It's for Sam. I would risk my life for her." Nicki looked down at the last bit of her sandwich. "Heh, she's done the same for me and wouldn't think twice to do it again. It's the least I can do."

Claire walked over to Nicki and took her hands. She stared intently into Nicki's eyes as to give the sense of seriousness this all was. "You know what might happen if you're caught or if we're caught while you are gone."

"Stop trying to talk me out of it and tell me what I need to look for." Nicki knew the consequences that she faced by soaring, but didn't care. She wanted to find Sam just as much as anyone else did.

Claire grabbed Nicki into a big hug and then smiled from relief. "Thank you, Nicki."

Claire escorted Nicki to the farthest side of the fire, near a fallen tree branch. She pulled Nicki to the ground as she explained what she needed to look for. "Check out any buildings, cabins, tents, other fires, and things like that. Thank you for doing this."

"Don't worry about it. Besides, what do we have to lose?"

"You," Claire stated dryly.

"Ah, I wouldn't get lost. And hey, if I do, I can just spend the time in the trees until daylight. We need to have a signal or something for me to look for, if I truly get lost."

Claire sat and thought for a moment. "I've got it. If you get lost, I will send a light wisp to dance just above the tree line. Just make sure you sneak up on it because the moment it detects you, it will want you to chase after it and then you will get lost all over again."

"Great, that's all I need. Ok, I can make sure I look for the flashlight first. If not, the little annoying wisp." Nicki succeeded in making Claire smile.

"If you end up lost, we'll guard your host body, but might have to move so I will make sure we keep you safe while you're out."

"Minor details. Ok. Let me finish this sandwich so we can get this over with."

Nicki finished her sandwich and after taking a few sips of water, she began to position herself for her meditation. She laid her head on Claire's lap and began the process. She closed her eyes and began to breathe. She heard Claire's voice soothe over her skin like a warm blanket as Claire began the ritual. Nicki felt her body ripple under her skin as if she were an underground earthquake. That ripple started in the center of her body and preceded outward, towards the very ends of her body and down her limbs, lastly her head. She felt her whole body buzz by Claire's voice. Her words formed and shaped the energy vibrating through Nicki's body. Nicki felt a tugging from outside of her body, pulling her insides out. She felt a source of energy escape her body through her breath as she exhaled.

Kenny and Chaz looked on silently while Claire performed the ritual. They watched as Nicki's body shook under the words. They saw Nicki's chest fill to capacity and then deflate to produce a breath of light. A radiating mist came from Nicki's mouth. The golden white color mist hovered above. It flowed over towards the guys where they backed up to keep it from touching them. Claire spoke to the mist and it turned to make its way back to her. Claire said another set of words and a large barn owl landed on a branch next to the group. The mist floated up to the owl and entered it. The owl received the mist with an inhale. The owl blinked and ruffled its feathers. It jumped off the branch and flew down to perch next to Claire. The guys looked at Claire and the owl and then to Nicki's body. Her body wasn't breathing.

Chaz looked at Claire and asked. "Is Nicki ya know?"

Claire looked at the owl. "Nicki?"

The owl bounced on its fallen branch.

Claire smiled and turned to Chaz and Kenny. "She will be fine as long as she is not killed in her host body or as long as her own body is not harmed."

"What's she going to do?" Kenny asked in wonderment.

"She'll go further in one hour than we could in one night. She can scour the hills and get back to us with any information."

Claire turned to the Owl. "Nic, be careful. Remember, any buildings, campfires, anything unusual."

The Owl nodded and turned to squawk at the guys. She jumped into the air and flew off above the treetops. Nicki soared through the air, high above the canopy. The night was cold against her face as she flew. The trees below her were grayer shades of their daytime color, lit only by the light of the moon. She looked to the horizon and saw many columns of smoke to investigate. She made them her targets. Her night vision was as good as if she were looking around during the daytime.

She circled the first pillar of smoke she reached, spiraling down until she was able to perch on a tree branch high above the campsite. She looked upon a group of campers, probably a family, turning down for the night. She took off for the next. She got to the next column and perched on the roof from which the smoke was coming from. She flew over to a nearby branch and looked back at the building. It was a cabin. It was normal looking, nothing out of place. She saw a flashy car in the driveway and a truck with a boat. She looked through the windows and saw a bunch of men sitting around a table, playing cards. Just to be safe, she flew around to look through the other windows. She didn't see anyone else, so she took to flight once again. She looked back for a moment, to make sure Claire had the light on, which she did. It looked like a beacon of light coming from the earth. She turned to the next set of smoke columns. She checked three more campsites and two more cabins before she found one that seemed out of place. She flew up to the cabin and perched on a nearby tree. It was more of a shed than a cabin made up of stone and mortar, a door and a couple of windows

She looked at the intricate markings on the walls but could not make out any particular sign. She looked around. There was a fire burning inside, but no vehicle near the building. In regards to the area she was in, that wasn't too suspicious, but she was going to check out the building just to be safe. She flew around the roof to one of the windows. She was able to perch close by and peer inside. Something moved in the room.

The shadows were thick and kept her from seeing much more. Being an owl with nocturnal sight, Nicki felt the powers of magic present. It was an old magic that had most worn away but what was left made her feel as if she was trying to find a needle through a piece of screen. She heard chains rattling in the building. Nicki's pure curiosity made her move closer. She found a large crate by the front window and dared to fly to it. She landed softly on top of the crate and moved her head inside. To the left, she saw a cot with someone asleep on it, their back turned to the window. She looked to her right, into the shadows and heard mumbling. She could hear the chains rattling as if someone or something was shaking. She needed to see.

She brought her body as close to the inside of the building as she possibly could. She strained her neck to see what was making the noise. She tried to move just a bit further. In her efforts, she knocked over a ladle that sat unbalanced on a bucket. It fell to the floor in a clank. The person on the cot bolted up, Nicki could sense it. She saw something jump in the shadows. She saw long dark hair and hands. She heard the person on the cot scream.

"What the hell?"

Nicki knew she had to act quickly. She backed out of the window just as a hand reached for her. She had to fall backwards off the crate to keep from being caught by the hand. She took off in flight only to land on the roof where she couldn't be seen. She heard them talking.

"I am going to die of hypothermia, please."

"Walk around, it will keep your blood flowing."

Nicki's blood ran cold. She had found Sam. At least she was alive but Nicki didn't know for how long. Nicki took off above the canopy once again. Her heart pounded as it were to burst out of her chest. She flew back in the direction that she came. She flew for about 10 minutes before she even saw the beam of light from Claire. Once she saw the light, she flew as hard as she could to the group.

Nicki dove into the trees and landed on the fallen branch behind Claire, which startled her. Nicki began to dance and squawk uncontrollably.

Chaz spoke out. "What's that? Timmy's stuck in the well again?"

No one looked at him, which Chaz didn't mind. He was content with his own humor. Claire began to chant the spell once again. The owl poised without moving. The mist that had come out of Nicki before, was now exiting the bird. It hovered around for a moment and quickly made a nosedive into Nicki's chest. The force sent Nicki gasping for air. Her back arched as she dug her fingers into the cold, dark earth.

"She's, she's alive," Nicki said as she breathed.

John and Marc were in their hybrid form, finishing a deer when they heard Nicki's voice. John sprinted over to where they were. Claire stood up.

"She found her."

"Where?" John asked.

Nicki was still trying to catch her breath. "10 minutes flight... southwest of here... in a building... two windows, one door, no vehicle... a stone building, looks, looks like a shed. She's chained."

John turned to Marc. "Nicki found her. I'm going to start on foot now. I'll leave markings."

Marc held up his hands. "Whoa, you can't go alone, not with that watcher holding her captive."

Chaz jumped up. "I'll go with you."

Nicki sat up. "We could all go, but I can't walk. It's taken all of my energy."

Kenny and Chaz both changed back into their hybrid forms and started to pack up their camp. Claire packed up their knapsacks, watched John and Marc change back to full beast form. It took only 5 minutes to be back on the trail once again. Kenny once again carried Nicki.

Nicki said. "Just to let you know, there are many campsites between us and them. We have to be careful."

Kenny smiled to himself. "Honey, we have been doing this for longer than you have known us to be what we are. We know the drill."

Nicki buried her head in embarrassment.

"Don't worry, Nicki. And thanks for the advice anyway. Forewarned is forearmed."

The group stayed together except for Marc and John who scouted ahead. They hoped to reach Sam before dawn. While John and Marc scouted ahead together, John had renewed hope of saving Sam. Marc could feel John's sense of hope and prayed that it was not in vain. Marc waited for John to catch up.

"I'm going to scout a bit ahead."

John nodded. John was left to his own thoughts of Sam. He knew that he would die for her. He knew that he would kill for her. He knew that he had come to terms with the undeniable feelings that he felt for her. His feelings went beyond any comprehension of the word love. He knew it when he first ran into her and had fought it ever since. He had talked with Claire and Marc about it and still denied himself the simple pleasure of loving another person. If they rescued her, he would not deny his feelings any longer. He would hold onto her and never look back. The resolution gave him more strength than anything he had felt before. His surety of his feelings and his acceptance of them bonded with his determination to get her back. He broke into a stride and quickly caught up with Marc. Marc kept up with his pace.

"What's with the sudden surge of energy?" Marc panted.

"I love her. I know it. I always have, I just hadn't met her yet," John answered as he ran.

"Don't go doing anything stupid."

"Let's worry about that once we get her back."

"Promise me that you'll not go after her without more than just me there."

John ran ahead of Marc. Marc knew that he would have to keep up with him, if he were to keep him from doing anything rash. He just hoped that Kenny and Chaz could get to them in time.

Chaz and Kenny were refreshed from their stop and from the meal that Marc and John had gifted them. Nicki was fast asleep on Kenny's back. He had rigged up a piece of clothing to hold Nicki in place as he ran. It wasn't pretty, but she wouldn't fall off as she slept. Claire couldn't sleep if she wanted to. She was too worried. Chaz wanted to break out in a summer camp song, but thought it might not be taken well in present company, so he kept the tune in his head. Kenny and Chaz were only 15 minutes behind Marc and John. They hoped that their pace would keep them only moments from each other.

Sam walked her area, swinging her chains and even broke out into humming.

Gabe tossed on his cot. Sam saw that it was irritating him and proceeded to add words to the song.

"Ninety-nine bottles of beer on the wall, ninety-nine bottles of beer... you take one down, pass it around." He huffed. "Ninety-eight bottles of beer on the wall"

Sam pressed on. She thought of summer days, splashing on the lake as the sun beat warmth into her skin.

"Seventy-six bottles of beer on the wall, seventy-six bottles of beer... you take one down, pass it around, seventy-five bottles of beer on the wall."

Sam twirled her chains like a jump rope. She started to walk faster and sing louder.

"Fifty-two bottles of beer on the wall, fifty-two bottles of beer."

In a flash, Gabe had tackled Sam to the floor. He held his clawed hand above his head. Sam made no movements under him. Gabe watched the moment of fear drain from Sam's eyes, only to be replaced with light. Her eyes began to burn in their sockets. Gabe lowered his face to hers.

"I want to feed you your own tongue after I rip it from your skull. I'll even cook it for you."

"Get off me," Sam said from a voice deep inside.

"What did you say?" Gabe hissed, letting warm saliva spill onto Sam's cheek.

She never flinched nor tried to pull away.

"You heard me. I will say it once more. Get... Off... Me." Sam snarled, with no emotion or expression to heighten the remark.

"I'd like to see you try," Gabe said as he brought his hand down onto her. His hand was caught in hers. He looked at his hand that was being crushed by her small, human hand. He looked back down at her and he saw the change starting. He saw her skin changing to a different color. He felt the pressure on his wrist, he knew that she was going to change. He jumped up off her and she went with him, never letting go of her grip. He took his other fist and knocked her out cold. Her grip loosened and he let her drop to the floor. He walked over to his side of the room, flipping any piece of furniture he had along the way. He got to the door and ripped it open. Once he walked outside and stood in the light of the moon, he screamed into the night. He took a few breaths and walked back into the dwelling. He walked over to Sam and saw that her skin was still a different shade. The lighting wasn't enough to tell her markings, but what he could see of them he knew that they were none that he had ever seen before. Her skin was a golden brown color, with certain shaded areas. He dared not touch her. He walked over to his bounded library and pulled a book from its shelf,

"Oct 13th, twilight. She started to go through the change and was mistakenly knocked out. Will proceed with the observation once she awakens."

He closed the book and kept it out. He had a feeling he would be writing in it more as the night progressed.

Sam began to dream. She dreamt of a house on a mountaintop. She looked into its valley and saw thousands of smoke pillars coming from beneath the forest. She was sitting on a porch, wrapped in a blanket with someone. She was warm and

content. Children playing in the background and it made her smile. She burrowed in closer to her blanketed companion. He held her tight. She looked up to reveal her partner and to her heart's desire, it was John. He kissed her on the forehead and whispered to her.
"Wake up."
"I don't want to."
"But you have to."
"I want to stay with you."
"I'm not too far away. Now wake up."

Sam started to come around.
Gabe was shaking her stating. "Wake up."
Sam opened her eyes and saw that she was now sitting up against the wall. She was panting hard and feeling dizzy.
"Don't fall asleep. You'll bring it on."
Sam couldn't bring herself to say anything. He handed her a bowl and a rag.
She reached for it and felt resistance on her arms from the blanket that wrapped around her. She looked around and then back to Gabe. He was standing away from her and was scowling.
"What?" he snapped.
"What… what's this all about?" she talked through each breath.
"I don't want you changing here. I have to get you calmed down, to take you to them."
Sam looked down at her hands and saw her skin. She gasped and spilled most of the contents in the bowl. She thrust her hands in front of her and examined them. She was freezing yet her skin was burning. Her body was aching and burning all at once.
"You need to calm down or it will just bring it on faster. We have maybe 4 hours at the most."
Sam was able to catch her breath.
She replied. "We have someone that was going to help me through it. Take me to her and I will go with you to…" Sam didn't know what else to say. "Them."

"HA!" Gabe laughed. "Take you to Carol? You would be better off with them." Gabe's tone changed and he looked off into the distance. "But if you take her there, they will surely kill her. That's what they'll do."

Sam just sat and watched him.

"I have to think. Think..." Gabe was once again back to acting how he had been before.

"Maybe I can help," Sam offered.

"Help? That's what they're afraid of. Your help is not wanted. Yet your help is needed. Your help will spread like a disease and will bring hell to the order." Gabe snarled the last of his statement.

"You aren't making any sense." Sam tried to keep her emotions down.

He got up and went to the counter. He got the ladle and a pill bottle and walked back to Sam.

"Take two of these."

"What are they?"

"They'll calm you down and stop the change for a while."

Sam was hesitant until Gabe screamed at her. "Take the goddamn pills now!"

Sam took them and sat there watching him.

Gabe continued. "Unruly, unorthodox, anarchy, but is that all bad?" he said to himself.

"Who are they?" Sam tried again.

"They are the ones that want you dead. They are the ones that sent me on this baby-sitting assignment almost 20 years ago. They are the ones that have tried to reassign me after I had done all of their dirty work. They sent their messengers. I sent their messengers back, piece by piece."

Sam began to feel the effects of the drugs. She continued to listen to Gabe as he rambled on.

"They are the ones that had taken a general in his prime and assign him to observe a 5 year old human girl. They didn't want to get their hands dirty. They didn't want to waste their time. It would serve them right if I were to let you go."

"I won't..." Sam started to sway. "I won't tell them that you let me go..." Sam tried to hang on to consciousness.

"You wouldn't have to tell them, they would know. They would know."

Sam watched as Gabe blurred, then vanished before her eyes before she fell into her drug induced sleep. Gabe sat there for a long period, watching her skin change back to her human color. Once he knew she was asleep, he got up and grabbed his book.

"Last entry, October 13th. Samantha Harris never made it through her initial change. She was killed during the process. Her body will be burned to cover any traces of blood lines."

Gabe shut the book and stared at Sam. From here on out, he would not need to log or catalog any events in her life. He would not have to observe her actions. He would not have to put her life before his. He felt a sense of sadness come over him. He cleared his throat, stood up, and placed the book on the shelf.

"I'm better off. I can get back to my men. They need me I'm sure. A good leader is always missed." He looked at his hand that was still holding onto the book that he had carefully put on the shelf. He shook his head and started for the door. Before he went outside, he grabbed the fawn's head and glanced over at Sam one last time. He opened the door and headed for his shed.

Gabe set the fawn's skull on the table to be cleaned. He looked at his collection, which had begun to gain light from the morning sun on the horizon. He took precise care of his collection. He would clean it and then leave the skull in the sun to bleach before adding it to his collection. He started out the door when he heard movement outside. He opened the door and saw a Were motioning to someone outside his range of sight.

"What business do you bring?" Gabe sounded official.

"We have come with a message and to relieve you of your post." The Were returned the niceties.

"You can go back and tell them that I will relinquish my post once my assignment is complete."

"But you see, you haven't sent word in some time. They were beginning to fear that you had perished and they feel that this is a…" trying not to sound condescending. "…delicate matter that needs to be followed."

"I have sent word for months, letting them know that I will NOT relinquish my post until I have completed my assignment. They know very well that I'm alive." Gabe couldn't hold back the smile of satisfaction. "And steadfast to my duty, that they have assigned to me."

"They feel that it's time you retire." The Were was growing impatient.

"Then tell them to come and tell me themselves."

"We have another message." The Were began to close the distance between them.

"And that message is?" Gabe humored.

"If you denied our services, we were to relieve you one way or another."

"If you try, you will be sent back to them as all the others have… a piece at a time."

"Gabriel, you don't want to do this."

"How DARE you use my sir name. I'm your ranking officer and you will address me as such."

"They have unanimously approved your retirement, so you are now just Gabriel."

Gabe roared and raged for the young Were. He stepped aside and let Gabe fall to the ground with his own power. Gabe could hear the young man's laughter, as he righted himself and stood in a cloud of dust, glaring at his subordinate.

John and Marc heard a roar and knew that they were close. They broke out into a sprint. They ran until their lungs burned for air. John began to sense Sam and used that connection to power himself on. He passed Marc up the hill and reached the cabin. He grabbed the handle of the door and ripped it from its hinges. He ran in and found Sam slumped on the floor in the corner. He ran to her and turned her on her back. He checked and found her pulse but she was knocked cold. He wiped her hair from her face and she began to come to.

She opened her eyes and saw a Were hovering over her. She tried to get away from him but he grabbed her hands. She tried to struggle and started to scream when John put his hand over her mouth. She tried to wince free but was unsuccessful. Her eyes widened when she saw another beast come through the door.

She heard the two conversing but couldn't understand what they were saying, still under the influence of the medication she had taken earlier. She saw the morning sun gleam through the door as the new figure searched around the cabin to find a set of keys. The Were brought them over and unlocked Sam's shackles. The beast holding her, held her firmly yet gently. Sam eased up and he let go. She sat there as her shackles were carefully unlocked.

John saw the broken skin were the shackles had worn through. Her wrists and ankles were bloodied and bruised. Sam tried to stand, but was unable to without help. She grabbed onto John's arm to steady herself. He placed his hand behind her, to help her balance. He knew that she didn't know that it was him at that moment but didn't know why. There was no time to ponder why.

Gabe began to concentrate. The young Were got the best of him for just that instant. Gabe channeled his rage and anger into power for his survival.

"Gabriel, that was uncalled for." A second Were mocked as to alert Gabe to his presence.

"Yes, it was. Trust me, it will not happen again," he said calmly.

"Now... back to business. Are you going to cooperate or are we going to make you change your mind?"

"Try if you dare." Gabe smiled sadistically.

The young Were sighed and shook his head. He walked over to Gabe and crouched into a fighting stance. Gabe took a cleansing breath and dropped down to match the stance of his opponent. They circled each other until the Were made the first move, slashing at him wildly. Gabe was able to swerve and miss his attack, and countered it with a jab to the beast's side. The Were turned and tried to hook Gabe, but was knocked to the ground when he swept him off his feet. Gabe continued his attack. The two Weres wrestled on the ground until Gabe kicked the young one off. The young Were came at Gabe with a knife in his hand. Gabe was on his feet and ready for the next attack.

He taunted the young one. "A knife? Who is teaching our troops to use weapons? Come and get me with your knife, you pansy-ass faggot."

The young Were slashed with the timing of each step he took towards Gabe. Gabe was unimpressed. He dodged each blow effortlessly. He blocked the last swipe and felt a searing pain in his side. The other assailant had stabbed him in the back when he was not looking. Gabe cursed himself for not paying more attention to his surroundings. It had been a while since he had to battle more than one messenger.

Gabe turned and saw the satisfaction on the knife wielder's face, drain to shock as he grabbed the young Were's head and bit into his neck. Gabe locked down and ripped away, taking a large chunk of thorax with him. Gabe was immediately drenched in blood from the neck wound. He was also instantly energized from the blood lust. He turned his head and spit out the chunk of flesh that he had torn from the Were, as he let the lifeless body fall to the ground.

The other Were was immediately on Gabe in a berserk rage. Gabe invited the attack. He swung at alarming speeds, but Gabe easily blocked each one. Gabe was begging to feel the effects of the knife still stuck in his side. He felt himself begin to slow which could mean his life to a berserk Were. He waited for an ideal opening, and grabbed his head with both hands. With a quick twist, he snapped the Were's neck in one pop. The Were's body instantly went limp. Gabe simply allowing the useless corpse, to unceremoniously slip from his grasp.

He couldn't catch his breath. He felt along his side, found the knife and pulled it out. He knew it was silver, he could tell by the pain it left. It wasn't a fatal wound, but it would bleed as if he were human and not Were. He knew that he needed to stop the bleeding soon. He grabbed both victims by the hair and dragged them to his shed, leaving a large bloodied trail behind him. He hung each one on a meat hook suspended from the ceiling. He would tend to them later, to ready them for sending back to THEM.

John, Sam and Marc made their way outside. Sam tried to run for the tree line, but fell to the ground. Sam was unconscious for only a moment before she came to. Marc helped her to her feet and they made their way to the edge of the clearing when Sam turned.

Gabe was on his way back to the cabin when he heard commotion. He ran to his home and saw Sam and the two Weres.

Gabe shouted out. "Where do you think you are going with her?"

"She's coming with us." John stood his ground.

"Your buddies are dead. Give her back to me and I might let you live."

"You are insane if you think that we are going to give her back to you."

"Then you can join your friends. I will send you all back in due time."

Marc came up to John's side. They circled Gabe, and Marc made the first attack. Marc was slicing away at Gabe as Gabe blocked what he could with his arms. John came up from the other side, punching and slicing at him as well. Sam started towards the bunch. She watched as the two Weres took Gabe to the ground. Marc backed off too let John finish him off. John was rearing in for a killing attack when Gabe used what strength he had left to push John off him, and stand up. He attacked John but he countered the attacks. John dodged and backed away and saw Gabe stall, gasping for breath. John watched Gabe use what strength he had left to fend him off. John enjoyed the satisfaction of Sam's captor gasping for air, to see him suffering. John could see Gabe begin to change into his human form.

The rest of the group caught up to the melee and stood to watch. Claire was calling out to Sam but she could not hear her. She ran to Gabe. She watched as John brought his hand up to make one last blow to Gabe and she stood between them. John, startled, looked at Sam. Gabe tried to grab at Sam's shoulders but she pulled free of his weakened grasp. She looked straight into John's eyes and that's when she realized who he was, she finally recognized him. John saw the recognition in her face along with the pain and fury, and yet she stood her ground.

"Don't you dare kill him."

"Get out of his way, girl. Let him do what he must." Gabe tried to push her away again.

She moved away from Gabe's reach, which put her closer to John. She stood there and stared at John.

"Don't!" She said as if she could stop him. He knew that she could. The sheer power of his emotions would keep him from killing Gabe if Sam prohibited it.

John got closer to her, roared with fury in her face, and ran off. Tears streaked down her cheeks as John screamed, yet she still stood her ground. She knew that it was wrong to kill him. He had not really hurt her. Somehow, she knew that he wouldn't have. She felt Gabe fall to the ground and she turned to him.

"You silly little girl, you fool. He had every..." Gabe breathed. "Every right to his conquest."

"No, he didn't. You didn't do anything."

"I stole you. That's... that's enough." He couldn't speak anymore. She looked up in search for something to help him when she saw Nicki and Claire as if they had been standing there through the whole event.

"Aunt Claire, Nicki. I want you to heal him."

They all just stood there, watching.

"HEAL HIM!" Sam cried out.

They didn't move.

"HE DIDN'T DO ANYTHING. HE DOESN'T DESERVE TO DIE LIKE THIS. NOW HEAL HIM, PLEASE!!!" She pleaded to them.

Claire and Nicki walked over to Gabe and Sam. They stood over Gabe, who was struggling for breath. Nicki said a few words over his body, followed by Claire and a small light flashed over him. Gabe sucked in air and his body went limp. Sam looked down at him and then to Nicki and Claire for explanation.

Nicki answered. "He won't die now, but I'm not helping him anymore."

Claire just looked at Sam with no expression on her face. Sam knew that they would never understand her actions or her pleas.

She drew on her sorrow and found the strength to stand. She walked over to Gabe's home and grabbed a blanket for him. She returned to cover Gabe and to look at the rest of the group.

"I will not leave until he's awake. He's been watching me since I came to live with Claire. I want to find out why. He has to come with us. There are hundreds of books inside, all logging my life. They need to come as well."

Sam turned and went back inside the house. She came out, trying to drag the kitchen table with her.

Chaz walked up to her. "Why are you doing this?"

"It was an invasion enough to have the books written, I don't want to leave them and have someone use them against me."

"Why not torch them?"

"There has to be clues in his writings, something I can pull from. He wrote on things that I might not have remembered. I need the books and I need your help bringing them back." She looked at him with tears in her eyes.

"If he tries to kill you, you know that we'll not be slow about his death, right?"

Sam nodded, never breaking eye contact. Chaz sighed and then asked. "What are you going to do with that table?"

"If we turn it over, we can load all of the books on it and we can pull it with us." Chaz answered without looking at her. "I'll handle this. You go to Nicki and Claire."

CHAPTER TWELVE

Sam hung her head. She didn't want to face them right now. She turned and walked the small path to the edge of the woods where they sat in silence. She never looked up to meet their gaze. Claire was sobbing, while Nicki only allowed herself silent tears.

"I know you don't understand why I needed you to save him. I know-" she was cut off when the two stood up, and grabbed and hugged her. Sam gave into their embrace and began to weep with them. Claire and Nicki held onto Sam tightly as Claire covered Sam's cheek with kisses.

"Don't you ever do this to us again," Claire sobbed.

"I promise this wasn't intentional, really. But he didn't harm me. This..." She held up her wrists. "... is from me being stubborn over my logical thinking. A human cannot rip thick chains from the walls."

Claire began to wail.

"Aunt Claire, it's ok. I'm ok."

Claire tried to stop herself, which only ended in hiccups.

Sam added. "Do you understand that we need to take him with us? He could be very vital to helping us."

Claire only nodded.

Marc walked over to the girls. Sam looked up at his Curreno form. She smiled. "Thank you for saving me."

Marc's expression was that of concern as he spoke to her. "I need to find John. We will meet you back at the house if you don't catch up with us."

Sam laid her hand on his arm. He nodded to her and walked away. She could feel energy from the sun's rays and looked up. She let the heat of the sun warm her dark hair, which in turn warmed the rest of her body.

"Do you have some water that I could have?"

Nicki handed her a canteen without expression.

Sam noted the look but had neither the time nor the energy to deal with it. She drank the canteen dry then handed it back to

her. She walked over to Gabe, who was sitting up, and knelt by him.

"Are you alright?"

"Silly, foolish girl. Helping me is not going to help your cause. I'm but a mere waste of your time."

"But knowing that I saved you might also obligate you to some answers that I need."

Gabe just smiled at her with dead eyes.

"You will need to get dressed," Sam said. As she ignored the expression he silently made.

"I'd rather change back," he answered.

Sam looked up at Chaz and the table filled with books. Chaz and Kenny had rigged the table where it would hold all the books. There were over 150 altogether. Kenny had taken strips of cloth and tied them to each leg, making a wall on each side. Chaz had made up a makeshift pull for someone to bear the weight of an awkwardly made sleigh. Sam looked back at Gabe.

"You may change. You will be the one to carry your books to my house. Is there anything else in there that you would like saved?"

Gabe, startled, looked at Sam. "The journals are all I had."

Sam stood up. "Then change and get to it. Chaz?" she called out to him. "Burn it down."

Sam walked away, ignoring the look on Gabe's face. She felt the pain of hunger race over her but kept on. She was too pissed to give in now. Once everyone was ready and Gabe was hooked up to his table, they were off. The sounds of the building burning gave Sam a false sense of hope. She felt as if a part of her darkness was being destroyed by light and fire. Good, she thought to herself. Kenny led the way as he followed their trail back. Gabe was next, followed closely by Chaz. The girls were last in line to follow. Chaz wanted himself between Gabe and the women in case the old fart got a second wind. As the group trudged through the barely seen trails, no words were spoken.

Marc finally caught up with John, who was sitting on a boulder looking over a valley filled with lush trees and steep hills.

"Hey man," Marc said.

"Hmmm," John answered, never taking his eyes off the valley

below.

"Look, she's alive. She's also right; he needs to stay alive if we are going to get any answers as to why he had been assigned to watch her."

"He kidnapped her, held her in chains that wore through the skin, didn't feed her and god knows what else, and she puts her life on the line for HIM?" John's voice rumbled over the valley floor making nested birds take flight from the trees.

"She obviously knows something that we don't." Marc tried to reassure his friend.

"She just stood there. If I were in a complete Berserk, I would have killed her for merely being in the way." John lowered his gaze to the boulder he sat on, ashamed to have even thought the worst.

"No you wouldn't."

John just sat there.

"Dude, she seems like a bright girl. I think that if you just ask her, she would have a good reason why she did what she did."

"I don't want to talk to her," John tried to convince himself. He stood up and began to walk back to the trail. He didn't fool his old friend.

Marc blocked John's path and answered. "Yeah you do. You want to hold her and thank the gods that she's alive. But you are too pig-headed to lay down your pride and just do it."

John turned to the side and passed his friend. Marc let him, too tired to try to battle words with him.

"Not after what she did," John said as he kept walking.

Marc threw his arms in the air as he walked after his friend. "Dude, she also figured out that it was you when you were about to kill him and she didn't freak out. In fact, she stood her ground."

"Because she knew that I wouldn't be able to do it."

"Because she trusted that you wouldn't, not that she knew you wouldn't. She trusted you to do the right thing. Just because we don't know what that is yet. Ah hell, John, just fucking talk to her will ya?"

"I gotta cool down first."

"Then you can cool down with the group. We can't just leave

Kenny and Chaz to watch that looney."

John kept walking. "Let Sam save herself."

Marc stopped and scoffed at him. "Oh, now that was not right and you know it."

John stopped and turned to his friend. "I'm just so pissed." He wrenched his hands in the air as if he was strangling the stubbornness out of Sam's brain, at least that's what he would have liked to have done.

"Then go kill something, hit a tree, anything. Just get your ass back to that group."

Marc nudged his friend and walked away.

John stood there for several moments with so many emotions running through his system that it made him numb to anything. He couldn't focus on one thought clearly. His mind was suddenly like a hundred TV's all playing different channels at once. The only thing that he heard loud and clear was his heart, and it pained him. He was so relieved to know that Sam was alive and relatively unharmed. He didn't even want to let his mind go to that dark place where thoughts of, 'what if,' laid low beneath the murky waters. He didn't want to feel pain that was not needed. He took a few breaths and walked back towards the group.

Marc made it back to everyone and walked on the other side of Gabe. He could hear Gabe laughing and talking to himself.

"Hehe, what they need is Sam to know. Yes. Sam will know, I will tell her. I will log it. Wait. No more logging. What to do with the time."

Marc stopped and let Chaz catch up. "Has he been doing this the whole time?"

"Yeah, fuckin' psycho. He needs a straight jacket. There's like two of 'em up there." He twirled his finger at his head.

"Keep an ear as to what he says. I want to see if there's something that he'll let out that he might not later."

"Oh, I'm sure we'll get out a lot, later," Chaz said seductively as he strolled dramatically in sync with the group.

Marc stopped walking as he left Chaz with one statement.

"You're just out right scary, aren't you?"

"Only when the mood hits me... And I'm so... in the mood." Chaz rubbed his hands together, never taking his sight off Gabe.

Marc smiled and shook his head and added. "We will use your expertise later, I'm sure."

"Use? Hell try and stop me."

Sam walked slowly with the girls. Stars began to cloud her vision. She tried to concentrate on putting one foot in front of the other, but she knew that she was at the end of her rope. She was captured over 36 hours ago, her head still hurt from the whack she took compliments of Gabe, and she hadn't eaten since Sunday night. The medicine had finally worn off, but it didn't help her that she was so drained. And to top it off, she had seen John in his Curreno form. She didn't know why he hadn't told her before she found out. She didn't know if he would talk to her after what she had done. She agreed with Gabe, he had every right to his kill and she took that away from him. If she were in his shoes, she would be pissed too. She couldn't think about that now. Her head hurt enough, she didn't need her heart to hurt too. She wondered where her boring life had gone. For a fleeting moment, she missed it.

They walked for only a few more minutes before Sam's exhaustion began to be noticed, by everyone. Marc walked to the women and made them wait as he talked to Sam.

"Sam, you ok?"

"I don't think that I'm going to make it, if it's much farther."

"We're about 4 or 5 hours away. It wouldn't normally take that long, but we have gramps up there, pulling the books."

"Those are important. We need them."

"Understood."

Sam tried to think. "I need to rest but I don't want the group to stop. Would you stay with me and we will catch up with them later?"

"Sure. I'll go tell them."

Marc took Nicki and Claire to the side to talk with them. Sam watched them as they nodded and then looked back at Sam. What she didn't hear was that Marc told them that they would be ok and that John had been following the group but decided to keep his distance for the time being. He would stay with Marc and Sam and that they would be safe on their own.

Marc came back to Sam with a small bag and handed it to her. "Claire said you're to eat this."

Sam opened the bag to find an apple and a sandwich. She tore into the apple before she could say thank you. As soon as she started to eat it, her stomach became queasy.

"Whoa Sam. Eat slowly or you're going to make yourself sick."

"I didn't think that I was that hungry." Sam's body began to shake from the food. The adrenaline began to race through her body once again and she was buzzing with ringing in her ears. She pulled the sandwich out of the baggie that held it.

"Just eat slowly." Marc sat with her in the darkness and watched her eat.

"Thanks for staying with me," Sam replied, between bites.

"I couldn't let you stay behind alone." Marc tried to lighten the conversation. Sam wasn't paying attention. He knew where her mind was. He watched as her eyes scanned the area for someone.

"You know John will get over it, right?" Marc stated. He could see Sam's shocked expression even in the darkness. She focused on Marc and asked. "HUH?"

"If you would just explain to him why you needed to save that crazy old fool, he will get over it," Marc added for further explanation.

Sam looked at her half eaten sandwich. "I don't fully understand myself why I didn't let him to kill Gabe. I know that right before Gabe left the cabin the last time, he gave me medicine to help my pain and to stop..." Sam hushed.

"Stop what?"

"Stop the change," Sam continued. She hadn't told them yet.

"You've got to be kidding me," Marc said in disbelief.

Sam's appetite subsided. She didn't feel like eating the rest of her sandwich.

"It's just you're so old. I mean, not the normal age to be going through the change. Are you sure that's what's going on?"

"Not the time to knock my age, man." Sam was tired. She forced herself to eat the rest of her sandwich. She drank the rest of the canteen that Kenny had given her and placed it back around her shoulders.

"No, what I meant was if you are Trueblood that they go through their change at puberty."

"I know, that's what Chaz told me. I'm new at this."

"So, have you changed yet?" Marc began to look Sam over for any visual signs and wondered to himself why he didn't notice before. He could tell now that there was something definitely different about her. Her scent was strong and true, but her features were not yet defined.

"No. But it's getting closer, and don't look at me like that." Sam drew her arms close to her body.

"You haven't told John yet, have you?" Marc suddenly said, still in disbelief.

"Like how he hasn't told me about his either. No, I haven't told him yet because we didn't truly know what was going on and I didn't want to scare off a perfectly good man with the old 'Hey, I might be a werewolf story'. Oh god, that sounded confusing to me. I'm not into explaining myself right now. I just didn't tell him."

"So you knew that was him."

"Not at first. But there is no hiding the eyes. That's how I figured out who was holding me hostage."

"You knew him in human form?"

"I use to see him all over town. He disguised himself as a homeless person. He's blind in one eye, I think. A scruffy old guy. Nuts to boot."

"He was talking and laughing at himself before I stayed behind. I told Chaz to keep track of what he was saying."

"Do you think that John will ever talk to me?" Sam's heart went to her sleeve.

"If you're honest with him? Then yes. I understand now why you guys have such an attraction to each other. It just wasn't normal, but come to find out, neither are the two of you. So it fits."

"Thank you."

"For what? Talking with you? Someone has to. Silence bugs me," Marc scoffed.

"Me too Marc, me too..."

Marc didn't bother talking, while Sam sat quietly as she stuffed the baggie into the bag and rolled it up to put away in a back pocket.

Sam had enough rest for the time being and so they started again. They were about an hour away from the rest of the group when her ears started ringing. She stopped walking and held onto a tree. She could see Marc's mouth moving but she couldn't hear him past the ringing in her ears. She shook her head, unable to catch her breath.

"I'm... I'm about to black out. I'm sorry," she finished her statement and collapsed to the ground. Marc walked over to her and at the same time, John came out of the distance.

John picked up Sam. "I'll carry her the rest of the way."

Marc nodded and watched his friend tear himself up with unspoken issues as he carried her. He walked with John in silence.

John held Sam close to him. He rested her head on his shoulders and cradled her like a child as he walked gingerly through the rough. He could feel her breath on his neck and her body warm from physical contact. He strained his head to look at her in the moonlight and saw the lines that her tears had made across her dusty face. He held her close to his heart, relieving the pain that he felt.

John broke the silence between the two.

"I overheard your conversation with Sam."

Marc just kept walking.

John continued. "So, she's a Trueblood," he made a statement rather than a question.

"Does it change things?"

"It should. You and I know that it's a big no-no."

"But..."

John lightly placed his cheek against Sam's head. "I guess we will just have to see what goes on. I'm still angry, but hearing her explain it to you, I have to give her the benefit of the doubt. He'd better answer our questions though."

"The guy's a few beers short of a six-pack."

"That is a bad mix, being that strong and not right at the same time."

Sam stirred in John's arms, which made him hush. She turned into John a bit, wrapped her arms around him to fall back to sleep. John repositioned her slightly and continued on.

John and Marc caught up with Nicki and Claire who were still bringing up the rear. Marc kept walking until he reached Chaz. Claire saw John holding Sam and gave him a sorrowful smile. John smiled back at her, through pain filled, grief-stricken eyes. Nicki never paid attention to either one of them. She walked fast to catch up with Marc. She needed support of her own, whether Marc was furry at the time or not.

Marc tapped Chaz on the shoulder. "So, how's the Schizoid?"

"Entertaining. He's talked non-stop."

"Has he said anything that might be useful?"

"Who knows? He's been talking a lot about a council. He's run through many battles he's been in. This guy was a major player in the Ferros clan. No wonder he's a bit off his rocker. Look at the guy. I don't think there's an inch of him that doesn't have a scar of some sort."

"We're almost to the property. Another hour you reckon?"

"Yeah, if GRAMPS!" Chaz shouted. "Hurries his ass up."

"Shhhhhhh...." Marc hissed. "Sam's out right now."

"How is she?" Chaz turned his gaze to see John holding Sam close.

"Tired... very tired. I have a feeling this'll not be the end of this."

Chaz noticed how Sam had snuggled against John. "They make a good couple."

"John's worried with him being a Turned and she being Trueblood."

Chaz laughed. "I've known that girl since we were kids. You saw what she would go though for what's right. If she and John are meant to be... well... let's just say I wouldn't want to be the one to stop her?"

Chaz proceeded to tell Marc about a time they were at the lake, fishing...

Gabe chimed in. "May 16th, 1984, 2:45 in the afternoon. A puppy wandered onto the property. Sam hid that puppy for three

202

whole days before Claire found it...."

Chaz stiffened. Marc looked over to Gabe. "You will speak when spoken to and only then. You got me?"

"I did get you," Gabe said, sarcastically.

Marc started for Gabe when Chaz grabbed his arm.

"Don't. Let's gain our strength for the interrogation."

Marc looked at Gabe. "You're lucky that Sam's apartment is on the third floor."

Gabe just laughed to himself as if someone had told him a joke.

CHAPTER THIRTEEN

Everyone reached the house around 11:00pm. John took Sam straight to her apartment but not before Claire grabbed his arm to let him know, that she would be bringing up dinner for two. He thanked her and headed up the stairs. Kenny and Chaz followed John with the table of books. Once they had the books settled in Sam's living room, John laid Sam down and searched through to find the most recent volumes. He pulled out a few of them, and took them to the bed. He lifted Sam, laid her in his lap, opened the oldest of the books, and began to read. John gave Gabe what credit he could give on the logging that he had taken on Sam. John was able to read the logs and almost see the activity-taking place. He read on.

"December 17th 2003. Claire is consoling Sam on the upcoming holidays. Sam has always found it particularly hard to get through the holidays without her parents. She only grieves now during such events. She is stronger than first noted in volume 16."

As John read, he began to see a pattern to Gabe's writings.

"February 19th, 2004. Danny pulled Sam over again. She tried to be polite and ask him to stop the harassment. Danny is not one to give up that easily. He should be taught a lesson. If it didn't compromise my position, he would not be an issue any longer. Though it is good observation to see Sam under such scrutiny from a previous lover."

John's face grimaced. How could she have been lovers with that asshole? His thoughts went back to their earlier conversation at Randy's. He tried to put it out of his mind and read on.

"June 5th, 2004. She is beginning to have the nightmares more often now. Claire should have someone there to help her through her change by now. If she does not send someone soon, she could kill Sam without even knowing it. How ignorant humans can be at times, trying to keep the inevitable from happening. She is a Trueblood and there is no denying that. I have not sent word in many months to the council. I'm sure that they are not pleased with my actions. I have observed Sam for many years and I do see the potential threat that she may pose if the prophecies happen, but if the prophecies were just the act of a feeble woman trying to hold onto her title... then an innocent woman will die for it. That is neither noble nor right. I will not let that happen."

John's head began to hurt. He shut the books and closed his eyes. He dreamt of Sam being attacked by Danny while Gabe watched, pen in hand... writing each account down. John had to force himself awake. He was not in the mind frame to go dreaming about such things. When he woke up he found himself lying on his back and Sam lying across his chest, sleeping. He wrapped his arms around her and tried not to fall back asleep. Moments later, there was a knock on the door. Claire entered the room with a large tray of food. The aroma made John salivate. She had made a baked chicken, two baked potatoes, a large side of green beans, a large salad and a plateful of brownies. She laid the tray down on the chair next to the bed and walked over to John.
"I hope I didn't wake you."
"The smell alone would have. You didn't have to go through all this trouble. She's still sleeping."
"I know. This is for you. Hers is still downstairs."
"I couldn't-" John was interrupted
"Yes you could, but you're too polite. You need your strength. Now eat and enjoy. How's she been?"
"She hasn't woken up yet. I've read some of the volumes."
Claire raised an eyebrow.

"I hate to say it, but I can see where he started to have a change of heart on his assignment as he kept calling it in his writings. It's like over the years, he's grown to…" He couldn't find the right word so he just said the one he thought of. "… like her, in a way a parent does for a child."

Claire scoffed at the idea. "Oh I doubt that." She turned towards the bathroom, returned a moment later with a wet face cloth, and began to wipe Sam's face clean.

John continued his conversation. "In a Major… General… strict grandfather way… yeah. You should take these last few and read them. Maybe you can see into it a bit better, since many of them have you in them anyway."

"WHAT?"

"Just read them. You'll see. Oh, and thanks again… for the meal."

"Anytime. Thank you for carrying her home." Claire picked up the bound volumes skeptically and left the room.

John sat up and began to eat the feast that Claire brought.. Sam stirred and finally woke. She saw John in his naked human form, eating in her bed. She didn't know which looked more inviting. She thanked the gods that at least he was covered with a blanket. She also thanked the gods that he was there, with her. John smiled at her as if he were saying 'oops'.

"Sorry, I didn't mean to wake you."

Sam looked around in amazement and asked. "How did I get back home?"

"You passed out when you were walking back with Marc. I came out of the distance and carried you the rest of the way."

"When did we get back?" Sam yawned.

"Before midnight. You've only been asleep for a few hours. You should go back to sleep and rest up."

"So what you're telling me is that you carried me, home?" Sam's eyes began to fill with tears.

John just nodded. He was choosing his actions very carefully.

"After I kept you from killing Gabe, you still cared… Carried me?" Tears began to roll silently down Sam's face. Sam felt the tears make chilling paths down her face and lowered her gaze to the bed. She made a futile attempt to wipe the tears away nonchalantly.

John noted the slip along with her actions.

"I'm not going to lie. I was very angry. I didn't understand why you wanted him alive."

Sam's head began to pound once again. John felt Sam stiffen for the blow of bad news and he tried to recover.

"I read through some of his volumes though."

Sam shot John a look.

"Look, I needed to find out for myself if this guy had any credibility to keep me from finishing what I started. To my frustration, he does." John's gaze softened.

"How far back?" Sam could feel her face flush.

"A couple of years worth. I gotta hand it to him. He was good at what he was doing."

"Thorough?" Was the only word she could bring herself to say. She couldn't even look John in the face. She could only imagine what was written in the journals.

"Frightening." John felt that it would hurt less if he kept his answer short and to the point.

Sam felt herself blush even harder. "I guess you read about things…"

"Things that I didn't want to? Yeah. Nevertheless, I had to know. Does it make me feel comforted to know what you had gone through? No. But I had to know. I hope you're not mad at me." John handed her a brownie as a peace offering.

Sam took the brownie without making contact with him and began to break off little bites to eat.

"I should be, but I'm not. I guess you got a free pass into my past. A much unedited version, I'm sure."

John ate some salad, replying. "You could say that."

Sam decided to change the subject. "I still can't believe that you're here."

John was puzzled. "Why wouldn't I be? Sam… I care about you. I trust that you have a reason why you kept the old man alive. I may not like it, but I trust your intentions. They don't change the way that I feel about you."

Sam's eyes began to fill with tears once again. "I have such bad timing."

John smiled at her and laid his hand on her leg. "What do you mean?"

"I mean that I can never find Mr. Right, at the right time."

"You've met Mr. Right before?" John tried to lighten the mood.

Sam just looked at him. "Mr. Right, yeah, I met him a few days ago. We have a lot of things in common, like jam."

John scooted closer to her, on the bed. "Sounds like a nice guy." He took his napkin and dabbed away her tears as she spoke.

"The nicest man I've ever met. I just wish that I could have met him under different circumstances."

"If he's as good a guy as you're making out, I bet it's not the timing that's the frustrating part, just the events during the time that have taken place since." His eyes met hers.

Sam grabbed his hand and held it to her cheek. John opened his hand and obliged.

"There's so much I want to say," John's voice came out suddenly strained.

"It's that timing thing, isn't it?" Sam hung her head.

"I'm just glad that you're back home safe… with me."

John felt a smile form in his hand that held her face.

"Me too," she answered.

They sat for a moment in the silence of the room and enjoyed being together. Sam took in the feeling of security, if only for a moment. Who knew what the future held and if it was anything like her recent past, it wasn't going to get any easier. She knew that she would have to steal chances like this from now on, when she could. She gave herself a moment to look around at her room. Her gaze went to the door where there were still signs of her attack. Claire had cleaned the blood from the floor and wall as best she could, but both would have to be repainted to match the rest of the room. Sam's stomach growled, which startled John and Sam both into nervous chuckles.

"Why am I so nervous?" Sam thought to herself, but she knew the answer. Such traumatic events would bring anyone closer and bond them with that one special moment, even as horrific as it was. That combined with the attraction that she already had for John brought so much more to the table, so much more to enjoy.

"So why am I not enjoying?" Sam asked herself. "I can taunt a monster to kill me, but I can't take the next steps into giving away my heart? There is something seriously wrong with me."

"My stomach's growling at me. I think it noticed your food and that brownie was a teaser."

John held up a potato. "Would you like to join me?"

Sam smiled in acceptance. John leaned over, grabbed the tray and sat it between the two on the bed. He then leaned over, cupped Sam's face in his hands, and gave her a chaste kiss. He caressed her cheek with his thumb and then pulled away. They both sighed relief and looked down at the tray. There was only one plate and serving of silverware so they both ate whatever food they could with their fingers. The rest they would share the silverware. John carved the chicken and handed Sam a leg.

Sam raised her hand to it. "I'm more of a breast woman."

John's eyebrow raised as he intended to keep her spirits lifted as best he could. "I would have pegged you for a leg woman."

Sam let herself be happy in the moment. "You know what I meant."

"Hey, everyone has their preferences. Breast it is." He pulled the breast away from the rotisserie chicken and scooted it to Sam's side of the plate. Sam tore bits off and ate as John prepared the two potatoes.

He stopped mashing butter into one of the potatoes and asked. "What in the world did you get in your hair?"

Sam's hand immediately went to her hair. The feeling alone was enough to make her cringe. It was caked and matted with blood and dirt.

"It's some type of salve that Gabe gave me to stop the bleeding. It smells like shit, but it stopped the bleeding almost immediately and it also helped with the pain."

"How? By knocking out the person wearing it?" John's nose wrinkled.

Sam looked down and smiled. "I *am* kind of stinky, aren't I?"

"Not that bad. I've smelled worse."

Sam looked at her meal partner and smirked. She tilted her

head to the side and asked. "Would you mind if I took a quick shower? I don't think I could eat without gagging from my own smell."

"I don't mind. I'll call down to Claire and have her bring up more food. I'm sure she'd like to know you're back in the land of the living."

Sam got up and walked to her dresser. She pulled out a large t-shirt and a clean pair of underwear and headed to the bathroom.

"I should only be a minute. I guess it depends on how hard it is to get this goop out my hair."

She raced to the bathroom in an attempt to hurry back to John, and the food. She disappeared behind the door. John could hear the water start to run as the shower turned on. He smiled as he envisioned her enjoying a hot shower after her whole ordeal.

Sam did enjoy her shower. Her head wound was still sore, but it had healed quickly. Sam saw the water that poured into the drain and about chased it down with the brownie she ate earlier. The water was brown and red from all of the dirt and blood caked all over her body. She washed her hair three times before she got the smell out. She scrubbed her body, rinsed and scrubbed it again. A notion came over her that she had to stop trying to wash the incident from her body, because no matter how hard she scrubbed, her mind would always be stained. She immersed herself in the droplets of water from the shower and rinsed off one last time.

Once she finished her shower, she got out and brushed her teeth. She ran a comb through her wet hair and dressed. She thought for a second that maybe she should have grabbed more than what she had, but it was too late now. "Besides," she said to herself. "He's naked in a bed with me and we have been very good." Happy with her answer, she came out to find John in her bed with her sheet wrapped around his waist and wanted to melt where she stood. She reiterated to herself. "John is in my bed, naked." She shivered and grinned, noticing that there was another tray of food there.

John's attention was on his food as Sam opened the bathroom

door. He began to answer as he turned his attention to Sam.

"Claire said that she's glad that you're feeling better. She said that if you need some of her tea just to call down... to... um... her."

John's last words were lost on the last bite that he had to will to swallow as he watched Sam walk towards him. The woman who went into the shower just moments prior looked as if she had been dragged through a hedge backwards, being that she was filthy and badly shaken from her ordeal. The woman standing before him now could have been plucked straight from a shampoo commercial.

He watched as her wet hair stayed in place against her back, leaving a wet mark on her shirt. He followed the shirt down to the hem, which hit her just above mid-thigh. He had to bring his mind back up, to focus on anything besides that hem and what lay beneath. He focused on her hair and how it looked black when wet. Sam was without make up, without some made up hairstyle and definitely without a stylish outfit and yet she felt more beautiful than ever. She noticed how John looked at her.

"This is the Sam that is underneath make up, dust, dirt, grime, shitty smelling salve, blood, tears, and god knows what else. This is me."

John sat there and stared at her in amazement, to the point that it made Sam a bit nervous.

"What is it?" Sam became self-conscious.

"I have never witnessed a more beautiful creature in my life."

Sam flirtingly turned her gaze and giggled. "You're just silly"

"No, I mean it. You're absolutely radiant."

He leaned over and ran his fingers through her cold, wet hair. The fragrance from her shampoo immediately permeated the room, filling John's senses.

Sam leaned her head back and let John play with her hair.

"What the feeling of safeness will do to a person's physical appearance."

"Wow," John breathed.

"Stop it. You're making me feel all squidgy inside."

"You and me both," John suggested.

Sam closed her eyes and savored the intimate, and very brief moment, before she was hit with hunger pains. Her stomach rumbled once again and John couldn't help but laugh.

"Maybe we should eat."

"I'm so sorry, but I'm so hungry," Sam tried to explain.

"Why are you sorry? You never have to be sorry with me. I completely understand. I should be the one apologizing for distracting you."

John had to force his gaze towards his plate to keep from staring at her. He felt truthful in what he had just professed to her. He had never seen a more beautiful woman, look more enchanting. He couldn't wipe the smile from his face as he continued to eat.

Sam was famished. She knew that she had to eat slow and keep a pace or she would make herself sick.

"Thank you," she said under her breath.

"It was my pleasure, whatever you're thanking me for." John replied as if he were to give the gratitude. He finished his last bite and added a statement as if it were mere conversation.

"Ya know. I can understand why he's so senile."

Sam looked as though the statement perplexed her.

"Think of it this way... If you had to spend your whole life... well... a good chunk of your life doing nothing but watching and writing down things about a person, wouldn't you be a bit loose in the marbles too?"

Sam swallowed her last bite as she pondered the question.

John continued. "He had to put his life aside to watch yours. There were many times he could have and even wanted to step in, but didn't. Strange old bird."

"Where is he?" Sam asked as she began to arrange her dirty dishes on her tray.

"I think the guys have him chained in the basement. Nicki has put a bind on him, where he's unable to turn while in the house. So, there is a naked old man sitting on a chair in your basement. He's sorry looking when he's in his human form."

"I want to ask you something. When were you going to tell me about you?"

"I had planned on telling you this Friday, after treating you to dinner and a movie first. That was the plan at least. I'm sorry you had to find out the way you did." John leaned over the bed strategically, to safely set his tray down without mooning Sam in the process.

"I'm sure you know about me by now... reading the books and all."

"Actually, I had followed you with the group until you and Marc fell back, that's when I heard your conversation. I stayed with you and him, partly out of extra protection. Partly..."

"Partly what?" Sam got out of bed, took her tray over to John's, began to transfer the plates to one tray, and stacked the trays near her door.

"You have to understand something first before I explain further. I was so pissed, Sam. I couldn't see past the fact that he had taken you from me, from all of us. I wanted him to pay at all costs. You put yourself in a very dangerous position when you put yourself between him and me. You didn't know that it was me when you put yourself there. You could have been killed. But I still..."

John stopped.

"Partly what?" Sam asked again as she returned to her side of the bed.

"Partly, that I was concerned. I have this undeniable bond with you that makes me crazy at times. I couldn't just leave you. When you were taken from us, I was ready to do whatever it took to get you back. I would have done things..." John looked away from her.

Sam moved closer to him. She suddenly was aware of the potentials of John being completely nude. She felt her body begin to react to him. She placed her hand on his bare chest. She felt his heart dance under her touch.

He continued. "And mostly because I can't keep denying how I feel about you. I had a lot of time to come to terms with it, while I carried you in my arms. I have had nothing feel so right and so terrifying at the same time. At times, it's just too intense and I feel like I'm going to explode from the immense emotions. But I just can't bring myself to say it yet. It's just too soon. "

"I do know how you're feeling. Know that I feel the same as you. It's inevitable, undeniable, completely irrational, but it's right. You were the one thought that kept me warm, gave me hope and filled me with strength. I am very lucky to have bumped into you."

Sam leaned over and kissed his cheek. John nodded and then looked into her eyes.

She knew that it wasn't the right time to invoke anything between them, knowing that just a short time ago, she had been chained to a wall, but she couldn't help it. The security that she felt with John being there didn't help her one bit.

"Would you mind if I took a shower too? I don't want to be the only one who stinks."

Sam got up and walked to her dresser. While she searched, she replied. "If I would have known you wanted to take a shower too, I would have invited you to mine." She stopped searching for clothes for John, the moment that she made that statement out loud. She couldn't believe that something so brash just came out of her mouth. She looked at John and saw his dropped jaw reaction as well.

"I'm sorry. I don't know where that came from. Ok, that's a lie. I have a feeling I know where that came from." She turned back to the dresser and answered. Go, go now... hurry."

She heard John rush past her, chuckling as he did.

"It's not funny. I'm glad that you find this funny." Sam shook her head and continued to look for something that might fit him.

Sam went to her closet and finally pulled out a large T-shirt and a pair of sweatpants. She walked over to the bathroom door and heard the shower running. She knocked on the door.

"I've a shirt and pants for you. They should fit."

"Can you come in and lay them on the sink?"

Sam hesitated for a moment. She looked at her badly bruised wrists and tried to keep her mind serious if she was going to have any control. She bit her lip and opened the door. The steam immediately filled her lungs with aromatic scents and John. She walked over and laid the clothes on the sink. She turned and her eyes looked directly at the frosted shower curtain. She could see John behind it, and imagined the water hitting his tanned skin. She stood there enthralled by the glimpses of flesh that silhouetted up against the curtain and sighed.

"You know, I could really use your help with this one pesky spot on my back," John said disarmingly.

Sam could feel her body heat rise with the steam. "You are an evil man, Jonathan Michael DesRosiers."

John peered out of the shower, his top half hanging out of the curtain, the side of the bottom half plastered up against it. He pointed to a spot on his back. "It's right back here... I... can never reach it." He looked at her and smiled seductively.

"Not in the shower, I don't want our first time to be the night you save me from being held captive and definitely not in a shower." She walked out with conviction.

"What? What'd I do?" John teased. He felt better than he had in days. He knew that she was where she belonged and that only through death would someone take her from him again. He was not going to leave a chance for that this time. He let himself dwell in the feeling of happiness amongst other things.

Sam returned to her bed and snacked on another brownie from dinner. She tried to think of what she was going to ask Gabe. She pulled out a pad of paper and a pen from her nightstand and began to jot down questions. She knew the first thing she was going to ask was who in the hell was 'THEM' that he kept referring to. Why are they so worried about her and her life? Why did he abduct her and then reconsider? She tapped the pen against her teeth and lost herself for a moment in thought. She couldn't get out of her mind, the slickness of John's skin in the shower.

She couldn't see past the water that had collected on his long eyelashes. She replayed the vision of seeing his bare body pressed against the shower curtain. How easy it would have been to forget her troubles for just a moment and give into her needs. She shook her head and looked over her questions again. She wrote down a few more before picking up another brownie.

She heard the shower turn off and imagined John toweling off and getting dressed. She saw the doorknob from the bathroom turn and she hurried herself to look deep in thought with her questions. She heard the door open but she did not sense him walking towards her. She tried not to notice until she heard him clear his throat. She looked up and saw him standing in the doorway with her clothes on.

The sweatpants were drastically tight on him, accentuating certain areas on his lower body. He had to wear the pants low to make up for the height difference in the legs. Even then, they still hit him above the ankle. The shirt hit him above his navel, exposing slight ripples in his toned stomach and a small trail of hair that lead into the pants. The shirt was also too tight for him around his shoulders. She forced herself to look at his face. He stood there with a look of skepticism on his face.

"I look ridiculous."

"No you don't. You look..." Sam paused. "Fine."

"They're not made for guys. That much is true." He took off the shirt slowly and let his gaze fall back on Sam. He watched Sam's focus move to his abdomen and he smiled.

"Are you still hungry?"

John practically poured himself into bed. Sam acted as if she wasn't paying attention.

"Huh? Oh, I'm just snacking." She ignored the double meaning to his question.

He sat down on the bed with her. He leaned in closely to peek at her notepad.

"Whatcha writing?"

"I'm trying to come up with some questions to ask Gabe. I can't think of anymore. Here." She positioned the list towards him. "Can you think of any?"

John reviewed the list as Sam watched his expressions. He was nearly sitting behind her, looking over her right shoulder. His chest touched her back as he examined her questions, or at least *tried* to examine them.

"No, I think those are pretty good questions. Why don't you let one of us ask them for you?"

"I'm not afraid of him. I know that I should be but I feel that after I go through my change, that I will be able to handle myself pretty well."

"It takes some getting used to, trust me."

"I'm going to tell you something, but you can't get mad."

He just looked at her, waiting for her to finish.

"I was provoking him yesterday." She saw the disapproving look stream across his face as she continued. "I didn't like to be captive. I thought that a fast death would be better than anything else that he was planning, so I started to taunt him."

John's expression never changed.

"Let me explain. At the time, I didn't know what was going to happen, so to be dead was better than where I was at that time. Anyway, I taunted him to the point where he tried to hit me."

John sat back and looked to the door. Sam grabbed his arm and held him. "Like I said, he TRIED to hit me, but I caught his arm in mine. I started to crush his wrist."

"Was he in hybrid form?"

"Yes."

John sat there for a moment. "That's why he gave you the medicine. You started to change, didn't you?"

"Something started to happen. I started to writhe in pain. That's when he gave me the meds."

John eased but Sam still held his arm, more for contact than to restrain him.

"You were asleep just a few hours ago, why didn't you dream?"

Sam shook her head. "I think that physical and mental exhaustion stopped it for the time being. I don't know what's going to happen tonight. Lately it's tried to come on even during the day."

"When?"

"When a cop pulled me over on Monday."

"You mean Danny, your ex?" John added as a statement, not an accusation, but it just as well could have been. It hit Sam harder than he meant for it to.

"Yeah, Danny. How did you, oh yeah… Never mind, the books right? Anyway, he pulled me over and I was keeping control, but once he pulled away I started to hyperventilate in the truck and I looked at myself in the mirror. I was all splotchy… my skin had turned to some dark grey brown color… and my eyes…" She whisked away in the memory.

"I had a run in with Danny too."

John broke her concentration.

Sam looked into his deep blue eyes. "When?"

"After Claire called to tell us that you were missing. It took all I had not to kill him. He's nothing but a prick in uniform. Guys like that give good cops a bad name."

"What did you do to him?"

"He pulled me and Marc over. I was able to control myself for a while, but he kept pestering and pestering until I snapped. I changed just as he unloaded about three shots into my chest. I grabbed the gun from him and threw it in the woods. I then threw him in the same vicinity. I ripped out his car radio and slashed his tires. It's better than disemboweling him on the side of the road. I had been in form since we got back here."

"For the record, when I went out with him, I was young and very stupid. I stopped going out into public because he would always be there. I don't know why I ever started dating him. I'm going to hate to see what he's going to get when he pulls me over from here on out. He's not even that good of a cop." Sam put her hands in her lap. "I'm sorry."

"Don't be. I just hope that I'm there when you wolf out on him the next time." Sam sighed from mental exhaustion. John decided to get her mind off things.

"Let me take a look at your wrists." He took her hands and held them to expose the bruises.

"You're healing nicely, and fast. Yes, I can see you're getting close. Does it still hurt?"

"A little," Sam answered nervously.

John leaned down and kissed the inside of each wrist. Sam's body warmed as his body made contact with hers.

"Your ankles were bound as well, right?" He lifted up each foot and gently kissed the inside of her ankles and then placing her legs on each side of his body.

"Did he hurt you anywhere else?" He leaned into her and nuzzled his nose against hers.

"No, but I could lie." She met his lips.

They kissed each other as if to say I'm glad that you're safe and with me. They held back any other feelings or desires. They pulled away from each other and returned with a warm embrace. He pulled her onto his lap and just held her.

"Thank you for saving me," she whispered in his ear.

"It wasn't just me, everyone was there." He kissed her neck lightly.

"I mean before that. Thank you for saving me."

He knew what she meant and held her tighter for it.

She smiled and said. "I... I ... I can't breathe."

They laughed for a moment and he released her. He got out of bed to head downstairs.

"I'm going to check on everyone. Do you want to come?"

"Sure, but give me a minute. I need to put on more clothes."

John walked over to Sam who was rummaging around in her dresser for a pair of jeans. He put his hands on her shoulders and quickly turned her around. He pulled her shirt above her waist so that he could run his hands over her bare back. He caressed her gently as he leaned down and nestled his face into her neck. Sam held onto his body, welcoming him. He took a deep breath to capture the scent of her clean body. He lightly kissed her shoulder as he pulled away from her. Sam was flushed from head to toe. John looked down and sharply back to Sam's face.

"We have to wait a minute," John chuckled.

Sam dared not let her eyes wander down his body as she answered. "Then you'd better sit over there or we'll never be able to leave."

Sam found a pair of jeans and put them on in front of John. He had seen her at her best and worst, underwear wasn't going to make a difference. John watched Sam wiggle into her jeans and couldn't help but smile. Once Sam was buttoned and zipped, she slapped her thighs.

"Well, I'm ready if you are."

John stood up and took her hand before leaving the apartment.

CHAPTER FOURTEEN

Once they were on the main level of the house, John headed for the basement and Sam went to the kitchen. She found Claire asleep at the kitchen table, the morning sun creating an angelic aura around her. She looked around the kitchen and marveled at the cleanliness. She knew that there had been a storm cooked up in here not too long ago, but what always seemed to amaze her was the cleanup. Claire always said that no job is complete without a thorough clean up. It ties up loose ends. Sam smiled to herself at the irony that presented itself with Claire's words of wisdom. Sam walked over and sat next to her. She put her hand on Claire's arm and kissed her on the cheek.

"Hmm? Oh... oh hi dear," Claire said in a startled tone. "I must have fallen asleep. Are you hungry?" Claire tried to push her fallen hair back into place of the bun that she was wearing.

"I woke up when you brought John's plate to him. Thank you for bringing me an extra plate while I was in the shower."

"I had fed everyone but you. I thought that I would wait until you called down for something. I sat down after taking your plate to you. I guess I must have dozed off."

"I'm sorry about earlier."

"Oh that?" Claire waved her hand in the air because she knew she was speaking of the event with John and Gabe. "Don't worry about that. I understand now why you did it. I read some of the journals. It's definitely disconcerting to know that half your life is recorded in volumes of books."

Sam winced. "Are they bad?"

"I'm sure there are things in them that you wouldn't want me to know about, but I only skimmed... I don't want to pry."

"How's the rest of the gang?" Sam looked around the empty kitchen. She could feel the presence of people in the house, but they were nowhere to be seen. It was a familiar feeling to Sam from the many years that Claire took in boarders. The kitchen was quiet and becoming brighter every moment from the rising sun.

"Kenny and Chaz have stuck it out. They are waiting for Brad to show up. When we got back to the house, Aimee was here with Katie. She said that she would call Brad and tell him that it was urgent. She said that he should be here sometime today. I'm more worried about Nicki though. She's pretty upset over it all."

"Where is she?"

"With Marc, in the library."

"Are you sure you don't need my help for anything?" Sam asked one last time.

"No, I'm fine. I'm going to go up and go to sleep though. You know where I am if you need me."

Claire got up and kissed Sam on the top of the head as she headed out of the room. Sam sat for a moment before heading over to the coffee pot. There was about a half cup left that was being warmed by the burner underneath the pot. Sam knew that one of the guys must have left it that way. She dumped out the remaining coffee and started a fresh one.

She sipped on her coffee as she watched the sun finally break over the trees. She smiled and welcomed the morning as a new day. Once finished with her liquid breakfast, she headed towards the hall.

Sam knocked on the library entrance as she walked in. Nicki and Marc looked up at Sam. Nicki looked away as Marc got up and made his way to her.

"I've tried to talk to her, but she's highly pissed. Good luck." Marc patted Sam on the shoulder for encouragement as he walked out of the room.

"Thanks for trying," Sam answered before she walked over and sat in front of Nicki.

Nicki never once looked at her.

Sam positioned her body to be directly in front of Nicki when she spoke.

"Everyone understands why I had to keep him alive, everyone but the person I need the most."

Still no response.

Sam continued in her plea. "You of all people should know that I wouldn't do anything too stupid…"

Nicki looked up, but not at her as she interrupted with one word. "Danny...."

Sam sighed and tried again. "You should know that I have LEARNED my lesson of doing stupid things such as Danny, and that I wouldn't make that mistake again. I believe in my heart and in my gut that not killing him was the right thing to do. I don't know why just yet, but I knew that I had to go with it. I love you Nicki, and the last thing that I want is for you to be mad at me, but I had to do it."

Nicki faced her, which gave Sam a front seat to the pain that dove deep into Nicki's eyes.

"It's not even the Gabe thing that pissed me off, Sam."

Nicki rolled her eyes and walked to the window, mindlessly playing with the curtains as she spoke.

"It's the fact that it's all going to be different now. I thought that it was going to be ok, finding out that you were a Trueblood and all, but going through this, it's too much."

"What do you mean?" Sam got up and walked to the window where Nicki stood but didn't stand too close. She wanted to give her the space she needed.

Nicki turned to face Sam. "Are you going to start putting your life on the line for people that you don't even know now?"

"What in the hell are you talking about? I knew Gabe and I knew that he had useful information." Sam tried to defend herself.

"You find out that not only are you a werewolf, but that you are this Trueblood thing, and since then you've gotten into trouble, where you put your life on the line not once, but twice in a three-day period."

Sam put her hand on her hips and answered. "Hey, one of those times was not even my fault."

Nicki moved away from the window, obviously annoyed with Sam's answer. She worked her way to the bookshelf and ran her fingers across the spines of the books.

"But is this how your life will be, from here on out?"

"What if it is?" Sam shrugged.

Sam didn't follow her, but rather stayed at the window. It was her turn to gaze out onto the forest. Nicki walked back over to the window and leaned against the sill.

"I don't wanna have to constantly worry that I might lose you."

Sam took Nicki's hands in hers and smiled. "Whether I was Were or not, you should always worry. That's life."

Nicki didn't try to let go. She looked down at her best friend's hands and smiled sorrowfully. "But this is no ordinary life."

Sam began to swing Nicki's arms like two school children. "Then maybe it's time for a change. That's what life is, right? I want you there with me. I don't think that I could go through the rest of my life without my best friend. I would die of the heartache alone. I do promise to try to be more careful though. Promise."

Nicki's eyes brightened a bit in attempts to let go of the worrying. "This is going to take some getting used to. I can't say that I'm going to be peachy-keen about all of this, but I will at least try. Just don't die on me anytime soon, I couldn't go through the rest of my life without my best friend either, you know."

Sam hugged Nicki for a long time. Sam broke from her when she heard her coughing.

"What's wrong?" Sam asked.

"I was inhaling your hair. Blah!" Nicki said as she tried to brush Sam's hair from her face.

The girls began to laugh quietly to themselves.

Nicki went back to leaning against the windowsill. The day was clear and beginning to brighten. The heat through the window felt good to both the girls.

"I put a bind on Gramps, downstairs."

"Oh yeah, Gabe," Sam thought.

"How's he holding on?" Sam asked sincerely.

"Well... you might want to tell the guys to be gentle. He's looking a little worse for 'wear', for want of a better word. Not that he looked like a spring chicken before. Oh and get this, I hear Brad's on his way."

Sam thought back to Claire's conversation about the different 'Turned' people in town. Brad was a Werebear. He and his wife had been turned on a hunting trip to Alaska. Brad, from what she knew, was a certified bounty hunter. Now, she questioned his assignments and bosses for that matter.

"Did Aimee say when he would be here?"

"Sometime, today. I guess we should get some rest before the big event."

Sam looked at her in question.

"The interrogation by Brad. I don't know about you, but I want to be there for that."

All Sam could do was nod slowly. She knew that Nicki didn't want to be there. She was just mad for what he had done.

"Come on. It's time to get some rest." Sam put her arm around her. "So, are we good or what?" Sam bumped Nicki in the side, which was intended to bump her on the hip. Sam always forgot how much shorter Nicki was to her, inches worth.

"AH!" Nicki laughed. "We're good." Nicki put her hand around Sam's waist and gave her a quick hug as they walked out of the room. Nicki and Sam headed for the basement.

The girls made it down to the basement where they had Gabe tied up. The basement was as old as the house, so there were parts that were still nothing but a dirt floor. There were additional rooms that made up fruit cellars, storage and some secret rooms. There were tiny windows at the top of the walls, but most were grown over on the outside. The basement was lit more by the exposed light bulbs that hung from crass ceiling fixtures. Rows of jars and other questionable items were stacked neatly on shelves. Even the basement, with the partial dirt floor, was clean.

Nicki examined the chains around Gabe's chest that were secured to latches in the concrete floor. Gabe did not try to fight the restraints. He knew that he was useless in his human form and that the bind that Nicki had on him was stronger than any chains that could hold him.

Sam walked up to Gabe but stayed a good distance away. She felt Gabe's intense stare through his swollen and bloody face. His body was in the same shape as his face. His breathing was ragged and uneven. She noticed that Chaz had most of Gabe's blood on him, which meant that he was enjoying himself a bit too much.

"Chaz!" Sam called out without breaking eye contact with Gabe. "I said to keep him alive."

He never looked at her. "He's still alive... just."

"He's going to answer some questions first," John added as he walked up behind Sam.

Gabe laughed aloud. "Answers will not help you, little one, when you don't know which questions to ask."

Chaz backhanded him across the cheek. Gabe swung back from the momentum, righted himself, and spit out a tooth as he replied. "Watch it, pup. You're getting pretty good with you're aim."

Chaz went to swing again when Marc grabbed his arm. "That's enough for now. Sam started to pace in front of Gabe. She had known him for a while and was able to observe his patterns while she was held captive. She stopped and spun on her heels to face him. His head snapped to attention to watch her actions.

Sam moved in closely, daring Gabe to make a move. She squatted down and rested her arms on her thighs.

"I'll get the answers I want."

"You're brave with your friends around." Gabe sputtered between swollen lips.

Sam's expression was that of death on a fieldtrip. Her eyes went cold and her smile matched her intentions. "If you had not drugged me, I would have killed you."

Gabe returned her stare and let a large smile jump sporadically over his face.

"You wouldn't have had the heart."

Sam stood up slowly and sighed.

"There's a new me on the brink, my friend. I would think that you would befriend me rather than become my enemy." Sam turned to walk away.

She added. "You'll get to meet another one of my good friends really soon. I don't have the heart? Well, his is as black as night when someone wrongs one of his own. He will ensure I get the answers that I seek. Rest up, Gabe, you are going to need all the strength you can muster." She looked at Chaz who was still in amazement over Sam's reaction and stated. "Don't fuck with him anymore until Brad gets here. Give him some water and then leave him be." Sam started up the stairs and John followed behind. She stopped and called out. "We all need to get some rest. We should set up some type of watch for a while. Who'll take first turn?"

Chaz smiled sadistically.

Marc saw him and said. "I'll take first watch."

Chaz pouted and walked to the other end of the room. Nicki announced that she would stick watch with Marc. John agreed that there should be two at all times, to control the treatment of the prisoner.

Marc heard Chaz's voice ring down the stairs. "Oh goodie, I get to rest up in time for Brad to get here? It's like all my Christmas' rolled into one."

John ushered Sam up the stairs. Once they made it to the main floor, John told Sam to head up to her apartment and that he would be up shortly. John went to the kitchen in hopes to find the number to Aimee and Brad. He searched through the personal address book until he found the number. He wanted to find out if Aimee had any news.

"Hello?" Aimee answered the phone.

"Aimee? It's John."

"Hey, what's up?"

"I just wondered if you had heard from Brad yet?"

"I thought he would have been here already. I talked with him about twenty minutes ago. He might be stopping for supplies." Aimee stated as if it were a normal occurrence.

John was perplexed. "Supplies?"

Aimee was silent for a moment, trying to find a way to explain herself. John didn't give her time to answer.

"Don't answer that. Ok then, I'll just tell everyone that he should be around shortly in say an hour or so?"

Aimee answered. "More like two or three. Does he need to be there sooner because I could call him back...?"

"No, no that is fine. It will give us time to rest. Are you coming out?"

"Yes, we aren't sure if we will be together or driving separately. I don't like to have Katie around while he's...."

working."

"Understood. Ok, well if anything changes with his timing I guess... give us a call."

"And the same goes for you if something there arises."

John and Aimee said goodbye and John headed back up to Sam's apartment. He was worn out.

John knocked on Sam's door before entering. He heard Sam's voice, and he opened the door. The room was completely dark except of a single candle burning next to her side of the bed. He could see her glow in the candlelight. He walked over and climbed into bed with her, all the time Sam watched him out of the corner of her eye. He turned down the covers and slid in under with her, pressed his body to hers and pulled the covers back over both of them. She turned over and faced him. They laid there for a while in silence. Sam could not hold back the silent tears that slowly streamed down her cheek.

John wiped them away with a finger.

"What are these for?" John asked.

"Too many emotions at once, I guess. Real highs and lows."

"I hope I'm one of the highs."

"My only high..."

"To be honest, you're mine as well. It's been too long."

"Yes, but with you here with me, it's been worth the wait."

John wanted to let go of all of the foolish human faults of second-guessing himself and just tell Sam how he felt about her, but he was afraid that, being so soon, he would scare her off.

Sam watched as his eyes began to show his turmoil.

"Do you want to tell me something?"

"I'm not sure yet. No. I'm sure about what I want to say, I'm just not sure of my timing. As you said, it's all about the timing. But I could tell you what it's like to be a Werewolf."

Sam knew he was changing the subject, but she was ok with that... for now.

"That would be better than some dated book I got from the market."

"I remember that book! It flew out of your bag. AH-HA! I knew it wasn't just for novel reading!"

"So," Sam said teasingly. "Tell me what it's like."

"It's the most terrific and most terrifying thing that could ever happen to you, and they happen simultaneously. It's feels like your body is being ripped in two but the power you feel replaces that pain, and then you feel unstoppable. You gain powers that you would have never dreamed of, your senses, your strength, all increase. Your mind becomes crisp and clear... focused."

Sam was enthralled. John continued, all the time running his hands through her hair.

"But when you change in complete form, it's like your mind takes a backseat to the beast. It takes someone a long time to override their beast's mind."

"Can you?"

"Most of the time I can. I normally only change to that form when I'm hunting, or when I'm in need to track something."

"You hunt?" Sam looked surprised.

"Oh yeah, that is something that you will have to get use to. You won't have a choice in it. Normal food will not sustain you long while you're in form, especially when it's for a prolonged period of time."

"How long were you in form when you were looking for me?"

"The whole time..." John didn't miss a beat.

"Did you hunt?"

"Yes, a few times. I settled for things like rabbits and squirrels, you know, easy things to catch. If you go hunting with a buddy, you can get bigger and better prey like deer or cattle, though that's a pretty big order."

"You killed a cow for a meal before?" Sam looked at him in disbelief.

"When you're on an assignment that requires you to stay in form for up to 10 days straight, you have to keep your energy up. So yeah, I was in a party of four that took down a cow. Just think of it as a really rare steak." John smiled.

"I don't know if I will ever get use to it." Sam broke eye contact with John for only a moment before she ended her sentence. "I'm scared."

"Everyone goes through that. It gets easier after your first time. Think of it as, well, losing your virginity. They say that for women, it hurts the first time and each time after it gets where it doesn't hurt anymore and then finally can be pretty good. I have never been a woman before, so I couldn't attest to that, but I can imagine."

His last statement rewarded with a grin. He continued. "I hope that you will let me be there for you, for your first change. I went through mine alone and I would never wish that on anyone I know."

Sam moved her head to lie on John's arm. "I wonder how Aunt Claire would take it if I told her that I didn't want Carol's help."

"She'd probably freak."

"But I don't want her help. Why should I get any special accommodations when you didn't, when so many others didn't?"

"Why does it bother you so much?" John sounded as if he really wanted to know.

"I don't know. I guess it's personal. No one should be treated like a lesser person. One rule for all ya know."

"You could run for president with that kind of speech," John teased as he tickled her under her chin.

"Hush, you know what I mean." Sam played back.

John put his hand over his heart and stared at the ceiling as he replied. "Thank you, Ms. President."

"That's so not funny." Sam smiled.

John grabbed a hold of her and pulled her close. "Whatever you say, Ms. President."

Sam snuggled her head into John's neck. He laid his head on top of hers and squeezed her body to his.

"I wish that we could erase the past two days from the books," John whispered.

"I don't. I'm not glad that I went through it, but I'm a better person for it by surviving. I have learned what I shouldn't do and what I could have done to make things different. My motto is if you can't learn from life, that's when it's bad."

"I think it's way past your bedtime. Your clichés are getting worse."

"It's just not normal to feel this way for someone I met just a few days ago. I feel like I've known you all my life," Sam said, as she ran her hand down John's side.

"We have something that most people don't though."

"Fur?" Sam chuckled.

"No, we have a bond. We've both been discouraged by past relationships and to find a nice person who is truly interested in you... I feel it makes a person fall harder, faster." He almost didn't finish the last part.

"So, they fall harder and faster?" Sam pointed out the one part of the statement that he had stumbled upon without knowing.

"Tell me you disagree."

"I wasn't saying either way, I was asking you the question."

"Why ask me again if you already heard what I said?"

John's human side skirted the question. "I just liked hearing it, that's all. It's been a long time... oh wait, it's been never since someone has fallen hard and fast for me. I like the idea."

"You really have some dumbasses living in this town."

"So hard and fast, huh?" Sam couldn't let it go.

"How about this?" John leaned in and kissed Sam in the most romantic way that he knew how. The kiss lingered on Sam's lips even after they parted.

"Good answer," was all that Sam could say before swallowing hard.

"We'll continue this conversation later, but for now I want you to get some rest. Brad will be here shortly."

Sam buried her head in John's chest.

"Do I have to?" Her angst turned quickly to the revelation that her mouth was pressed to John's bare skin. She was also suddenly and tortuously aware of how close their bodies were to each other. She ran her lips across his skin and felt him react to her.

John slid his hand up the back of Sam's shirt. He wanted to be in contact with her body with no barrier. Sam could sense his need and stripped off her shirt, leaving herself bare from the waist up. He pulled her to him, letting their bodies mingle with each other. He kissed her gently on the lips to try and not provoke any further actions to be taken. She welcomed his touch. He pulled away and put her head back in the crook of his neck. She knew that it wasn't the right time and didn't pursue him any further.

She relaxed her body in his and quickly fell asleep. John lay there holding Sam's body to his, for as long as he could, before he fell victim to slumber too.

CHAPTER FIFTEEN

John was awakened by Sam nuzzling his neck. He tried to pull away from her, but she was able to keep her intended position. John finally moved to his back and Sam followed only to end up straddling him. She sat on him, looking down into his slate colored eyes. The only thing that he could see of her, were her luminous eyes.

"What's wrong, John?" Sam purred. "Would you rather me be on bottom?"

"What are you doing, Sam?"

"Don't deny yourself what you want. Don't deny what I want."

Sam leaned down and started to tongue his chest while her hand descended his body. John tried to push her back by her shoulders when she caught a hold of his wrists, pinning them forcibly above his head, and began to kiss his neck.

John tried to break free of her grasp, but her strength was too much for his human form.

She paused for a moment to look up and glare at him. "Why are you fighting me? Oh," Sam purred. "I see. You like it rough, Boy Scout?" Sam slammed her weight into his arms and made him wince.

"Sam!" John tried to wriggle free. "Sam, stop it."

He felt his beast frothing forward. She squirmed on his body, making him react to her. She took his hands, put them on her chest, and squeezed his hands to her breasts.

"Sam, NO!" He pushed her off and stood up to evade her advances. He turned on the light to find her positioned on all fours, on the bed. Her skin had completely mutated to a darkened gold color. Her markings were a cross between a wolf and something unknown.

She slinked over to the edge of the bed like a cat and growled at John.

"If I have to fight you for what I want, I will," she stated.

John stood his ground and readied himself to change if

necessary. "What did you do to Sam?"

Sam threw her head back in pure sexual style. "I needed to get out, stretch a little, and maybe even get some exercise while I'm at it."

She got off the bed and stood for a moment, letting her hair fall around her shoulders. She walked slowly to John arousing his inner savage through his connection with Sam. She was using Sam to get what she wanted. He felt himself start to reshape and fought to keep it at bay.

"I will not let you use me, and I sure as hell will not let you use Sam."

"I've grown stronger now and I'll do as I please. I have no master."

"You'll kill her if you don't go through the proper steps. If you push her body any further, you'll both die."

"LIES! ~" Sam shouted at John.

"No! Truth!" John tried to rationalize with her. "Now you need to finish your slumber and come when you're called."

Sam wrapped her golden arms around John and went in for a kiss.

"You would send me away?" she pouted.

"I want Sam, not you." He wrenched her arms from around his neck so hard that she fell onto the floor and went limp. John picked up Sam who was out cold, and started to place her back into bed where they were before. He watched her body return to its human state before he pulled the blankets over the both of them and waited a moment before he tried to stir her. Sam began to wake. Her eyes opened wide and she shot up to a sitting position.

Before Sam could say anything, John hushed her and eased her back to the pillow she had been laying on.

"I think that you were beginning to have another nightmare."

"How could you tell?" She looked alarmed.

"I've learned the signs."

"What time is it?"

"You've only been asleep an hour. Would you like to sleep more? I didn't want to wake you, but I didn't want you to fall into a nightmare either." John didn't want to tell her yet what had just happened moments earlier.

"I'm afraid to go back to sleep now. I started to have a dream that I was chained to a wall again. I could hear a conversation far off in the background, but I was too far away and couldn't make out what they were saying. I could have sworn though that I heard your voice. It was probably you trying to wake me."

"Maybe..." John caressed her face. "Why don't you try and sleep a little? I'll wake you if you go under again."

"Thank you." Sam closed her eyes and let exhaustion overtake her.

John wiped the beads of sweat from his brow. He hoped that his control would last until she finally made her change. He didn't know how much longer he could keep himself under thumb. He lay there and let his body finally relax while he watched the sun struggling to shine through the slits in the blinds.

Brad let Aimee and Katie enter the house through the front door. They had decided to ride together since Brad didn't feel that Katie would be in any harm while he worked.

Brad strode down the stairs to the basement, letting the thump of his boots announce his presence. Brad was able to see where Gabe was chained to a chair and walked over to stand behind him. Brad cocked his head forward so that the brim of his Stetson just touched the hair on Gabe's neck. Gabe flinched and snorted out of the slumber that he had fallen into.

"So sorry. Did I wake you?" Brad finished his cigarette then dropped it to the floor, grounding it out with the toe of his cowboy boot. Gabe mumbled a reply as he tried to turn to see who stood behind him. Brad grabbed the back of Gabe's head, stopping his movement. "Here are the rules. You'll do what I say, when I say it. You'll answer all questions as completely and thoroughly as though your life depends on it. Because it does..."

"Sam doesn't want me dead." Gabe laughed as only an insane person could mimic.

"Sam's not here and I don't give a flying fuck what happens to you. My loyalty is to myself. Sam's a friend, so she'll forgive me if you die. Do we understand one another?" The entire time Brad spoke, his voice stayed emotionless.

"Who are you?" asked Gabe. "I know your smell, but never knew who it belonged to."

Brad stepped around in front of Gabe, his hands in the pockets of his barn coat. Gabe sat there and inspected the new member of the group.

"You are the Parks boy. You aren't home much. They wouldn't have sent a human down here, but you're no wolf."

Brad drew his right hand out of his pocket and held it out towards Gabe. Brad willed his hand to morph into his beast. The hand before Gabe began to grow. Hair poured slowly from the back of it, and the 8-inch long claws slid slowly out towards Gabe. There was no fear in Gabe, only curiosity.

"That's right mutt. I'm a bear. In addition, I have more control over the change than anyone you've ever seen. So remember that if you die, it won't be an accident." Brad let his hand return to normal as he took off his coat and hung it on a nail in the wall. He removed the Stetson and placed it on a shelf, resting on its crown. Brad pulled a cigarette out of the pack stashed in his pocket and placed it between his lips, staring at Gabe the whole time. Gabe watched him, trying to size up the man who stood before him.

He bowed his head slightly as he smiled. "You really don't know who I am, do you? Let me introduce myself." Brad took a drag off his cigarette and continued to talk making his words look as if they were on fire. "Brad Parks. Big game hunter, bounty hunter, and finder of stray Weres, commissioned by the Council, strays... like you."

"I'm not a stray!" Gabe spat at Brad. "I'm a general in the Ferros! I have led men into battle and seen the horrors that one Were can do to another! You cannot scare me! You cannot hurt me! There is nothing, nothing you can-"

Gabe's words were cut off as Brad lunged forward and slammed a knife through the back of Gabe's hand, securing it to the arm of the chair that held him. At the same time, Brad covered Gabe's mouth with his left hand in case Gabe tried to scream. Gabe swallowed his pain in an attempt to breath. Brad watched Gabe's eyes glaze over with determination. Brad grinned at him.

"Good. I can see we're going to have some fun." Brad walked over and removed his lighter from his jacket. He held it between his thumb and middle finger, snapping them together to open it.

"You see, it's been a long time since I've interrogated anyone with some stamina... a little determination."

"Go fuck yourself 'Teddy'." Hatred glared at Brad from deep within Gabe's eyes.

"My apologies. Tell you what, I'm gonna go up and grab some coffee. You think about everything that I might even want to know, and we'll talk when I get back." Brad walked over to Gabe and grabbed the handle of his knife, pulling it slowly out of his hand. Gabe stared at him, feeding off the pain. Brad then took his cigarette, tore off the filter, and placed the lit cigarette in the wound so that it would slowly burn down to Gabe's hand. Brad patted Gabe on the head. "Stay."

Gabe growled and tried to twist his head, snapping his teeth at Brad's hand. Brad turned slowly and started for the stairs.

Gabe strained and shouted into the air. "Pain is a source of power, 'Teddy'. No matter what you do to me, I will pull from the pain."

Brad never acknowledged Gabe, as he slowly climbed the stairs.

When Brad reached the kitchen, he called for Nicki. "I might need you to heal Gabe from time to time. I don't want to take away the pain or heal the wounds, just keep him from dying. I don't plan on killing him, but it'll be close."

Brad poured a cup of coffee and headed back downstairs.

"Chaz, grab a pair of tweezers then come down. You'll get a kick out of this." He walked past Gabe when he returned to the basement. As he did, he poked at the stab/burn on Gabe's left hand, causing him to wince. "You should really be more careful." Brad chortled. "Think of anything you want to tell me yet?" Brad lit another cigarette.

"You smoke too much, and you're ugly."

Brad grinned. Chaz came bounding down the steps, a smile splitting his face from ear to ear.

"Oh this is going to be good." As he passed Gabe, Chaz let

his elbow catch his ear, snapping his head to the side. When Chaz tried to hand Brad the tweezers, Brad shook his head.

"Start on his eyelashes and work your way out for me." Brad thought Chaz was going to orgasm. He was the only person he'd ever met that liked the idea of inflicting slow pain. They would make a good team to work on Gabe.

"You mean he's already refusing to answer questions?" asked Chaz.

"I don't know," Brad replied. "I haven't asked him any yet."

Chaz giggled and walked over to Gabe. "Just one hair at a time."

Gabe winced at the first hair being plucked. "You realize it will all grow back the first time I change."

"Good! Guess then we'll start over." Brad took a drag off his cigarette.

Gabe was about to smart off when Chaz reached from behind and yanked out another hair. Brad looked at Chaz then dropped his head to hide a smile. Chaz was worse than a kid in a candy store. He took his time trying to decide which lash to yank next.

An hour later, Gabe had no eyelashes left, no eyebrows and other small spots on his face. "How does that feel Gabe?"

"It tickles. I like the way you operate. At this rate, I will be able to heal and then we will see what you can do."

"Okay, how about this." Brad strode over to Gabe and placed a collar around his neck, flipping a switch on the black box attached to it. Then he tossed a coil of wire under the chair Gabe was chained to and grinned at him.

"You know what this is?" He held up the end of the wire with a plug.

"A neck massager?" Gabe smarted back. "Why don't you rub my feet while you're at it, gimme me the spa package?"

Brad's response was to reach over and plug in the wire. Gabe thrashed and whimpered in his chair until Brad unplugged the cord.

"You can start talking, or you can suffer. It's that simple."

Gabe brought his focus back to Brad. "You'll have to do better than…" Gabe's words were sealed in his throat as Brad plugged the cord back in. After about thirty seconds, which seemed like an hour to Gabe, Brad unplugged it.

"Ready to talk?" Gabe's only answer was to yawn and stretch to pop his neck.

Brad walked behind Gabe and placed his hands on either side of his head. "I think it's time you changed into something a little less comfortable." Brad closed his eyes, and concentrated. Hair sprang from Gabe's body everywhere that it would during a full change, but that was all that happened. Gabe didn't change in size, gain any muscle strength or any other of the numerous benefits that accompanied being Were.

Gabe groaned at the pain of having a partial change forced upon him. Gabe realized then just how powerful the bear was. Brad continued his torture and drew out Gabe's claws.

Gabe screamed. Unlike the usual meld of the change, Gabe's claws tore their way through his fingertips, extending to their full length. He tried to force the rest of the change, but Brad didn't allow it and caused the muzzle to retract.

Kenny and Marc came running down the steps. When they reached the bottom, they froze. They saw Brad concentrating with his hands on Gabe's head. Chaz stood next to the table in front of them, his mouth hanging slack from the shock of what he witnessed.

Brad let go of Gabe. "Still having fun, Mutt?"

Gabe was breathing fast, trying to get used to the pain. He stared out at Brad. "You're not old enough to perform such a talent. Where did you learn that?"

"My secret bucko... ready to talk?" Brad lit another cigarette.

"How long exactly, have you been watching Sam?"

Gabe closed his eyes briefly. When he opened then, he had a look of boredom in his eyes. He sighed and looked off to the side. Brad opened a toolbox and pulled out a hammer and chisel. He walked over to Gabe's injured left hand. Gabe had dug his claws into the chair when Brad called them out.

Brad rested the chisel against the claw of Gabe's left pinky, just before the fingertip, the hammer held loose at his side. "Last chance Gabe. How long?" Gabe just smiled.

Faster than anyone in the basement could see, Brad brought the hammer down on the claw, severing it completely. Gabe howled in pain. Blood ran onto the floor, pooling next to the leg of the chair.

"Tell them nothing," Gabe said. "You've been through worse, you miserable lapdog. But they need to know."

Brad plugged in the fence cord for fifteen seconds, adding to Gabe's misery. "We've got nineteen more Gabe. You want to start talking?"

"Never! I'll never tell you anything you worthless-" Before Gabe could finish, Brad used the chisel and hammer to remove the claw from Gabe's ring finger. The howl of pain and rage echoed through the basement.

Marc was headed back upstairs. He didn't care to watch Brad work. Kenny nodded to him once before turning to leave, still no expression on his face. Chaz moved around to get a better look at the damage Brad was inflicting on Gabe, grinning like a little boy who just received his first BB gun.

"How long?" Brad asked

"Since the beginning," Gabe hissed. "You weak minded fool. You'll heal as soon as you change! Tell them nothing!"

"Were you in any way responsible for her parent's death?"

Gabe glared at Brad. "Hurt me all you want. I won't tell you anything else."

Brad shrugged and took off the middle claw. Gabe whimpered, controlling himself enough not to scream. Brad plugged in the fence cord again before proceeding to remove the index and thumb claws. Gabe's eyes were starting to roll back in his head, his breath coming short and fast.

"We're only a quarter of the way through Gabe. Keep talking and I'll stop."

Gabe shook his head violently. "No."

Brad shrugged and turned to Chaz. "You want a turn?" he asked. He held out the bloody tools to Chaz.

"Really? You mean you'll let me help?"

"I need some coffee and a pack of cigarettes. Take off one claw every three minutes." Brad unplugged the fence. "You can stop if he starts to talk."

Chaz took the hammer and chisel with awe, nodding in agreement.

Brad went back up to the kitchen and poured a second cup of coffee. He turned around to face Claire as she walked in.

Brad went into the living room and sat with Aimee and Katie to see how they were doing. "How are things going?" asked Aimee, with a twinkle in her eye. She didn't have the stomach for Brad's work, but lived vicariously through him. Punishment of evil was what she craved, just couldn't hand it out on her own.

"It's going. He's being stubborn."

"It's the bad man," said Katie. "The good man wants to tell you, but the bad man won't let him."

"That's why I'm trying to make the bad man go away."

"Ok. Tell Gabriel that he'll be okay," Katie replied.

"Well, daddy has to get back to work. I will be back in a bit."

Brad topped off his coffee on the way back to the basement. When he reached the bottom of the steps, he saw Chaz still grinning, if a little pale. The front of Chaz's clothes, covered in blood.

"I don't have quite the knack you do. I couldn't get them off in one blow."

Brad looked at Gabe's mangled right hand. It appeared to have taken Chaz two, sometimes three strikes to remove the claws. The stubs that remained were ragged wounds that seeped a dark steady stream of blood. Brad went over to the workbench and motioned Chaz to follow. "He admit to anything?"

"No. He'd begged for mercy, almost weeping, then started cussing at himself, and me."

Brad returned to Gabe and looked into his eyes. The one did seem to be begging while the other glared. "Gabriel? Can you hear me?"

"Yes." Came the feeble answer. "Shut up weakling. I'm in charge here." "Why won't you let me tell him?" "Because he's a worthless Turned. He has no rights to the information. Only the council of Truebloods has the right." "But I want to help Sam." "SHUT UP!"

Brad took the conversation in and made up his mind. Gabe was very much insane. He just hoped the old lunatic would survive to give them answers.

Brad retrieved a pair of pliers from the toolbox and picked up an object in a small pouch he carried on his belt. Brad stood before the chair and smoked silently, waiting for Gabe to look up. When he did, Brad held up the pliers that held the small nugget of melted silver for him to see.

"This isn't enough to kill you. But it will prevent any wounded part of you from changing. If I put this in the remains of your claw, unless you're able to dig them out they'll never change, they'll never heal, and you'll be stuck with those wounds forever."

Gabe just glared at him. Brad crouched down in the puddle of blood under Gabe's left hand. He tried to take the hand, but Gabe curled his fingers into a fist, refusing Brad access to them. Brad went and pulled a nail out of the toolbox. Returning to Gabe, he began to press the nail into the center of Gabe's wrist. The pressure point where the nail entered caused Gabe's hand to flex open, but Brad didn't stop. He pushed the nail through into the arm of the chair. Gabe's glare did little to penetrate Brad's cold gaze.

Brad picked the pliers back up and slowly but deliberately began to push the silver into the exposed wound of Gabe's severed little claw. The howl of pain was deafening. Curses filled the basement along with the terror of knowing that what Brad had said was true.

"Talk to me Gabriel. Tell me what I need to know."

"IT was the Council. They sent the Ferros after Sam's parents. I tried to stop them, but they turned on me. They fought me and took me back to the council. My punishment was to watch Sam to see what would happen." Gabe dropped his head, breathing hard to regain himself.

"What else? What did you plan on doing with her at your place?"

"I was supposed to kill her. The council found out that she was changing and realized the prophecies might be true... I was supposed to kill her."

"Would you?"

Gabe shook his head no, but hissed. "Yes."

"Tell me about the prophecies Gabriel." Brad realized that the other, Gabe, was fighting his way back to the surface.

"The prophecies say when I get out of this chair, I'm gonna kill you and have a little fun with your family."

Brad punched Gabe in the face, sending the chair over backwards. It came to rest on its side fifteen feet away.

"Holy shit!" Exclaimed Chaz. "That was fucking unbelievable." Chaz glided over to Gabe. "He's out cold. Want me to wake him?"

"No. Let him sleep for a while. I need to regain my composure. No one threatens my family." Brad tossed the pliers onto the workbench. "He's dead Chaz. No matter what Sam says, I'm going to kill him."

Chaz nodded in agreement. "Family is all there is Brad. Should I set him up?"

"Nope. I want him to remember what happened when he comes to. Let's get something to eat."

Chaz was on his feet, following Brad like a puppy waiting for a treat. Brad looked over his shoulder at Chaz when they got to the kitchen. "You need to watch yourself Chaz. I know you like this, but if you're not careful, it will consume you, and you'll wind up hurting an innocent one day, just because you like to see it."

"Brad, I wouldn't do that. I-"

"Chaz, I've seen it. And you don't want me hunting you." Brad took his necklace out from inside his shirt and tossed it to Chaz. It was a bear claw, six and a half inches long. Chaz let out a low whistle. "You kill this thing?"

"That belonged to the Were that turned Aimee and me. It's kind of a long story. I'll tell you some other time. But know this. I was human at the time, and I used a knife."

Chaz's mouth dropped open. "Are you shittin' me? A knife?" With that, Brad whipped out an oversized, military issue knife. He handed it to Chaz while he went about getting coffee ready for the two of them.

"I had no idea. How bad were you mangled though? You got to tell me that."

Brad grinned. "Well, my shoulder got pretty chewed up."

Chaz stood there waiting for the rest.

"Oh…" Brad added. "… and I broke my ankle trying to get

back to camp. But that was before I fought the Were."

Chaz shook his head and laughed. "You are un-fucking-believable. But you're right; I don't want you hunting me. I don't think I could handle it."

"Survive," Brad corrected. "You wouldn't survive it." Brad handed Chaz a coffee mug and took back his knife. "Let's finish it."

Chaz nodded and the two went into the basement. As they walked down the steps, they heard Gabe arguing with himself. "We cannot tell them." "But we must." "Then we die. We take our secrets to the grave." "I don't want to die." "Neither do I, but we can't tell about the council's plans to harness Sam and control her. If they know how powerful she is, how much she could control all the Were's, they will use her themselves." "But I..." "Shh... I think they are back."

Brad went over to where Gabe lay on the floor, still chained to the chair. He grabbed the chair and lifted it up with one hand, smacking Gabe's head against the floor in the process.

"Oops. I guess I should be more careful." Brad righted the chair and sat it back where it had originally been in the room.

"Now then, we were discussing the prophecies. Which ones have come to pass, which ones haven't?" Brad took a drag of his cigarette as he finished speaking.

"Let's see... I've been captured, tortured, so those have come to pass." He closed his eyes as though he were thinking. "Yet to come is me killing you, fucking your wife, and eating your little girl. I think that's it."

"Gabe, you're an idiot. I'm going to let you have a taste of what your life, what's left of it at least, is going to feel like." Brad took his time, sauntered over to Gabe, and stood behind him. He placed his hands on either side of his head. "Remember how this felt last time? It's going to be worse this time."

As Brad finished speaking, he forced Gabe to his human form. Gabe screamed. Brad then forced him into his Curreno form. The shift back again to human was quick, followed by a brief change into full wolf before going back to human. After the quick succession of changes, Brad drew out what was left of Gabe's claws. The changes had been so fast that there was no time for them to heal.

Brad let go of Gabe as he continued to scream and thrash. Chaz looked at Brad with a mixture of awe and horror. "How do you do that?" Chaz whispered.

"It's a gift." Brad stated matter-of-factly before lighting another cigarette. Gabe slowly stopped thrashing, and his screams tapered off to moans, but his body began to shake of its own accord. The pain and fury of the changes had rattled him, possibly sent him into shock. Brad looked at Gabe without emotion, and then started to grin.

Gabe's fury took over. He refused yet again to tell any information. He instead began to sing. "99 bottles of beer on the wall…"

Brad turned and picked up the pliers. As he approached Gabe, his determination set, he changed his mind. "Chaz, work him over." Brad paused and lit another cigarette. "The old-fashioned way."

Chaz grinned broadly, as he cracked his knuckles and stretched out his hands and arms. He took his time, making sure that every muscle in his body was loosened up before he began. Chaz's first swing took Gabe under the jaw, ending his song. The second punch cracked one of Gabe's ribs. The next few throws landed on arms and legs.

Brad was impressed. Most people beat a captive in the head only. Chaz knew enough to spread out the pain and damage, giving each area time to recover, if only a little, before it was assaulted again. Brad watched for a while before excusing himself.

"What," asked Chaz. "You getting squeamish on me?"

"Nope. But I am out of coffee. Can I bring you anything?"

"Water, maybe some lunch if Claire's cooking yet."

Brad nodded and headed up the steps. He found Claire and Marc in the kitchen. Brad nodded and poured a cup of coffee before taking a seat at the table. Marc passed him the sugar before asking.

"Well, how's it going?"

"He is very determined not to tell us anything. Chaz is working him over now." Brad sipped his coffee. "You want to help?"

"No. I'm not much on physical violence."

"You're a fucking werewolf. How can you avoid violence?"

"Bradley!" Exclaimed Claire.

"Sorry ma'am. I forget myself sometimes."

"At least you don't smoke anywhere but the basement." Claire had her back to Brad as she bent over the stove, so she didn't see him place the unlit cigarette behind his ear and drop the lighter back in his pocket. Marc smiled over his cup.

"It was decided that there should always be two people with Gabe to make sure that he is treated right, or at least not abused."

Brad sprayed coffee across the table. "You're kidding, right?" Marc shook his head. Brad continued. "In case you've forgotten, we're interrogating a prisoner. A prisoner, I might add, who spent countless years as a Were general for the Council. He has more constitution and determination than anyone that I've ever met. He hasn't broken yet because there's a second person in him that gives him the will power of two men. Chaz isn't going to do anything permanent to him. Just beat him up for a while."

"How long's a while?" John asked from the doorway.

"A few hours, maybe less. That okay with you?" Brad made the question a challenge.

John held up his hands. "I just wanted to know how long I could let Sam sleep. We're on the same side here."

"Sorry," Brad said. "I don't like my methods questioned. I took stock of him from the beginning, that's why I know he'll break soon. You see, I could break him in five minutes." Claire turned to look at Brad as he continued. "But everyone in this house, with the possible exception of Sam, wants this guy to suffer. I'm doing for everyone else what they aren't allowed to do."

Marc looked at Brad in a new light. John nodded his agreement, and Claire announced that breakfast was ready, and if he'd like to take it down to Chaz.

"I'd say call him up, but I do not think eating while doing that kind of work would bother him."

"I think you're right Claire."

By 1:30, Brad was bored watching Chaz beat up Gabe. Brad went over to the workbench and retrieved the pliers and silver particles. He never even hesitated as he approached Gabe's mangled left hand. The first piece of silver slid effortlessly into what was left of Gabe's ring finger claw. Gabe howled. Brad shoved one into his middle finger. When Brad got to the index, he stopped with the silver half way in, looking up at Gabe. Then slid it out slowly, letting the pain wash over Gabe like fire, before shoving it all the way in. Brad decided to do the thumb too, for good measure, before standing up and turning away from Gabe.

"You're not talking yet," Brad said it clearly, so Gabe could hear him. "I want to know who all is on the Council, where they meet, what the prophecies entail, what happened to make you decide not to follow the council's orders, who killed Sam's parents? Gabe, I want everything. But I want Sam to hear it first. Take a few minutes to recover Gabe. Chaz, go get the others, they'll want to hear this too."

Brad caught Gabe's attention with the change in his voice.

"My daughter told me to tell you that everything will be all right... Gabriel."

Gabe nodded and lowered his head.

John was the one that woke Sam up.

"Sam, it's time. Gabe's ready to talk."

Sam stirred and then bolted up from her slumber.

"What? He's going to talk?"

"We need to hurry. We don't know how much longer he will comply with answering."

John didn't have to tell Sam again. She threw on her shirt and shoes and ran for the stairs, followed closely by John.

When the others came down, they stood at the workbench, glancing at the array of tools that Brad had used, trying without success not to imagine how they had been used. Sam stood in front of Gabe, looking at the damage that Brad had inflicted, but showing no emotion. She knew it would be bad when she asked Brad to do it, but this was the first she had ever seen of his work.

"I have a few questions," Sam said. Gabe stared up at her.

"Will I get the answers I want and need?"

Gabe nodded his head. "Yes."

"Did you kill my parents?"

"No. I refused, and that is why I was sentenced as your watchdog."

"Why refuse?"

"Because I knew of the prophecies. I knew there was a good chance…" Gabe paused to catch his breath. The torture had taken too much out of him. His words were slow and measured in an attempt to keep from moving anything that didn't have to.

"Good chance for what?" Sam prompted.

"A good chance that you'd be the one to fulfill the prophecies."

"What prophecies?"

Gabe's eyes began to fog over and his voice went monotone. It was as though he spoke from another place. "There will be one born with the spirit of the ancients. She will be the vessel to those who choose to heed the calling and bring forth a new way, the right way. Once she is reborn of two houses, this will come to pass."

"How do you know it's me?"

"She will be pure of heart. Her eyes will hold the fire of legends burning within them."

"Why did you kidnap me?"

Gabe came back from the far place and took a few staggering breaths. "Please… a few moments to catch my breath?"

Brad looked to Sam to see if he should make Gabe continue. She shook her head once before turning back to Gabe. "Rest. I'll be back in a few minutes."

Sam went upstairs to get some fresh air followed by Nicki, Claire and Aimee. They all stepped out onto the porch in the late afternoon sun.

Nicki sat down and hung here head. "How does he do that?" She hadn't directed the question at anyone, but they all knew it was for Aimee.

"He says that when he has to do this kind of work, he sees nothing. People aren't real to him. It used to scare me, but then I realized that he would never hurt Katie or me, so I accepted it."

Sam continued to look off in the distance. Claire sat next to her and put her arm around Sam's shoulders.

CHAPTER SIXTEEN

The men were still in the basement. Marc, John and Kenny stood rigid, their stares trying to bore into Gabe. Chaz was pacing, waiting for Gabe to try something so that he'd have a reason to hurt the prisoner again. Brad leaned against the workbench smoking, not seeming to be paying attention to anyone.

The girls came back down and Sam handed Brad a glass of water and motioned to Gabe. Brad took the glass and knelt down by him.

"Gabe," he whispered. Gabe jerked away, anticipating the pain he thought was coming. "Gabriel. Here's some water." Gabe looked at Brad, uncertain what was about to happen. Gabe saw in his mind's eye, Brad trying to drown him with the glass of water. "It's okay Gabriel, I won't hurt you."

Gabe's eye flicked towards Chaz.

"I won't let Chaz hurt you either."

Chaz's physical bearing changed visibly. His shoulders slumped, he dropped his head, and Brad could have sworn that he saw the lower lip pout. Chaz walked over to the wall and slid down it to sit on the floor.

Gabe took a drink, Brad holding the glass for him. Gabe looked to Sam, thanking her with his eyes before continuing.

"I am sick of writing. Writing, logging, following. What you are doing, who you are with, where, when. I've had enough. I long for battles, blood, and victory. I was born a warrior, trained to fight and lead men. I was tired of babysitting. All I had to do was to take you in or kill you myself. So easy. They would have been fine with it either way."

"Who?"

"The members of the Council... the Directorate. At first, they scoffed at the prophecies, until the union was made between your parents, a forbidden union. I was watching them, reporting to the Council anything that happened. It was spy work, not babysitting. But still, I would have rather done something else.

You were born and still I was ordered to watch. Then you began to show signs."

"What kinds of signs?"

"Your ability to communicate with animals... Sensing, and even absorbing others auras... Yes, all signs... all strong." Gabe stopped and looked at Brad. Brad picked up the glass of water and held it for Gabe to drink.

Gabe continued. "Your parents got wind of me and rushed you here, to your Aunt Claire. I reported the aversion and was ordered to eliminate them. I returned with my orders but couldn't do it. I confessed the Council's intentions to your parents. I then called in my men who were loyal and ordered them to defend Paulette and Thomas." A tear ran down Gabe's cheek. "Our attempt at protection was futile. I lost thirty men that day. Others along with me were taken away. Afterwards, they made us watch your parents' deaths." Gabe's eyes were filled with tears now.

"They didn't deserve to die the way they did. No one does." He turned his gaze on Brad, hatred swimming in the tears. "The council forced the change on them. Their beasts ripped through the human shells. I can't forget their screams of agony as they died in the process. There just wasn't enough room for the beast to shed its human skin."

Gabe turned his attention back to Sam. "I was hung by my arms. They ripped the skin from my body in strips. Strip by strip, taking their time. When one man would tire, another took over." Gabe paused and looked at Chaz. Chaz merely stared back at him, letting him know he'd start again now if he were allowed. "They made tiny cuts along my exposed muscles with silver knives." Gabe shuddered visibly. "It lasted for three months... every day... from morning until night. Never letting me change to heal... I never found out what happened to my men. After I was allowed to heal, I was taken before the Council.

"I was sentenced to watch you and keep records and to report any signs of the prophecies. I did, until six months ago. Then I stopped reporting. I rebelled."

"Why?" asked Sam.

"I can see nothing but good in you, and in the prophecies being fulfilled."

"Explain the prophecies."

"It is hard to explain." Gabe sighed

"We don't have much time, but I will let you rest a moment longer." Sam turned and went up the stairs, John following.

As the two of them stood there, holding each other, they let the silence speak for them. It was a lot of information to assimilate. Brad came upstairs and checked the time. 7:30 pm.

"It's going to be dark soon. I told Claire I'd grill so that she could hear the rest."

Sam walked up to Brad and gave him a hug. "Thank you. It's not easy to hear about your parents' death, but I'm glad I heard it."

Brad squeezed her hand gently as she headed down the stairs. John started to pass Brad but was stopped dead by a giant paw on his chest. John looked up at Brad.

"You hurt her, and you'll answer to me." John nodded, knowing that Brad was being sincere in his 'protective, older brother' actions.

Gabe was talking as John came off the steps. "I can't explain prophecy. Once you hear it, you just know it when you see it. You are the prophecies coming true... the living prophecy."

"Stop saying that!" Sam snapped, taking a step towards Gabe. John stepped forward and put his hand on Sam's shoulder to comfort her.

"But you are. The way you are progressing, the time frame. It's all written, and you're fulfilling it."

"STOP IT!" Screamed Sam.

"You will be reborn unto the beast and bring revolution from the Turned and serve it to the Truebloods." Gabe's voice and eyes had changed. He was quoting prophecy again.

"The One, will obliterate the union of the clans, our way of life will crumble, and the structure as it is known will have to be rebuilt from the ruins. The One will do these things." Gabe's eye's returned to normal. "You are doing these things."

"I haven't even 'turned' yet."

"It's close. Even your union with the Turned has been foretold. You are the epitome of anarchy."

"Why didn't you kill me?"

"I couldn't. Over the years, you have weakened me."

Sam crossed her arms. "If you weakened, it was because of yourself. Maybe you just got old."

Gabe tried to lunge out of his chair, barely moving with the chains holding him down. "I did not weaken! I am not old! I have commanded hundreds of men and killed scores!" Gabe was panting heavily, a thin line of spittle running from the corner of his mouth. I DO NOT WEAKEN!" He screamed.

Chaz chose that moment to strike Gabe in the side of the mouth, ending his tirade. "Cool it or I'll do it for you."

Gabe glared at Chaz and spat blood at his feet. Chaz looked at Gabe and smiled.

Brad had the grill going and was sitting in the kitchen letting the charcoal settle. Katie came in and threw her arms around his neck. "You sent the bad man away daddy."

"Did I? I wasn't sure. He's still there though right. He's still in Gabe, just sleeping."

"He's still here, but not in Gabriel."

"What do you mean honey?" Brad asked as he swung Katie up onto his lap.

"He's hiding." Katie looked around to make sure no one else was around. "He's outside… in one of the soldiers."

Brad bolted out of his chair with Katie in his arms before setting her gently on her feet. "Go downstairs with mommy. Tell the others I sent you down and that I'll be right there." Katie nodded and skipped down the steps.

Brad walked out onto the porch and stretched his back, scenting the air. They were out there, and there were a lot of them. Brad lit a cigarette and walked out to his truck, trying to get a fix on the soldiers. There were too many.

"Who were the members of the Council at the time of my parents' murders?"

"There were three other than your parents. A Valden, a

Saedar, and a Ferros."

"Was it a unanimous decision between the three?"

"No."

"Who opposed?"

"The leader and Commander of the Ferros. Klasos Duncan."

"Then I guess he doesn't have to die when I find them." Sam turned her back as she walked away.

Brad grinned to himself as he opened the cab of his truck. He dropped the seat forward and pulled out two oversized duffle bags from the extended cab. Pushing the door closed with his foot, he headed back up to the house.

While he walked, Brad took a mental note of what all he had in the bags. There were 100 rounds of .45 auto for his custom pistols, a Springfield XD 9mm, two Uzi's with four 20-round clips each, a Colt M-4 carbine assault rifle with six 30-round magazines, a Beneli semi-automatic twelve gauge that would hold nine shells, and a handful of special hand grenades.

Brad nonchalantly locked the back door as he entered. He went to the basement steps and heard Sam as he started down.

"I'm done with him, for now."

"We've got problems," Brad said, as he reached the bottom step. He set down the bags and went over to Gabe.

"Nicki, heal him." Brad went over to the bags and unzipped one.

"His left hand won't heal with the silver gunk in it. There's a nail in his wrist too." Nikki rhymed off the problem heal spots.

"Chaz!" Brad said without looking up. Chaz grabbed the hammer and removed the nail, slowly.

Brad pulled the 12 gauge out of the bag and tossed it to Aimee with a box of shells. She turned to the workbench and began loading it without a word. Brad then produced the two Uzi's, tossed them to Kenny and Marc without hesitation, and then tossed them the magazines for the guns. Brad moved to the next bag as Chaz came over and looked inside.

Chaz let out a low whistle. Brad passed him the M-4 and a belt that held all of the magazines. He looked up at John as he tossed him the Springfield XD and one spare magazine. Everyone was still silent as Brad stood up.

"There are over thirty soldiers outside, surrounding the house. All of the guns are loaded with my own personal bullets. Titanium tipped silver jackets with compressed silver powder." The Were's all looked around at each other uncomfortably.

"The tips will penetrate the body armor. The jacket will keep the wound from closing, and the silver will penetrate the blood stream, killing them in about three seconds. If, and this is a big if, they are in some state of change. Otherwise, it's just a bullet, so watch your shot placement." Brad paused and looked at Nicki. She nodded to him and he went to stand in front of Gabe. The old man looked up at him.

"Gabe, when the fighting starts… run. If I see you with any of the soldiers, hostage or not, you die." Everyone but Sam started to object. Brad held up his hand and silence returned.

"We're not through Gabe. Not by a long shot. I will find you, no matter where you run." Gabe nodded once very slowly, returning the welcome in his eyes. Brad changed his left hand and pinched the chains holding Gabe to the chair in two.

Brad turned back to the group. "Kenny, place them."

"Aimee, you've got the back door. Marc, the front. Chaz, go up to Sam's place and provide sniper fire covering the vehicles. Claire, I want you, Nicki and Katie in the bomb shelter."

Nicki began to protest.

"You have to be safe, we might need some healing when this is over. John, once it starts - get Sam to a vehicle and get her the hell out of here."

"I'm not running and leaving you all behind," Sam demanded.

"No, you're surviving. You heard what Gabe said. You have to live, no matter what." The others agreed.

"Alright?!" Brad proclaimed, a question as well as a command. "One more thing."

He moved around the group.

"These are a last resort. We all know too much to be taken. If you are overrun and there is no chance you'll make it, pull the pin. These are sterling silver hand grenades. They have a blast radius of thirty yards. You won't survive." Brad knelt on the floor and removed his t-shirt. He slid his arms through the shoulder holster that held both of his .45's.

"Where will you be?" asked Aimee. "Not that I need to ask."

Brad grinned at her and winked. "I'll be around." He placed the spare magazines for his pistols into his pockets. "Everybody ready?" They all nodded. "Good. Let's play."

Claire, Nicki and Katie all climbed into the shelter while the others went up stairs to take their places. Brad was about to shut the hidden door when Katie piped up.

"They're scared daddy, outside. They're afraid because you aren't supposed to be here."

"I know sweetie. That's why we'll win." Katie giggled and gave Brad the thumbs up.

Brad stopped at the top of the stairs and made sure all his knives were n place. The oversized military grade knife strapped to his back, and each boot held its Safe Keeper III snuggly. Brad grinned at Aimee as he walked past her. "I love you."

"I love you too. Just be sure you leave some for us. And don't play the hero."

He looked over his shoulder at her. "I never play." With that, he kicked the back door open, surprising a soldier on the steps.

"Howdy, fucker!" Brad said cheerfully as he shot the man between the eyes. Brad took two steps and dove off the porch as all hell broke loose around him. He came up running, a pistol in each hand firing into the darkness, his heightened eyesight allowing him to make each shot count.

Aimee let her beast surge just below the surface as she opened fire, killing two with her first shots.

Mark's Uzi sprayed death into the night, tearing the legs or arms off those his bullets found.

The sharp crack of Chaz's M-4 reigned death from above.

Kenny charged straight out the front door making a beeline for the vehicles. Sam was right behind him with John on her heels. A solder ran out in front of them while Kenny was firing to his right. John pulled up his 9mm and placed a round through the center of the body armor, sending the soldier over backwards. The shot had been next to Sam's ear, but she was more focused on getting to the truck than her hearing at that point. Kenny leapt into the back of John's truck, providing cover fire for Sam.

Aimee was on the back porch using the shotgun to decorate blood and body parts over the yard, stopping only to reload the gun. Marc was doing his fair share of damage, once he learned how to handle the recoil from the automatic pistol.

Sam yanked the door open and dove into the cab, landing on the floorboard. John was right behind her, turning the ignition without shutting the door. He heard the sound of bullets punching through the bed of his truck. He was about to check on Kenny when he heard the yell. "GO GO GO!"

As John hit the gas, he caught a glimpse of something out of his right eye. Without even looking, he raised his pistol and fired as he sped off down the lane.

Kenny was crouched behind Nicki's Camaro and thought he heard laughter. He glanced around and realized it was coming from the direction of the house. He looked up over the hood and saw Chaz standing on the third floor porch off Sam's place, laughing hysterically.

"Come on you pussies," Chaz tormented. "Is that the best you've got? Come and get it you sons of bitches."

"Ain't that he truth." Kenny heard from right beside him.

He spun towards the voice only to have his turn halted by Brad. "Careful. Don't worry about looking around, just kill the enemy."

Brad reloaded his pistols and slapped Kenny on the shoulder.

"Damn that boy needs help." Brad said in reference to Chaz.

"See ya later." As he disappeared into the night.

Aimee spun around and sprayed the head of a soldier over the man behind him with her shotgun. The second man froze in place by the gore that covered him. Aimee knew she was out of shells and took advantage of his hesitation, stepped forward and kicked him in the groin with all her might.

The man gasped and doubled over in pain. Aimee slid one shell into her gun, chambered it, and shot the man in the neck, removing his head with no amount of delicacy. The wall next to her erupted in splinters as she dove back inside to reload. She was feeding shells into the gun when three soldiers charged in after her. Her beast roared to life and her change into Curreno was instant. Her 8 foot Were opened the first soldier from groin to neck, leaving him dead on his feet. The second died when she shoved her claws through his chest and out his back, grabbing the man behind him by the throat. There were others outside who witnessed this and decided to find an easier target. Aimee's instinct to protect Katie was in full swing. She went out into the night, rampaging and killing.

Marc emptied the magazine in his Uzi. He reached for another and realized that he was out of ammunition. As he turned into the house for cover, he saw what happened with Aimee. As she left the house, Marc ran to get her abandoned shotgun. He shouldered it and turned in time to annihilate two soldiers coming in the front door. He loaded more shells and decided to remain in the kitchen to guard the basement door. He shot a soldier running past the window and was answered with a volley from somewhere else on the porch. He knew from the angle where the shots were coming from and started to shoot through the walls. His attempt was answered with a scream as one of the soldiers tried to run away, his right arm missing below the elbow.

Brad ran through a group of solders, shooting each of them in the back without missing a step. He dropped his pistols and drew his big knife from behind his back. He was out in the woods, hunting. The gunfire was lessening, the fight almost over. Brad slowed his pace and scented the air. He found what he was looking for and set out again.

The Were commander was standing alone. Brad crept up behind him and spoke softly. "Hello, General."

The General spun and felt the knife blade pass through his ballistic vest, slicing the top of his heart. The General refused to give up though. He raised his pistol towards Brad's head. Brad smiled at him and twisted the knife in a figure 8, quartering the General's heart. The knife pulled free as the General's lifeless body sank to the ground.

Brad crept back towards the house, hearing only the occasional report from Chaz's rifle. Chaz was good. He was slowly searching the night from his perch, finding those few soldiers living, and correcting the problem.

Chaz was having the time of his life. He began to whistle the theme of the seven dwarves in Snow White, as he calmly and methodically assassinated the soldiers. He realized from his vantage point that he was able to shoot most of them through the heart or lungs as they gave him a profile. Then he discovered a new game. If he shot them in the throat, they'd flop around like fish on dry land. Chaz giggled to himself. He remembered Brad's warning from earlier, but decided it didn't apply under the present circumstances. This was war.

As he moved, Brad scented the wind. He could smell only death away from the house. He smiled to himself. He had counted over 30 soldiers while stalking the woods and dealing death. And the group he was part of, five of them not counting John and Sam had annihilated them all. Brad reached the drive after retrieving his pistols. He stopped and looked off in the distance, hoping Sam and John were okay.

As Brad walked into the house, he looked at the group assembled in the hallway before him. They were all covered in blood and gore. Marc and Kenny had obviously, and literally, fought tooth and claw, as had Aimee. Aimee sat quietly, waiting to hear that it was clear. It was obvious she had changed. She was naked and covered in blood, and there was a glassy look in her eye that Brad only saw when she was very, very aroused. Brad winked at her.

"Go get the girls from downstairs. Then get a shower. They're all dead. You all did well. Tell Nicki to hurry."

Brad called after Aimee. "Kenny needs that leg looked at."

Kenny looked down for the first time and noticed that he was injured.

"Shit. When did that happen?" he gasped.

"When you leapt out of the truck bed, the bullet hitting you probably saved John's life."

"I guess he owes me one," Kenny grinned.

"Yeah. Good luck getting him to pay up," responded Marc. They all laughed, the tension of the fight easing a little.

Chaz came skipping down the stars, his eyes bright with excitement. "That was fun! Can we do it again?"

Brad shook his head. "You, my friend, need serious help."

John drove through the evening. The sun was touching the horizon, throwing shadows through the cab of his truck. Sam stayed huddled in the floor of the passenger side, shaking. They rode in silence for nearly 20 miles. Only when they were through town and closing in on Moorehead did John speak.

"I think it's safe to get up now."

Sam just sat there.

John looked over to Sam for only a moment, and found her crying silently into her knees. He wanted to stop the truck and comfort her, but he knew that he needed to get her to safety first. He tried talking to her again.

"Once we make it to Moorehead, I'm going to find a hotel."

Sam spoke in panic. "But you can't. You always have to give your driver's license. Who knows who would be working the counter?" No, we can't do that." Sam shook her head violently.

"Sam, there are hotels that don't require ID. I'm sure it won't be the best of accommodations, but we can rest and wait until it's safe to go back."

"It'll never be safe, never be over."

John didn't try to reason with her. He just sat quietly and drove. After a while, Sam climbed up to the seat of the truck, deliberately staying hunkered down.

As signs started popping up announcing Moorehead, John pulled off one of the exits and headed down the road. He drove through more questionable outskirts of the town and found what he was looking for. The motel was a small, two story building. There was a dirty neon green and blue sign out front that buzzed, "Mo-rehead Motel." Someone had obviously knocked an "O" for a joke. John pulled up to the front entrance and put the car in park.

"I want you to stay in the truck while I get the room. If anyone comes out, take off."

He leaned in and gave her a quick kiss of reassurance before heading inside.

Sam scooted over to the driver's seat and put the truck in drive. She sat with one foot on the brake and one on the gas. About five minutes later, John came out and got into the passenger side.

"We're round back, 214."

Sam drove around to the back and parked in the most inconspicuous place she could find. John grabbed a bag from the back of the seat and took Sam's hand as they exited the truck. He lead the way up the back stairs, past the unconscious wino on the floor, past the walls of non-descript wallpaper due to the grime and bad lighting. The carpet tended to stick to the soles of their shoes as they made it down the hall. Once they were to the room, they locked the door behind them and immediately pushed the dresser against the door. John pulled out his .45mm and laid it on the table, near a broken mirror. Sam went into the bathroom and found two towels. She brought both out to the bed and sat on them. John tried to call Marc but couldn't get a signal in the room. After much silent frustration, he turned to Sam.

"I'm going to need to walk outside to call Marc. I'll leave the gun with you. Point it at the door. If you don't hear this knock..." he knocked three times slowly on the table where the gun sat. "... once the door opens, start shooting." Sam took the gun and took the safety off. She handled the gun, getting used to the weight and then looked up at John and nodded. John smiled slightly and headed to the door. He turned before leaving and asked. "Would you like me to call in some pizza? I know that I need to gather some energy and I would rather do it the human way..." John shrugged.

"Sure. Get some water too. Thanks"

John walked out the door and Sam sat in the dark room lit by only a tiny window that no human could pass through over the age of eight. The window threw light on the door, putting Sam in the shadows of the wall. She crouched down in the corner of the room and aimed for the door. She had positioned one of the chairs to place her hands on, to steady herself. The silence was deafening as she sat and waited.

Brad, Kenny, Chaz and Marc all scoured the area. They made sure the dead were in fact dead and then proceeded to place them in the mass grave they dug with a backhoe about a half mile from Claire's house. They loaded the bodies into the bucket of the backhoe after searching the bodies for additional information and weapons. Out of the thirty bodies, they collected eight boxes filled with firearms, ammo and ID's. Claire and Nicki went through the wallets of the deceased and set a plan to track down more information on who attacked them.

Claire pushed one of the boxes away from her. "There's nothing here to help us."

"There must be something here, that can help us," Aimee said, as she peeked into one wallet. She held the wallet in her hand as she slumped in her chair.

"I... I can't go through these anymore. I can't keep opening wallets to see family pictures staring back at me. I just can't." Aimee knew that it could as well be one of their own wallets being peeked through. She held back her tears and turned to the weapons. She began to unload each weapon to get an inventory of their defense.

Claire topped her head over one of the many boxes excitedly. "Look, what do you think this might be?" She handed Aimee a business card that had archaic tribal signs on it. Claire knew the symbols but could not depict what they said. Aimee peered down at the small card and squinted to see the print.

"This is Valden. Only pompous asses would advertize themselves this way. Let me take this out to Brad."

"Does he know how to read that?" Aimee shrugged. "I don't know. At least it beats walking out to find Kenny and Chaz. They are setting up trip flares right now and I really don't want to set off a booby trap."

Claire sighed with the thought of the battle that had just taken place on her property. She was far enough from town that no one would pay much attention. She was sure though, that she would be getting a nosey cop out soon. She got up from the table and decided to start on dinner. It was going to be a hodge-podge of meals for the group but she didn't care.

Aimee went out to the porch where Brad sat on one of the chairs, writing out his list. One would think by the way he sat so leisurely that he was planning a grocery list. Aimee came up from behind and put her hand on his shoulder. "What did you come up with?"

Brad put out his dying cigarette and picked up his coffee mug to take a drink before he answered. "I have Kenny and Chaz setting up trip flares and mortars around the perimeter. Kenny knows what he's doing and Chaz needs to keep busy. We have points laid out here, here, and here." Brad pointed to a makeshift map of the property. "If I know how they work, they will attempt to take the house through this pattern." Brad ran his finger down three different areas.

"Do we have enough weapons?" Brad took Aimee's hand from his shoulder and kissed it lightly. She smiled as he did.

"We have enough weapons, but we need ammo. I have jotted down the type of weapons that we have acquired." Brad let a slight chuckle escape his lips.

"Acquired? You sound so... professional."

"Business is business, right?"

Aimee never smiled during her answer. Brad cleared his throat and continued talking out his list. "We'll need to make a run into town."

"Where are you going to get all that is needed?" Brad grinned.

"I have most of it stashed away, as for the rest.... There are a few people who owe me big. It's time to make them pay up. We'll have more than enough."

Aimee handed the business card to Brad. "Can you make out what this says?"

Brad reached in and grabbed his reading glasses. He ran his fingers over the symbols and mumbled to himself before he answered. "It's a card for Riley Green. He's the second in command for the Valden, like the Vice President or such. Heh - be it like those guys to have business cards printed up."

Aimee took a seat next to Brad. "Does this mean that we're in big trouble?"

"Well, if this guy has a business card like this in his wallet, I'm sure it's not a great sign, but nothing that we can't handle."

"Are you kidding me? We're not an army, Brad. We're going to get killed."

Brad turned serious for only a moment to respond to her. "You're safe with me." Brad tried to ease his soberness. "I might just give ole' Riley a call. It's been awhile since I have talked with him."

"Oh, so you know the guy?" Aimee said shocked. "Yeah, biggest faggot you'd ever meet. He has a way about him that makes people fall under his spell. I never get too close or look him straight in the eye. I'm not going to be one of his boy toys."

Claire was stirring a pot of noodles for the big serving of spaghetti when the phone rang. She rushed over, hoping that it would be Sam or John.

"Hello?" Claire answered earnestly. "Ms. Autry, this is Sherriff Clark. I got a call on some gunfire that was going around your property. Is everything ok?" Claire tried to sound nonchalant. "Sherriff, it's so good to hear your voice! How have you been?"

"Fine, Ms. Autry. Are you ok?"

"Oh yes, we have a lot of people staying with us. Brad Parks has asked if he could bring a hunting group onto the property. They have set up a firing range by the lake. Oh, I guess I should have called to let you know. I'm so sorry. It's just been a long time since we have had so many… visitors." Claire strained her last word.

The Sherriff replied. "Are you sure that everything's ok?"

"Yes, Yes. Everything is fine. I just get so nervous around the gunfire, that's all. Oh, there might be, more. But don't be alarmed. Target practice and hunting."

"Ok, I'll take your word for it. You know that you can call me if you get into any trouble, right?"

"That is very kind of you Sherriff, for thinking of my safety. But I'm ok. Well, I don't mean to be rude, but I have a pot of noodles boiling over. I need to go Sherriff; it was nice talking to you. You should come out for dinner some night. Bye." And she hung up the phone before he could answer or say goodbye. With a wipe of her brow, she went back to preparing dinner. She just hoped that she had enough to feed them all.

Kenny and Chaz began to strategically place the different colored trip flares Brad had devised on an area map. They set different colors to mark where the opponent would be coming from as well as how fast they were closing in. Green for the farthest parts of the property, clear across the lake. Yellow just in front of the lake. Orange for the front of the property and red for everywhere close to the house.

Chaz held the bulk of the antipersonnel items as they trounced through the woods that outlined the property. Chaz became bored quickly and began to sigh heavily and roll his eyes at Kenny, as he was instructed to place the next device. Kenny, still filled with anger and frustration from the previous battle, became agitated with Chaz's attitude. "You know, you could go back to the house, I can finish this myself."

Chaz seemed to be looking for some type of confrontation for some unseen reason, or maybe he wasn't finished with the battle that ended so abruptly earlier.

"No, old man, I can carry your load for you." Chaz, not knowing what hit him, found himself on his back with a full-blown wolf on him as it reared down on his throat. Chaz began to struggle, but the wolf locked down harder to show that he meant business. Chaz lay still even through his own growls of anger for being bested by an old geezer. Chaz had 20 years on Kenny at least, he thought to himself, and here he was, getting bested by an older man.

Chaz tried to swallow but was unable to due to the hold.

He tried to speak. "OK, OK... You got me."

The Wolf began to bite down but then stopped when it saw the fear begin to creep up in Chaz's eyes. The wolf backed completely off him and began to morph back to human. Chaz lay on his back for a moment to give himself time to rub his neck, weighing up the decision whether to continue the confrontation. He watched as Kenny changed back quickly and decided not to further the discussion.

Kenny picked up the map where he had laid it off to the side, and continued as if nothing had happened. Chaz never once sighed nor showed any signs of contempt for the rest of task.

Once the claymores and tripwires were set, they made it back to the house. Chaz went straight for the kitchen where the smell of food lured him in. Kenny made a Bee-line for Brad. Aimee had just stepped back inside when Kenny walked onto the porch. Brad let a grin slip his lips. "Uh Kenny? What happened to your clothes, man?"

Kenny grinned back as his chest puffed out a bit.

"I had to teach a young pup a lesson."

Brad shook his head. "Disobedient? Chaz?"

"Yeah, that lil' turd was trying my patience. I know he thinks that just because he's about a foot taller, and a lot younger than me, that he can take me. Maybe with the right training he could. But I had a hold on him before he even knew to shit himself."

Brad began to laugh. Kenny joined in just as Chaz came out with a sandwich in his hand.

Chaz spoke up, spitting chunks of bread out everywhere. "Yeah, you got me, old man. I don't know how, but you got me. Truce already."

Kenny came up to Chaz and put his arm around his shoulder.

"Chaz, I am a retired special forces sergeant. I was trained on honing in on my abilities for killing. I could be eighty years old and still take your untrained ass. Now, if you're a good boy and do as you're told, I just might begin to train you."

Kenny didn't wait to see his expression; he could sense the excitement in Chaz as walked into the house to fetch something to wear. Chaz stood there with a mouthful of half chewed food, daydreaming about the chance to move like Kenny. Brad motioned for Chaz to join him in going over the plans for any other attack that might ensue. As Brad marked out all of the spots that would more than likely be popular for an ambush, Marc and Kenny came out to join in the strategizing.

They went over the plan laid out before them. Chaz would take the roof since he proved himself to be situated where he wouldn't berserk. They had already set the patio area of the step to secure it more as one would a bunker. Brad also mounted an M60 on the banister right outside Sam's apartment door.

John made it down to the truck and called Marc's cell phone. He didn't get Marc, so he left a message that they were ok and would check back later. He hung up the phone and noticed that his phone showed a message. He listened to his voicemail.

"John, I hope everything is ok. Call when you can. Hey, Kenny, Chaz and Brad are securing Claire's property. If anything happens your end, head to Claire's." John finally called the delivery place and ordered. He walked back to the room and before entering, he knocked slowly, 3 times. He opened the door carefully and found Sam in the corner, gun aimed right on him.

Her eyes were as wide as the barrel of the gun. John squeezed through the door and closed it quickly. She relaxed and sat in the chair as John locked the door and put the dresser against it once again. He turned on the lamp near the table and turned on the TV for background noise. The sounds of moans and screams coming from the TV, made John and Sam both look in surprise. John chuckled and turned the channel.

"This place is a dump but yet they provide soft porn on HBO."

"Did you talk to anyone?" Sam asked.

"I left a message. They left one for me too. We must get bad reception out here."

The drowning sounds of commercials filled the air like white noise. "Marc said something about the guys securing the area."

Sam sighed in relief. John noticed the sudden change in posture and looked at her in question.

"I hate the fact that others around me are in danger because of me, but Kenny and Brad know their stuff. I know that Kenny was in some special forces while in Vietnam. He spent a lot of time over there from what I gather. Brad, well he's a bounty hunter. I can't even imagine what he has up his sleeve. But I know that they would never let anything happen to any of us if they could help it."

John mindlessly flipped through the channels with the remote that remained fixed to a chain on the nightstand.

"I wouldn't let anything happen to you either, if I could help it." Sam took the comment as a defense to her comment ,that she didn't mean to sound as a put down to him, but she feared that's what happened.

"John, I'm not saying that you couldn't or wouldn't take care of me, of us. You are protecting me now, aren't you?" John just flipped through the channels, never landing on one he felt to be interesting.

Sam sighed and walked over and sat next to him on the bed. "I mean it. I feel safe with you. I'm just glad that they're there to keep everyone else safe."

John flipped it to a digital music station since that was the best thing on the TV. Sam went over to the vanity and pulled a small plastic cup from its cellophane wrapper to get a drink of water. She turned the water on and heard the pipes knock and bang before rusty water came spitting through the pipes. She jumped back as she shouted "ewww." She shut the faucet off and sat back down at the table. She ran her finger down the gun, observing the intricate markings throughout the stock.

A knock ran out on the door and before John could sit up on the bed, Sam was back in the corner with the gun pointed to the door. John moved cautiously towards the door to answer it. A knock rang out again and it was followed by the sound of a gun being cocked.

"Who is it?" John said, his voice going deep and unnerving.

A non-descript voice rang out from the other side of the door.

"I got your pizza."

"Yeah?" John answered.

There was a pause and the voice became evidently frustrated. "You want it or not?"

"What's the total?" A huff followed the answer. "47.28 dude, you wanna open the door? These boxes are heavy."

John gave instructions to leave the pizzas on the floor behind him. There was a silence for only a second, which was probably the delivery guy looking behind him. "Are you sure you want me to put them on the floor?" The voice asked dubiously.

"Do it, and I'll slide the money under the door. Then I want you to move fast and get the fuck out of here. If we see you in the hall when we open this door, we'll shoot ya."

"Don't flip out man. I just deliver the pizzas, man."

John slipped $60 under the door.

The voice added. "Do you want change back?"

John's voice deepened even more as he shouted. "I said go!"

The next sound heard was someone running down the hall, away from the door. John waited a few seconds and started out the door. He checked the hallway, and in seeing no one was there, he picked up the food and brought it quickly inside. A car could be heard screeching away from the motel. He took the pizzas over to the table where Sam had been sitting. She was still crouched in the corner with a death grip on the gun.

John knelt beside her and put his hands on hers. She reluctantly gave the gun to him.

"That's better. Now sit up here and I'll get us some water." He pulled her chair out and then opened his bag. He pulled out a gallon jug of water and placed it on the table near the stack of pizza boxes.

"I need more light to eat." John turned on an overhead light, it barely lit the room. The nicotine stained light bulb burned a dirty yellow in a very retro looking room. The light itself made sizzle and popping noises, which were deafening in the stressed air. It wasn't as bad as in the hall, but it was still dirty feeling. John handed Sam a box. "I have a pepperoni, a sausage, a meat lovers, a supreme and a veggie lovers. I didn't know what you wanted so I bought a few of each."

Sam looked at the stack of boxes in front of her in amazement.

"How many pizzas do you think I'm going to eat?"

"Oh, I dunno, one at least. I'll probably eat 5 or 6. I'm not leaving you to hunt, so I'm settling." John looked down at Sam's hands still creased from holding the gun tightly. He took her hands in his to examine them more closely.

"I know you're frightened, but you don't have to worry so much. I'll not let anything happen to you."

Sam was busy staring at her hands, too ashamed to look into his deep blue eyes. "What happens if I get you killed in the process?"

John smiled and kissed each of her palms. "If you haven't noticed, I'm a big boy and I have taken care of myself pretty well thus far. I think I can manage."

Sam pushed the box from in front of her. "I'm serious John, what happens if I lose you? I don't think that I could live with myself."

"Are you going to cast me aside, send me away just to keep me safe? What if I tell you that I wouldn't go? You wouldn't be able to stop me."

Sam huffed. "And you think I'M stubborn?"

John pulled her chair closer to his and put his arm around her.

"Besides, I bet there has to be something to this life mate thing. It has to be like some dynamic-duo or something."

"You believe?" Sam tried to retort, but John interrupted her before she could go on.

"I'm saying that I'm willing to take that chance." Sam smiled from the inside out. She grabbed John and hugged him with all her might. "Ack, I'm choking on pizza," John teased.

Sam's fears seemed to lessen over the amount of warm fuzzies that were soaring through her body. She felt her shoulders loosen and become sore. She didn't know that she had been holding them tight. She picked up a slice of pizza and began to eat. The first bite sent her salivating. She was hungrier than she thought. She began to eat heartily as she struck up conversation with John.

"So." She talked between swallows. "Does that mean that we're going steady? Do I get to wear a pin or ring or something?"

John let himself go to her humor and laughed. Sam snickered with him as well. "I left my letterman's jacket at home, sorry."

"Oh that figures, let me guess…. Football?"

John pushed the second empty pizza box from him and continued to the third as he answered her. "For your information I played all types of sports. But I wasn't a jock. I was the defensive end in football, forward in basketball and trombone player in band. I was more of a band geek than jock. The jocks never made fun of me because I was bigger than they were. The band geeks took refuge in my friendship. It was a great time in high school. Well, as much as teenage angst can get anyway."

Sam had finished half her pizza and never thought twice about it as she started on the other half. "I was 4H all the way. I knew what I wanted to do in life. I don't know how the animals will react to me now though, well after I mean."

"Animals are very intuitive creatures. They even know when humans are out to do harm. Even though you are or will be, they will know Sam. I don't think you'll have any problems. Now some dogs however, sometimes want to fight you for dominance."

"Has that happened to you?"

John finished the last bite of his third pizza and as he opened his fourth box he replied. "Yeah, it's happened on occasion."

Sam was curious at this point. "What do you do when that happens?"

"I eat them," John said in fact.

Sam was in disbelief. "WHAT?"

John shrugged. "It must be a guy thing, or a Were thing but no tiny Chihuahua is going to tell me that he's my alpha. No, the mutt is more a tiny morsel than a threat."

"You have really killed and eaten a dog?" She was still stunned as to the veer that the convo had taken.

"Dogs," John answered.

"Oh, I can't believe this," Sam said, not accepting what she had just heard.

"Hey, in some countries, dogs are a delicacy. Most of the time they're just strays anyway. Hey, I've eaten wolves too. It's par for the course."

"Oh my. I can see Nicki's pooch trying to growl at me now. I will look at it and see a roasted dog, like the cartoons when they see a character roasted like a turkey."

"Yep, that's about it. And you'll eat more for vengeance than food."

"This is going to be nuts."

"It's different, that's for sure."

Sam looked into his eyes, searching for an answer. "Do you miss being human?"

"I won't lie to you. Sometimes I do. But only like five percent of the time. The other ninety-five percent, I'm glad that I'm Were. I must have been chosen for this, so who am I to argue."

Sam looked down at her pizza box and went to take another slice when she realized that she had eaten the entire pizza. "Oh my god, I'm such a cow."

"No honey, that's wolf. Wolves eat cows." John teased her.

"Haha, very funny. I can't believe that I just ate an entire medium pizza."

"Um," John added insult to injury. "That was a large."

She buried her face into her hands. "Oh my god."

"Hey, you're a lightweight. I'm on my fifth pizza. I'm about done now, so we can save the other two for later."

CHAPTER SEVENTEEN

Sam got up and walked over to the bed. She lay on her stomach and stared at the TV screen while she rubbed her right shoulder. John turned off the overhead light and dimmed the lamp on the nightstand as he climbed on the bed and on top of Sam to properly massage her.

"Oh, you *are* tense. Here, this should help." John gave Sam's shoulders a squeeze and Sam let out a slight moan. John, satisfied with his quick thinking replied. "I could do better if you lost the shirt."

Sam looked over her shoulder but couldn't actually look at him from the angle that she was laying. John let her up while she slid off the bed. She stood with her back to John, took her shirt off, and quickly covered her breasts. She lay back on the bed, her shirt still covering her chest. John sat back on top of Sam and proceeded to unfasten her bra. She tensed for only a second and then relaxed. John slid the straps down to her elbows and started on her back.

John worked out knots that Sam didn't know she had. He started with her shoulders and worked his way to her neck and then down her spine. He massaged her back for a full hour before he asked her if she wanted more.

"Are you kidding me?"

"No, why?" John answered as he continued to kneed away at the knots in her back.

"This is amazing. I think you loosened my toes."

John smiled to himself as he leaned forward and whispered into her ear. "I'm just getting started. I'll make your toes loosen and then curl back up again." He finished his statement with a kiss on the top of her ear. He continued on a path to her neck and kissed her as he moved against her. His movements made Sam's eyes close and her body react to him. His hands glided down her sides to her hips and he continued his trail of lingering kisses down the middle of her back. Sam was enraptured. She was no longer afraid, afraid of what laid ahead, afraid of taking chances with John. She was not afraid of the feeling she had for him and those that she's had since the day she met him. She welcomed him into her heart where he would stay as long as he wished. He gently laid Sam on her back. He looked down on her as she held her shirt to her chest. Her hair fell around her like a dark shadow. He bent down slowly and when he was too close to see her chest; he moved her hands, along with the shirt, away from her body. He nuzzled his face into her neck and inhaled deeply. He dug his hands underneath her and wrapped her up in his arms. He held her as he whispered into her ear.

"I want you to know that I have never felt this way for another person. I want to be with you always. I will be yours if you will have me."

Sam wrapped her arms around his body as she spoke to him.

"Forever I will want you. Forever I will want this. I don't ever want this to change."

He pulled away from her just enough to lovingly kiss her lips. He was a kind and gentle man, but Sam could sense that the passion and heat simmered just underneath. John kissed her with held back intentions. Sam wanted him to give way to his actions so she kissed him harder. It did the job. John ravished her with lingering and hard kisses. John began to be swept away and pulled away abruptly.

"We...we can't." Panting hard by now.

Sam sat up and lightly touched her lips to his as she answered.

"Yes, we can."

"I... I don't want to rush things." John held firm.

"I do." Sam was persistent. It was her turn to cover his body in kisses. She gently caressed his shoulders down to his arms with her fingers. She followed her hands with her lips, covering every inch of his upper body with undivided attention. Once she made it to his belly button, she teased him a bit before rising up dragging her bare chest against his. She ran her hands over his chest. John took back the lead. He pulled his shirt off and pressed his body to hers. She let her shirt and bra fall to the bed beside them. He gently glided his hands down Sam's arms and then down her back. He gently grabbed a handful of hair and kissed her neck passionately. Sam held on for balance. Her world was spinning. John slowly laid her on the bed as he followed. He continued kissing her, as he undressed her. Before he joined her, he undressed in front of her. The light of the room was not enough to make out details of John's body, but the silhouette of his muscular body was just as inspiring. He climbed into bed and lay next to Sam. "All you have to say is no." John said sincerely.

"We have been through hell and back, John. If I don't give into to my desires now and I'll lose my chance, I'll die of a broken heart."

John caressed her cheek. "You're such a beautiful woman." He leaned in and kissed her as they proceeded to make love, for the first time.

Sam lay intertwined with John's body, her head on his chest. "Your heart is racing."

"Yours too," John answered.

"I've never... in my life... experience anything like that." Sam exclaimed between inhales. She couldn't seem to catch her breath.

"I must say, I haven't either." John smiled in his euphoric state. Sam snuck a peek at his back and noticed the nail marks were already beginning to heal. Dried traces of blood ran down his back and sides.

"I'm sorry bout the nail thing," she stated as she gingerly ran her hands over his wounds.

"Don't be sorry, be proud. A little bit of pain at times always intensifies the pleasure." He leaned over and kissed her shoulder where he had bitten her during their interlude.

Sam teased. "But aren't you afraid that you might turn me?"

"If I turn you, it will only be to get you on your stomach." He playfully responded.

"Jonathan DesRosiers!" she gasped.

He moved so that he could rest his head back upon her chest, and caress her bare skin.

"Sam?" John paused. "I think I've fallen for you." He didn't look up to see her reaction, but he could hear it in her heartbeat that instantly sped up.

"You think or you know?"

"I don't want to scare you. I just thought that I would be honest," John chose his words carefully.

"Well, I'm not scared. In fact, I'm happy." Sam smiled to herself.

John smiled too at her remark.

Sam continued. "I feel the same way, John. I've been completely enthralled; or rather obsessed with you since the moment we bumped into each other. Where we are right now… here… it feels right. I hope that we're here for a while."

John smiled and replied. "We only have the hotel until eleven tomorrow morning."

Sam and John rested for only a while longer before Sam got up to take a shower. She kissed John before leaving the room. He watched her as she made her way to the bathroom door, and she knew it. Before she entered, she turned and lost herself for a moment and couldn't hold back her smile. Her heart raced as her body yearned for more.

She turned and entered the bathroom.

As she started the water, she looked at herself in the mirror. She had a perfect human bite mark on her shoulder, near her neck. She touched the bruised area and grinned. 'Pleasure and pain' she thought to herself, before she turned and got into the shower. She let the hot water relax her achy muscles. She began to wash up when she heard John enter the back of the shower.

"Remember that pesky spot on my back?" He turned his back to her. He obviously wasn't finished with her.

She looked at the full profile presented of his backside. She pulled him into the water. "Let me take a look at it." She pressed her body against his back and ran her hands over his shoulders, down his arms. She intermittently kissed his shoulders and the nape of his neck. "Yes, I can see what you're talking about." She paused to kiss him again. "Don't move. Let me get it for you."

She reached down and grabbed the soap. She lathered his back and then turned him around to continue her cleaning. He started to grope her body when she remarked.

"Uh-uh. I don't need help. Now, be good and let me finish."

She continued to soap his body. She pressed her breasts against his soapy chest as her hands ventured further down his body. "Oh, I see you need lots," she breathed into his ear. "Lots of cleaning..."

Sam and John continued their night of passion from the shower back to the bed. Their encounter created energy that flickered as if the room housed a hundred candles. The room began to dim as he collapsed onto Sam. She held him close to her as he rested his head against her neck. He had not even the strength to keep his eyes open. Sam gave out a sound that was almost a purr.

John responded to her as he drifted off to sleep in her arms. "I love you."

"I love you too," she replied, without a moment's hesitation.

She could feel his body give way to complete relaxation. She pulled the covers over them as best she could and curled up beside him, laying her head on his chest and joined him in his slumber.

It was 4:00am when John was woken by the bed shaking. He jolted up. Sam had begun to convulse. He tried to shake her, to break the trance, but was unsuccessful. The room was hot from the energy permeating from her. He knew what was happening and knew that he needed to get her to Claire, fast. He jumped out of bed, dressed quickly and picked Sam up in the sheet she laid in and ran out the door. He put her in the passenger side of the truck and ran to his side to get in. He dialed Marc's number as he sped away.

"Hello?" Nicki answered.

"Nicki, its John. We have major problems."

"What is it? What's wrong?"

"It's Sam. She's changing."

"WHAT?" Was all that he heard before the phone dropped to the floor, he tried to pay attention to the road as he sped down the frontage road that led to the highway. He knew that he was about an hour and a half away from the apartment. He heard someone scrambling to pick up the phone.

"John?" Marc answered this time. "What in the hell is going

on?"

John looked at Sam who was now sitting in a trance-like state, panting as she stared into nothingness.

"Her change has started. She's really far into it now. I won't be able to stop her. I am about an hour and a half away. I don't want to get pulled over, but I need to get there quickly."

John could hear Nicki screaming in the background and Claire trying to comfort her.

"Ask Claire if there is anything that I could do to help her."

He heard Marc relay the question, and then silence. Marc answered. "She said that there's nothing that we can do for her, besides keep an eye on her. She said to be careful. She might begin to show signs of... aggression."

As Marc was finishing his last statement, Sam grabbed the wheel to jerk it towards her. The truck began to squeal towards the median as the truck drifted sideways, barring against the tires. John righted the movement.

"I have to go," John said as he hung up the phone. He needed an extra hand to keep her at bay. He was lucky that he had a large sized truck with tinted windows. He pulled over to the side of the road only for a moment. He needed to change. He had only driven a few times in his Curreno form, but it was the only way to keep her from wrecking the truck. He needed to be in a form that would match her in strength, hopefully. Once in form, he got back into his truck. He had to ease his seat back as far as it would go and was still having a hard time driving. Sam was also a distraction. She was plastered up against the door, glaring at John and growling. John just sped away. Occasionally, Sam would try to grab for the wheel and John would catch her hand in the process.

The last time she tried, he held her arm in the air.

"Don't!"

Sam, or whoever possessed her at that moment, glared at him and replied.

"Die."

John ignored the statement. He knew that it wasn't Sam doing the talking. He remembered what it was like the first time that he changed. He knew the mental battle that Sam was under.

He just prayed that she was strong enough to prevail over her beast.

Sam woke to the surroundings of the lake, by a howling scream. She tried to gain her bearings when she heard it again. At that moment, Sam knew that the primal screams were directed towards her.

"RUN!" Is all she heard from within. Sam began to run for the house. Her journey seemed endless, her lungs burning from the hot air that she was breathing in.

"TOO HOT!" She was telling herself as she began to lose momentum. She came to a stop, just long enough to catch her breath when she heard footfalls coming quickly upon her. She heard a breath piercing the night air, so loud and crisp against the oddly silent night. Sam's heart began to race. Her mind once again filled with the notion to run. She didn't give her body time to protest. Something instinctive set in and she ran faster than she ever had before. The sounds of the footfalls were so close that she could swear she felt the breath of her attacker upon her. Sam reached the house opened the door and slammed it shut. She waited to hear something hit the door as she suspected it would. But all she heard was a huff and someone, or something, run off. She ran to the closet and grabbed the shotgun. Sam raced to the back door and secured that as well. She sprinted through the first floor, making sure that every window had been locked before heading back to the living room.

John drove as fast as he could. He could feel the surges of power emit from Sam's body. Her body jerked and writhed where she sat, her gaze fixed on nothingness. Every so often, he would see Sam's body contort into all too familiar shapes. John tried to pay attention to the road and drive as fast as he could. He tried to dial Marc, to let him know that he was about 20 minutes from the apartment, but his gigantic form became an obstacle to the small buttons on the phone. He had voice activation on his cell, but it didn't recognize his voice while in Curreno. He fought the urge to throw the phone out the window. He could only hope they would be ready for them to arrive. He dodged between cars and semi-trucks as they blared their horns at him.

John made it to the apartment complex. He drove his truck through the back of the property. He literally parked his truck on the patio that led to his apartment. He grabbed Sam and dragged her over the seat as he got out. His actions didn't faze Sam. John banged on the glass door and looked around at the other apartment lights coming on nearby as Marc finally opened it for him. John came pouring through the room with Sam. The sight of Sam brought screams of anguish from Nicki and Claire. They ran to her as John dropped to his knees. Claire examined her quickly. Nicki tried to grab for Sam when Claire stopped her. Nicki fought Claire until Marc came to Claire's rescue. He took Nicki from Sam and John, to his room. Claire could hear Nicki's pleas and sorrowful mourning through the thin walls. Claire tried to hold back her terror.

"I... I called Kenny. He should be pulling up at any time. We have to leave soon, before one of your neighbors calls the police."

John nodded. He stood and motioned for Claire to follow him to his room. He laid Sam on his bed and ripped drawers open from his dresser. He turned to Claire with a large shirt. Claire and John clothed Sam while she was still unconscious. Claire looked tearfully to John for answers.

"I didn't hurt her. I woke up and she was like this."

Claire shook her head. "I know you didn't do this... I know."

John was packing a small gym bag when he heard a knock on the front door. John zipped the bag shut, picked Sam up in one big swoop and followed Claire out to the living room.

Kenny was in the room with Marc and Nicki. Marc had obviously eased Nicki's mind, since she was no longer hysterical. Nicki couldn't bring herself to even look at Sam lying in John's arms. She just stared down at her dirty jeans.

"We've got to leave now. I have a police scanner in my van and there's been a call. They will be here any minute."

John made it out the door with Sam, followed by Claire. Marc and Nicki brought up the rear.

"Nicki and I will follow in your truck," Marc called out to John.

John nodded as he clambered into Kenny's van.

Kenny drove Randy's cargo van. It was black with the name 'Randy's Bar and Grill' painted in blood red, on the sides. There were no windows in the back of the van, to John's relief. The inside of the van lined with numerous sized crates. By the writing on the sides, John knew that they were more than likely ammunition and artillery. Sam was on the bed of the van, her body jerking from unseen forces. John lay next to her as best he could, to keep contact with her if nothing else.

Kenny sped off without waiting for Nicki and Marc. They knew the destination. Kenny took off down a gravel road, just off the main interstate and met up with the highway that would bypass most of the town. Claire kept looking back into the van, into the darkness in hopes to catch a glimpse of Sam by the streams of lights created by the street lamps they passed. All she could hear was the panting that Sam began to do, and the small pops and snaps that came from the darkness, mottled in low gurgling sounds. The last thing that was heard was John shouting.

"Kenny, you'd better hurry."

Sam reached the living room as she saw a form come out of the shadows and up onto the back stoop. She clambered to get the hutch and push it in front of the door.

Sam loaded the gun as fast as her shaking hands could work. Just as she saw the beast starting to stir, she shot it in the chest at almost point blank range. Blood coated Sam as it made an outline on the wall around her. As Sam pumped the gun for one last shot, the beast jumped up and tore into Sam's shoulder, creating sensations of pain throughout her body. Sam struggled to bring the gun up just as the beast slashed at Sam's chest as it tried to swing the gun away. The beast's nails dug deep within Sam's chest, piercing her heart. Sam fired one more time into the Beast's abdomen and both fell away from each other. Sam lay on her back, staring at the ceiling as she felt the pain begin to leave her body. She lifted her hand to her chest and pulled back to see nothing but blood covering her palm. She blinked slowly and tried to swallow only to choke on herself. The taste of blood was prominent in her mouth. She turned her head to the side in time to see the beast had turned into something more human, a woman.

This fur-covered woman was awash of blood and wounds. Sam watched her crawl and cover Sam with her body. Sam looked into the woman's eyes and saw herself staring back at her. She and her other self were staggering for breath, rattling in their own life.... Sam knew that there was no winning. She had failed. She had let down her family, her friends and her newly found love. She let herself selfishly think of John for only a moment. If this was the end, she wanted him to be with her in mind and spirit. She let herself sink deep inside herself, piercing the earlier memory of being wrapped securely in John's arms. His warmth engulfed her, warmed her blood and began to ease her pain.

Kenny was leaving a trail of dust in his wake as he sped down the gravel road. The van would fishtail at times, but Kenny was an experienced enough driver to know how to tame the vehicle. They were ten minutes from Claire's house when they turned onto the main highway. Kenny looked in his side mirror and cursed to himself then shouted.

"I got cherries. I have to pull over."

John pulled a mover's quilt over Sam as best he could, and tried to sit back in the shadows. Claire sat quietly in the passenger seat and thought of ways to help divert the officer. The van stopped and it was only a few minutes before the officer made it to the window.

"Kenny, what's the hurry?" Danny asked jovially as he peered into the van window. "Oh, hello Aunt Claire." His voice held a sign of discontent.

"Danny, we really need to get to the house," Claire added. "I left my stove on. I hope that I didn't burn my place down."

Danny smirked. "Yeah that would be a shame."

Kenny spoke up. "Look Danny, we really need to get to her house. How about letting us go, just this once."

Danny stood up straighter and smiled. "Now Kenny, you know that a police officer has to do his duty. I'm gonna have to check the van."

"You really want to let us go," Kenny said seriously.
Danny cocked his head and put his hand on his gun.
"Get out of the van."

Kenny sighed and started to get out of the van. As he was positioning himself, he whispered to Claire. "As soon as I'm out of the van, take off."

Claire's eyes about popped out of her head. She nodded nervously and looked back at John. John nodded slowly and pulled Sam closer to him. Kenny shut the door and Claire waited to hear him round the van's rear before she lunged for the driver's seat. She readied herself and started the van. She threw it into gear and slammed onto the gas.

Danny didn't know what was happening. He went to go for his gun. Kenny backhanded Danny into his car. Danny hit the hood and slid down to the ground unconscious. Kenny walked over to Danny's car with his gun, intending on shooting out the tires. He had a better idea. Kenny handcuffed Danny and threw him in the back of his police car. Kenny looked around to make sure that no one was coming, jumped in the driver's seat and took off.

Claire skidded to a halt in front of the house just as John was jumping out of the back with Sam. Claire went directly to the door. Brad had been waiting for them to arrive. He looked past her, to John and knew what was going on.

"Aimee. Get the room ready. Sam's turning."

Aimee came popping through the room. Her expression was that of concern and excitement all wrapped in one. She grabbed Claire by the arm.

"Come on, Claire. We have lots to prepare for."

Claire followed Aimee in a lost world. Time seemed to be running in both slow and fast motion all at once. She couldn't keep her bearings. She heard nothing but the sound of her heart beating in her ears. She stopped in the doorway, watching Aimee buzz around, preparing for Sam's arrival. Only when she felt a hand on her shoulder, did she come to. Kenny was behind her.

"Claire, we have to make room for John to come through."
Claire mindlessly nodded and was ushered back by Kenny. John

came through with Sam and laid her on the bed then he turned and looked for the 'everything's gonna be ok' speech.

Claire could no longer hold back the tears. She began to weep as she stared at John. Even through his Curreno form, John's expression showed that of compassion. He walked over to Claire and put his arms around her. She held onto him and cried. Claire only came up to his lower chest while he was turned, but it didn't matter. Claire rested her head on his abdomen and cried into his fur. His massive hands were gentle as he caressed her head. Aimee was busy tending to Sam and the room. On her final trip out the door, she put her hand on Claire's back.

"Claire, how about I make you some tea? Maybe a bite to eat? If we are going to be up for a while, we will need to keep our strength up."

Claire sniffled and looked up at John. "Thank you."

She motioned John to bend down, so that she could plant a kiss on his muzzle. John patted her on the shoulder and watched as they walked out of the room. Once he was alone with Sam, he allowed himself to melt back to human form. He pulled a chair close to the bed, sat down and watched Sam's silent struggle. Her skin would change colors, fur had begun to spout from different places and then disappear just as fast, leaving tiny prickles of blood on her skin. John watched Sam's facial features begin to change slightly. He took a cool rag from the basin of water that Aimee had placed on the nightstand and dabbed it across Sam's forehead. His heart was breaking, seeing her in such a state. He felt helpless because he knew that there wasn't much he could do for her. All he could do was be there, and hope that was enough.

Aimee poured hot water into Claire's cup and then into Nicki's. Nicki had arrived just as Aimee and Claire made it to the kitchen. She had poked her head into the room where Sam was, but didn't go in. She couldn't handle the current state that Sam was in and felt ashamed of it. Nicki stirred her tea and listened to Aimee.

"She will be ok. We know that Sam's a fighter. She will make it through." Aimee was convinced that Sam was going to make it.

Claire and Nicki couldn't help but think the worst. Aimee was about to continue when Katie and Brad joined them. Katie walked over to Claire and rested her head on her shoulder.

"Aunt Claire, don't be sad. Sam has the power to overcome her beast. She doesn't know it yet, but it's in her. She's fighting her beast with logical thinking. She doesn't know that she must give in no matter what the beast does. Only when she is reduced to emotions only, will she then know how to triumph."

Claire kissed Katie on the head. "What would we do without you, Angel?"

"I don't know. The Ancient Ones are watching her. They told me to tell you that Sam is too stubborn for her own good."

Such words from the mouths of babes, Claire thought. She began to fill her spirit lift into the clouds of a little girl's blue eyes. Katie smiled.

"There, that's better. That's my special ingredient." Katie stated as she winked at Claire.

Nicki took a sip of her tea. "What are we suppose to do now?"

Claire got up and headed for the pantry. She pulled out a worn cookbook and thumbed through the recipes. Nicki gave her a strange look. Claire smiled and answered.

"I have five Weres in my house right now. I know that they must be famished. I have to stay busy or I will be reduced to a blubbering idiot. I will kill two birds with one stone. Nicki, would you like to help?"

"Why not? Like you say, anything to keep busy."

"I wanna help!" Katie squealed in delight. "Can I help, mommy?"

"Sure, baby. I'll go check on daddy."

Claire and the girls began to run throughout the kitchen. Nicki even turned on Claire's CD of Big Band swing. Though it was playing very low, it still helped ease the tension. Katie's presence was also helping them relax.

On her way to Brad, Aimee stopped to talk to John. John sat naked from the waist up. He had let himself fall back to human form. He had taken a sheet and wrapped it around his waist.

"How's she doing?"

"About the same. Her features are starting their progression. So far, so good. Well, you know what I mean."

"It's all part of the process. She's doing fine. Katie says that there's hope for her, if she looks hard enough for it."

"Do you remember your first time?" John was looking for a diversion.

Aimee came in, sat on the edge of the bed, and caressed Sam's arm gently.

"Yes. I don't think that anyone could ever forget his or her first time, not even a Trueblood. It's like a nightmare that never leaves you. It was the most frightening thing that I ever had to face. I think that it helped me in the end though. Since my own transformation, I have not faced another adversary that scared me so. I guess the saying is true, we're our own worst enemies."

Aimee was describing her first turn to John when he pressed himself against the chair and lost his breath for a moment.

Aimee reacted quickly.

"John, what's wrong?"

John's eyes began to tear and his breath became shallow. "It's her. She's here."

Aimee's eyebrow lifted as she answered. "In the room?"

"She's giving up. I can feel her giving up the fight. There has to be a way to help her."

Aimee put her hand on his. "John, that's not possible."

John shot up out of the chair, sending it to the floor.

"I tell you goddamnit, I can feel her!" He continued to feel in the area where he stood.

"It's like I can feel her in my soul…"

Aimee didn't try to touch John again, but answered. "Then send her love, John. Send her your heart. There is no way to enter her world. Make that connection with her soul and give her the strength she needs to win."

John buckled under his own weight, fell to the floor on his hands and knees, and mumbled to himself. Aimee took that moment to exit the room and closed the door behind her. John needed his time to concentrate. She made her way down the hall to the aroma-filled kitchen.

"Sam's not doing so hot."

All three girls turned to look at Aimee.

Nicki was the one that spoke up. "Huh?"

Aimee smiled and answered. "Her battle, she's having her battle here in the house. Her soul has found John. He says that he can feel her giving up. He's trying to connect with her. It's not much of a link, but there's one there."

Claire started to make her way around the island when Aimee stopped her. "You can't go in there. You might break the link between them."

"It's not fair! I should be able to help her!" Claire tried in vain to struggle out of Aimee's grip.

"Claire, we would all love to help her but we can't. You need to focus yourself, for her sake."

"I don't want to! I'm tired of being the one that is the wise and the strong. I want my little girl back and I will do whatever it takes to get her back." Claire was clearly raging now.

Katie spoke out in a voice that was not her own.

"SILENCE! This is not for you to interfere, for doing so would surely kill her. Know your place." Her voice was that of many voices speaking in unison, both male and female.

Everybody turned to face Katie who was floating about 3 feet above the island. Her arms stretched out as if she were holding her body up by the wind suddenly blazing through the kitchen.

"It is written as such that one of a forbidden union will bring forth a new life for thousands. If it is to be Samantha Harris, we have to let her take the steps towards the prophecy." Katie began to descend back to the top of the island where Nicki stood close to steady her landing.

Claire took a deep, shuddering breath and wiped her tears away. She felt foolish for her outburst and apologized to Aimee for such a display.

"Of undying and unfaltering love? Every mother has such love for her children. Don't ever be ashamed of that," Aimee took Claire in her arms and gave her a warm hug.

"What did you put me up here for?" Katie was speaking to the ceiling. She smiled big and then looked at the women and spoke again. "What they will do to get attention."

Nicki chuckled as she helped her down from the island.

Sam was able to open her eyes. She saw the woman smile triumphantly and strain to speak. "I have beaten you. I... I have won." This other woman tried to laugh but only let out coughs that racked her body. Sam knew that it was time. She sent one last loving thought of everyone she held dear and let John be her anchor as she began to drift into darkness. Her vision began to close on her, darkness began to overtake her. She saw the woman's mouth turn from a smile to that of horror and through the darkness, Sam saw a burst of light stream out. The contrast was that of a bat trying to fly into the sun. The sound of static began to buzz in Sam's ears and her body began to take on a filling sensation. Her vision started to return to normal as she watched the woman above her begin to dissolve into a fine mist that swirled around her, around the light as a moth to a flame. Sam could make out the sounds of pleadings.

"It's not fair, I beat her. I won. This can't be happening." The sounds of screams tore through the air as the wisps of mist that the woman had turned into, slammed into the wound in Sam's chest. The light disappeared and Sam blacked out.

"No, NO, she's gone. SHE'S GONE!" John screamed from the room. He came running out into the hallway with his arms out in front of him. "She has to be here, she has to still be here"

Brad came running in from the porch when he heard John shouting. He ran to John. "We have problems buddy."

John was in a daze. Brad laid his hand on John's shoulder, forcing his power into his joint enough to gain his attention.

John shook out of Brad's hold and his trance. "What?"

Brad made a quick and low whistle and within a few seconds, Kenny and Chaz were at his side.

"I have spotted at least 10 soldiers on the front flank."

Kenny added. "About that many or more in the back. Chaz? Have you seen anything?"

"I'm in the crow's nest. If they come in on the property opening, I would see them. I think they know this from last time. I haven't seen anything, but I've noticed that the night is too quiet."

"Shit. Ok, we need to get the girls in the basement."

"We aren't going anywhere." Nicki brought up the rear. "Someone has to watch Katie"

"I will watch her." Claire had Katie on her hip. "Gimme a gun. I don't want to take any chances."

Kenny handed her his .45mm after he cocked it and put the safety back on. "You push this button here to take the..."

"I know how to use a goddamn gun, Kenny. We'll be in the basement." Claire turned and hurried down the stairs.

Brad made eye contact with everyone as he spoke. "We are going to run it just as we planned. We will give Claire and Katie ten minutes to get settled before all hell breaks loose." He grabbed Aimee at that point and pulled her close. "Smoke'em if you got 'em." He told the group as he walked away with Aimee at his side.

John raced back to the room where Sam was and pulled her to the floor. He wanted her as far from the window and door as possible. If he felt comfortable doing so, he would have stuffed her in the closet. At least he knew then that she would be hidden in case he was, well he wasn't going to finish that last thought. "Think positive," he said to himself. He moved some of the furniture around and placed the bed on its side to use not as much for a shield than for a place to hide from onlookers from outside. He pulled Sam behind the bed, and covered her once again with a blanket.

Kenny slapped Chaz on the back. "I hope your night vision is as good as your day."

Chaz couldn't help but grin. "It should be. Santa brought me toys." With that he pulled out a set of night vision goggles.

Before Brad and Aimee walked through the front door they heard Chaz's remark as Brad chuckled out. "Ho, ho, ho."

Brad kissed Aimee lovingly and then whispered into her ear. "Once this is over, I would love to take you out on a date."

Aimee's smile couldn't cover up the sadness in her eyes. "It's about time. I've missed you. Friday night?"

Brad stole one more chaste kiss.

"7pm... and don't be late. We'll have Claire watch Katie."

Aimee's smile melted from her face as she replied. "I love

you."

Brad tried to reassure her in the best way he knew how. He smacked her on the rear and teased. "Girl, you'd better. I love you too. Let's git us some vermin."

Aimee unsheathed two sawn off shotguns from leg holsters that Brad hand made for her two years prior. She swiveled the guns in her hands and readied her grip. She kept what looked to be a hard case fanny pack around her thin waste, filled with extra ammo. She had been taught by the best. Brad readied his semi automatic assault rifle and pulled on the LBV to ensure none of his extra magazines would fall out. Brad walked out the door first. He cleared his throat and spoke into his Individual Tacticular Radio.

"Check team. Brad on point, north flank."

"Aimee on point, south flank."

"Marc on rear point, north flank."

"Kenny on rear point, South flank."

"Chaz in the coo coo's nest, sights set and flying high."

"Nicki guarding base."

"John... guarding life."

"Claire guarding ... um... Me and Katie?"

Brad answered to the entire group. "Listen up, we'll run through this like we planned. They know how we operate, but they will not be ready for what we have in store for them. Chaz, ready the clackers, make sure the safety is off."

"Check." Chaz answered as he picked up the clackers for the set claymores that he and Kenny placed around the perimeter. Before he squeezed the triggers, he shouted out over the radio.

"On three... THREE!"

Chaz squeezed the triggers until he finally saw the explosions surround the area. Horrid sounds of pain and carnage screamed through the night, and with it, came the rain of men and Weres alike. Chaz began shooting at the crowd rushing the house.

Meanwhile, John carried Sam to her apartment. He felt it would be safer there, being on the third floor; Chaz guarding the outside entry, John would only have to focus on the inner house door. He picked Sam up in his arms and quickly ran up the stairs. Once he had Sam placed on her bed, he began to secure the room.

He moved her armoire against the inner door. It wouldn't stop a beast, but it would give John more time to react to the intruder. He also began drawing the blinds for more safety measures. He finally made his way back to Sam who laid in a trance like state of terror. Her mouth was locked in a silent scream.

Her body had made its final transition to true form right before his eyes. Her true form was more than wolf alone. Her coat was a light caramel color and her fur was thicker than that of a Lykoi. Her body slender... almost... aerodynamic. Her muzzle was smaller and her paws wider. She looked to be crossed between a wolf and a mountain lion.

Sam lay there, panting in her new form. Her fur was wet with sweat and blood mingled together in the scent of musk. John ran his hand down her body and she whimpered. John patted her on the shoulder and shushed her. John grew silent as he began to hear the sounds of battle ringing from outside. He looked back at Sam as she started on the downhill ride of the transformation. She had made it past the halfway mark, but the last half was the most critical. John radioed to Claire.

"Claire, she's made it past true form."

There was some static and a faint voice came over the other end. "John, Claire told me to answer you because she's crying too much." She pulled away from the radio, but John could still hear her. "What was it you called it?" Katie's mouth was back to the radio. "OH yeah, John she said that they were happy tears. She wanted me to thank you too, for the update. Over."

John smiled at Katie's innocence and replied. "I will keep you in the loop."

"Ok, over and out," Katie peeped. John could tell that Katie was enjoying talking on the radio. John was about to set the radio down when he heard another call on the line.

"John? Where's your location?" Brad asked.

"Sam's apartment," he replied.

"Good, I was just going to advise you of that. It's getting hairy out here."

John focused in on the gunshots ringing outside.

"Chaz is on the balcony. I thought it was the best place to be. Keep me posted."

"10-4," Brad said.

John put Sam in her walk in closet to put to rest his initial idea. It was the safest place for her to be. One way in, one way out. He kept the door open so he could keep his sights on her through her progression. He pulled all of the clothes out the closet and threw them to the floor, making room for her.

John utilized his fear and anger to bring on his change. He stood through the ripping and popping of tendons, and of bones remaking themselves throughout his body.

The final stages of John's Curreno form were accompanied by loud bashings at the apartment door. With each bang, John readied himself further into a pouncing position.

The last bang ended with the apartment door bursting into splintered pieces. Two Weres came running through the door. John didn't give them time to think. He lunged for the two, taking one down with him to the floor. John had torn the throat of his victim out faster than the other had time to react. He was to his feet, and steadied himself for the next attacker. The body of the slain creature twitched, and jolted and finally lay still on the floor… human female.

John and the remaining assailant circled and growled at one another. Chaz, who was still outside, knew that the two had snuck past him and was able to enter the room. He was too busy guarding the balcony to turn to offer assistance. He hoped that John would be able to handle the situation

CHAPTER EIGHTEEN

John let his sight move to the closet for just one moment, but it was enough for the Were to see, and deduce, where he'd hidden Sam. The beast turned and started for the door. John tackled it, causing the closet door to slam shut. John and the Were wrestled until they were unexpectedly interrupted by an explosion. The Beast and John looked up and saw another Were standing there. They didn't have enough time to stand before the Were, obviously female by her movements, was on them. She was strong and agile. She fought with precision and morbid grace. John stood up and froze as the female finished the attacker. The female Were turned and looked at John. At that moment, it hit him as plain as the nose, or rather, 'muzzle', on his face. It was Sam.

She ran her forearm across her mouth in attempts to remove the blood, but only furthered the line of gore across her muzzle. Her eyes were shining bright with all the amber in the world, captured within her. John could only stare, as she bounded through the closed window next to the balcony.

Chaz pointed his gun and gave way to the running targets. One by one, he dropped the enemy down. He started to turn his attention to the stairs when the window beside him exploded into shimmering shards of glass. He halted his fire, trying to get a target on the new figure. Through his scope, he still couldn't tell whether the addition was a friend or foe.

Sam landed on all fours and quickly stood up. She turned and looked up at Chaz and grinned. Her eyes were on fire. She winked at him before turning towards the forest. Chaz knew then, what, or rather who, it was. A chill ran down his body and all he could do at that point was to watch her through the scope.

Sam was a running death machine. She met up with a lone Were and grabbed his head, ripping it off in a fluid motion as she continued to run. The headless body slumped to the ground, quickly changing back to human form. She ran down the path that headed to the road, all the while leaving bodies in her wake. She had no weapons, no tactics, only the instinct to kill or be killed. Blood lust began to rise inside her, giving her even more enthusiasm to her rampage.

Chaz watched Sam work as she made her way around the property. She was ruthless and swift in her attacks.

He murmured to himself. "Damn. I gotta get me one of those." He was almost taken over by an attacker sneaking up the stairs to the balcony. Chaz quickly turned his M60 towards him and smiled.

"You almost had me! Almost." He shot the beast through the bridge of his nose which sent the back of his skull exploding from his head. The wolf tumbled backwards from the momentum of the bullet. Dead people do not fall gracefully. Each step he tumbled, head over feet. Chaz heard crunching and looked on with enjoyment at the amount of blood that had now painted the side of Claire's house, like a bad abstract painting. Chaz turned his sights back to the battlefield.

John was on his way downstairs when he heard screams and gunshots. He jumped the remainder of the stairs and made it to the basement. He rounded the corner with his weapon aimed. He could hear the girls whimpering.

"Nicki!" John called out before seeing the girls. He didn't want to get shot or shoot anyone in the process.

"It's John, I'm coming round the corner"

John made it around the corner and found Claire hovered over Nicki.

"There was a soldier that came through the window. He had Nicki. I had to shoot through her to get to him.... I... I."

John inspected the wound and Nicki's vital signs. Nicki was only unconscious. She had a bullet wound in the shoulder. It would hurt when she woke, but she would live.

"You need to keep pressure on her wound, to keep her from bleeding to death. I'll take the gun, you keep her set."

John rifled through the clothes that lay at the washer and threw on a pair of dirty sweat pants. They were tight on his sculpted body, but now that he was in human form, he felt uncomfortable being nude in front of a little girl. He took his position near the entrance to the basement, and waited. He could hear the exchange of fire ring through the broken glass of the window. The racket of gunfire had lessened somewhat, due to the group, and to Sam. He watched more in shock than amazement at the carnage that ensued. He handed the gun to Claire and made his way outside.

Marc sat protecting the north side of the front porch. He had gone through most of his ammunition and thought he would have to change in order to keep guard against any onslaught, when he heard the battle sounds diminish. He watched a lone figure dart through the thicket, almost too fast to track. He didn't know who it was, but was thankful that it was on his side. He watched as his enemy fell like dominoes. He strained to watch the being round the house, continuing the killing spree. Marc turned, and in amazement, looked at the myriad of lifeless bodies strewn about the front yard.

The group came to realize that the battle was over. Sam had made her way through the barrage of soldiers, tearing away at the life that stood before her. No one in her way was safe. Her rampage went on until there was silence. Blood, gore, and bones followed her down her quite literal path of destruction. She came to the clearing at the back of the house and faced the group. She threw down the detached arm of one soldier and the head of another. She held her blood soaked hands in front of her. She clenched her fists and cried out victoriously through the air. Her scream pierced the air and individuals alike. It ended with her falling to her knees.

John watched from the porch. The love of his life enthralled in a horrid state of blood lust. She cried out in victory. He went to her as she fell to her knees. He stopped in front of the beast that knelt before him. She was hyperventilating from exhaustion. John knelt down and held her head in his hands. He wanted to look into her alien eyes. He wanted her to see him.

She looked ahead at the stranger that held her. She looked and found familiarity in him. He stroked the side of her face with his thumbs, encouraging her to remember. Sam found her way back as the lust bled from her eyes, and her body dissolved to human form. John pulled her to him, he held her. She couldn't hold on any longer. Exhaustion took over and she fainted. Her deep, long breaths were reassuring to John. He turned and presented her to the rest of those left standing.

Sam stirred. Her head pounded and the elevated noises didn't help. The moment she tried to sit up, eight hands were on her, and insisting that she lay back down. She agreed only because of the sudden feeling of dizziness. She tightened her shut eyes and sputtered. "Too bright."
With that came a scampering sound, like that of keystone cops, to draw the shades.
"Better," she said. She blinked a few times and the first face she saw was John's. He brushed her forehead with a damp cloth and he smiled. She was still a bit unsure of what had happened. John helped her sit up and Claire was right there with a nice hot cup of tea.
As Sam sipped her tea, she was told of the battle, the entire five days that she'd been asleep, of her survival. It was almost too much for Sam to swallow. The tears welled up and streamed down her face in their silent fall. She tried to look away, but John made her look in his eyes. She saw validation, acceptance, and love in his gaze. She tried to shake away.
"How could you look at me like that, after all that I've done?"
John tsked at her humility. "Sam, we're all monsters in our own right, be it human or not. You saved your family, your friends. You saved me."
He didn't wait for a reaction. He held her. The rest of those tending to her left the room to give them privacy. He held her close, against her protests. She gave into his embrace and let herself go.
He reassured her. "You're an extraordinary person with extraordinary abilities. You saved us, do you understand that?"
Sam just shook her head into his chest.
"But will I be able to control it?" she wondered.
John finally exhaled a breath he didn't know he was holding. Finally, he was getting through to her. She was ready to learn, to understand.

The next few months Sam spent catching up on all of her family history, going through different exercises to strengthen her control, as well as her new found skills. She found a love for hunting with John and the rest of the group, and attained better grasp of who she was, in any form she chose.

Sam knew that the road ahead would not be an easy one, but the only road not taken, is a wasted opportunity. She would continue onward, down her path of life, to see where it would lead. To answer the questions, and to find a better future in her new, Trueblood form.

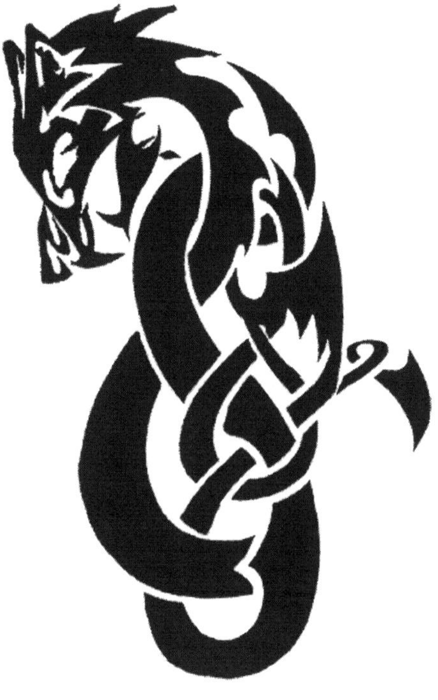

Chains of the Turned
Volume II of the Lykoi Series

"But you can't go, Sam. You don't know what's going on!" Claire tried to reason with the girl. She sat helpless as she watched Sam pack her rucksack.

"I haven't heard from John in over three months. I know that something is wrong. I told him not to take the newly assigned project. I told him that it sounded shady."

Claire handed Sam the shirts that lay beside her on the bed.

"You know that he had no other option. He's not like you."

Sam snapped at Claire. "I KNOW! It's unjust how the Turned are treated. He's not someone's house pet. He's my John!" Sam sat on the edge of the bed, tears burning down her cheeks. Claire took her handkerchief and dabbed the frustration from her face.

"There there my child. You need to think clearly. Have a plan. Be safe and come back to me in one piece."

Sam finished packing and set out in her AMC Scout. She stopped to pick Chaz and Kenny up and was instructed to meet up with Brad once they hit the Missouri/Kansas border.

Chaz sat in the back, his headphones blaring music loud enough for everyone to hear. Kenny said very little and Sam said even less.

They had their plan to rescue John. What they didn't know was what waited for them...

Made in the USA
Charleston, SC
08 February 2012